Also by Stew

MILLIONAIRES ANONYMOUS (a play)

Contents

"Data is a precious thing and will last longer than the systems themselves."

—Sir Tim Berners-Lee

ONE

Her heels felt tacky on the tough, balding carpet. Detective Inspector Alison Farber remembered her wild university days quite vividly, but in retrospect they seemed fairly tame compared to students nowadays. A case of rose-tinted glasses on her past, perhaps. A generational thing. Students were students; they got pissed a lot and smashed things up, and the corridor Farber was walking through was cold proof of that.

Discarded beer bottles, cans and plastic cups lined the walls of the corridor like runway lights, each one frozen in the state it was left in barely a few hours earlier. A pungent aroma of stale booze and cannabis filled the air, bringing back memories of every hangover Farber had ever had. She passed a stoved-in pumpkin on her left, the red candle wax having spilled out across the carpet and solidified like a dried bloodstain. Somewhere behind her a collection of glass bottles clattered like bowling pins.

'Bloody students,' said Detective Sergeant Leonard Staedler. Farber stopped and watched as he crouched on one of his dodgy knees, letting a compressed breath hiss through his lips as he righted the bottles he'd knocked over. A pair of curious students passed, one wearing a skeleton costume with black and white makeup smeared over his face – undoubtedly a work of art before he'd spent the night lip-locked with the bloodied nurse who walked alongside him. *Halloween costumes are getting more impressive each year*, thought Farber.

The Detectives continued and turned a corner, making their way towards a room buzzing with police activity. A girl with black hair and a yellow blouse scurried by, tear-streaked mascara running down her pale cheeks. A few doors away they came to the backs of a group of gathering adolescents.

'Out of the way please,' said Farber, her stern, authoritative tone making their heads spin like startled owls. Farber and Staedler finally reached their destination where they were greeted by Constable Buchanan, a short man in his forties.

'Messy bastards, aren't they?' he said, pushing open the door to room 412.

It was dim in there, most of the light coming from a solitary window that was partially blocked by an ageing wardrobe. The room was a standard student dive. A single bed occupied one wall, with a cream duvet peeled back haphazardly. Against the opposite wall a long mirror was propped up next to a small wash basin, scabby with limescale from years of neglect. Farber overlooked the other details of the room as her attention was quickly drawn to a lumpy white sheet on the ground in front of her, a burgundy patch soaked into the carpet at one end.

'Single shotgun wound to the head,' said Buchanan, notepad in hand. 'We're still canvassing, but the lad's name is Nikolai Guskov. He was 21. We think it's him anyway, the blast took his face clean off. Forensics will confirm the identity.'

Farber crouched and lifted the sheet at the burgundy end, revealing an unsightly mess; about 75 percent of the young man's face was missing, exposing a sticky composition of blood, sinew, bone fragments and raw grey-pink matter. The vague shape of a skull could only just be made out, but the jaw and some of the lower left eye socket were gone, most likely on the far side of the room.

'He was a third-year computer science student,' said Buchanan. 'Ukrainian born. Here on a scholarship. We can't get hold of his mother, the number doesn't work.'

'Ukrainian number?' asked Staedler.

Buchanan nodded. 'A place called Kosmak,' he said, '…at least I think that's how you say it.'

'Kos*mach*,' corrected Staedler, 'it's in the far west of the country. I wouldn't put much stock in the uni's student database. A lot of that info gets compiled the day they arrive and doesn't get updated again.'

Farber watched as Staedler stepped around the body and homed in on a sawn-off shotgun lying on the carpet by the bed. He tensed before getting down on one knee again, grunting through the pain.

'This is some serious kit for a computer nerd,' he said, leaning over and sniffing the barrels.

'Home connections?' said Farber.

'Maybe.'

Farber looked back at the corpse and peeled back even more of the sheet, exposing Nikolai's bare, sallow neck, then his shoulder where his T-shirt had stretched to one side. Taking a Biro from her jacket, Farber prodded the end just above his collarbone. It was tough with no give. The smell wasn't too bad though.

'I wouldn't say he's been dead any longer than 12 hours,' she said, checking her watch. 'Which puts the earliest time of death around 11 last night.'

'Who heard the shot?' said Staedler, grunting back to his feet.

'Funnily enough, no one,' said Buchanan, prompting inquisitive looks from the detectives. 'Well, half the students are still in bed, but you saw the mess on your way in. Students on Halloween? Bloody maniacs. This place was bouncing last night. We even had a few call outs – noise pollution, lads fighting in the street, one drunk and disorderly. You could have set a bomb off in here and no-one would have blinked.'

'Then who raised the alarm?' said Farber.

'Erm, Professor…' Buchanan quickly consulted his notepad, then gave up, 'one of his lecturers. She got worried when he didn't turn up to class.'

'And all the other pissheads from last night *did*?' asked Staedler.

Farber lifted even more of the sheet, revealing the left-hand side of Nikolai's body. Stopping at his hands, she tilted her head curiously at the sight of white surgical gloves.

'Weird, isn't it?' said Buchanan, shuffling over to Farber. 'One of the girls outside said he suffered from an obsessive-compulsive disorder among other things.'

'Like?'

'Paranoia. Anxiety. Said he was a bit of a loner. Don't think he had many friends, not in real life anyway.'

Farber carefully placed the sheet back and stood up, letting her bored eyes survey the room autonomously. It appeared to be an open and shut suicide, and there was nothing much more they could do. Almost a waste of petrol. Still, she'd picked up some milk and eggs on the way over.

'*In real life*?' repeated Staelder, questioning Buchanan.

'He was a computer nut, wasn't he?' said Buchanan. 'My lad's the same. Locks himself upstairs all day every day on the bloody internet, chatting to god knows who.'

Farber glanced over the corpse once more, then up at the ceiling. Blood spatter had painted the Artex as if someone had thrown a water-bomb filled with red paint. Farber brought her head level and found herself staring at a computer sat on a flat-pack desk straight out of Ikea. The screen was off, but on top sat a webcam with a glowing red light.

TWO

His fingers glided over the computer keyboard like Mozart at a grand piano, rapping the keys with expert efficiency. Forget the mouse, it was too slow – he used key combinations; shortcuts to navigate the screen without having to constantly move his hand from keyboard to mouse. Those extra milliseconds added up when you spent all day plugged in.

The office was an ex-storeroom, cramped with no windows, and about as long as the inside of a minibus only not as wide. There were four computer workstations, two on each side. The desks were littered with computing equipment, peripherals and electrical sockets. Any visitor would think the place was a mess, but there were no visitors – only authorised personnel were allowed in there.

'See these here,' said Detective Sergeant John Beckford, clicking the last key and pointing his index finger at the middle of the three screens that faced him. Peering over Beckford's shoulder was Chief Inspector Graham Noakes, a man of advancing years (or an 'old sweat' as they were called in the service) who oversaw operations in the High Tech Crime Unit.

'Ordinary system files, sure,' said Beckford. 'Only they don't match up to the standard installation of the operating system. More noticeable than that is they're all of equal file size, so I ran a sig-check on them and turns out they're compressed files. I did a little renaming and…'

He rattled a few more keys and hit enter, opening a newly renamed zip-file that filled the screen with a list of images. Beckford sensed Noakes straighten up behind him, which confirmed what was about to happen next and flooded the pit of his stomach with nervous bile. Beckford tapped a few keys, highlighting a random image file and waited for the order. Whatever was about to hit their retinas with a mere click of a button would be burned there forevermore.

'Go on,' said Noakes. Beckford inhaled slowly through the nose and then ripped the plaster off with a stab of the enter key.

On screen appeared a high-resolution photograph of bright, ultra-sharp, sickening human behaviour. Beckford averted his gaze in an instant, almost giving himself whiplash, hoping the fraction of a second glimpse of youthful abuse didn't have time to embed itself into his memory like so many others had in the past. It was ammunition for nightmares but an unfortunate part of the job.

He blindly pressed Alt-F4 on the keyboard, closing the image and dropping it back into the long list of files that had immortalised barbaric moments in time.

'Okay,' said Noakes. 'Good. That's one down.'

A stalwart of the job, Noakes appeared to be wholly unaffected by what he saw. But Beckford knew better. Sure, Noakes was a 30-year man in the Metropolitan Police, 15 of which have been in computer crime, but in that time the extent of heinous things he'd been exposed to hadn't numbed him. He'd just had more practice appearing that way.

Due to the sensitive material that staff were routinely exposed to at the HTCU, counselling and an assessment was required every six months. And yet, even regular therapy and an iron stomach wasn't enough to fight back the nightmares. Their office had a relatively low staff turnover, but in the year he'd been working there, Beckford had witnessed two officers fall at the first hurdle.

The mental toughness of officers involved in such work had to be strong enough to maintain a certain level of desensitisation or disconnect. The job's difficulty doubled if the officer had children of his or her own. Luckily, Beckford didn't have that cross to bear. A blessing in disguise, but that's not to say it didn't mess with his head every now and then.

'All right, crack on to the finish line,' said Noakes, patting the back of Beckford's chair and heading for the door. Noakes pressed his ID badge to a sensor and the lab door unlocked with a click. As he exited, an audible wave of activity from the main office flooded the room, then the door sealed shut again and locked once more, plunging the lab and Beckford back into the low drone of running computer fans.

Beckford turned back to the list of images and quickly closed the zip file. The hollow feeling in his stomach was back, always emerging at the same time every day of the week. It was reminiscent of the first time he saw a dead body, an anecdote that could now be told to friends over a few drinks – intense at the time, but softened in retrospect. Officers could walk the beat for years without ever seeing one, but Beckford popped his cherry on the first day of his two-year probation as a Police Constable. A jumper from a multistorey car park. The sound of the body hitting concrete was one he'd never forget, but as the years went on, desensitisation had kicked in. The more bodies Beckford saw, the less affected he was. It got easier.

Being exposed to images of child abuse *never* got easier. In fact, it got worse. The desperately unfortunate yet exclusive club of innocent children grew bigger month by month, fuelling Beckford's suspicions of what went on behind people's closed doors. There'd been a time when he wanted children of his own. There'd even been a false alarm the other year. But now he wasn't sure it was a good idea anymore. Maybe it was the best way to protect them from the evils of the world.

Beckford turned to the screen on his left and started filling in details of the examination report. The computer belonged to a Mr Tadhg Hamilton, a 40-four-year-old who was currently residing in prison awaiting trial. He had a wife, three teenage children and worked for a logistics company. On his lunch breaks, Mr Hamilton used his work computer to connect to a chat room on the 'dark web' – a part of the internet not easily accessible and not indexed by popular search engines. The chat room was used by paedophiles to anonymously distribute child pornography, but unknown to Mr Hamilton – or the other six people who frequented the room – one of them was an undercover police officer working for the Child Exploitation and Online Protection centre.

Over the space of three weeks, the undercover officer managed to socially engineer Mr Hamilton into giving up his mobile phone number for the promise of meeting a young boy whom the officer had said he'd 'groomed specifically.' Once the number was in CEOP's possession, it didn't take long before Mr Hamilton's front door was smashed in and he was dragged away crying and protesting in cuffs. His home and work computers were confiscated and delivered to the High Tech Crime Unit on Water Street, where DI Beckford began his forensic examination of the data.

Due to the sensitive nature and volatility of the files stored on any computer, an extremely strict chain of custody had to be followed to preserve the integrity of the digital information. If a conviction rested on the found evidence, there could be no room for doubt and no room for human error. That was where Beckford's obsessiveness came in handy. He was as thorough as humanly possible.

The lab door beeped, unlocked and DI Linda Kilburn – the unit's second in command and chief Forensic Investigator – poked her head in along with a rush of office noise.

'Psst, John,' she said, unable to get Beckford's attention from the computer screen. 'You'll never guess who just walked through the door.'

This time he turned, and his stomach – which had already flipped like a pancake just moments ago – flipped back over again. It could have been a number of people who had walked in, but Beckford took the shortest route to the person he dreaded seeing the most, and he didn't need Kilburn's subtly blended look of apprehension and glee to know that Alison Farber was indeed stood out there. After all, their past had become police folklore among the bored coffee breaks and work nights out.

Kilburn backed out of the lab, letting Beckford emerge into the office as she watched his reaction with fascination like a scientist observing an experiment. Whatever reaction he gave was only a bland representation of what was going on behind the facade.

And there she was, exchanging casual pleasantries with Noakes by the reception desk. Her hair was longer than the last time Beckford saw her and just generally looked different. Was it straighter? Curlier? Darker? Lighter? A million memories flooded his head, kick-starting dormant emotions like rusted pistons.

Beckford had spent the past year building a mental block between them, brick by brick, but as her eyes met his across the office he felt the cement soften and the wall tremble slightly. It was a brief glance. He smiled. She smiled back, then carried on chin-wagging with Noakes.

Oh, she's here for work, thought Beckford as he noticed

her arm resting on a bagged computer unit on the reception desk.

'Who's that?' said Sergeant Liam Davis, two desks down. A younger member of the unit who had one hand on his computer mouse and the other in a packet of ready salted crisps.

'Never you mind,' said Kilburn. Beckford sidled to his desk, taking a seat and logging into his workstation as casually as possible. Davis' head rose over the partition.

'John?'

'She's homicide,' he said, '…someone I used to know.' He was staring at his computer screen, but in his peripheral he saw movement… and it was heading his way. When the blurred figures were in spitting distance Beckford looked up, his heart hammering in his ribcage.

'Another one for the queue,' said Noakes, planting the wrapped computer unit on the edge of his desk. 'It'll give you something to do,' he added, winking before walking away, revealing Farber behind.

'Thanks, chief,' she said after him, but she was looking at Beckford. Another tight smile. Beckford stood up and held out a hand.

'A *handshake*?' said Farber, '…really?'

Beckford dropped his hand and shrugged, trying to smile it off. 'I thought Hadley's unit was your first port of call?'

'They're snowed under with some multinational phishing scam apparently.'

Multinational phishing scam? Beckford hadn't heard of any such case, which led him to suspect the base unit on his desk was just a ploy. But why now? Was she coming to tell him she was getting married? Pregnant? Moving abroad? Anything to rub his face in the shit.

'Contacts?' said Farber, aiming V-shaped fingers at her

eyes.

'Oh, got them lasered.'

'I always liked you without glasses. I always liked you with them, too. I mean, you look good.'

'So do you.'

Farber hooked some hair behind her ear. Beckford's mind raced, desperately trying to grab a topic of conversation that would distract them from the obvious awkwardness. He could hear Davis crunching his crisps. Might as well have been popcorn.

'Thanks for the card by the way,' said Beckford. Farber furrowed her brow, then remembered what he was referring to.

'Oh.'

'I'm sorry I didn't—'

'No, it's okay'

'I was in a bit of a—'

'John, it's okay, I understand. I wasn't sure if it was appropriate or not, but it was the verdict we were all hoping for.'

'It was very appropriate. It helped a lot. So… thanks.'

Farber smiled, satisfied.

'So?' said Beckford, changing the subject not-so-subtly and patting the base unit on his desk like a dog. 'What's the story?'

'Nothing Earth-shattering,' said Farber. 'A student at Harper College killed himself in his dorm room last night with a sawn-off 12 bore. He was very tech savvy, bit of a loner.'

'Aren't they all,' said Beckford, unravelling the plastic bag the computer was wrapped in. He dug a hand in and slid out papers from a plastic wallet stuck to the side of the case. The first sheet was a chain of custody form, the second a seizure form listing relevant information about the computer, including where it was seized from, date and time, name and address of owner.

'We're thinking he purchased the weapon online,' said Farber, 'possibly through underground sites or social networks. It'd be good if he left us some footprints. I'll copy you in on the preliminary as soon as I've done it.'

'What sort of timescale?' said Beckford, not lifting his head from the forms.

'Anything quicker than Hadley's unit and I'm happy. Shall we say two weeks?'

Beckford was fully aware of their own backlog of work at the HTCU. Two weeks would be lightning quick, and yet despite being completely conscious of his ulterior motive behind it, Beckford would push Farber's job to the top of the stack. He wanted to see her again, and as soon as possible. It was as simple as that.

'I'll see what I've got on,' he said.

'Great. Anyway, I best be getting back. It was good seeing you, John.'

'You too.'

Farber turned on her heels and headed for the exit. *How very amicable*, thought Beckford. *Formal. Cringeworthy, even.*

'Alison!' said Beckford. She turned. Beckford held in his hand the chain of custody form. 'You need to sign this,' he said.

Farber nodded and returned to his desk, scribbled her name, then as she handed the pen back their fingers touched. Farber smiled once more and headed for the exit, saying goodbye to Noakes on the way. Beckford watched until she was out of sight.

'Just someone you once *knew*?' said Davis, dropping the empty crisp packet into his bin and licking his salty fingers. 'I've seen less sexual tension in porn.'.

THREE

The frenetic, almost psychotic dubstep beats of Skrillex blasted from the car stereo as Beckford pulled up outside the pharmacy, securing a spot on the double-yellows. He tapped his phone, closing the sat nav, then cut the engine at which point the deafening synths and drums ceased. No one at work knew he listened to that kind of music, but they'd be even more amazed by who turned him onto it. In fact, they'd be amazed at a number of things that Beckford kept in his closet.

The dashboard clock said 5:49 pm – 11 minutes until the pharmacy closed. With nights getting darker, traffic was getting worse. Living a stone's throw from Wembley Stadium, travelling to work by train was a must. However, on occasion when he needed to get somewhere fast after his shift, he deluded himself into thinking the car was quicker. It didn't help that London's roadwork pandemic seemed to have no foreseeable cure, making his journey from the HTCU in Hammersmith to the pharmacy in Camden even more troublesome.

He never used the same pharmacy, and despite being 11 minutes early it wasn't his dashboard clock Beckford was concerned with, it was the countdown timer on his phone. Four minutes remaining. He waited for a cyclist to pass his door before he popped it open and hurried across the pavement.

It continued to amaze Beckford what people could do with computers, and although he already had quite an extensive knowledge of the digital world thanks to a computer-centric upbringing by his programmer father, his first year in the High Tech Crime Unit opened his eyes to the scary realisation that computer crime was expanding at an exponential rate.

The landscape had changed. With growing numbers of lives, money and businesses now online, it was natural that crime would follow close behind. And crime was changing too. No longer were groups of hardened criminals breaking into banks with masks and guns – kids barely into their teens were breaking into multinational corporations from the confines of their own bedroom.

Over the past year, Beckford had witnessed the handiwork of many young hackers. The broad strokes of their crimes were fairly self-explanatory to someone still new to the field, such as exploiting security holes to steal databases containing the personal information (bank details, passwords etc.) of millions of people and auction them off to the highest bidder The fundamentals of their crimes, however, he still struggled with – how they actually did what they did. Beckford was still learning and while he attended numerous training seminars and spoke to experts within the industry, his education on hacking came mostly from the hackers themselves.

Willow O'Donnell was arrested under the Computer Misuse Act for a Distributed Denial-of-Service attack on the website of a video game publisher. Willow owned a botnet – an army of remote computers infected with a particular virus that allowed her to take control of those computers and get them to perform her bidding. It was like having a personal militia of robots, hence the name, and for many months before her arrest Willow made a healthy living hiring out her botnet to other hackers, providing them with access to the 'Command Server' for prices on a per hour, day or weekly basis. It was a thriving business for a 15-year-old.

Her slip-up came after a video game developer

announced the cancellation of their latest title, a fantasy RPG called 'The Knights Realm.' Having been swept up in the development hype, yearning for the game for well over a year and even starting her own fan-based message board that had over 10,000 subscribers, Willow was outraged by their announcement. So much so that she instructed her botnet, known as MagNet, to flood the developers' website with internet traffic, causing the site to crash and become unusable for as long as the DDOS attack went on for. Which would be a while.

Beckford was part of a team that had been tracking the then famous botnet and its activity for months in an operation called 'Leviathan.' This time, Willow had kept her head above water just long enough for them to trace the internet traffic to a house in Enfield, north London, where she was arrested in front of her shocked mum and dad in her messy basement bedroom. The HTCU took control of the Command Server, shut down the botnet and Willow was given a six-month sentence at a youth detention centre.

But Willow also had value. She had skills and connections in the digital underground that the police didn't have, and so they struck a deal with her by waiving her sentence if she agreed to cooperate in exposing an underground phishing ring; a group responsible for scamming users into giving up their bank details. It was during this time that Beckford got to know Willow quite well, and – amazed by how inferior he felt watching the young hacker do her thing – started to think of ways the girl's skills could selfishly benefit himself.

Desperate times called for desperate measures. Beckford's decision to leave homicide had been easy, but it was supposed to make things better for him, not worse. The panic attacks didn't go away and the numbness he felt towards everything around him persisted. If his therapist truly knew what was going on inside his head, his position at the HTCU would undoubtedly be at risk. She'd have him on a course of antidepressants and talking therapies in no time at all and have no choice but to recommend he be removed from service until he was all better.

Fuck that. Beckford's job was a necessary distraction. If he could just get a little help without anyone knowing… that's where Willow came into the picture.

One night, when dropping her off at her house Beckford broached the subject carefully. Having researched General Practice computer systems himself, he innocently mentioned an ongoing investigation, one that he'd fabricated, in which someone had been creating false prescriptions and selling them on.

'Fuckin' piece of piss,' said Willow. 'You think the NHS has money to spend on decent security? Those systems are wide open, dude.'

Next step for Beckford was to get some collateral. What he didn't want was the kid to have him over a barrel, so for the next couple of weeks he kept a close eye on Willow's online activity via a keylogger that had been developed in-house at the HTCU and which delivered every stroke of Willow's keyboard directly to Beckford's inbox. Hacking was a drug, and he knew she wouldn't wait long for her next hit. Then, sure enough, Willow dropped the ball.

She'd started work on a new botnet virus.

Waiting until Willow's parents were out, Beckford thumped his fist on the front door and staged a raid, telling Willow that the police had been monitoring her computer activity and had proof of her intention to release another virus with the sole purpose of recruiting computers for a new botnet. It was a mean move. The girl even started crying as Beckford unplugged cables from the back of one of her desktops.

With the con in full swing, Beckford let Willow squirm for a bit before he told her he could sweep it all under the rug as long as it didn't happen again. The relief on Willow's face said it all – Beckford had the leverage he needed. Letting it simmer for a day or two, he finally showed his hand while driving to the Water Street offices.

'I'll pay you £50 for a prescription. I'll give you a week's notice before I run out so you can get the next lot lined up.'

'How the fuck do I know you're not just baiting me into some trap?' said Willow.

'Why would we want you behind bars? You're too useful.'

After that, with both of their guards lowered, a real friendship formed. Beckford turned a blind eye to whatever small-time hacks Willow was involved with, and Willow wouldn't say a word about Beckford's anxiety disorder. Tit for tat. A perfect arrangement.

For Willow, the prescription hack was child's play. GPs used a service called EPS or Electronic Prescription Service, which electronically submitted prescriptions to the dispenser of the patient's choice, such as their local pharmacy. To get to the EPS, Willow had to first access the computer network of Beckford's registered GP, which she did with ease by going through a back door of the surgery's public website. Beckford couldn't believe how something so important in government rankings – database after database of personal and medication information – could be so wide open to blatant misconduct.

'More holes than a Thai hooker,' said Willow, glancing over at him to see his reaction. Beckford had heard worse stuff come out of younger mouths, but it was still disappointing to hear.

Once on the GP's network, Willow could access the patient database and records of any prescriptions handed over that day. She could also submit new ones through the EPS to local pharmacies on behalf of one John Beckford. But there was a caveat: Beckford didn't want there to be any record of his illegal prescriptions. So Willow built in a timer that would delete all evidence of her nefarious online activities after a preset period of time elapsed.

On the day of each hack, Beckford would call Willow and they'd settle on a time. When that time came, a prescription under Beckford's name would be submitted through the EPS to a chosen pharmacy. Beckford then had 30 minutes to pick up the prescription before the submission was automatically withdrawn from the EPS and erased from the GP's database. It had worked pretty well so far, but he had to be quick.

At 5:56 pm, Beckford was back in his car with a white paper bag – a fresh batch of Xanax to treat anxiety and panic attacks. He watched the timer count down the last 10 seconds.

Job done. He put the car into first and headed home.

* * *

Beckford stuck his fork into the last piece of rigatoni and swept it around the bowl, gathering the last scraps of his homemade sauce. On the TV was a police press conference where Chief Inspector Ray Michaels stood outside Scotland Yard – microphones, audio recorders, cameras and phones thrust into his face. Michaels was a colossal six-foot-five-inches tall. A bear of a man. Everything about him was grizzly, from his deep, gravelly Invernessian accent to his five o'clock shadow and hairy arms that continued across the back of his hands.

'...and I would personally like to thank the staff who worked tirelessly throughout the investigation and to let this be a warning to members of organised crime, or any crime for that matter: Roger Uttridge is only the beginning, and the Metropolitan Police will never give up until London's criminal underworld is taken down piece by piece and justice is delivered. Thank you.'

Beckford was only half-listening. He'd spent most of the evening on autopilot, thinking about nothing but Farber – their past, their present, the possibilities of where things could lead. It was the same thoughts looping over and over like the tired lyrics of a crappy song. Dangerous territory, but he knew that suppressing his thoughts was entirely counterproductive, like trying to hold a beach ball underwater.

He shouldn't have been watching the news either. When Michaels appeared on screen, Beckford smirked with disbelief. It seemed the whole world was shoving his recent past into his face.

A few months prior to his transfer to the HTCU, Michaels had been Beckford's chief at homicide, albeit for a brief period of time. Beckford liked him, though. Michaels was a great leader. Someone you could go to with a problem who'd work out a solution and leave you feeling like you'd found it all by yourself. It was just an unfortunate time back then.

After washing up, Beckford sat on the carpet cross-legged. He played meditation music on his phone, closed his eyes and focussed on his breathing. He practiced mindfulness every evening, but depending on his day its purpose flitted between general cleansing to desperate antidote. On a day when the world had crowded in on him, he badly needed to disconnect.

Drawing air in slowly through his nostrils, he breathed out again. Over and over. He counted too. It was difficult. He tried focussing on the sounds in his flat. The ticking of the thermostat clock. The distant rumble of traffic outside. Someone, somewhere in the building talking. He tried visualising rolling hills. Valleys. Blue skies. A trickling stream. He tried sensing fresh, cool air blowing on his face. He exhausted every mental trick he knew battling his gloomy thoughts. It was no use.

After 20 minutes, Beckford opened his eyes wholly dissatisfied. He changed into his running gear and left his flat where he pounded the streets of Wembley for just under two hours. He tried to take a different route each time, steering clear of the main roads and stadium rat runs. Random side streets.

With hard trance music blasting in his ears courtesy of Willow and the darkness shrouding every road, house and car with an ambiguous cloak, Beckford felt like he could have been anywhere in the country. Away from it all.

FOUR

The fridge at the Water Street offices was always packed, overflowing with jars, yoghurts and Tupperware boxes, half of which had surely been there for weeks, if not months. Beckford rejigged a few tubs like a game of Jenga before he found the one he was after. Popping the lid, he tipped the contents into his porridge. A handful of blueberries. Burying a spoon in to stir he suddenly stopped. It was there, somewhere in the back of his mind. A familiar thought. The blueberries were like tiny sinkholes in snow, but there was something telling him to count them. If he stirred, they'd be lost in the gloopy porridge; although it wouldn't be the first time he'd sifted through hot porridge before to make sure there were 20 berries in there.

It had to be 20. Not 19. Not 21 – 20. Why 20? *Why not?* It didn't matter how many blueberries he had each morning, all that mattered was Beckford had picked an arbitrary number a while back and every now and then it had to be adhered to as if his life depended on it. Because in some totally irrational way, it did.

Beckford sucked a deep breath in through his nostrils and stirred, the blueberries disappearing into the mix. *Let it go John,* he told himself. To interrupt his thought pattern further, he moved onto his decaf coffee. It was there too – the amount of granules on the teaspoon, the desire to get just the right amount. He'd weighed it once, but now it was more a visual thing. He quickly tipped the granules into his mug and poured on boiling water before he could second-guess. Thankfully, at that moment Noakes entered the kitchen and opened the fridge. Beckford breathed a quiet sigh of relief.

'You nicked all the bloody milk again, John?'

'I'll pop out in a bit to get some more,' said Beckford, leaning back against the cupboard and spooning in a mouthful of porridge.

Seroxat is a selective serotonin reuptake inhibitor – an antidepressant – that normally kept Beckford's obsessive habits under control, but he had his off days. Sleep played a big part. A restless, disturbed night's sleep was asking for trouble. Caffeine was avoided at all costs, as was alcohol and eating late. His bedroom was temperature controlled. The consequences of a bad night's sleep had moulded Beckford's neuroses, causing him to optimise any aspect he could in order to improve his sleep. But there were some things he couldn't control. Such as his dreams, and last night he'd made an appearance again.

Woodhill Prison in Milton Keynes was Category A, housing some of the most dangerous criminals in the country. Beckford had never been. Never even seen any pictures. And yet, with his experience of other prisons he'd visited, his unconscious had managed to piece together a building that appeared architecturally sound. Like many dreams, however, the structure was misshapen and the order nonlinear. Moments where he'd be sat in the car park but somehow be in the visitor's centre at the same time, talking to a receptionist who had no face.

A blueberry crushed between his molars as Noakes flitted around the kitchen talking to him. Beckford hadn't heard a word. He was busy decoding the residual memories from his restless night. He remembered dropping keys, money, phone and his belt into a plastic tray and being padded down by one of the wardens. Then there was a strong sensation of guilt and worry… but what was it…? oh yes, fuck – that was it. He had a six-inch plastic shiv taped to the small of his back. They didn't find it. He was buzzed through a heavy steel door and walked down a corridor that went on for ever. The ushering warden talked, reeling off the rules and regulations of Woodhill's visiting policy. Beckford could have probably transcribed it if he really concentrated.

Then they were in a room that looked like a college staffroom. Blue-cushioned chairs grouped around tables set out in rows. Beckford suspected the tables were occupied by prisoners, but he never looked – their presence was just sensed in his peripheral. The prison officers lining the room, however, he did notice. Their postures tense, their faces stone. It was around that time that Beckford had roused, the anxiety over the blade lifting him back to reality.

'You think that'd be okay, John?' said Noakes, buttering some toast.

'Erm, I don't see why not,' he replied, taking a gamble. Beckford quickly dumped his bowl in the sink and let it soak, then headed back to his desk before he agreed to anything else he might not have heard.

It had been a few weeks since he had thought of convicted murderer and rapist Peter McGregor, but it didn't take Sherlock to deduce why his past was being dug up again. Alison Farber might as well have turned up at the HTCU with a hard hat and pickaxe. All Beckford kept asking himself was, *why now?*

* * *

Dominic Peltz sunk his teeth into the burrito, forcing excess beef, rice and onions to ooze into the cardboard tray. A stray jalapeño slice landed in his lap, which he delicately picked up and threw into his mouth before brushing the brine stain on his jeans with the back of his hand. Peltz had lunch at Kelly's pretty much every day, having sampled every deli, snack bar, bistro and sandwich shop in the Kensington area. He always sat at the window if he could, the constant stream of tourists outside providing him with the sense he was still in touch with the real world.

The sight alone of other living, breathing human beings was becoming a necessity and a daily ritual for Peltz. In his line of work, real people were something of a rarity. Skype video conferences, emails and telephone calls were as close as he usually got to his colleagues. Real-life interaction was dissuaded outside of the Studio. Therefore, at lunch he always stared out of the window, observing the most eclectic mix of human beings the planet had to offer.

If he was honest with himself, Peltz people-watched primarily to fuel his erotically charged fantasies. It had been a while. His success rate in and around Soho was diminishing and his one-click McFuck app wasn't reliable. Bunch of psychos. Peltz was bored of the locals, but the exotic mix of foreign tourists gave his brain and dick new possibilities. What he wouldn't give for a tall Caribbean man to screw him senseless. Or a big Maori – their tattoos drove him wild.

Placing the half-eaten burrito back in the tray, he licked his fingers clean then pulled his wallet out of his back pocket. A folded tenner peeked out at him and he stuffed the wallet back into his trousers. He paid for everything in cash and needed toilet roll – the stuff at the hotel was like rubbing sandpaper on his haemorrhoids.

To Peltz's left, a young man in a sharp suit sat down and placed a boxed meal on the table; a burrito without the wrap. *Must be on a low-carb diet*, Peltz deduced. Something he'd considered himself. Lord knew he needed to shift the weight, but then again diets were for people who gave a shit. Sharp Suit obviously did. If it wasn't for his big nose, he'd look like a Hugo Boss model. His hair was preened to perfection and his aftershave so strong the smell of burritos occasionally disappeared altogether.

Peltz remembered the days of aftershave. The days of personal appearance. Burritos certainly didn't help but they were cheap, tasty and quick. He wasn't meant to be away for long and his toilet roll errand had just added another five minutes.

The smart young man pulled a newspaper out of a rack on the wall and opened it awkwardly in the cramped bar, shovelling a forkful of Mexican fast food into his mouth as he did so. Peltz had already fantasised about fucking him, despite his big nose, but playtime was over and he needed to get a move on.

Taking a larger bite of out of his burrito, Peltz stole glimpses of the paper's front page as the man skim-read. Out of the window, a dishevelled homeless person in an oilskin coat stood talking to himself, avoided by anyone who came in his proximity. Peltz chewed and watched, then glanced at the paper again. In among the noise of words and pictures, one image stood out in a small, bottom-right article. The man flipped the page—

'Could you go back, mate?' Peltz said, causing the bloke to jump slightly. He was a Scouser, born and bred in Liverpool, and even though his accent had softened since living in London, it still had enough of a twang for people to look at him differently. Most of the time untrustingly.

The man turned the page back and Peltz leaned over. The article's bold headline said: "Genius Student Takes Life" and was accompanied by a profile photo of Nikolai Guskov. Peltz sat like a mannequin, his eyeballs speed-reading the article. The man was motionless too, holding the paper like a butler to his master. His face looked like he wasn't sure what he was doing.

'Thank you,' said Peltz, turning back to his tray and stuffing the last bite into his mouth. He picked up two paper serviettes and wiped his lips, then took his tray to the waste receptacle and disposed of it. The young girl behind the counter waved a plastic-gloved hand and Peltz waved back before leaving.

Once he was out on the street, he ran.

FIVE

He huffed and puffed, running upstream against a river of tourists carrying a thousand Harrods bags. "Police were called to the scene early on Tuesday morning," the article said. It was now Wednesday. *Fucking Wednesday*, he thought.

Peltz passed South Kensington Station and took the corner, slowing to a light jog to give himself enough stability to read his phone. There'd been no calls and no messages. Not today or yesterday. He couldn't believe it. The system would have picked it up. It should have alerted him.

He needed to speak to Silver. Each quiet side street he passed looked inviting, but he knew better than to make a private call in an unsecured area. It was never worth the risk, not unless he wanted to become a target of his own kind.

The hotel wasn't far, he just hoped his heart would last the distance.

By the time he stumbled up the steps and into the lobby, Peltz was heaving like he'd crossed the finishing line of a marathon. Shuffling towards the lifts, he pressed the button and rested a hand on the wall, taking in huge lungful's of air.

'Been for a run, Mr Barrett?' said Keisha, a young brunette whose head poked up over the front desk. Luckily for Peltz he'd given up on formal wear around the same time he started living out of a suitcase, so his standard attire of trainers, joggers and a sports jacket disguised his condition perfectly.

'Thought I better start before the old ticker packs in for

good,' he said in between breaths. Keisha's sent him a wide Colgate smile and got back to her computer.

The lift arrived on the fourth floor and Peltz squeezed through the opening doors. He speed-walked towards his room, keeping at bay any thoughts that he was actually having a heart attack. *If it's going to happen*, he thought, *now is as good a time as any*. He didn't particularly want to be around for the shitstorm that was about to hit.

Inserting his door key, the lock beeped with a green light and he barged in. The place was a standard double room, but a total mess. Two black suitcases lay open under the window, spilling clothes out onto the floor like volcanic lava. A crude washing line had been constructed out of plastic rope stretching from the hinge of the bathroom door to the curtain rail, most of its load being socks and boxers.

There was one main difference between this room and the other 109 at the hotel. Every area of wall, floor and ceiling was covered in a dark-grey acoustic foam. The floor was flat, enabling people to walk on it, but the walls and ceiling were spiked with foam stalactites, making the place look more like a recording studio than a hotel room.

The soundproofing had been set up by a third-party company who'd been informed that Peltz – or Mr Dominic Barrett as he was known to them – worked from his room with VIP government clients. The company demanded that the room be set up in such a way and that no one, not even the cleaners, had access, and the hotel agreed. It was the primary reason the place was such a shit-tip.

Peltz unzipped his jacket, threw it on the bed, then dropped into the chair at the dressing table where three laptops sat open side by side. He knocked the mouse of the middle laptop and the screen came to life, revealing a login box. His sweaty hands unlocked his phone and opened an app called Tork2Me. As the app went through an authentication process, Peltz affixed headphones and rattled login details into the laptop. Once authenticated, Tork2Me offered up a list of contacts, each of them portrayed by anonymous silhouettes with pseudonyms like "Kevlar", "Banshee" and "Drogo". Peltz was known as "Plasticuff".

Anonymity was strictly adhered to in the Studio. It wasn't to protect their identities from each other – they were fully aware of the names and faces that lay behind each avatar. It was to protect themselves from "the outside". Peltz was head of security and responsible for keeping their existence unknown. They'd never once been breached, but there'd been times where moths had fluttered too close to the flame. However, prevention was always better than cure, and this time it looked like Peltz needed a miracle.

He tapped the contact "Silver" and a connecting tone rang in his ears. Peltz knew full well that they had to schedule calls, but this was an exception. A *massive* exception. The call rang and rang and rang, and just before Peltz was about to hang up it was answered by a digitised voice, vocoded to disguise the person behind it. That's how they all sounded.

'What is it?' the voice said, the low register obviously male.

'Please tell me it's a scrub job,' said Peltz.

'Who?'

'…and if it was, why wasn't I kept in the fucking loop? I was his contact, no one else. *Me*. So why the fuck—'

'*Who…?* The Ukrainian? I'm unaware of this, explain what you're talking about.'

Wiping his sweaty face with the bottom of his T-shirt,

Peltz froze, the realisation sinking in.

'Fuck,' he said. 'Tell me we know. Tell me we know he's dead. The fucking Ukrainian. Tell me we know that.'

'The Ukrainian's... *dead?*' said the voice, his surprise registered by the rising modulation. Peltz opened his mouth, but his brain was flatlining. He quickly jumped on the keyboard, his fingers typing at supersonic speed. A series of windows and login boxes appeared and disappeared as he went through security steps to connect his laptop to a Virtual Private Network or VPN.

Every device on the internet, whether a computer, fridge, phone or TV, had an Internet Protocol address – a sequence of numbers that acted as a digital postcode. An IP could be traced from one side of the world to the other in as long as it took to sneeze and wipe your nose. But there were ways to mask it. The most popular option was an anonymising system such as a VPN, or a TOR browser, which routed the device's internet connection through a number of nodes – hundreds, if not thousands – burying it in the mass of traffic that filled the web. It made it near impossible to trace. Perfect for criminals.

'What do you mean he's...' the voice tailed off. 'How dead?'

'As dead as it says in the paper,' said Peltz, working away. 'They found his body Tuesday morning. Blew his fucking head off.'

'Are you sure?'

'That's your job. I'm not sure of anything anymore. It was in the *Metro*. Today's edition.'

'Why didn't your system pick this up?'

'His name and variations are in the metadata. The crawlers should have sent out alerts, unless the *Metro* decided to jump back 100 years to do everything analogue!'

'Hold on...' said the digitised voice.

Peltz finally connected to a remote computer; a Virtual Machine or VM for short. By name, the computer wasn't real. Its digital existence consisted of software on an apportioned area of shared disk space, nestled in among 100 other VMs. Its physical existence was a single hard disk in an array of hard disks connected to a mainframe, stacked in an eight-foot cabinet that stood in an air-conditioned cargo container next to 30 others in a secluded industrial site north of Hamar in Norway.

It was sunny in Hamar, but Peltz wouldn't know and didn't care. On the VM, Peltz opened up the desktop version of Tork2Me. The application wasn't available to the public, having been developed in-house to ensure security was tight and the code unavailable to bored hackers looking for a challenge.

As well as hosting secure phone calls, Tork2Me had chat channels. Entering one called #StudioB, Peltz was presented with a chat box and a list of channel occupants. There were about a dozen of them, all with random and sometimes bizarre nicknames. Not all users were active though; most of them idled in the channel, which let them dip in and out at a convenient time to review the day or week's activity.

'You there?' said Peltz into the phone, '…he's still online.'

He shouldn't have been there, though. The user "Espresso" had put both barrels of a sawn-off shotgun through his brain two days prior and his computer had been confiscated by the police. Yet there he was, a digital ghost among the other channel occupants.

'Could be a fucking puppet,' said Peltz, typing a command into the chat box. He hit enter and Espresso disappeared from the user list. Peltz then loaded status information about him, her or it.

'Hello?' said Peltz into the phone.

The voice came back, 'I can't talk now.'

'He's been idle since Monday,' said Peltz, '…9:20 pm—
'

'This is unacceptable.'

Peltz's teeth locked. 'I'm not in his pocket 24/seven,' he said. 'We promised him space.'

'I'm not blaming you. I can't talk. Inform the others and drop everything, this takes priority. I want it sterilised like a surgeon's glove.'

The line went dead. Peltz dragged the headset off and bounced it off the table where a hundred coffee rings were stained into the wood.

Hands clasped together, Peltz regained focus. He had things to do.

First, he logged into Notitia, their system that monitored more live traffic than all the world's stock markets combined. Its job was information, specifically language – words, syntax, phrases, patterns, modulation. Governments had used something similar to track down terrorists, but the whistleblower Ed Snowden exposed their use of such invasive systems in the summer of 2013. The Studio learned from their mistake.

Peltz loaded a database of metadata that Notitia referenced 1000 times a second. He searched for the terms "Nikolai" and "Guskov" separately at first, then combined. Neither existed. The only explanation Peltz could think of was that the Ukrainian had been in and removed himself from the library of terms, which explained the absence of system alerts, but how the lad had got into the protected system in the first place made Peltz's stomach turn over.

What else had he done?

Peltz's team would be tasked with comprehensive system health checks, but for now his next priority was the whereabouts of Nikolai's computer. While the lad was vigilant – like they all were and had to be – he was only human after all. It only took some slight misjudgement or slip for a breadcrumb to be left behind. And what Peltz didn't want is for some jobsworth cyber-crime officer to pick it up.

SIX

The metal case came away from the chassis with ease, exposing the guts of the computer. Beckford wore latex gloves, because despite the unfathomable wealth of data stored on a computer, fingerprints and DNA could very well be the only evidence left behind. Often the best convictions were the simplest.

BBC 6 Music squawked out of a pair of tiny speakers balanced precariously on a shelf. The examination room was soundproofed, but unless audio was an important part of the task at hand, the radio was a necessity; the hypnotic drone of computers had been known to send officers mad.

With the computer lying on its side, Beckford peered in and noted the make, model and capacity of each component – hard drive, RAM, motherboard, graphics card etc. Then with one of the many cameras the HTCU had at their disposal, Beckford took a few snaps; close-ups of individual components, then a wider shot, one of the computer sat upright and one from every side.

The physical state and makeup of a computer often gave great insight into its owner, so much so that Beckford had become pretty good at building a picture of them without even turning the machine on. Age was important. Technology moved at such speed that an old dusty machine running outdated software wouldn't typically be owned by someone au fait with computers. A pre-built, branded machine pointed to a standard consumer whereas a custom-built spec pointed to someone of higher technical ability.

The components gave clues too. A high-end graphics card suggested either a gamer or graphic designer. A specialist audio card could be fitted for a musician or producer. Multiple hard drives depended on the setup – a mishmash of different makes and sizes inferred the user had upgraded as and when they needed more space, possibly a casual user who liked to download a lot of illegally sourced movies, music or software. If the hard drives were all the same size, they were possibly configured in a redundant array of independent disks, also known as RAID – a way of combining multiple disks to span the storage and share the processing of data. If this was the case, it meant data integrity was important to the user, pointing a finger at a developer or systems analyst, possibly someone running their own server.

Farber had sent over her preliminary report, but Beckford hadn't read it yet. Where was the fun in that? The challenge kept things interesting and if the picture he built in his head turned out to be correct, the resulting smart-arse euphoria never got old. Unfortunately, as he inspected the components of the computer he realised there was to be no ego-boost today. Everything about it was standard – standard case, standard components, standard software. And standard meant faceless, anonymous.

A faceless computer for a faceless kid. Beckford smirked at that one.

* * *

'This is cosy,' said Farber, the door sucking shut behind her.

'Sometimes I just come in here to get some peace and quiet,' said Beckford. 'Especially working with that lot out there.'

'I thought computer nerds were the quiet, antisocial types?'

'At parties, yeah. Drop them in an office full of tech and it's like a Doctor Who convention. Anyway, who are you calling a nerd?'

'No shame in that, John. Nerds are super cool these days.'

'Well, in that case, yeah: I'm a nerd,' said Beckford, swaggering over to a spare chair. He sensed Farber rolling her eyes behind him. She hated it whenever he acted cocky, but it amused Beckford tremendously.

'Madam,' he said, wheeling the chair over to her. They both took a seat in front of Nikolai Guskov's exposed but whirring computer. Farber planted her bag on the floor and placed a plastic wallet of case notes on the workbench in front of her.

'Saw Michaels on TV last night, said Beckford, flicking the mouse to kill the screensaver. 'Thinning a bit on top, isn't he?'

'I'll tell him you said that,' she said.

'Please don't. He'd kill me with his bare hands.'

'He'd kill me if he knew I was here for a suicide,' said Farber. 'Please give me something juicy, and don't tell me it's just a bunch of porn. Although does anyone actually download porn anymore?'

'You'd be surprised,' said Beckford. 'Collectors like anything they can hoard, especially if they can count it in gigabytes.'

Farber grabbed her notes and slid out a few pages, 'The firearm report came back. Remington 12 bore… or gauge if you're American.'

Beckford took the photograph. 'As common as Ford Fiestas,' he said.

'Forensics only found one set of prints,' said Farber, 'which means he sometimes took off those gloves. What I'm finding hard to believe is someone as quirky and antisocial as Nikolai Guskov buying this gun from a local gangster. Makes me think he purchased it online, possibly from people back home. Maybe I'm jumping the gun a bit.'

'Nice pun.'

'Oh God, sorry. Unintentional.'

'But yes, you are jumping it,' said Beckford. 'I wasn't able to glean anything like that, primarily because there's nothing on here.'

'Nothing? No accounts? His social networks would be useful.'

'Nada,' said Beckford, clicking the mouse. A window popped up showing a list of files and folders. 'It's very odd. You'd expect a young lad, a student especially, to have all sorts of crap on here. Games, music, grotty bookmarks, weird downloads, coursework, maybe some porn, but the hard disk is as clean as you like. Just a standard installation of the operating system. No third-party software. No internet history. No images or personal documents. Apart from the dust, you'd think it was a brand-new system. So, I dug a little deeper. You know how when you delete a file it's never truly gone for ever?'

'Yes,' said Farber, searching her brain. 'It can still be recovered unless the space it occupied is overwritten by something else…?'

'That's right. Well, I ran our data recovery software on it. Nothing. I checked file logs, system logs and went right to the root of the computer. Not a thing.'

Farber's disappointment was apparent. Beckford let it sit a moment, having weaved his summary like the three-act plot of a film.

'But there is one thing,' he said, minimising the window and revealing the computer's desktop. He dragged the mouse cursor to the only icon on there; a file called, "*WATCH ME.*"

He looked at her and said, 'It's a bit nasty.'

Farber gave him a nod and looked back at the screen. Beckford double-clicked the file and a video appeared showing a young man who they both recognised as Nikolai Guskov, his face gaunt and pale. Nikolai was sat in his dorm room, staring at the camera. The video quality wasn't great; the ceiling light had created a flare across the lens, worsened by a smudge in the bottom left-hand corner – possibly caused by a greasy finger or some other residue.

There was sound too; a dance beat, loud but distant, pulsating in the background.

'Halloween party,' muttered Farber.

At the centre of the screen, Nikolai's eyes penetrated the lens with intensity. He spoke with a thick Ukrainian accent, his voice low and shaky.

'We live our lives in the digital world more and more each day. It's not a safe place. Your every move is recorded with excessive amount of data. At home, work, on holiday. You cannot avoid it. Chatting to friends. Doing weekly shop. Walking down street. Yes, just walking down street – CCTV films wherever you go. Your mobile phone conversations recorded. Your GPS location tracked. There is nowhere you can go, there is nowhere you can hide. You are being watched all the time. There is only one way to disconnect.'

In the video, Nikolai stood up, his head and shoulders leaving the frame of the shot but his hands coming into view, revealing the sawn-off shotgun – the Remington 12 bore that Farber still had a photo of clamped between her thumb and forefinger.

Before she could even comment, Nikolai jammed both barrels under his chin and pulled the triggers. A blast, distorted like a digitised cannon, exploded from the computer speakers in the lab causing Farber to shudder.

Nikolai's corpse dropped out of frame like a giant sandbag, leaving behind a soft nebula of discharge smoke suspended in the air and a spray of blood on the wall and ceiling behind him. The relentless dance beat continued pounding, ominously, like the beat of a heart. Beckford clicked the "X" in the top right corner of the window and the video disappeared.

He turned to Farber and could see that she was stunned. Despite the numerous dead bodies police officers dealt with as part of their job, they rarely witnessed someone die up close and personal, even if it was low resolution. Farber stood up and turned from the computer, brushing her sweaty palms on her skirt.

'You all right?' Beckford asked. Farber turned back and nodded with a false smile, perching herself on the other workbench. Beckford added, 'It's a lot better than most of the stuff we get here.'

Farber took a deep breath and dragged her fingers through her hair, ruffling her brown curls. Beckford remembered her tics like it was yesterday. The hair ruffling was one of her ways to snap back and focus. She looked at him, ready to continue.

'The video runs for 14 hours after he pulls the trigger,' said Beckford. 'It shows you lot arriving and doing your thing, right up to the point where the computer's unplugged. It's nine hours and 58 minutes between Nikolai killing himself and the concierge coming through the door, putting his death at 11:46 pm, give or take.'

'Okay, so at least the video proves there's no sign of foul play.'

'The postmortem come back yet?'

Farber nodded to the wallet on the workbench, 'Knock yourself out.'

Beckford dragged out the report and pored over the

pages. After a moment Farber said, 'You miss it, don't you?'

Beckford heard her straightaway but took a moment to consider his answer.

'How about a coffee?' he said, regretting it the moment the words left his lips. It was the look on her face.

'Now? I really should be getting back—'

'I meant after work,' he said, cursing himself again for speaking before thinking. *What are you trying to achieve here John?*

The silence was unbearable. Beckford could see the cogs behind her eyes turning over. A question like "how about a coffee?" would have felt innocent and casual between most people, but not Farber and Beckford. Not with everything that had gone on before. Beckford held her gaze, trying everything in his might to exude innocence and casualness.

Coffee with an old friend, he said in his head, hoping she'd hear him.

'Actually…' she said, 'I have yoga on Wednesdays. I hate to miss a class. Sorry.'

Beckford sucked his lips in and nodded. 'Some other time then,' he said, but inside he was thinking, *that's right up there with the most stupid things you've ever done.*

Before the awkwardness could get any worse, Beckford pointed at the computer.

'I'll try to wrap this up quickly,' he said. 'There are still a few more things I've got to… well, these procedures usually take for ever and I kind of skipped a few things, you know, to speed it up for you.'

'That's fine,' said Farber. 'Just let me know when to pick it up and I'll be right over.'

After Beckford had amicably shown Farber the door, he went back to the lab for solitude where he stewed over the last few minutes of their conversation. The coffee question, her reaction. Had it been too long? Was she seeing someone new? Did she just find the whole thing a bit much?

After a few minutes more, he realised he was on dangerous obsessive territory. Hoping to break his thought patterns, he turned his focus back to the exposed computer on his desk.

Strange, isn't it? he told himself, feigning interest in the hope it would distract him.

But it *was* strange and the more Beckford thought about it, the more it took centre stage in his mind. There was something just not right about Nikolai Guskov's computer. The video proved no sign of foul play, but why go through the trouble of restoring the machine back to a forensically blank state? It wouldn't take a digital expert to suspect that if a computer genius like Nikolai had done that, they must have had something to hide.

SEVEN

It had just passed midnight; a rare time of the day when the Dunning Street halls were hibernating, the lack of activity accredited to it being late enough to have missed the drunken students heading out for cheap nights in crappy dives in and around East Twickenham and early enough to avoid their return.

The road was also quiet, with most of the pubs and takeaways having closed for the night. By a bus stop, a man waited while his Yorkshire terrier urinated on a bin. He carried on walking and the dog caught him up with a sharp pitter-patter of claws on concrete. Peltz used to have a Yorkie. He reminisced briefly about Chappy before checking the dashboard clock again and gulping down the final third of a scalding Americano. It wasn't the best idea, as his stomach had been churning like a washing machine all day.

When the coast was clear Peltz left his car, lugging a heavy holdall from the passenger seat. No sports attire this time – Peltz was wearing a full suit and tie. Within seconds of leaving his car he'd crossed the road, swiped a keycard at the Dunning Halls entrance and was inside. With the lift already waiting on ground level, he got in and pushed the button for the fourth floor.

When the doors opened again the corridor was dark. As Peltz stepped out and turned right, motion-sensor lights flickered into life. He'd only been to the Ukrainian's room once before, but he remembered exactly where it was, what colour the door was, even the dings and chips out of the wooden doorframe. He remembered everything.

Apart from the faint sound of a panel show coming

from one of the rooms, the floor was quiet. Peltz kept light on his feet, and on his journey he neared the sound of the TV show and passed it, localising it to room 407.

When he eventually reached 412 he crouched and unzipped one of the bag's side pockets. He lay a lock-pick set on the carpet and quickly slid on some surgical gloves. The lock only took 12 seconds to click open. Peltz had counted. It wasn't a personal record by any means, but it was close. He entered the room slowly, quietly, closing the door behind him and locking it again.

When he flicked on the main light he was looking directly at the computer desk opposite, ignoring the blood stains on the carpet and bone fragments still embedded into the rose-splashed ceiling. The keyboard, mouse, monitor and speakers remained, but there was no computer, just a clean rectangle on the desk surrounded by dust – the computer equivalent of a chalk body outline.

Peltz hadn't expected to see the Ukrainian's machine as he knew it had been confiscated. Taken from the scene by a DI Alison Farber and delivered to Water Street police station at 3:32 pm on Tuesday afternoon where it was signed in by a DC Michael Fitch and assigned to a DS John Beckford for forensic analysis.

Peltz had read Beckford's report.

Peltz had watched the video.

In fact, Peltz knew as much information about Nikolai Guskov's suicide as the police did. But that wasn't enough. Not by a long shot. The Studio didn't operate by matching the pace of the police. In almost all cases they were always ahead of them by quite some margin. It was the only way to cover their tracks. The fact that they were now playing catch-up made Peltz's ulcer scream in protest.

Not wasting any time, he found an uncompromising area on the carpet to dump his bag. He lay his suit jacket on the bed, undid his tie, then pulled a laptop from the main compartment of his bag, opening it up on the floor. Then, with a camera in his hands, he stood back against the door and snapped a wide-angle photo of the room. The first of many. It was going to be a long night.

* * *

At around half three in the morning, a herd of inebriated students flooded the corridor outside, forcing Peltz to take a break and sit in darkness for 20 minutes. He listened in as the students were berated by a fellow undergraduate trying to get some sleep. About five minutes later, a girl in tears was being consoled by her friend about a boy named Carl. Anyone else would have been amused by their adolescent drama. Not Peltz. He was pissed off. He was there to do a job with a very limited timescale in which to do it in.

By the morning, piles of books, clothes, bedding and other unearthed paraphernalia scattered the carpet. With no margin for error or complacency, Peltz had searched every square inch of Nikolai's room with a meticulous attention to detail. Both the wardrobe and computer desk had been pulled away from the wall, taken apart piece by piece and screwed back together again to ensure nothing was hidden within the wood or metal. The pipe under the sink had been removed and checked for clogged waste. The carpet had been lifted and tacked back down. Even the cheap generic wallpaper had been scrutinised for signs of tampering.

In the desk drawers, Peltz had found stacks of coursework and lecture notes. Each page was photographed and uploaded there and then to one of the Studio's servers, where the images would be run through an Optical Character Scanner to search for specific keywords or phrases that might compromise their organisation.

Across two shelves were 27 textbooks. As Peltz leafed through number 24 – *Computer Architecture: A Top-Down Approach* by Adam Longhorn – the sound of a door closing in the corridor broke his concentration. He turned his head and saw light easing in under the curtains. It was time to go.

He fanned through the final three books quickly and stacked all 27 back on the shelves, consulting a photograph on his laptop for the exact order and positioning of each volume. He then toured the room like an estate agent, tabbing through a number of other continuity shots on his laptop, ensuring everything was in place and exactly how he found it. Once satisfied, he packed his laptop away and used baby wipes to give his face, neck and armpits a rub down before dousing himself with antiperspirant.

In Nikolai's murky mirror he put his tie back on, his jacket and then combed his hair to make himself look somewhat presentable. He patted his jacket pockets, confirming which side his false warrant card was on, then slinging the bag over his shoulder he put an ear to the door and yawned for the first time all night. Next stop would be quick fry-up and a double espresso, then back to the hotel. He'd done his bit, the others would take over from here.

When a sufficient stretch of silence filled the corridor outside, Peltz took a deep breath and left the room.

EIGHT

Beckford sat up in bed, his head muggy. His alarm was due to go off in 10 minutes, but he'd been restless in the night and decided it was time to call it quits. His dreams were strange and made little sense, but it was clear Farber's reintroduction to his life was the catalyst.

Sifting through the cacophony of fragmented sounds and images from the night, Beckford tried to piece them together like a film editor. In his dream he'd been where they found her again. A ditch in an unassuming woodland just off the M5 motorway. His sister Sally, her body had long gone, taken away by the coroner in a black PEVA bag. The crime scene circus had also been and gone, and all that remained was the dirt, the grass and some of the foliage her corpse had been found under. And Farber. She was there.

It was the case he wanted to be apart of but couldn't. Sally, the wild child who ran away from home at 16, a prostitute in her late twenties. Beckford could have been there for her if he'd known. If she'd told him. If he'd asked.

Searching further through his fading memory, Beckford assured himself that Peter McGregor made no appearance in his oppressive dreams; it was something at least, and yet the simple act of thinking about him, coupled with a lack of quality sleep, could easily send Beckford down an unwanted, obsessive path.

Typical of many OCD sufferers were the intrusive and unpleasant thoughts and the dread that they may act upon them. In times of stress, Beckford's obsessive focal point was nearly always Peter McGregor. The thoughts, taking on a reality of their own, would show Beckford arriving at

Woodhill Prison, sneaking the plastic shiv beyond security, facing the man who raped and murdered his sister and then violently stabbing him in the carotid artery again and again and again until Beckford was dragged off the man's blood-soaked corpse by wardens.

It was a fantasy born out of pure and unmitigated vengeance, but Beckford was a police officer, not a killer. He knew right from wrong, and yet no matter how irrational the wild fantasy, the pang of terror that accompanied it felt like a personal promise that it was destined to become a reality. And that's what he feared the most. Irrationality was often bypassed in the mind of an obsessive-compulsive.

Beckford watched the news for a while, distracting himself with equally disturbing events. Flicking between the channels, he stopped at a clip showing police officers holding back a baying mob of journalists and angry bystanders as a prisoner transport truck flanked by police outriders was escorted from the Old Bailey.

'*…Uttridge, one of London's most notorious crime lords, will spend tonight in Woodhill Prison before being transferred to Wakefield tomorrow where he will begin a life sentence.*'

'Sayonara,' said Beckford.

Although he had never dealt with Roger Uttridge directly, Beckford had come in contact with many of his underlings and the rackets they ran. Guns, drugs, trafficking, prostitution and money – they did it all. Nailing the kingpin was sending the right message, and despite the fact that there was always someone else standing by to take the throne, the initial unrest and instability of a toppled king often produced a period of criminal inactivity until the vacuum was filled. It gave the Met enough time to make headway in other areas, giving themselves the breathing space they needed to prepare for the inevitable approaching storm.

It was clear that things at the Metropolitan Police were on the up. Beckford didn't trust stats, because he knew what often went unnoticed or ignored in order to gather them, but what he couldn't deny was the increasing respect and appreciation from the capital. Public confidence was one of the most important factors and something the Met had put significant effort into acquiring and maintaining. And right now, they were flying.

* * *

A fluorescent strip flickered to life, flooding the HTCU lockup with a bleached hue. Beckford entered, followed by DS Rebecca Hayman, a tall natural redhead with glasses and a friendly face. The lockup, nicknamed "The Graveyard," contained rows of metal shelving units that stored a variety of bagged electronic devices – computer base units, laptops, tablets, mobile phones, cameras, hard drives, memory sticks, satellite receivers, games consoles and even the occasional pager. It was the archaic technology that garnered the room's nickname, with the majority of hardware that was sent there, dying there, submitted as a precautionary response but never called upon.

The legal cases that the items were affiliated with either closed successfully without the aid of digital evidence, which meant the device was awaiting return to its original owner (or to be destroyed if there was no owner to go back to) or the case never got off the ground in the first place and was stuck in evidential limbo, the device waiting to be summoned for evermore. It put storage space in the Graveyard at a premium. Noakes had been in negotiations for some time to take over an empty room on the first floor, but internal politics kept delaying the move.

'He's doing great,' said Hayman as they walked and talked. 'Started nursery last month, which was a little scary. More for us than him to be honest, he never wants to come home.'

Beckford scanned the shelves as they passed. 'I can't believe he's nearly three,' he said, 'and I still can't believe Ben procreated if I'm honest.'

Hayman laughed, 'My dad said something similar. Actually to Ben's face. Gave him a bit of a complex, I think.

'Another one to add to the list,' said Beckford. 'Just don't let Declan grow up to be a copper, all right? There's a million better jobs out there.'

'I was thinking professional footballer.'

'As long as he doesn't play for Man United you have my blessing.'

They stopped at one of the many clear-bagged computers in the racks and Beckford checked the label.

'Here it is,' he said, tugging at the plastic knot on top and burying his hand inside. He slid out a form and handed it over.

'Use that,' he said, pointing to a nearby base unit on the floor. Hayman placed the form down, scribbled her signature and passed it back to Beckford who added his own, dated it and slid it back into the bag.

'Job done,' said Beckford, lifting the machine. 'Want me to carry it to your car? You are a woman after all.'

'Fuck you,' said Hayman with a smile. Beckford loaded the unit into Hayman's waiting arms. 'Maybe see you at Declan's party?' she said.

'Maybe,' said Beckford as a formality, although they both knew he wouldn't be there.

Hayman shifted the machine under one arm, gave him a salute and exited the lockup. When he heard her close the internal door to the corridor, Beckford took a small bottle of antibacterial hand gel from his pocket and squirted a five-pence amount into his palm. The bags got dusty and he just hated the feeling on his skin.

Next, he logged the computer transaction on another form hung from the rack shelf, listing every item that had been deposited and withdrawn from that particular space over the past six months; another crucial measure to the complex and sometimes overwhelming chain of custody.

As Beckford scrawled, his attention suddenly switched to the adjacent space. He stopped writing and side-stepped in front of a different bagged-up computer.

One benefit to Beckford's OCD was that it made him scrupulously tidy, forcing strict organisation of things, promoting order, good aesthetics and efficiency. Some people saw it as a hindrance, but Beckford knew it was a perk, especially in cybercrime. Ones and zeros were the atoms of the digital world, infinitesimally small in the grand scheme of things, but each one having a logical purpose and reason for being. That's what made Beckford such a good forensic investigator – his attention to detail. And it was a detail in Nikolai Guskov's bagged computer in front of him that piqued his interest.

For the purpose of efficiency, Beckford's method of choice when tying the bag was a slip knot, allowing them to be opened easily with one tug. He'd done it hundreds of times with all the devices he'd ever investigated and packed away. He'd done it to Nikolai's computer the day before. But when he reached up, took a firm hold of the plastic above the knot and tugged… the knot tightened.

Most people would have shrugged it off – they'd tied a different knot, *so what?* Not Beckford. The slipknot was an action ingrained in him on a subconscious level. It was a habit. He'd *never* tie an ordinary knot, that would have required a conscious decision and one he'd certainly remember.

He stood staring at the computer, his brain whirring and clicking. His investigatory thought process was the same every time. He'd ask himself the question, answer it to the best of his ability with the information he had at hand with an added spoonful of logic, and it would offer up another question, which he'd also answer… and so on. One after another they'd come, linked together like an ancestry chart.

Why would anyone else look at Nikolai's computer? A simple misunderstanding, perhaps? Like, "Whoops, not that one." Bag re-tied. Yes, possible.

Maybe I made a mistake in my investigation and someone wanted to check? No. People in the office rarely step on each other's toes, but if anyone makes a misjudgment or error that someone else is aware of, it's always communicated in an informal one-to-one. We're loyal here, not snitches. No one has said a thing to me, and they've each got a list of jobs as long as their arms, so why would they voluntarily get involved with someone else's work?

Maybe we've been audited? I haven't seen any dour-faced suits in the building, and Noakes would have mentioned it. He doesn't keep things like that from me.

On bad days, Beckford could sometimes get stuck in a loop. Most of the time he'd exhaust all questions and would be left with two options: leave well alone or take pursuit. And pursuit was always the more alluring option.

For the conundrum in front of him, Beckford battled hard, presenting himself with enough reason and rational thinking to emphasise how irrational the pursuit would be, not to mention a complete waste of time and energy. Unfortunately his OCD fed on resistance, and despite physically removing himself from the scene and tricking himself into thinking he'd taken the mental high-road by burying his suspicions, Beckford was well-versed in its relentless control over him.

The issue gnawed at him until late into the afternoon when the frustration and annoyance reached boiling point and he couldn't concentrate on anything else. Managing to steal a few minutes, Beckford locked himself in one of the labs where he logged into the door security management system – a system that recorded entry and exit times of all ID card holders at every secure door in the building. It was an open system, meaning anyone could log in and check if they wanted to, but Beckford didn't want to be seen doing so. That would only raise questions.

A list of dates and names scrolled down the screen, but straightaway he could see the only person who'd entered the Graveyard in the past 24 hours was… him. He didn't buy that, not for a second. Security was extremely vigilant at the HTCU, but people had been known to be complacent. He'd done it himself, jamming the Graveyard door open with a computer case or not checking he had closed it properly on leaving. It was possible the entry system was faulty. A bit of a stretch, but possible.

Next on Beckford's list was the CCTV footage.

With the HTCU being a relatively new but growing department, their basement office at Water Street was a hand-me-down that they'd started to outgrow. Because of this, the Graveyard wasn't part of the main office, but a room further down the corridor. Getting to it unseen was a doddle, but there were two security cameras, one outside and one inside. Beckford sunk his teeth into a pink lady apple and fast-forwarded through footage from the previous day.

At 19:14 he'd entered the Graveyard carrying Nikolai's PC, bagged and tied. Unfortunately, the video quality wasn't good enough to see the knot, and he'd done the bagging and tying in the lab where there was no CCTV. He was so certain he'd tied a slipknot he would have bet his life on it. Three minutes late at 19:17 he left the Graveyard.

Beckford fast-forwarded and didn't see another soul through the whole evening. When the timecode hit 22:00 the lights inside the Graveyard automatically turned off and the camera switched to infrared, illuminating the racks of gear in shades of ghostly monochrome. The timecode fluttered on and on, past midnight and through early morning. Not a soul. If it wasn't for the timecode, Beckford would think he was looking at a static image.

At 07:00, the Graveyard lights turned back on and the camera switched over to colour. There was no movement until Beckford saw himself enter with DS Hayman. He paused the video and leaned back in his chair, chomping the last morsel of apple before dropping the core in a nearby bin. It didn't make any sense. He wished it did, he could have let it go and got on with more important matters. Instead, he headed back to the Graveyard.

Taking Nikolai's computer from the rack, he placed it on the ground and removed the bag. With a Phillips-head screwdriver, he took two screws from the back of the unit and with a bump of his palm, the case came away. Beckford could see the hard drive was intact. Four screws later, it came free from its metal chassis.

Each computer component had a serial number, either stamped on the device directly or on a label stuck to it. The serial – typically a series of eight numbers and letters – was issued by the manufacturer, allowing them to catalogue and identify each item they produced. It also played an important role in the forensic examination process. With the large quantities of devices that went through Water Street each week, it was the only definitive way to tell them apart.

Beckford grabbed a biro and scribbled the hard drive's

make, model and serial number on a Post-it note before putting the computer together again and loading it back onto the rack. When he got back to the lab he loaded up Nikolai's computer report he'd typed the day before and held the Post-it up to the screen.

Same make, same model, same serial number. He was half-relieved and half-annoyed.

Did I really tie the wrong knot?

His eyes focussed on the Post-it stuck to his fingers as he assessed himself. He knew he hadn't slept very well. He blamed Farber. There was no warning, no preparation for her turning up like she did. Why didn't he take the job in Glasgow? London was a big place, but obviously not big enough.

Beckford stuck and unstuck alternating fingers to the gum of the yellow Post-it note. Tying the knot differently meant more than just a simple mistake. It meant disorder, which meant he was starting to lose control. He took the Post-it to the other hand and wiped his sweaty palm on his chest.

It always started with sweaty palms. The sensation was like a rollercoaster, slowly ratcheting its way up the chain lift hill. He could feel his chest tightening, his heartbeat pounding and his breathing become laboured. It was the early signs of what was to come.

Jolting up out of his chair he started to pace the room, using movement as a distraction. Sometimes it worked, most of the time it didn't. His thought process had been caught in the suction of an anxiety whirlpool, the revolutions quickening like the wheels of an accelerating bike. He stuck out an arm and rested his elbow on a shelf, closing his eyes and taking in long deliberately slow breaths.

Not now. Please not now…

The more he battled it, the more self-perpetuating it became. His therapist always advised him to just let it happen, to run to the edge of the building and jump, trusting that he'd land safely. Easier said than done when a panic attack was developing into raw terror.

Just as the swell of fear started to overwhelm him, a thought entered his head like a stick thrown into the revolving spokes.

If someone were to remove the hard drive from Nikolai's computer for malicious intent, they would cover their tracks. They would doctor the report.

During the examination of Nikolai's PC, Beckford scribbled serial numbers and other details onto a notepad, just like he did for all examinations. It was easier to gather the information longhand before inputting it into the report. Once in the system, the notes were torn out and disposed of in special "confidential information" bins that were emptied, shredded and incinerated nightly.

The empty notepad stared at him from the desk, but using the oldest trick in the book Beckford took a pencil to the pages, and with the graphite edge started lightly shading the paper. Agatha Christie would have been proud. The details of yesterday's report shone through as clear as day and when he held the pad up to the screen his stomach twisted like a hooked eel.

'John?'

Beckford turned. Noakes was stood at the door, leaning in. He hadn't even heard it unlock.

'Is everything okay?' asked Noakes. Beckford was hot and sweaty, his heart still battering against his rib cage.

'I think the air-con's bust again,' he said. 'You know what it gets like… these machines on all the time.'

Noakes looked up at the air conditioning unit. It wasn't on, but the temperature in the lab wasn't abnormal. In fact, a thermometer dangling from one of the shelves would have told them it was a perfect 21 degrees centigrade if either of them had checked.

'Corden's up in reception for you.'

Beckford swung a quick glance at his watch, amazed at how late it was. Noakes retreated from the door, then leaned back in.

'Are you sure you're all right?'

'I'm fine. I just had… well, it's passed now. I'm fine. Didn't sleep too well last night. Thanks. Tell her I'll be five minutes, will you?'

'You want *me* to ask a Commander to wait?' said Noakes. Beckford gave him a smirk and Noakes left the room, the door locking behind him.

Beckford turned excitedly back to the notepad, his eyes flitting from page to screen. Same make. Same model. *Different* serial. He double-checked the numbers 20 times or more, disbelieving his own eyes.

Has someone replaced the hard drive or is my mind playing tricks?

There must be a perfectly logical explanation for what I'm seeing.

Did I scribble down the wrong number?

Beckford grabbed the hard drive and checked his watch again. Before data interrogation could be carried out for a forensic examination, hard drives were 'cloned,' which meant duplicating their entire contents from the original hard drive to another of the same size, make and model. The cloned hard drive was then the device that the analysis was carried out on, ensuring maximum integrity of the data on the original source hard drive.

Beckford only had four minutes. He quickly slotted the original hard drive into a disk caddy connected to his computer and power flooded the device. It was recognised by the operating system and after a few mouse clicks Beckford was looking at the contents of the drive once again. The same drive where Nikolai's suicide video had originated.

It was empty.

NINE

They sat at a table as multicoloured bowls of Japanese cuisine passed them on a conveyor belt like game show prizes. It had been all fish and rice so far and Beckford couldn't stand anything that came from the sea apart from tinned tuna.

Commander Amelia Corden was a stern-looking woman in her early fifties. She wore the same rectangular tortoise shell glasses that she had done for years, but Beckford thought her hair looked a little darker than last time they met. Coloured possibly, although there was still an occasional grey wisp that poked out of her mousy-brown bob.

'I did ask you if this place was okay, John,' she said.

'To be honest,' said Beckford, 'I was a bit distracted when you mentioned it. Thought I'd trust you instead. They do noodles, surely?'

'Ask them to make you something.'

'Hold the phone, what's this?' Beckford picked a bowl off the conveyor and peered into what looked like chunks of something familiar, possibly potato. He took the lid off and when the smell hit his nostrils he dumped it back on the conveyor.

'Fish is excellent,' said Corden, tucking into something slimy looking. 'Good for the brain. Omega three. Protein. I'm surprised you of all people aren't into it.'

'There's only so far my neuroses will stretch.'

A brief gap opened up on the conveyor before another row of bowls came trundling along. Beckford reached out and grabbed one by chance: vegetable gyoza – dumplings with a miniature container of soy and vinegar sauce.

'I think we have a winner,' he said, dismissing

chopsticks and going straight for the fork. Corden had three empty bowls stacked to her side already and all Beckford had consumed was some yellow miso soup.

'As I was saying,' said Beckford, sticking his fork in the first dumpling, 'this fella's phone had about two-million pounds of cryptocurrency on it, and it became like the diamond from that film *Snatch*. Have you seen *Snatch*?'

'Jason Statham?'

'Yeah. So, people are robbing the phone from each other left, right and centre until it lands in the hands of some mid-level crook called Sam... Sam... *shit*, what's his name? Anyway, his *son* finds the phone one day, and – wanting to impress his dad – reformats its memory and installs a newer operating system. Two million quid, gone.'

'Oh dear.'

'This all blows up because the crook owed a ton of money to someone higher up, and so he gets his legs broken. That's how the phone ended up on my desk.'

'Did you recover the money?'

'Of course. And by the time I did, it was worth two-point-five.'

'Madness,' said Corden, taking a swig from a bottle of Asahi. 'Tulip mania for the 21st century. Still enjoying it then?'

Beckford had his mouth full and nodded – a kind of lazy side-to-side nod that could be construed as "so-so".

'Busy,' he said out of the side of his mouth, then chewed as he talked. 'It's fine. Nice people. Passed my probation last week, if you can believe that. I'm now an official digital forensic specialist.'

'It's *not* been 12 months,' said Corden, aghast.

'It sure has. We'll all be dead before we know it.'

'Christ on a canal boat. So why only "fine" then?'

Beckford finally swallowed, 'I'd prefer to get out a bit

more if I'm honest. I should have known that going in, it's not exactly the most active or healthiest of professions, hunched over computers for 10 hours a day.'

'What job is these days?' said Corden. 'I've been stuck behind desks for as long as I can remember, and let me tell you the higher you rise the worse it gets.'

'At least you've got a standing desk now. When's that money filtering down to us lowly peons? You know we'd work harder if we were standing up all day.'

'The Met only throws money at problems,' said Corden. 'Stop trying to change the subject, John. Your job?'

'My job, right. My job. So yeah, at least in homicide I got to use my legs, but let's not go down that road again. It's *fine*. Who knows? Maybe cyber crime is just a stopgap. Something for me to get some distance from all that… other stuff.' Beckford took a sip of his beer then added, 'Maybe I'll go back.'

A smile crept over Corden's face.

'Hold your horses,' said Beckford, 'I've seen that smile before. Don't go telling people I said that. It's just a loose idea that's been floating around my battered brain.'

'I won't tell a soul, John. But this is good. Things are… I mean, she's good then? What's her name? Your therap—'

Corden stopped as a waitress came in earshot and passed them by. Beckford took the opportunity to dip a dumpling in soy sauce and take a bite, nodding as he chewed.

'Dr Hampton-Smith,' he said. 'And yes, she's helping.'

'You're not sleeping with her, are you?'

'Best therapy there is,' said Beckford without missing a beat. Corden's eyes widened, then shrunk back when a smirk crawled onto his face.

'There's still time, I guess,' said Corden.

'I don't need to get under someone to get over someone.'

Get over someone? It was a slip of the tongue and Beckford prayed that Corden wouldn't notice.

'Graham told me you had an unexpected visitor the other day,' said Corden, the statement loaded with C4 explosives.

'The pigeon outside my window? Nah, he's always there.'

When Beckford made eye contact with her again, she could have been a statue, her stone eyes penetrating him. Beckford scoffed and added, 'For a 60-something-year-old, Noakes is quite the shit-stirrer. Yes, she came to the office. For work.'

'Couldn't have sent someone else?'

'Absolutely,' he said, chewing and nodding. 'But maybe she was just trying to be helpful.'

'She's a DI now, isn't she? Don't you think she's got better things to do than be a delivery driver? You're forgetting, Farber worked under me for a good couple of years before you joined CID. We played squash together.'

'How could I forget? You… playing squash.'

'Perhaps there's something still there.'

Beckford forked his final dumpling and raised it to his mouth. 'Of course there is,' he said, 'but it's not going to work.' He bit the dumpling off the fork and placed the dish to the side before scanning the flow of new bowls coming from the kitchen. Corden let him have a moment.

'CID will always be there for you John, but I've got something better.'

'Early retirement?' he said, picking another dish off the conveyor before putting it back.

'Retirement? John, you'll be working for as long as your body allows you to. No, I can't say too much about it apart from it's a specialist unit that I head up. I've wanted to bring you on board for some time, but then… Sally, et cetera et cetera.'

'What kind of specialist unit?'

'It's top of the heap. Our remit outstrips anyone, backed by the Commissioner himself, and for the last three years our annual budget has gone in the opposite direction to everyone else.'

'So that's where our money's gone,' said Beckford.

'A tighter budget is the reason we're doing so well. You understand, don't you John, that cost-cutting forced everyone to look closer and harder for better solutions to problems that riddled our organisation for decades?'

'Then why is your 'special unit' rolling in it?'

'You'll find out… if you want to.'

Beckford let the offer hang in the air between them. He took a sip of beer and glanced around the restaurant. A duet of high-pitched laughter pulled his attention to a couple of young Asian girls sat at the conveyor a bit further down from them. For a second, Beckford's train of thought was sent down a track of its own, wondering if the girls were actually Japanese tourists or British-born citizens. And if they were tourists, what did they think of the English equivalent of their local cuisine?

'Still taking medication?' asked Corden. Beckford looked at her, then down at his hands. Without realising it, he'd straightened two chopsticks out on the table, perfectly parallel to each other.

'No,' he said. It was easy to lie with only one syllable.

'And what about your thoughts? Does *he* still feature?'

Beckford's eyes stayed on the chopsticks while he softly nodded.

'I thought she was good,' said Corden, 'this therapist of yours?'

'You think that kind of shit gets erased after a handful of sessions?' said Beckford. 'There was an article about him in the paper the other week, what with it being the anniversary.'

'I saw it. I hoped you hadn't.'

'Couldn't help myself. Not exactly hell, that prison, is it? Sounds like it's got more books than the London library.'

'Peter McGregor is paying for his crime, John, don't let the papers—'

'He's not paying for a fucking thing!' he spat. 'We are. *I am*. While we're sat here, right now, I don't think of him locked in a cage crying pitifully in his own filth. I picture him laughing, his disconnected eyes beaming into me with a crude, evil smile plastered across his ugly fucking face. He's *comfortable*.'

'You'd rather he was dead?'

With one hand, Beckford took a napkin and started folding in the corners, ensuring the edges were equidistant from each other.

'It doesn't… it doesn't *feel* like justice, that's all I'm saying.'

'Justice?' said Corden. 'Justice shouldn't feel like anything. The more removed we are, the fairer the sentence. Philosophy one-oh-one, John.'

Corden was good at spinning the right perspective on things. Their catch-ups were getting fewer and farther between, but each time Beckford came away with renewed sense of purpose and place. She was good for him.

By the time the bill came, their conversation had steered onto more neutral subjects, such as what television programmes they'd been watching and how Corden's husband broke his radial bone while skiing in Austria. Gradually, as tiredness seeped in, Beckford's attention started to wane and his thoughts went back to Nikolai's computer.

It was clear that someone had broken into the Graveyard. Clear that they'd replaced the hard drive and then covered their tracks. With the only thing on the hard drive being a video, which Beckford had multiple copies of, Beckford struggled to think of any clear motive as to why someone would do all that.

When they left the restaurant into the cold, crisp evening, they said their goodbyes and went their separate ways. On the walk to the tube, Beckford got out his phone and called Farber.

TEN

They'd agreed to meet at 10:00 pm. Farber had just got out of yoga and needed to go home for a quick shower, she then swung by HQ for the key and fob from the lock-up. To burn some time, Beckford headed back to Water Street to double, triple and quadruple check the hard drive.

At 9:45 pm, Beckford left Water Street and grabbed the tube from Hammersmith, taking the District line to Richmond. Farber was already waiting for him outside the station, hands buried in a thick coat with a ruffled hood.

'That's a warm-looking coat,' said Beckford. 'Can we swap?'

'I'm bloody freezing,' she said.

Beckford was glad she'd driven. Dunning Street halls was in East Twickenham, about a 25-minute walk from Richmond over the bridge.

'Still listening to Smooth?' said Beckford, the radio kicking into life with Zoom by Fat Larry's Band when she turned the key in the ignition.

'I listen to whatever's playing a song I like,' said Farber, pulling out into traffic. Beckford detected a hint of defensiveness in her voice. He tried to keep the conversation amicable and lacking in awkwardness, but it was an unusual situation they'd found themselves in. After some menial chit-chat, Beckford's dislike for elephants in the room forced his hand.

'Who'd have thought we'd ever be in the same car again?' he said.

'Not me, that's for sure. It's weird, I know. Want me to turn around?'

Beckford glanced over and caught a smile on her face. It settled the mood somewhat, but there was an even bigger elephant that Beckford was hoping to steer the conversation towards – why had she dropped the computer round at Water Street in the first place?

Had she just wanted to see him again or was that Beckford's wishful thinking? Maybe it was *him* who wanted to see *her* again. Was their organised trip to Dunning Halls part of an ulterior motive?

No, he reassured himself. Someone had definitely broken into the Graveyard and covered their tracks. It was a genuine breach of security.

Beckford decided to leave the elephant alone, worried that if he brought Farber's own motives into question she might turn the car around. And he didn't want that, the mystery over Nikolai's hard drive had him hooked like a trout.

'We only dated for a few weeks,' said Farber, their conversation suddenly taking a natural detour from formal pleasantries to personal cross-examinations. 'He was a barrister.'

'Ah,' said Beckford with an unsavoury tone.

'He was very nice, actually. But… well, just very nice.'

'I guess we live in a world where very nice isn't nice enough.'

They drove over Richmond bridge and Farber knocked the indicator, taking a left.

'What was his name?' said Beckford.

'I don't think so, John.'

'I know him then?'

'I never said that, but I know what you cybergeeks can do with a name. That's a bit unfair on him, don't you think? Like I said, it was only a few weeks.'

'*Cybergeeks?*'

'Anyway. What about you?'

'Why would I look him up?' said Beckford. 'I'm sure

he's undoubtedly better looking than me, that's a given. I think you don't want to part with his name because I know him. A barrister?'

'Is this really that important, John?'

'Wait a minute…' said Beckford, a realisation dawning on him. 'Lawrence? What's his name… thingy Lawrence? Fuck. Dark beard. Agh. Wait… *Val* … Val Lawrence?'

Farber slowed to a stop at a red light, eyes on the road. Beckford felt his back teeth clench.

'I knew it,' he said, '…I just knew that prick'd swoop in. Man of the match through the Huffington case because he wouldn't leave you alone. Did you… no, don't answer that.'

'No I didn't!' protested Farber. 'Not that it's any of your business.'

Beckford stared straight ahead, half-regretting prying an answer out of her and half-relieved it was the answer he wanted.

'I'm sorry, Ali. You didn't have to say anything. It's none of my—'

'I kind of did though, didn't I?' she said. The lights flicked to green and she pulled away with enough gusto to pin Beckford back in his seat. 'So there we go,' she added. 'Now it's your turn.'

'You already know the answer.'

'There must have been someone…'

'Nope.'

Flashing blue lights approached in the oncoming traffic. The police car passed and turned out of sight in the rearview. Farber set her eyes back on the road and shook her head.

'No one? I find that hard to believe.'

'Believe what you want, it's the truth.'

As the awkwardness that had threatened to arrive finally

settled in, they drove for a few blocks relying heavily on the radio to fill the silence. Beckford didn't quite believe Farber either. A woman as attractive and confident as her, having slept with no one since their split over a year ago? What was she waiting for?

Unable to find a suitable space around Dunning Street, Farber parked two roads over and they made the rest of the way on foot, filling the journey with idle chit-chat about old friends.

'Staelder still got his mug?'

'Of course.'

Beckford let out a disgusted groan and laughed. Staedler had been drinking from the same grotty mug for 20 years. The piece of ceramic – which was originally gleaming white but now sported a thick layer of coffee tar – had followed him up and down the country, sitting proudly on any number of desks in each borough he'd been stationed.

'Jeanette still grinding him down?' said Beckford.

'Oh, she's still there. Or should I say *he's* still there. They make me laugh, those two. Still talk about you.'

When they got to the front entrance of Dunning Street halls, Farber produced a plastic fob. Beckford wasn't used to being ushered. From the moment he called her up, asking for a favour, he'd felt – for the first time in a long time – a sense of professional inadequacy. Working in the HTCU certainly had its perks, but they mostly existed in the digital domain. Out in the real world it was still the common or garden plod who ran the show.

'What's this all about then John?' said Farber, swiping the fob over the sensor. A thunk came from the heavy glass door and she pushed through, holding it open for him while he took a photo of the sensor on his phone.

'Thinking about getting one of those for your flat?' she said, her sarcasm laid on thick. 'This was a suicide, remember?'

'I just had to see something for myself,' he said, reviewing the image on his phone, wondering whether the model was connected to a backend system that logged exits and entries.

'Are the fobs divvied out per room or randomly?' he added.

'I'm just throwing fuel on the fire here, aren't I?' said Farber. 'Come on, I'm not heating the outdoors.'

Once inside, a short corridor led them to two lifts and a door leading to a flight of stairs. Beckford registered a CCTV camera in the ceiling and they took the lift to the fourth floor where they caught the attention of a group of congregating students outside one of the rooms. Farber and Beckford glanced at each other as a heavy sweet stench of marijuana hit them, but they carried on down the corridor without saying a word.

At the door to 412, Farber handed over some purple nitrile gloves, only to see that Beckford had brought his own.

'Moonlighting as CSI again?' she said.

'Only for TV.'

Upon entering Nikolai's old room, Beckford had a sudden overwhelming sense of familiarity. It wasn't the room itself, even though it did remind him of his own dingy dorm back at university, right down to the same miniscule sink and drab decor. No, it was the familiarity of a crime scene.

Every action had a reaction, and an incomprehensible number of each had led up to that point, leaving the room in the exact state he was looking at. A piece of the world, frozen in time. To uncover truth in the mystery of a crime scene, those actions had to be reverse-engineered, like turning the clock back, slowly and ever so meticulously.

Farber stood to one side and watched, getting her own sense of familiarity, seeing Beckford stood there, eyes searching, brain ticking. It was like the smell of an old aftershave. A pleasing echo from the past.

From a folder, Beckford slipped out a handful of crime-scene photographs showing various angles of Nikolai's corpse – his obliterated face, the way his legs entwined, his gloved hands. The autopsy photographs also showed his uncovered hands. Nikolai's fingernails were almost non-existent, the skin around them chewed away through habit. It made Beckford look at his own ragged nails with disappointment. It was a hard habit to crack.

Rifling through the photos he came to wide-angle shots showing the room as a whole. He stepped around the bloodstain on the carpet and held the photos up one by one, turning to place them against their origin. One photograph showed the original position of the desk chair, which had since been moved in order to remove the body.

Beckford wheeled the chair back to the desk and made eye contact with Farber – only a glance, a subconscious action as a result of being watched and nothing more. He looked at the chair for a full 10 seconds then sat down. Facing him on the desk was the monitor and webcam from where Nikolai had recorded his suicide.

'There's only one way to disconnect,' muttered Beckford under his breath. He stood up from the chair and mimed putting a shotgun under his chin, during which the chair had wheeled back just over a foot.

He pretended to fire the gun, opting for a garish sound effect that wouldn't go amiss during a children's game of soldiers, then he dropped lifelessly to the floor, hitting the chair and landing in the crimson patch. The thud would be heard downstairs, and even Farber found herself jumping at the impact.

'Christ, John.'

Beckford sat up nonchalantly and turned to look at the chair. It had been knocked as far as the bed, much further than in the video or photographs. Beckford bit the inside of his lip, then Farber said, 'Is this where you tell me you've got a strange fetish for re-creating snuff videos?'

Beckford stood up and faced her, letting his arms hang by his side in a display of vulnerability.

'I've changed so much since we last saw each other,' he said, the conviction in his voice so serious it made Farber's stomach turn over. Then he smirked.

'You prick,' she said. Beckford snickered and rounded the computer desk, lowering his head behind the monitor, trying to see what the webcam would see.

'You going to tell me what this is about?' said Farber, getting impatient. Beckford hesitated, wondering whether he should spill the beans about the hard drive, but he didn't know enough yet. The serial number, while wholly suspect to an obsessive like Beckford, could be dismissed as a glitch in the matrix and nothing more by someone not afflicted with his mindset.

'I find it strange that his computer had nothing on it,' he eventually said. 'It wasn't just clean, it was forensically spotless. That can only mean he had something to hide.'

'Like a dodgy music collection nicked off torrents?'

Beckford stayed where he was and retrieved more photos from the folder – printouts of individual frames from Nikolai's suicide video.

'Like something important,' he said.

'Did you see the video?' said Farber on an out breath, her patience waning. 'He was a paranoid loner who thought the government was tracking his every move.'

'He didn't say government.'

Farber uncrossed her arms, hands landing on her hips.

'Wow, you really do miss it don't you?'

Beckford held his left eye closed – his right eye the stronger of the two – and lined up a printout, shifting his head from side to side, trying to recreate the exact perspective.

'This monitor's been moved.'

'Most likely, John. We didn't realise we were dealing with a member of a terrorist cell at the time.'

'I'm not having a go,' said Beckford, 'I just wanted…'

He shifted the monitor out of the way and finally found the matching angle of the webcam. He waved Farber out of the way and she rolled her eyes, positioning herself over by the bed. Beckford took his phone out and snapped a couple of photos from where the webcam would have been, then came around the front of the desk and started rifling through the rest of the case paperwork.

'Why gloves?' he said. He saw Farber was only half-paying attention, so held up a photo of Nikolai's gloved hands, 'Obsessive-compulsive?' he added.

'And the rest,' she said, then nodded to the computer desk. 'Middle one.'

Beckford turned and slid open the middle drawer. It was brimming with medication: boxes, bottles, packets, tubs, creams. Everything ranging from over the counter stuff – ibuprofen and Sudafed – to prescriptions of Xanax, Librium and even Valium. Many of them hadn't been opened and for a brief moment Beckford wished Farber wasn't there; he could have given many of those pills a good home.

'Jesus.' He then added quickly, '…where was his GP?'

'Only people who exist have GPs, John. Nikolai was off the grid. No medical records at all.'

'You're telling me that's not the least bit suspicious?'

'He was an immigrant.'

'An immigrant studying at a fairly well-respected university.'

'I don't think you need to be registered with a local GP to enroll on a course there.'

'You *don't think*?' said Beckford, raising his eyebrows. Farber twisted her mouth at him.

'I know you understand how these cases work John, so why are you being such an arse about it? Are you just bored or something?'

He wasn't listening, his attention focussed on a toxicology report.

'Have you read this?' he said, angling the page for Farber to see. She huffed and shook her head. Beckford looked back at the page.

'He had enough paracetamol in his blood to kill him without putting a gun to his head.'

'Well, if you want a job done properly,' mumbled Farber.

Beckford could have taken her comment as sarcasm, but it was true; a gunshot wound to the human brain didn't always kill, even from something as powerful as a sawn-off 12 bore shotgun. Then again, overdosing on paracetamol wasn't definite either. Statistically he knew that only 15.5% of male drug-related suicide attempts were successful in the UK.

If you want a job done properly.

He flopped the report down on the desk and approached the bookshelves, loaded with a wide selection of academic textbooks covering many of the core computing subjects: networking, operating systems, programming, databases, security and algorithms. A pattern formed, one that Beckford identified quickly.

'Did he have a part-time job?' he said.

'Nikolai? No, he lived off the grants from his

scholarship.'

'He was a hacker,' said Beckford matter-of-factly, not taking his eyes off the books. For the first time that evening Farber's interest piqued and she stood up and joined him, tilting her head to read a few of the spines.

'I don't see any hacking books,' she said.

'You think Jamie Oliver reads cookbooks? These are fundamental subjects, everything a hacker needs in his arsenal.'

'Newsflash… computer science student reads computer books!'

'A *first-year* computer science student,' said Beckford, 'I saw the syllabus; Linux isn't covered until year two, and yet he's got…' he quickly tallied them up '…11 books on it. All security-based too.'

'Linux?'

'It's an OS… an operating system, used by most web servers. A computer that hosts websites, basically.'

'I know what a web server is John.'

He waved a hand over the shelves and said, 'No library books either. All purchased. That shows dedication.'

Farber looked closer at the books, sliding out copies at random. There wasn't a single library label or tag among them.

'So he bought them,' she said.

'They're academic books, Ali. You remember how expensive these were when you were at Manchester Met? And for a student with no job? There must be a grand's worth here, easy.'

He gripped a couple of books from the shelf and scanned the back covers.

'These aren't just hand-me-downs either, they're the latest revisions. It's costly being a computing scholar. Technology moves so fast and you have to move with it, especially if you're a hacker.'

Turning the book edgewise, he showed it to Farber and said, 'Look at the spines; read cover to cover a hundred times.'

'Someone could have supplied him with them.'

'You're right,' he said, the insinuation in his voice crystal clear.

'I meant as part of his scholarship,' said Farber, turning away and receding back into the room. 'Look John, if work at the HTCU isn't challenging enough, Michaels would have you back in a heartbeat. You know that, right?'

Beckford placed the book back on the shelf, stopped, then pulled it back out. It was titled *Advanced Database Design and Technology* by J H Mathers.

'John…'

'I can't go back,' he said, studying the glossy deep-blue cover of the book in his hands. There was an inset image with a gradient hue of yellows and oranges displaying numbers and symbols interconnected by arrows.

'Fine, it'll be awkward,' said Farber, 'I get that, so apply to be stationed elsewhere. Go north. You think their homicide squads wouldn't welcome an ex-Met detec—'

'I *can't* go back,' he said and the room fell silent.

A moment later, Farber's mobile rang from her bag. 'These bloody sales calls,' she said, 'same time every day.' She answered it and turned away.

Beckford looked back at the book in his hands. It was a paperback but weighty. Over two inches thick. Flipping the pages cover to cover, all he saw was dense technical documentation. He opened the book again at the beginning, the first couple of pages displaying basic publishing information. The following few pages had revision updates and a foreword by J H Mathers himself, where Beckford discovered the 'J' stood for John.

After the preface, acknowledgements, a barrage of pre-reading advice and content pages came another half-title page to signal the actual start of the book. Beckford brought the page up closer to his face.

In pencil, scribbled between the text of the title, were the numbers 4 4 4 3, like so:

ADVANCED

DATABASE

4 4 4 3

DESIGN & TECHNOLOGY

Beckford thought it looked odd, yet deliberate. It could have been easily missed on a more impatient leaf-through or even ignored, seen as a memo and nothing else. He flipped the pages one by one until he came across a seemingly insignificant page where the numbers '4443' had appeared again, this time in the top left-hand corner.

Flip, flip, flip. And again, page 208, bottom left.

Flip, flip, flip. Page 491, right in the centre.

When he reached the end of the book he'd found six more occurrences of the number sequence, all scribbled in pencil and with no bearing or correlation to each other. He turned back to the half-title page, set it down on the desk and took a photo.

Farber finished her call and turned back to him, 'No matter how many times you ask them to remove you from their sodding list…'

Beckford quickly placed the book back on the shelf.

'Well?' said Farber. 'What's happening John?'

He tried to not get ahead of himself. Notes and scribbles in books – student books especially – were 10 a penny. If the paperback had belonged to Nikolai and bought brand new as he suspected, then the scribbles would have been in his hand.

Another common symptom of OCD was finding importance in the least notable things, and to Beckford the numbers '4 4 4 3' were pure brain-bait. There was something else, too. It could have been the computer books, the chewed fingernails, the messy dorm, the loner aspect… but Beckford started to feel a strange affinity for the anonymous Ukrainian. Their commonalities were almost too close for comfort. On the realisation, Beckford stopped chewing his bottom lip and looked back at Farber.

'Time to go,' he said.

Farber lived in Clapham and dropped Beckford back at Richmond station on the way home. They sat in the car for a few minutes, delaying their goodbye by laughing and reminiscing about Beckford's 40th birthday.

He'd been called to a flat in a council block. A dead body, multiple stab wounds. It was only when Beckford crouched and got a closer look at the stiff that Staedler jumped up and scared the living shit out of him.

Beckford's terror was for ever etched on a photograph that he kept in the bottom drawer of his study. He was even more surprised that night to find out Corden – who was Chief Inspector of the department at the time – was the brains behind the jape. She'd even marked the event down as 'training' to keep the upper echelon none the wiser.

It was a great birthday. Everyone had a drink and then got back to work. It was the familial aspect of his old department that Beckford hadn't quite discovered at Water Street. Maybe it was the sense of belonging that he was yearning for.

Eventually, Farber yawned and Beckford took the hint. He didn't attempt any physical contact like a hug or kiss on the cheek, instead opting for a casual wave before shutting the car door. As she pulled away, Farber said something like 'See you soon,' but Beckford couldn't be sure.

He took the overground back to Wembley and kept his journey occupied by thinking of nothing but Farber. It was only in that final car ride together that things started to feel… comfortable, and he knew she felt it too.

By the time he'd entered his flat, his eyes felt puffy, his body heavy and his thoughts electric, having shifted now to Nikolai – the hard drive, the crime-scene photos, his dorm room and the shelf lined with books. Beckford desperately wanted to get online and deep-dive into questions that bombarded him, but before he could let his obsession have its wicked way he drifted off on the couch.

* * *

The men sat in the car, watching him sleep on a monitor. The camera, the size of a cigarette filter, was taped to the branch of a bonsai tree Beckford had on his shelf in the living room.

All day they'd been reporting back on his movements. They almost lost him in the crowd at Hammersmith station. And when he'd got off the tube at Richmond, Beckford had no idea one of them was breathing down his neck. With their containment operation in full swing, the target couldn't be let out of sight.

Satisfied that Detective Sergeant John Beckford was now asleep at his home, the men drove away from the apartment block.

They'd return first thing in the morning.

ELEVEN

'About time you updated your profile picture, isn't it?' Noakes asked.

Beckford was on Facebook. Unlike a lot of workplaces, social networking sites was a common sight at the HTCU. The likes of Facebook, Instagram and Twitter were fast becoming the go-to places to source personal information, each site containing veritable wealth of publicly accessible data.

'I get a lot of compliments on this one actually,' said Beckford, but Noakes had already disappeared into his office.

Two new cases had come in that morning. The computer of an accountant from a local solicitors on suspicion of fraud, and a collection of ageing laptops taken from the home of a businesswoman suspected of online scams, apparently having setup 40 separate websites with the intention of selling fake slimming pills. They both went into the queue and Beckford was assigned the accountant. It'd be weeks until he got round to looking at it properly, but at least he could use it a smokescreen.

Clicking into Facebook's search box, Beckford poised his fingers over the keys. The skin around his fingernails were pink and raw, the sight alone tempting him for another go. He'd not slept well again. At three in the morning he'd woken on the couch with a stiff neck and a dead arm. Once in bed, he lay there wide awake, wondering what Peter McGregor was doing. Sleeping like a baby, no doubt. A man with no conscience could do that.

Beckford had tried to break the cyclical thought

patterns, but things only escalated. They always did. Pacing his bedroom, eyes closed, he recited a monologue from Act III, Scene I of Shakespeare's Henry V. He couldn't remember when or where he'd learned the lines, but he knew them off by heart and used it as mantra, distracting himself in times of stress.

Once more unto the breach...

In the office, Beckford yawned. The smell of Kilburn's coffee wafted over the divider and for the first time in a long time he fancied one himself. Decaf was shit, everybody knew that.

In a subconscious, habitual move, he lifted a finger to his mouth, ready to start chewing, but he stopped himself. He made them bleed sometimes. Lowering his hand back to the keyboard, he looked at the search box, half-tempted to type "Alison Farber." That wouldn't be a good idea, he'd already been down one rabbit hole that morning.

Instead he typed "Nikolai Guskov" and hit enter.

A list of user-profiles flooded the screen. Some of the names were written in native Ukrainian, some in English, yet only a handful had an exact match, the rest of them being partial matches like "Nikolas Guskov" or "Nikolai Ruskov."

Of the correctly named profiles, half of them had photos, none of which showed the gaunt, pale face that Beckford was looking for. He visited each profile in turn, but not being "friends" with any of them, their privacy settings revealed nothing of interest apart from flecks of information such as gender, location and on the odd occasion their friends list. Grasping at straws, Beckford visited the profiles with no photos, desperate for any connection that could lead back to the faceless kid.

And there it was.

The profile had no photos and no personal information,

but the friends list was visible and consisted of 21 people, the majority of them appearing to be of eastern European ethnicity. But not all of them. Second from top was someone called "Robert Brown." Not very Ukrainian, Beckford thought.

Like the others, Robert Brown's profile was locked down with security, but there was one scrap of data that wasn't hidden and it was all Beckford needed.

Under "Education" was listed Harper College, London – the same college Nikolai attended. Like a star in the night sky, too dim to see directly, Beckford had found the Ukrainian in his peripheral.

Drawing his chair closer, he clicked through to Nikolai's now dormant profile, but there was nothing he could sink his teeth into. He clicked every link on the page, scrutinising any piece of information as if it were a viable nugget of gold. There was no gold, only rocks.

Ideally, Beckford needed Nikolai's login details, but he had the patience of a child on Christmas morning and getting full access to a user's profile would be done via a formal request from the office, a process that could take up to six weeks, not to mention requiring a valid case to put forward with it. A pencil-shaded serial number was hardly a bloodied dagger covered in fingerprints.

Clicking back to Robert Brown's profile, Beckford hit "PrtScn" on his keyboard, taking a screenshot of the page. He then connected his phone into the computer, browsed to his camera images and opened the last photo he took – the title page from the J H Mathers book on Nikolai's shelf, the numbers "4443" clearly etched into the centre of the page.

Beckford zoomed in on the image so the numbers filled the screen. It was indeed pencil and not a random scribble that he'd first surmised; it had been written with care.

Did Nikolai write all his work in pencil?

Beckford loaded Google, typed "4443" into the search box and hit enter with his pinky. It took 0.31 seconds to return 50 million results – about 49,999, 999 too many. It was a lottery search and Beckford knew that. The numbers were too generic to come back with any kind of unique match. Finding a needle in a haystack would have been simple in comparison.

* * *

'Four-four-four-three?' said Noakes, typing on his computer. Beckford was at the door to his office, arms folded, leaning against the frame. Noakes finished his paragraph and looked at him, 'Doesn't ring any bells,' he said, 'Programming language?'

'I've checked them all,' said Beckford.

'ASCII? Hex? What about low-level code?'

Beckford shook his head and said, 'Assembly and Machine. Checked.'

'Errrrm,' Noakes looked at the ceiling and let out a deep sigh. 'Could be a block of internet protocol version 6 or the end digits to a telephone number. What's it for?'

'Also, that access system we use,' said Beckford, sidestepping the conversation and hoping Noakes didn't notice, 'for the doors.' He lifted his ID card from around his neck, 'You ever known it to glitch?'

'Glitch? Glitch how?'

'Like not record an entry.'

'I've no idea,' said Noakes, 'can't say I've spent very long looking at the logs.'

Beckford saw he was confused and would want an explanation any second, but then his face changed.

'We're not being audited, are we?' he said, suddenly

alarmed. 'Did Corden mention anything? What did she say?'

Beckford couldn't help but laugh.

'Don't worry,' he said, 'nothing like that, just some guff about a cost-saving initiative, losing department heads to claw back a bit of money.'

Noakes didn't bite and turned back to his computer.

'Don't let the door smack you in the arse on your way out,' he said over his shoulder.

Once back at his station, Beckford continued his search. End digits to a phone number had already crossed his mind, but active numbers trailing with "4443" went into the tens of thousands in the UK alone.

After an hour of constant searches, Beckford felt his eyeballs catching fire. For a couple of minutes he sat back, ate a banana and let his gaze lose focus. Then he got straight back to it, clicking through page after page of the millions of search results that flashed in front of him. Time started to move phenomenally fast and his frustration increased with each interrupting phone call or colleague, to the point where he started to give blunt, one word answers, making it obvious he was too busy to assist.

During a toilet break he stood in a cubicle and thumped the door with his knuckles. Why had he let it get this far? A few numbers, doodled in a textbook… that's all they were.

'Stop making something from nothing,' he said out loud to himself, but no amount of mental reasoning or bargaining could reverse his desire to crack whatever code or mystery he'd perceived.

His therapist had talked about the way something so small, such as a simple doodle and nothing more, could grow into a compulsive anchor and start snowballing. "4443" had teetered on the edge of that all morning, and he could no longer see the numbers as raw, meaningless information anymore. He knew they were important. Extremely important.

Back at his desk, his tired eyes darted from link to website.

Scroll, scroll, scroll, back, click link. Repeat.

He could physically feel his brain turning to mush. The photo of Nikolai's textbook filled his screen again. Rolling his mouse wheel, the image zoomed in all the way, right down to individual pixels. He rolled it out again and repeated the action a few times, stuck in some sort of trance.

In and out, in and out.

In, then all the way out again, the full title page coming back into view. In the top right hand corner was the page number 13. His heart skipped a beat. Page numbers? 44 and 43, perhaps? It was the most glaringly obvious idea so far, but one he just hadn't thought of. If that didn't piss him off enough, the fact he didn't have a copy of the book at hand really ground his gears.

Maybe there's an online copy.

Beckford loaded Google and in the search box started typing the title, 'advanced database—

His finger slipped, hitting the '3' key instead of the 'e.' A common mistake with the keys being so close together. Reactively, his ring-finger shot to the backspace but then he froze, staring at the word he'd just typed:

```
databas3
```

The floodgates opened. Vowels. The numbers were used as vowels, typically known as "leetspeak" – or even just "1337" – popular among the younger computer generation. He tabbed back to the photo on screen, noting the spacing of the numbers:

ADVANCED

DATABASE

4 4 4 3

DESIGN & TECHNOLOGY

Beckford's heart pumped harder. He went back to the search engine, removed what he'd typed, then punched in:

```
d4t4b4s3
```

The page flickered, throwing up results. There were 1040 links in total. If he had to, Beckford would visit each and every one. He considered 1040 to be a manageable number – a lot more manageable than 50 million.

With new burst of energy, Beckford started clicking. The first few pages of results contained old blogs with no relevance and sites for pirated films, porn and software. A few of the links clicked through to pages that were no longer online. Fortunately, Google kept cached copies of most dead links, letting Beckford peruse them regardless, but the only information he found was immaterial.

To speed things up, on each page he hit CTRL+F and searched for "d4t4b4s3" to save him trawling. After the fourth page of results he was reminded of just how much useless garbage there was clogging the digital highways.

They should just wipe the whole internet and start afresh. Nothing quite like a bit of housekeeping to cleanse the mind.

Click. Click. Click.

It was on the sixth page of results where Beckford made a breakthrough. One of the links took him to a message board, where people could post topics and discuss them anonymously behind avatars and made-up usernames. The website had a red and grey banner and was entitled "Survivors."

Beckford would later discover the site was dedicated to discussions on psychology and mental health problems, but the link from Google took him directly to a message entitled: "Looking For Someone."

Like most online message boards, users were required to register an account to be able to post. Each message they posted was tagged on the left-hand side of the page with their profile information such as username, how many posts they'd made, what date they joined the site and an avatar – an image depicting themselves, which for an anonymous board could be anything from a cartoon character to a pair of tits.

The moment Beckford read the first message his heart skipped a beat.

The username was "d4t4b4s3." The location was London. The date of the message was exactly one week prior to Nikolai's suicide. And what cemented Beckford's affirmation that all arrows pointed to the Ukrainian was the content of the message:

hello, I am young man and in need of help. before you try to talk me out of this, I want to save you bother and say without any question of doubts that I will be end my life soon. this has gone on far to long, and its time that i face fears and do what is necessary.

the help i require is not disuasion but encouragement. I am been alone for most of `my life but want to leave this world with someone who understand the pain im in. who wants to join me? pm if interested`

Beckford had read the message too fast, impatiently skimming through most of it, looking for vital nuggets of information that would reassure him that his day wasn't a total waste of government time and money.

Had he gotten ahead of himself again? Was the user really Nikolai Guskov? Beckford re-read the message over and over, the broken English producing a thick Ukrainian accent in his head the more times he read it. Yes, he was almost certain it was Nikolai, although he often confused certainty with hope.

Scrolling the mouse wheel, the replies of the message rolled up the screen. Despite Nikolai's request, the responses were filled with dissuasion, not encouragement. But that was just the publicly viewable responses. Nikolai had asked people to "pm if interested." A PM was a private message, sent directly from user to user, creating a two-way private chat. If there was going to be any meat on the bone it was going to be back there, under the layers of security and in among the database of information that the website ran on.

Beckford stared at the screen and pondered.

During his time in the police, he had been witness to countless breaches of ethics that would have made Socrates whirl in his grave. Yet, when faced with difficult decisions that were strangled by the strict rules of the job, for some the only way to adhere to the Met's mission of "Total Policing" was to bend the rules. Corruption had found its place within the service and it was an area that Beckford purposefully turned a blind eye to.

Out of sight, out of mind. Clear of guilt.

It was only after Sally's murder that he started to travel down avenues previously considered off limits. Desperation could bend a person in ways they never thought possible. To mute his conscience, Beckford told himself that any unlawful act he carried out would be to facilitate the truth, not represent the truth. He had to get into those private messages and there was only one way he could do it.

TWELVE

Under the Computer Misuse Act, hacking a website could see the perpetrator serve six months to five years in prison. Beckford had only been in cybercrime a year, and even though he'd picked up a few things along the way he was still very much an amateur. There were colleagues at the HTCU who could break into a website blindfolded, but Beckford wasn't stupid.

Willow had agreed to meet him at Waterstones bookstore not far from the office in Hammersmith. Upstairs, they sat at a high table in the corner by the windows and Willow opened her laptop, ensuring the screen couldn't be seen by prying eyes. Public wifi was perfect for hacking. In and out with very minimal traceability.

Unlike the stereotypical image of a hacker, Willow wasn't pale, spotty or greasy-haired. She hadn't aped the character played by Rooney Mara in the film *The Girl with the Dragon Tattoo* either by dying her hair black, piercing body parts and extensively inking herself. She was a sweet-looking girl with long straight auburn hair. Her complexion was perfect, too. Beckford often saw her carrying a skateboard around, but had never once seen her on it. Maybe it was one thing she hadn't quite mastered yet. The physical world was often a struggle for wizards of the digital domain.

Beckford placed two coffees on the table and sat back down.

'Thanks dad,' said Willow. It was their cover story. Beckford wasn't comfortable walking around with a 16-

year-old girl at the best of times, and now she was a committing a crime on his behalf.

Hacking could be an arduous process, but once started the determination to access the unreachable only strengthened with each passing minute. To get what Beckford was after, Willow had to interrogate the "backend" of the website – the behind-the-scenes software and hardware that hosted Survivors, providing not only the functionality but the security measures in place to protect its users.

Beckford held a copy of *The Hobbit* in his hands, trying to remain calm, but his eyes were on Willow's screen, watching closely. He could follow most of the hack, but at times he had interrupted her with a 'what's that…' or 'why would you…' and she would reply quietly and cryptically without missing a beat.

Beckford sipped his instant coffee. They had no decaf, but he knew he needed to be alert for this.

There were two types of website hosting: shared and dedicated. With shared hosting, multiple websites ran off the same server, "sharing" the computer's hard drive space, processing power and memory. It was a less expensive approach and one used primarily by smaller, less complicated websites.

With dedicated hosting, an entire server, or indeed bank of servers, were used to host a single website. Much more expensive, but it provided the site with 100% of the computer's resources. It was a definite requirement for larger sites.

The physical location of the servers could differ too, either existing in the corporation's building itself, usually within the IT department, or off-site and maintained by a third-party company in this or any other country. Again, it mainly depended on the size and value of the website.

If Survivors was a message board for a large corporation such as a bank or department store, Willow – despite her technical ability – didn't fancy her chances. With such large volumes of sensitive data passing through the site each day, the ratio of budget spent on their network security would be significantly higher than a lot of others. Even if she did manage to hack the site, it was likely they'd make a bigger fuss of it; the breaching of a company's client database was a show-stopper.

Fortunately, Survivors looked like a non-profit organisation that maintained financial buoyancy through donations and advertising, so it was unlikely to be able to afford such worthwhile security.

To begin her hack, Willow ran a "WHOIS check" on the domain name http://www.survivorsboard.com, which listed information such as when the name was registered and who registered it, but more importantly the addresses of the nameservers:

```
ns1.webbylegacy.com
ns2.webbylegacy.com
```

The nameservers gave Willow her first clue as to where the website's files were being stored. A quick Google for "Webby Legacy" and Willow was on their company website. As expected, they were a web-hosting service provider and going by their "About Us" page they had been in business for three years and had eight members of staff (accompanied by some less-than-flattering photos). A relatively small company. Short client list. Lack of experience in the field.

'Fucking doddle, this,' said Willow, her potty mouth being another characteristic surprise at odds with her angelic appearance. Beckford's heart started to pound with nerves.

To breach the site, there were two routes Willow could

take: the front door or the back door. The front door meant using SQL injections – a technique whereby programming code was entered as part of the site's web address, exploiting holes in the security and allowing the hacker to pull information directly out of the database. The back door meant avoiding the website altogether and going through Webby Legacy's hosting server. Willow openly admitted to her SQL skills being 'rusty as fuck,' so she opted for the latter.

As a bystander, Beckford didn't feel at all safe. Willow was an informant of sorts for the HTCU and he'd accompanied her in public many times before. Nothing new there. But if shit did hit the fan, he probably couldn't play the ignorant card and say he was too engrossed in Bilbo and Gandalf's adventures to know what she was up to.

Beckford would soon be implicated further by actions that had occurred a few months prior. He had been at Water Street discussing viruses with Sergeant Davis after the Omaha.B virus broke out on machines in the HR department on the second floor. While the IT team above worked like blue-arsed flies to contain the spread of the virus, Beckford gloated about how their systems in the HTCU were more secure than Fort Knox. Davis disagreed, betting him £50 that he could install a Trojan virus onto Beckford's computer without going anywhere near it. What Beckford didn't take into account was that even though his computer was up-to-date with all the latest security and software to protect against viruses, Davis could write his own code.

Antivirus software scanned for patterns in digital activity such as the accessing of important system files, file mutation and network port access – comparing the activity patterns to a definitions library. AV vendors spend a lot of time tracking new viruses, reverse engineering their code and pushing out the deduced pattern to their customers as preventative patches. Davis' virus was one of a kind. An unknown entity. And being written for the sole purpose of hacking into one machine, it was unlikely any AV vendor would have a copy of it anytime soon.

A few days later, Beckford started to receive anonymous emails titled "I KNOW WHAT YOU'RE DOING," with screenshots attached showing his own desktop. He had completely forgotten about his bet with Davis and was halfway through explaining the situation to Noakes when Davis interrupted and pulled Beckford back out of the office.

It was funny in retrospect, but Beckford didn't like being had – £50 later Davis handed over the virus, which he had called "BeckBot."

Beckford smirked at the name and shoved the pen drive into his desk drawer, thinking it might prove useful one day.

'Where the hell did you get that?' said Beckford, lowering *The Hobbit.* In among the seemingly hundreds of windows springing open on Willow's laptop he had spotted a copy of BeckBot.

'You think I was going to use one of mine to do this?' said Willow. 'This is your fucking gig.'

Beckford was yet again amazed. Had Willow hacked his work computer at the HTCU? *The virus was on a pen drive for God's sake.* Maybe he'd taken the virus home at some point and she's gotten into his personal computer. It was like seeing a magic trick. Beckford wanted to interrogate her more, but she was in her element.

To put some digital distance between her laptop and Webby Legacy to minimise the chance of being traced, Willow connected to a free anonymising network – a nest of a remote computers that acted like relays, similar to how TOR operated – feeding her internet connection from one hop to the next, to the next, and so on in layers, encrypting the data all the way to the penultimate relay before her destination, where it was then decrypted.

Once anonymised, she fired up the web browser and loaded a web-based email service called Hushmail where she signed up for an account and pick the address sohnjmith@hushmail.com. After logging into her new account, Willow composed an email and directed it to the address admin@webbylegacy.com with the false subject line: "Acc No: 322341."

She copied a paragraph of text from a random news article on the web and pasted it into the body of the email, ensuring it wouldn't be suspected as spam for having no content. She then attached a copy of BeckBot.

Being one of the most popular and easy ways to spread viruses, security software often treated email file attachments with a high level of suspicion. How would BeckBot get past their defences? Davis had incorporated a workaround.

As the email process initiated, BeckBot was treated like an ordinary attachment, but it was during transmission that the virus would integrate itself into the body of the email, thus removing itself as a suspicious attachment before it reached its destination. When the email was opened at the other end, BeckBot would automatically install itself on the computer system then delete its email, leaving no trace. On seeing this, most people (including Beckford when he fell for Davis' wizardry) would presume the email was spam that had been automatically deleted.

Beckford's stomach lurched as Willow clicked "send." The virus was on its way.

Once installed, the Trojan had a few subroutines that

would initiate. Firstly, it would attempt to duplicate itself across all computers in digital proximity, scoping out the reachable Local Area Network (LAN) and even Wide Area Network (WAN). A communication port would then be opened on the target, or “parent” computer, which would channel a gateway through any subsequent device between that computer and the outside world.

Next, it would scan the operating systems of the infected machines and reset the local administrator accounts, changing the password to one that Davis had originally set (“pussinboots”).

Finally, it would send an email back to the sender – in this instance Willow, aka sohnjmith@hushmail.com – with a map of the network and information about each computer, including a list of IP addresses. They waited five minutes. At some point, Beckford looked up from his book and scanned the cafe and surrounding bookstore. A man had been looking at him. They made eye contact for a split second before the man carried on perusing books about the Second World War. Paranoia often visited Beckford when he wasn’t getting a solid seven hours a night, but he could have sworn he’d seen the man before.

‘Boom!,’ said Willow, making Beckford jump out of his skin. The BeckBot email had arrived, but when Beckford looked back at the books, the man had gone.

‘The pig who wrote this ain’t half bad,’ said Willow, scrolling through the email. Beckford leaned in for a closer look.

```
//////  ////// ///// /   /  //////   ///   //////
//   /  /      /     /  /   //   / /    /    /
/////   ///    /     //     /////  /    /    /
//   /  /      /     /  /   //   / /    /    /
/////   ////// ///// /   /  /////   ///      /
```

```
Infection Successful!

The following computers are available for DESTRUCTION (Muhuhahaha)

192.168.0.1
192.168.0.5
192.168.0.10
192.168.0.11
192.168.0.12
192.168.0.13
192.168.0.14

Connect: 198.51.100.9:666
```

The last IP in the list would be the "public facing" address – the machine on the outer edge of the internal network that connected directly to the internet and allowed Willow access from her anonymised location.

Time was now a factor. For all Beckford knew, BeckBot's proliferation could have been noticed by Webby Legacy's tech team, sending their office into full-blown red alert. Systems could be getting shut down and cables pulled left, right and centre.

Loading BeckBot's client graphical user interface, Willow was prompted by a dialog box asking for an IP address. She entered "198.51.100.9:666" and clicked "Connect." Her screen flickered and suddenly became the desktop of another machine – one of Webby Legacy's, filled with unfamiliar files and icons.

It was uncertain which computer Willow was connected to on Webby Legacy's network, but Beckford guessed it was the machine that the infected email was originally opened on, most likely by a tech-support employee.

BeckBot used a feature called "sessions" that let the hacker use the infected computer without the person who was physically sat in front of it knowing. From the infected machine, Willow loaded the operating system's own remote connection software and entered the internal IP "192.168.0.1." – the first address in the list and one synonymous with a primary server.

She hit enter and a login box appeared, asking for a username and password. Willow entered "admin" and "pussinboots" and the login box disappeared, revealing another desktop, one that Beckford surmised wasn't the machine that hosted Webby Legacy's websites, but more likely one that maintained their internal network.

On the server, Willow loaded the Domain Name System (DNS) configuration screen, which listed external to internal address mappings, linking addresses such as http://www.survivorsboard.com to an internal IP address. This directed users to the right place when they entered a web address in their browser.

A list of mappings filled the screen that Willow scrolled through, most of them appearing to be consumer websites. Then, halfway down:

```
Survivors - 192.168.0.9
```

Willow logged out of the current server and connected quickly to the new address. Another desktop appeared, this one bland and ambiguous. She loaded Internet Information Services (IIS) – the application that processed the website hosting – and sped down the page until she came to the Survivors web application. A couple of clicks later and she was looking at the site's configuration page where she discovered the files location:

```
f:\web\server\websites\public\S\Survivor
s
```

Willow browsed to the folder, which contained all the files for the website. But that wasn't what Beckford was looking for. He needed the database.

Being a dynamic and interactive website, the database held almost all of the information that appeared on the Survivors website – usernames, profile information, posts and most importantly the private messages sent between people. In a database, each specific piece of data was held in columns, and each column belonged to a table that contained only information of a certain grouping or category.

Willow opened the Survivors web configuration file that listed a "connection string" for the database. The string was an aggregated line of information that contained the IP address of the database server and a username and password to connect with. Beckford could see that the database was on the same server as the one Willow was logged into. *Perfect.*

Trawling through available software on the computer, Willow opened their database management tools that displayed the databases hosted on the server in alphabetical order. Willow honed in on one called SurvivorsDB.

Beckford inched closer, his *Hobbit*-reading charade now long abandoned.

Once inside the database, Willow oiled her rusty SQL skills and ran a query on the Users table, searching for the username "d4t4b4s3." It came back with the UserID: 2029.

Beckford wiped his palms on his sleeves. The thrill of the crime was like taking a deep whiff of petrol. It was wrong. Definitely wrong. But it felt so good. He understood why people hacked for a living – the challenge was addictive.

Finally, Willow typed an SQL query that asked the database to bring back any messages from the "PrivateMSGS" table that were linked to the UserID 2029.

She hit enter and the screen filled with text.

THIRTEEN

He hovered his finger over the doorbell of the same apartment door he'd walked through a thousand times before. It was a door he once had the key to.

Beckford had been stood there for well over a minute, shrouded in darkness, battling any discouraging thoughts his obsessive mind was throwing back at him. It was like playing a game. A horribly frustrating game where he had to cross a busy motorway but cars and vans and lories kept whizzing by, blocking his route.

Then he somehow did it, blanking his thoughts just long enough to finally press the bell. He stepped back into the cold night air and swirled his tongue around his arid mouth. Lights were on in the house, but for what felt like an eternity there was no answer.

Just as he thought he'd been let off the hook and could go home with a valid excuse, Farber opened the door. She was wearing grey joggers, a navy Manchester Metropolitan University T-shirt that was too big for her and a look of surprise.

'John?' she said, opening the door wider.

'Probably shouldn't have come round,' he said, 'but your phone is off and I—'

'It's a work phone. I wasn't in today. Bloody migraine.'

'You still get them?'

'Come on in.'

With apprehension, Beckford walked up and stepped into the warmth. The first thing he noticed was the smell. It was nice, but one that hadn't changed a bit since he'd last been there. The memories came flooding in. It was amazing how scents could do that. The aftershave English Leather always reminded Beckford of his dad, but it was a very direct, one-dimensional scent – Farber's house had a unique blend, difficult to set apart the individual elements yet Beckford instantly felt like he'd bumped into an old friend.

Farber closed the front door and nodded towards the living room.

'Go on,' she said, 'you want a beer?'

'Just water please.'

Farber headed for the kitchen. Beckford swept his eyes around the surroundings quickly, noting slight changes. A mirror on the wall opposite, a new lampshade for the hall light. Different wallpaper.

He walked on through to the living room that, at a glance, looked exactly the same. Then his eyes picked out finer details, such as new framed photographs and Art Deco prints on the walls. Her vinyl collection had grown too, and an L-shaped couch had replaced her old, battered two-seater that used to swallow people in its saggy springs.

Beckford took a seat on the couch and bounced up and down like a prospective buyer in a department store. As he glanced around the room, a feeling of anxiety started to trickle in. Memories were fickle; they could shift, alter and bend over time. One of the things that terrified Beckford the most was the thought of not being able to trust his own recollections. The trickle flowed faster and heavier as he started to bat questions and answers back and forth:

What if the serial number I'd found in the bin was from an old case? No, there was no record in the system.

What if I'd written it down but never entered it into the system? That's unlikely to happen.

But not impossible, right?

Before the mental tennis match got out of hand, the

sound of a tinkling bell caught his attention. Mitsy was a black and white cat, mostly white with a splodge across her face.

'Hey,' said Beckford, lowering a hand down by his ankles. Mitsy jostled over for a sniff and a rub, driving her head into his fingers. He scratched behind her ear, down her neck and under her collar. She usually avoided strangers like the plague, but was surprisingly comfortable in his presence. Did she remember him? Or was she as capricious as the next cat, wanting nothing more than to be lavished with affection no matter who dealt it?

Farber entered with Beckford's glass of water and a mug of tea for herself and Mitsy scooted out of the way, taking up position by a toy mouse that was waiting to be mauled.

'Thanks,' said Beckford, taking the water. Farber settled into an armchair to the side and hitched her feet up. Minnie Mouse socks.

'All right,' she said, 'let's have it. I presume this isn't just a friendly visit?'

Beckford took in a breath and cut to the chase. 'I need you to find a misper.'

'That's not my remit.'

'It might be,' said Beckford. 'His name is Joseph Winterburn. He went missing last week. Lived with his mother in North Finchley.'

Beckford gave her the short version and skimmed over a few details, technical or otherwise, of how a 16-year-old girl under his supervision had hacked into a web-hosting company's servers and uncovered private messages between Nikolai Guskov and one Joseph Winterburn.

Breaching the website was one thing, but tracing Joseph required a bit of extra work for Beckford.

Like most websites, the Survivors database recorded IP addresses of every single user who logged in. Nikolai's private messages had revealed a conversation between him and a prospective suicide partner going by the alias BeatBoy84. The IP corresponding to the nickname was nearly always the same every time, spanning a couple of days, which meant he or she was logging in from the same location, more than likely their home.

Depending on the severity of a crime, formally tracing an IP address back to a real human being was nearly always a slow process and a total pain in the arse. The Met used a third-party company called Shellstar that provided IP intelligence to e-crime units across the country. Their data centres held details for millions of IPs and even though this helped, it only ever gave the general whereabouts of a connected device, not the front door address. To get that they had to contact the Internet Service Provider directly.

Internet Service Providers held the bulk of that data and didn't give it up without a warrant. Beckford didn't have the time or patience to put together a warrant on some tenuous leads, so instead he enlisted the help of Sergeant Davis.

After Willow's highly illegal escapade, Beckford headed back to the office and pulled Davis to one side, cashing in a favour he'd been keeping for a rainy day. Having worked in British Telecom for some years prior to joining the police, Davis still had some extremely useful contacts within the organisation. By the time Beckford had been to the loo and made a drink, an email had been delivered to his inbox with BeatBoy84's real name and address.

With the information, Beckford searched the Police National Computer – one of the many vast databases used by UK law enforcement. The search results came back – Joseph Winterburn had one previous conviction for petty theft, but more importantly there was an open case regarding his recent disappearance.

'You *hacked* into a web-hosting company?' said Farber, doing a good impression of a stunned goldfish.

'And leave my fingerprints all over it?' said Beckford. 'Don't be silly.'

'Then who?'

'That's not pertinent. Anyway, these small companies leave themselves wide open. We left them a polite note on their domain server informing them of how someone hacked in and how they could tighten their security to prevent it if they wanted to. Corporations normally pay a shit-load to some white-hat for that kind of service.'

'A white what?'

'A white… doesn't matter. Nikolai was looking for someone to join him in a suicide pact and a man by the name of Joseph Winterburn answered the post.'

He reached into his jacket and pulled out a couple of folded A4 sheets, opening them on the couch. Farber left the armchair and took a seat next to him, picking up the printouts.

'You can have this copy,' said Beckford. 'They exchanged six messages in total. Joseph starts off talking about how he wants to end his life and asks Nikolai how he plans to do it. Paracetamol overdose is the response. Joseph then sends his mobile number, which checks out but hasn't been connected to the operator network for over a week. Since the night Nikolai died, in fact.'

Farber gave him a look that reassured him he wasn't simply going crazy.

'Leading up to that night,' said Beckford, 'there were four calls to Joseph's phone from an unknown number. I say unknown number not because it was private, but because it doesn't exist.'

'Disconnected?'

'No, just doesn't exist. Never *has* existed.'

Farber was confused, which Beckford relished for a second before continuing.

'Some bright spark on the service desk blamed it on a glitch in the system. In other words, he didn't know. Their engineers are "investigating," but you know how long that'll take. I'd be surprised if they found anything at all.'

Mitsy jumped up on Beckford's lap, but his mind was elsewhere to be able to fulfill her craving for attention.

'Who knows what Nikolai was involved in?' he said. 'But somehow – I don't know how – someone got into the phone operator's records and removed every single trace of his contract and number.'

Farber processed the information, letting silence fill the air. Beckford could hear ticking, isolating it to a vintage clock on the bookcase.

'Right,' said Farber, finally. 'Okay, so… why?'

'The same reason he removed 99% of everything from his personal computer and his university network account.'

Farber's eyebrows raised, 'You hacked into Harper University too?'

'I spoke to them,' he said, angling towards her. 'Their IT team couldn't find anything of his. Work. Browsing history. Emails. Nothing. Not only that, his registration details are also gone. He's literally deleted himself from digital existence.'

'No medical records either,' said Farber, getting sucked in. 'No dental.'

'I'd hazard a guess we won't find him on any system. His mates – if you can call them that – were right about him. Paranoid to the extreme.'

Beckford's hand found Mitsy's neck and gave it a good scratch, oblivious to an impending allergic reaction that usually kicked in around now. Farber picked at a loose strand of cotton from her sock.

'What about Joseph Winterburn?' she said.

'That's where you come in. Be a bit unusual for me to go chasing up a misper.'

'This better have substance, John. I can't go wasting my time running around after your suspicions.'

'Please,' he said.

Mitsy jumped down. Having remained steadfast from the lure of an itch in his right eye, Beckford finally succumbed and dug a knuckle in, rubbing vigorously.

'Shit,' he said, punctuating it with a dry snort through the nose. He felt caked in cat fur. 'You mind if I—'

'You know where it is.'

A pleasing aroma effused from a bowl of potpourri in Farber's downstairs toilet. Beckford scrubbed his hands and face with an aloe vera soap and dabbed his face dry on the Egyptian cotton hand towel. It was like being at a country spa. One of the many spas they both visited together, back when things were good. He hated reminiscing. The joy of feeling back in the moment was never worth the heartache of returning to the present.

When he walked back into the living room, he thanked Farber for her time and pleaded again that she look into the disappearance of Joseph Winterburn. She promised she would and saw him out.

FOURTEEN

On his days off, Beckford tried to get up at the same time as a work day, but this morning he'd overslept. Things were on his mind, causing him to dream endlessly and awake more tired than ever. He couldn't help but drift back off again.

By the time he eventually got out of bed, it was after 10 and his head felt filled with cement. He was supposed to be meeting an old school friend for an "all-dayer" – beer and football, putting the world to rights, ogling women and ending with a greasy kebab to regret in the morning. Beckford wasn't up to it though.

On entering his kitchen he remembered there was no cereal and the bread had gone stale. He'd known it the day before, but had forgotten to pick anything up. It was unlike him to forget. A threat of anxiety circled his perimeter walls, but he kept it at bay, deciding he'd treat himself and go out for breakfast.

The nearest cafe was Olaf's, a 12-minute walk from his apartment in Wembley, but Beckford wanted to go further afield and found himself behind the wheel of his car, aimlessly driving.

The roads were surprisingly quiet for a Saturday morning. At a set of lights he ummed and ahhed on which way to go and where to eat. He took a right. Then at a roundabout he went south on Bridgewater Road as Skrillex pumped from the speakers again. He observed a couple of cyclists keeping pace behind him. It was only when he got in spitting distance of his eventual destination that he admitted to himself he'd intended on going there from the moment he opened his eyes.

Having only been to Dunning Street in the dead of night, Beckford could now see it in all its glory. It was a haven for students – big brand fast-food restaurants, a hundred Starbucks and Costas, express supermarkets and a plethora of bars with wacky names like Boom Time and XYZ. In among the modern businesses were surviving newsagents and takeaways that were presumably struggling to keep up appearances.

Beckford wanted a coffee. A real coffee, but one to enjoy in a relaxed environment, not on a conveyor belt.

After passing Dunning Street halls on his left, he clocked a small bistro called Fork & Field on the opposite side of the road. Beckford took the next left and parked in a public car park that charged half a kidney for two hours. From there, he walked back to the main road and joined a gathering crowd at a crossing.

At first he didn't take notice of the man in front of him. Idly, Beckford looked him over. The man's head was freakishly large, with his hair shaved to the skin. Across the crest of his cheek Beckford could make out a full, bushy beard. That's when his stomach turned and sweat started to seep out into his clothes.

It couldn't be.

The man was wearing navy blue cargo pants, cream Timberland boots and a black bomber jacket. He was the same height as Peter McGregor too. The crossing beeped and the crowd herded across the road. Beckford felt his legs go weak. Keeping his distance he observed the man's gait.

It was him, Beckford was sure of it.

What the hell was he doing out of prison?

As the realisation set in, he started to feel light-headed and the crowd closed in around him. Fumbling for his mobile phone he dropped it into the sea of feet. Beckford crouched and a random foot kicked the phone, causing it to skitter across the tarmac. Scurrying like a frog, Beckford managed to grab the phone and surface by the time the crowd had got to the other side.

Peter McGregor was gone.

For a further five minutes, Beckford stood on the pavement, heart in mouth, scanning everyone up and down the road, his mind doing star-jumps.

Was it really him?

Beckford scrolled through his contacts, called Corden but hung up on the first ring. Maybe he was wrong. He leaned back against a shop window and closed his eyes, but the street was noisy and busy, and Beckford needed to shut it out. Quickly, he headed towards Fork & Field and kept his eyes on the pavement.

* * *

Two down: *Mandate.*

Beckford tapped the pen on his teeth, then looked at where his saliva had touched the end. It was a cafe pen, one probably groped by an assortment of people, of which – according to Beckford's paranoia – consisted of dirty old men who never washed their hands after taking a piss.

He placed the pen down and took another sip of his latte, hoping somehow the heat from the beverage would kill any piss-germs that might be in his mouth.

Mandate… Mandate…

It had been a while since he'd had a real coffee. Possibly six months. He felt naughty, like an ex-alcoholic falling off the wagon. He was in dangerous territory, knowing how much caffeine exacerbated his anxiety, but he was hoping it would snap his mental acuity back into focus.

Unfortunately, his brain was still reeling from earlier. It couldn't have been Peter McGregor. The man had been locked away for life. It was simply an irrational thought that had blossomed and deceived him. As it so often did. Yet there was still a part of Beckford that wished he'd seen the man's face, just to put it to rest once and for all.

Adding sugar to his latte, Beckford stirred and gazed out of the window at the passing shoppers and traffic. His eyes landed on the opposite side of the road and Dunning House, where gaps in the stream of vehicles would open up every now and then, revealing the front entrance to the building. Beckford stared and stirred, both the cup and his thoughts. He imagined Nikolai walking into the building for what would be the very last time.

Was it dark?

Was he carrying the shotgun?

Was he with Joseph Winterburn?

A whirring coffee grinder pulled him back to the cafe and for the first time he took notice of the decor. In one corner, a rubber plant drooped in the humidity, a nick on one of the leaves having drawn white sap that had dried. On the wall, a silver-framed picture showed a time-lapsed photograph of a waterfall, the rushing water blurring like smoke trails. It was generic, tacky, but Beckford quite liked it.

On the counter, adjacent to the till, were two tip-jars, one labelled *Star Trek* and the other *Star Wars*. Beckford dug into his pocket for loose change then stopped when his eyes landed on something that decided his path for the rest of his day.

A CCTV camera attached to the wall above the rubber plant.

Beckford dropped his coins back into his pocket and walked over, stopping to let a middle-aged couple in matching anoraks pass.

When the rubber plant leaves touched him, Beckford peered up at the underside of the camera. It was old, possibly late-nineties, stained with years of dust, moisture and evaporated cooking oil. A small sticker indicated it was a Hitachi. Following the direction of the lens, Beckford figured it overlooked the cafe enough to see through the windows, and very possibly have a line of sight to the front entrance of Dunning House.

Was it too dark?

Does the cafe have shutters?

'Is something the matter?' asked a young female barista, lugging plates tarred with breakfast scraps. Beckford froze for a second, hoping his latte would finally kick his brain into gear.

'Actually,' he said, pulling identification out of the back pocket of his jeans. The barista's eyes bounced off his warrant badge and Beckford expertly slipped into the professional demeanour of his past role as a detective, improvising a convincing story about a fist-fight that had taken place outside on the night of Halloween. Asking to see their security tapes, the woman seemed unphased and with the blessing of the manager she cooperated with enthusiasm, showing him through to the back office where the CCTV was recorded.

The system was an AVE RT-195 VHS recorder, which took one tape at a time. The woman said they cycled through seven tapes, one per day each week. Beckford took the tape for the 31st of October, promising he'd return it the following day.

A chilly breeze had picked up outside, dropping the temperature significantly. Wrapping his scarf tight, Beckford buried his hands in his jacket and turned back to face the cafe. It had shutters, but the metal links looked big enough to see through without much restriction. It was tenuous, but he needed a timeline of the night in question.

Had Joseph Winterburn been at Nikolai's that night?

Had anyone?

What if Nikolai hadn't left his room for days?

Video would confirm that.

Gazing up and down Dunning Street, Beckford identified only two security cameras in plain view. The first camera was definitely CCTV – high on a post 100 yards down the road, overlooking the dual carriageway. It was most likely stationed there for traffic disputes, but Beckford guessed it had a good view of the front of Dunning House and, depending on the quality, might even be able to identify residents entering and exiting the building.

The second camera was on the other side of the road, positioned over a bus lane. Beckford knew those well, having been fined a couple of times for using bus lanes during prohibited times. *Bastards.* The letters he'd received were accompanied by photographic evidence of his car and registration plate, but the scope of the shot only contained close-ups of the road and little else. It certainly wouldn't include the entrance to Dunning House.

Beckford dismissed waiting at the crossing and darted over the road, dodging cars and buses and skipping onto the pavement. At the entrance to Dunning House, he pressed the button for Concierge. There was no answer. He cupped his hands and peered through the glass doors, spying the domed security camera hanging from the ceiling straight ahead.

After a couple more minutes of interspersed buzzer pressing, Beckford gave up. He'd be back, but would have to start his investigation by talking to the council.

The Richmond upon Thames council owned,

maintained and controlled the closed-circuit cameras throughout the borough. Beckford made full use of his occupational authority by making a phone call and landing himself up in a control room above the St. Meller Shopping Centre, a 10-minute walk from Dunning Street.

Like a newsroom, the control room was filled with banks of screens all showing live video feeds from across the borough. Two CCTV operators looked after everything, but there was usually three.

'He's hungover,' said one of the operators with a Polish twang. 'I mean, he's sick,' the man added, smirking. Beckford felt his presence was probably a welcomed break from their mundane daily task of scouring endless screens for signs of crime and antisocial behaviour.

'Wanna cuppa?' said the same bloke, stretching out in an ergonomic office chair. Beckford took him up on the offer. A cup of tea was a very useful time anchor, an excuse to stick around once he'd outstayed his welcome. He'd sipped many a cold cup of tea back in homicide.

Looking about the room, Beckford was surprised at the quality of the equipment, especially for a council. Very slick and very modern. He voiced how impressed he was and the other operator explained that a city-wide initiative came into action the previous year that saw 150 of the 213 cameras across the borough replaced with state of the art digital IP cameras – hardware that broadcast over the internet. A cost-cutting investment, but also one that improved efficiency and availability, allowing operators in each control room to connect and view live video from any camera on their network.

Having been there only a few minutes, Beckford had identified the chatty one of the two fellas. Wookie they called him for some unknown reason. Beckford got enough information out of him to start up his own CCTV solutions business and found it difficult to cut him off mid-prattle. Wookie was one of those people who were oblivious to their surroundings when they got talking.

'Where does all this footage end up?' said Beckford, finally managing to squeeze some input into the conversation. In great detail, Wookie told him that the video from both the IP and analogue cameras across the borough were saved digitally to an offsite data centre, maintained by a security specialist company called Datasec Ltd. The video was kept for a maximum of 31 days, which Beckford was pleased to hear as it was well within his required time frame.

With his tea now lukewarm, Beckford interrupted Wookie's never-ending string of sentences once again, asking to peruse the footage from the night of Halloween.

Wookie set him up at the hungover employee's desk and after a quick tutorial on the system ('click here, drag this, select that') Beckford got a taste of a day in the life of a CCTV operator. He wouldn't be changing careers anytime soon. Wookie lingered by his side for the first 10 minutes or so, enquiring endlessly about the case. Beckford continued to weave his story, having enough police experience to swipe details from old cases to add to its authenticity. Then Wookie left him alone.

On a central screen surrounded by smaller ones, Beckford watched exterior footage of the entrance to Dunning House. There was 24 hours of this stuff, but a circular knob on the control desk enabled him to alter the playback speed, whizzing it by like a Benny Hill video, then faster still.

The daytime cohort who entered and exited Dunning House was a pretty standard fare – individuals, couples, groups, all mostly young with the occasional mature student or parent with freshly washed laundry. The camera was much too high, too distant and the quality not good enough for Beckford to identify faces, but clothing and hair colour was relatively easy. It seemed it was the best he was going to get.

Having only analysed CCTV himself once before, he was reminded of how tedious the whole process was. There was software available that made things easier – automatically analysing the video and indexing objects on screen, allowing the investigator to very quickly filter by categories or search terms. He could have tried that, but as daylight faded on screen he realised how not even the most powerful software would have helped.

Shit, of course. Halloween.

They came in droves; costumes and makeup covering the whole ghoulish spectrum. Beckford shook his head and sighed, watching the onslaught of creatures, ghosts and pop culture celebs pile into Dunning House. Then he got sucked into the guessing game:

Predator... Harry Potter... Ghost... Saucy Ghost... Zombie Nurse... Saucy Zombie Nurse... Captain America. Was this how Nikolai got back inside unnoticed?

Beckford had drained three cups of tea by the time he'd gone through the whole evening, night and morning after Nikolai's death, earmarking 14 separate unidentified subjects in the video that could be a match for the Ukrainian. He'd done his best.

Wookie copied the footage to Beckford's portable hard drive. Then with a thank you and a handshake, Beckford was on his way.

* * *

The Dunning House concierge was less courteous. After a garbled exchange on the intercom, Beckford was buzzed into the building. In the ground floor corridor he met the garbled man himself – Victor, a middle-aged nobody carrying the weight of the world on one shoulder and a massive chip on the other. Victor acknowledged the warrant card but still resisted.

'That'll take an hour out of my day,' he said, 'I don't have the time.'

Beckford could smell weed on him, but he left that ace up his sleeve, opting to befuddle him by citing segments of the Data Protection Act. It wasn't verbatim. In fact, Beckford made most of it up, but Victor relented, giving him free rein over the CCTV system to save him a job.

'Is this about that Russian chap?' said Victor, hanging off the back of the office chair Beckford was sat on.

'I can't disclose any information regarding my request. Sorry.'

'Terrible, that was. Almost lost my breakfast walking into that room. Can't get the image out of my head… that bloody hole where his face was meant to be. You must see a lot of that shit— erm, stuff, yeah?'

'I'm on a tight schedule here,' said Beckford.

Victor held his hands up and left him to it. The system was less extensive than the council's surveillance equipment but fairly intuitive, with a simple user interface and menu system. The keyboard was old and the mouse wheel was missing but Beckford put up with it, wanting to avoid any further involvement with Victor.

Exploring the system, he learned that there were actually four cameras dotted about the Dunning House building. Two external cameras covering both sides of the rear car park and two internal cameras used for the entrances, front and rear. The system was digital, the files all easily accessible. He grabbed three days of recordings, one either side of Halloween, and left Victor a sarcasm-laced, 'Thank you for your cooperation,' before he left. Victor's face barely registered it.

When Beckford got back to his car, he paid the car park's extortionate price for five hours and headed home.

The men followed.

Tracking his physical whereabouts was nothing more than additional collateral. The Studio already knew where Beckford was by the tracker on his car and the GPS in his phone. They knew he was interested in CCTV in and around Dunning House. They knew about Joseph Winterburn and they understood that Beckford had uncovered the switched hard drive in Nikolai's computer.

Their threat system was called "Comminatio," which ran machine-learning algorithms that computed degrees of separation between identified subjects and the Studio. It wasn't perfect and it was constantly being refined, but its assistance was irrefutable.

Beckford was still marked as amber, with a threat rating of 654 out of 1000.

But it was rising.

They could intervene, softly, but history told them intervention only exacerbated things. They just had to let Beckford run his course. Most of the time the threat went cold and disappeared altogether. But when they didn't, the Studio had no choice but to step in.

FIFTEEN

The picture frame was old and wooden. Joseph Winterburn stood proudly in his academic gown and mortarboard, his graduation certificate gripped firmly in his right hand. Farber placed the photo back on the shelf as a small woman of advancing years entered the living room, presenting a tray of mugs and biscuits.

'I'm sorry Mr Staedler, but I don't have any sugar,' said Elaine Winterburn, placing the tray on the coffee table and serving tea to each of them in turn.

'That's quite all right,' he replied, not wanting to detract from their task by pointing out the fact he didn't ask for sugar. Farber received her tea and motioned her head towards the photograph.

'Is that Oxford?' she said.

'That's right. First-class honours in psychology. He's a very smart boy. So well mannered too. We brought him up right, there's no doubt about that.'

Staedler scribbled notes while Farber set her drink down to cool and took a seat on a small wooden chair where she slid documents out of a folder.

'Our records show Joseph was arrested for shoplifting six months ago, is that right?'

Elaine picked a biscuit off the tray and fumbled with it in her hands. 'Just a blip,' she said. 'He'd never done anything like that before. I know he didn't mean to do it. Youthful angst, I say.' She took a bite out of the biscuit.

'Has he ever left home before?' said Farber. 'Maybe stayed at a friends without telling you?'

Elaine's eyes widened. 'I wouldn't have reported him

missing if it wasn't out of the ordinary, detective.'

Staedler's cheek muscles tightened, but he fought back the smile.

'I realise that, Mrs Winterburn,' said Farber, 'we're just trying to gather all the facts. What has Joseph's mood been like recently?'

'His girlfriend left him last month,' said Elaine, her eyes landing on the photograph.

'Were they close?' said Staedler.

'Oh, he loved her. He truly loved her. I think they were discussing living together. It didn't help that he did nothing all day.'

'Unemployed?' said Staedler.

'Ever since he graduated. But don't get me started on those Conservative bastards. It's their fault. A lad as smart as my boy, they need people like that working for the country. Wasted talent. This country's gone to the dogs.'

'Was he on any medication, Mrs Winterburn?' said Farber.

Elaine glanced between Staedler and Farber, then nodded gingerly. 'For his down days, yes. Leck… Lecks-something. I've got the bottle upstairs.'

'Lexapro? Also known as Cipralex?' asked Farber.

'That's the one, yes.'

A ringtone blurted out of Farber's blazer, interrupting the interview. Quickly, she pulled out her phone and glanced at the screen.

'Actually, do you mind if I take this?' she said. Elaine nodded and Farber got up and left the room.

'John?' she said into the phone.

'Can you talk?' he said.

'We're with Joseph Winterburn's mother as we speak, if that's what you're ringing about.'

'Sort of. Listen. You remember where I live, don't you?'

* * *

By the time Beckford got home with his collection of CCTV recordings, dusk had crept in. With no time to ponder the threat of a panic or the sleepless night ahead, he made another coffee, digging a jar of the real stuff out of the back of the cupboard and added some warmed milk.

When settled into his study, he loaded the first video on the computer. The footage from inside the Dunning House entrance. Initially disappointed by the poor quality, Beckford realised it was good enough to make out facial features. It wasn't easy, however – the video had a washed-out effect created by the daylight bouncing in through the glass doors, and the subjects only faced the camera upon entering the building.

In notes he'd written on his phone, Beckford had a list of 33 separate timecodes for Nikolai "possibles" that he'd identified entering the building from the traffic camera. A cross-check with the internal camera would validate or veto them.

Landing the mouse cursor on the video timeline, Beckford dragged the pointer until the timecode in the top-right corner said 10:23. On cue, the first match (young, white male with fair hair) entered the building but straightaway Beckford could see from his slightly pixelated face that he was obviously not Nikolai. One down, 32 to go. With each timecode he checked he became increasingly disheartened.

Too fat.

Too short.

Too female.

Too old.

At the 16:10 mark, daylight had faded outside the glass

doors to Dunning House and the interior lights had come on. That's when the fancy-dress parade started, although there was only one ghost Beckford was looking for and there'd been no trace of makeup on his body or a costume anywhere in his room.

Cross-checking the videos was tedious. Somewhere around the 20th timecode, Beckford blinked and his eyes stung. He didn't need a mirror to tell him that they were red, possibly even square. It was dark outside his window by then, and the more he sunk into a rabbit hole of obsessive video scouring, the more fatigued he felt.

The timecode was at 23:44 when Beckford shot up straight and slapped the spacebar, pausing the video.

There he was.

That hunched, slender frame protruding through a thin jacket not fit for the winter chill. That pale face with its ambiguous expression. It was undeniably Nikolai Guskov.

Beckford felt excited for once. He'd watched the suicide video possibly 20 times or more, and now he was looking at the same face, as yet whole and unmolested, but in a different setting and under different light.

Underneath Nikolai's jacket was the red T-shirt he would be found dead wearing in eight hours later. Slung over his shoulder was the dark green rucksack that was recovered from his room, which yielded nothing of interest.

Beckford hit the spacebar again and Nikolai sprung to life, disappearing through a door by the lifts that led to the stairs. He wouldn't come down them again.

For the next eye-drying hour, Beckford tracked down Nikolai's departure and arrival times on both the Richmond council and the Dunning House CCTV.

Nikolai had left his halls of residence in the afternoon, wearing and carrying the same items as on his return just before midnight. Thousands of people had crossed Beckford's raw eyes, and only twice had Nikolai appeared. Out and in. Both times he was alone and didn't talk to anyone. It would take one person weeks, possibly months, to trace exactly where Nikolai went during those 10 or so hours. With impatience bubbling under the surface, Beckford felt deflated by the idea of such a mammoth task.

In Beckford's world, it was 5:34 pm and he felt just about ready to crash. As a detective, he was accustomed to spending an inordinate amount of time to produce very little, if any, results. It was in those moments that his father's words kept him going. *Sometimes you're running a blind marathon. The finish line could be a mile away or a single step.*

It was said casually over a beer and Beckford had no idea how much it would stick. But now, with his growing obsessive tendencies, it was more relevant than ever.

Blind marathons.

Sometimes he wished he could stop running.

With a yawn and a stretch he felt the bones in his body creak and his muscles protest. He went to the toilet, then stepped into the kitchen to look for quick fuel and a distraction. He opened cupboards and took tins and packets out, then changed his mind and tried the fridge. It was then that his eyes locked onto a VHS tape sat atop the counter. The CCTV from the Fork & Field bistro.

Stop running, John.

He picked the tape up and looked at it. It stored a certainly-identical recording to the Richmond council traffic camera, only from a different angle.

Certainly identical?

It's not certain if you don't look.

Who had a VHS player anymore? The only place to buy them was from second-hand shops, surely.

Stop. Fucking. Running.

But… what if? What if? What-fucking-IF?

Beckford slammed his palm down on the counter and snatched his car keys. Some 20 minutes later he returned with a beaten Sony VHS player, missing the remote. He couldn't argue for a fiver. From his "cable drawer" he dug out an old scart connector.

You're losing it, John.

When it was all hooked up he slid in the tape, which disappeared behind a plastic flap. Gears and mechanisms buzzed and whirred from inside the machine and the screen flickered to life with fuzzy, washed-out images that sent Beckford straight back to the eighties.

How did we put up with this shit?

It was then, once he'd fast forwarded the magnetic tape, reeling from one spool to the other, that he made a discovery that turned everything upside down.

Nikolai Guskov had been murdered.

SIXTEEN

'John Beckford?' a deep, authoritative voice asked. 'Come out, you're under arrest.'

Beckford could only see blackness through his peephole. They'd covered it up. Had they caught up with him about the hack? His heart slammed in his ribcage. Before he let panic take over, he reasoned with himself that there'd be a way to explain things. It was enough to urge him to tear the door open – and then he didn't know what to do: laugh or punch Staedler in the face.

'Hiya pal,' said Staelder with a wide grin. Farber appeared and sidled up next to him.

'Sorry,' she said, 'Len's idea.'

'Pair of pricks,' said Beckford, awash with relief. 'You could have put my door through with that banging, Len.'

'I go the gym now. Four times a week. Must be that.'

Beckford stepped back and let them in. He was surprised to see Staedler, and had it been any other time it would have been a pleasant occasion.

Did Alison bring Staedler along as a safety net?

Beckford was certain he hadn't been giving off any vibes. Why would he have?

'My word,' said Staedler, smiling at Beckford in amazement, 'who'd have thought you'd look so good without glasses?'

Beckford snorted, 'You always look better when I didn't wear them too, Len.'

Staelder was one of the good guys. When Sally's murder investigation kicked off, Beckford naturally wanted nothing more than to assist, but being a relative of the victim he wasn't allowed. Instead, he was put on light duties and spent his days and nights stewing with frustration over his exclusion from the case. Then things started to get out of control and Corden had no choice but to send him home on compassionate leave.

Beckford knew Corden respected him as a detective; she couldn't afford to leave such an astute mind on the sidelines. And it was Staedler, under Corden's authority, who started to drip-feed him case intel – emails, calls and case files. They met in anonymous out-of-the-way bars late at night, wanting to keep their rendezvous as covert and inconspicuous as possible. It was Staedler's lifeline to the investigation that helped Beckford more than anything else. It gave him something to focus on, keeping at bay the ungodly sensation of helplessness that threatened to smother him if he was kept in the dark.

Acting as an unseen detective, Beckford collated information, scoured statements and hunted for evidence. He'd set up his very own incident room at home, but was vigilant in keeping his involvement a secret. Staedler's job was on the line, but it was Beckford's relationship with Farber that suffered the most. It was an unfortunate sacrifice, but in retrospect Beckford felt worthwhile now that Peter McGregor was behind bars.

'When was the last time you had an eye test, Len?' said Beckford, 'I think over sixties get them for free these days.'

'Speaking of over 60, I heard you shot a 67 the other month. Not bad for a nine-hole course.'

'Gentlemen,' said Farber, 'before you start sword fighting, I'm supposed to be at the cinema in an hour.'

Beckford shared a smile with Staedler, then led them both through to his study.

'What are we looking at?' said Farber, placing her handbag down by her feet. She was momentarily distracted by the extremely unusual sight of unwashed dishes littering Beckford's desk.

'Have you been outside at all today?' she added, leaning in closer to Beckford's desktop monitor where a video was playing. With only two chairs in the room, Staedler had to stand.

'This is from a camera situated across the road from Dunning House,' said Beckford, 'from the night of Nikolai's suicide. He'd been out of the building since midday and nearly 11 hours later he returns home. There.'

He landed his finger on the screen like a dart, highlighting a shadowy figure bathed in streetlight ambling up the pavement towards the entrance to Dunning House. At the door, the figure swiped a fob and disappeared inside.

'Now,' said Beckford, moving the mouse cursor to a second monitor with another video. 'This is from inside the foyer.'

Nikolai's ghostly image entered, his face caught briefly by the camera before vanishing beyond the door to the stairs. 'All normal, right?'

Leaning across Farber, he reached the VHS player sat underneath a small TV on the corner of his desk. 'This is footage from a coffee shop across the road.'

The tape spun up, the TV screen flickering and bouncing until the video settled, showing the pitch-black interior of the cafe, the combination of windows and shutters creating a crisscross of orange-lit squares from the street outside. The timecode showed 23:44, matching the other videos.

The quality was poor, but good enough as Beckford's finger traced an ambiguous shape, walking between slits in the shutters – Nikolai, approaching the Dunning House entrance. Then Beckford pressed a button and the VHS paused, the screen jerking indecisively between frames, littered with static scan lines. Slowly and silently he placed a finger on the screen.

Unconsciously, both Farber and Staelder leaned in closer. Out of the shadows, 15 feet or so behind Nikolai and Beckford's fingernail, was another person.

'Someone else?' muttered Staelder. Beckford pressed play and they watched Nikolai enter the building, followed a few seconds later by the other figure. Nobody said anything for a couple of seconds. It was like the stunned silence that followed a particularly impressive magic trick.

'How?' said Farber.

'Digital manipulation,' said Beckford, swivelling his chair to face them, ready to present his theory like Sherlock Holmes.

'The footage from the traffic camera and Dunning House were both recorded and stored digitally. Dunning House CCTV is recorded to a simple system, but the office security is lacklustre, managed by some Neanderthal concierge. The traffic camera is maintained by Richmond council, and is a much larger, cross-site system with remote access through the web, which makes me believe—'

'Someone hacked in and altered it?' said Staedler.

'Is that even possible?' added Farber.

'Anything's possible in the digital world,' said Beckford. 'It all boils down to skill. When you've got teenagers breaking into NASA, a council-run CCTV system isn't exactly a tough nut to crack.'

He reached out, pressed a button on the VHS player and the video rewound, zigzagged static and colour splitting the screen. He let go of the button and the video resumed again. All three of them stared intently at the screen, tracking the second figure. The ghost.

'Winterburn?' said Farber.

'For now, yes,' said Beckford, hooking a hand around the back of his neck and stretching.

'So what was he doing with Nikolai?' said Staedler. 'He obviously didn't go through with the pact or we'd have a second body.'

'Did his mum say anything about her son's interest in computers?' said Beckford. 'I mean, did he even have one?'

'There was a laptop in his room,' said Farber, 'but John, even my mum has a computer... who doesn't these days? Mrs Winterburn said he liked bikes. Cycling. And he worked at Halfords for a few years.'

'What about video production?' said Beckford. 'Graphic design?'

'He studied music in college,' said Staedler. 'His bedroom was all music. There were about three or four guitars, one of them a really fucking nice Stratocaster. Maybe he was in a band? Maybe he worked on music videos?'

'Anyone can cut a music video,' said Beckford, then pointed at the screen. 'This... this is movie magic.' He picked up a pen drive and started twiddling it between his fingers.

'Nikolai's computer was stripped like a professional,' he said. 'These videos, the acquisition and the manipulation, the council one in particular... that's a pro job. Maybe Joseph hired somebody.'

Farber said, 'Why would he hire someone to remove his presence from the scene of a suicide?'

Beckford held up the pen drive and said, 'I'm not sure how much stock we can put in that anymore.'

'What's that?' said Staelder.

'Nikolai's "suicide",' said Beckford, adding air quotes with his fingers. He could see they were confused.

'The software that's available now,' he said, 'anyone can

get hold of it if they know where to look. Tools literally straight out of Hollywood that can do all sorts of things – 3D modelling, green screen, compositing, motion capture and tracking. I saw a short film the other week on YouTube made by 14-year-old kid in his bedroom that looked better than most blockbusters. *Just 14*. Everything's so accessible these days. The tools *and* the information. Anyone can change anything. Create something from nothing by moving pixels around a screen. And someone here has put a lot of work into creating something that we perceive to be real.'

'John,' said Farber. The apprehension in her voice said it all. They both thought he'd gone mad. Before she could continue, Beckford butted in.

'Nikolai was murdered but his suicide video proves otherwise, until I can prove *that* otherwise to be fake.'

'How are you going to do that, John?' asked Staelder.

Beckford tapped the pen drive on his teeth and said, 'I might know someone who can help.'

SEVENTEEN

Beckford scribbled his name in the sign-in book and the receptionist handed over a plastic visitor's badge. The offices at GyroFX were bustling with young, hip, eager employees. Creative types who looked like they'd come straight off the university conveyor belt. Over the din could be heard a thick New York accent that made Beckford's head spin.

'John! Jesus, man!'

Hogan Hewitt had shoulder-length curls, golden in places, wood-rim glasses and he wore a lurid Hawaiian shirt with linen trousers. Not ideal for autumn going on winter, but the office heating was on full blast, which caused Beckford to de-robe his jacket on exiting the lift.

'Man, you look different,' said Hogan, clasping Beckford's outstretched hand and almost pulling his shoulder from its socket. The two of them were more like passing acquaintances than close friends, but they had bumped into each other on enough alcohol-drenched nights to be able to call one another up for a favour. Hogan squinted, taking a proper look at him.

'No specs,' said Beckford, pulling his crushed hand free.

'That's it. That's it. Lasered?' Beckford nodded. 'You've got balls, fella. They'd have to pay me to smell my burning retinas. Did you smell 'em burning?'

'Wasn't too bad. Bit like singed hair.'

'Fuck. No way, man. No. Fuckin.' Way. Anyway, been a long time, bro! This way.'

They headed through the open-plan office that looked like a lot of modern startups, replicating the relaxed and creative philosophy of Google or Pixar. The decor was so bright and colourful it made Beckford's eyes hurt.

In the far corner of the office was an area that looked like a playpen, filled with bean bags and a white wall covered in scribbled mind-maps. They passed a row of vending machines filled with soda and sweets – retro stuff like Tab Clear, gobstoppers and sherbet dip dab. If colour and comfort didn't boost creativity, sugar and caffeine certainly would.

'I was surprised you worked Sundays,' said Beckford as they reached the far side of the open-plan area.

'Deadlines, my friend. Couldn't survive without them.'

Hogan ushered him into a small office and closed the door. 'You sure you don't want a drink?' he said, rounding his desk and planting himself in a leather swivel chair. 'Red Bull?'

'You drink that stuff?'

'Runs like water in this place. Fuck, man, I'd make it company policy to drink that shit with the kind of workload we've got going on at the moment. Some of my team pull all-nighters coked out of their heads.'

Beckford's eyes widened and Hogan realised he wasn't just shooting the shit with a friend. Beckford was a police officer.

'Coke, the soda,' he added with a wry smile.

'How about some water?'

'Right there, my friend,' said Hogan, pointing to a water dispenser in the corner. Beckford grabbed a paper cup and filled it. After his fall off the caffeine wagon the day before, he needed to flush his system. Caffeine had a half-life of around eight hours and his nerves had been on edge all morning, threatening to boil over into panic attacks and obsessive behaviour. He'd been semi-conscious all night, unable to properly drift into a deep sleep. His brain felt fried, but he had to keep going.

On Hogan's desk was a triple-monitor setup – huge industry standard screens providing an almost 180-degree perspective. Displayed on the screens was a work-in-progress visual effect, the recognisable "green screen" hanging as the backdrop to a piece of video.

'What are you working on, a film?' said Beckford.

'An online commercial. It's all online content these days, we haven't had film work for over a year, but like I said business is booming. What about you? How's the doughnut diet?'

He made the same joke each time, failing to realise that police and doughnuts was strictly an American stereotype.

'Actually, I work in computer crime now,' said Beckford, taking a seat. 'Transferred out of CID last year.'

Hogan bit the inside of his lip. 'Yeah. Actually I heard, man. I'm so sorry about your sister. Jesus Christ, the world is a fucked-up place all right.'

Beckford gave a subdued smile and nodded.

Not wanting to linger in the solemn silence, Hogan swept his hand across his desk and said, 'Anyway, let's not talk about that. Life is good now, right? *Right?* So, what do I owe this unexpected pleasure?'

Beckford turned behind him and said, 'Does this door lock?'

On the largest and most vibrant computer screen Beckford had ever seen, they sat and watched Nikolai Guskov pump both barrels of lead birdshot through his head. Hogan didn't even flinch, his desensitisation a cause for concern for Beckford. *What other mad shit has this crazy bastard been watching?*

No sooner had the video finished, Hogan pressed play and they watched it again. Beckford had scrutinised the footage to the nth degree with his detective hat on, but now he was sat with a visual effects expert in the realm of movie magic, who viewed it from a different perspective. As if he was observing a piece of art in a gallery.

'Well?' said Beckford after the third viewing, if a little impatiently. Hogan leaned back in his chair, swivelling left then right, hands behind his head.

'It doesn't look fake,' he said, 'but it could be. You can't take anything digital as gospel these days. Some of the shit our guys pump out makes *Jurassic Park* look like it was done on a fuckin' Etch-a-Sketch.'

'I know,' said Beckford, 'I saw this short film the other day on YouTube. Some 14-year-old—'

'Adam Cole!' said Hogan, his eyes lighting up. 'Shit, yes! Lives in Brixton. We're trying to poach the fucker, but all the big guns in Hollywood and Wellywood have already offered him the fuckin' world on a silver plate.'

Hogan looked back at the screen and stopped swivelling. He leaned forward again and played the video once more. Nikolai's timid voice quietly intoned from his desktop speakers. Hogan's eyes narrowed, his face barely inches from the screen.

'This bit's got to be real,' he said, 'I've not seen facial animation this damn good. Not this *human*. I've seen pretty close to this, sure – mocap is getting better every year.'

'Mocap?'

'Motion capture. Where the actors have those dots on their face? They have these special cameras that track the dots, capturing every movement and nuance as the face moves, letting us guys recreate it using, well, anything we want. This isn't mocap, though. It's real.'

'How sure are you?'

'Yeah, 100% buddy. I mean, fuck me man, if this *is* mocap we're out of a goddamn job.' Hogan paused the playback. 'What's the video resolution?'

'It's 640 by 480.'

'Fuck, must be an old webcam.'

'It is – a Microsoft Lifecam VX 5000,' said Beckford. The information was on a printout in among the notes on his lap, but he knew them off by heart.

'And then you've got the slight fisheye going on,' said Hogan, 'which could easily be added in post.'

'Post-production?' said Beckford, although he already knew the answer. Hogan didn't answer anyway, resuming the video from Nikolai's closing speech.

'Okay,' said Hogan, 'so if we're taking this as real, why would he spout all this shit if you're saying he was murdered?'

'Maybe someone bribed him or had a gun pointed at his head. Or both.'

'Backup a sec, that Joey kid.'

'Joseph Winterburn.'

'Yeah, him. Say it's that guy on the VHS, the second figure. Do you see him leave the building in the footage?'

'No. The tape from the Fork & Field goes through the night and into the morning when our lot arrive *and* leave. It's hard to identify the second figure on the tape, but my guess is if Winterburn did leave it would have been via the back entrance, and those Dunning House videos have been doctored. It still doesn't explain why our pal Joseph would go through the trouble of fabricating the suicide.'

'Maybe it's not fabricated. Maybe it's real. Joey turns up, watches from the wings as Nikolai bumps himself off and then Joey couldn't go through with it, shits himself and leaves. It happens with some suicide pacts.'

'So why tamper with the videos at all then?'

'Like I said, people are fucked up. Maybe Joey is some paranoid nutjob who thought that even being associated with some kid's suicide would get him into trouble with the cops. Come on, man, are you being the dick here or am I?'

Hogan's theory actually made sense to Beckford. He could relate to it. A sufferer of OCD could fabricate connections between anything, however disparate and irrational they appeared. There was always a way to connect the dots. If Joseph Winterburn was a fellow OCD sufferer, catastrophising his loose involvement in the suicide pact could explain why he was on the run.

'But Winterburn doesn't have the tech skills,' said Beckford. 'You know what it would take to hack in, unseen, to the Richmond council CCTV system? Not just that, but the video from the traffic camera is flawlessly edited. The second figure, if indeed it is Winterburn, has been completely erased. Like the kind of stuff your team do on a daily basis. Professionals. *And* Nikolai's computer was wiped clean, remember? Forensically clean. Someone really fucking talented is hiding something.'

Beckford bit his tongue – the f-bomb was unnecessary, but Hogan's potty mouth was infectious.

On screen they watched as Nikolai stood up and put the side-by-side sawn-off barrels under his chin. Beckford stopped chewing the skin around his index finger and slapped the spacebar, pausing the video.

'What about this?' he said. 'His head going out of frame here…'

'I was thinking the same thing,' said Hogan. 'The old off-the-screen, we-don't-have-enough-money-to-do-that-so-use-your-imagination routine.'

'That's it, isn't it?' said Beckford. 'We don't actually *see* his head take the blast, just hear it. With the timestamps being alterable and no one actually hearing the gunshot on the night, there's no reliable way to pinpoint when he actually died.'

Hogan tapped a key, progressing the video frame by

frame.

Beckford added, 'They found a fatal level of paracetamol in his system, so he could have died from an overdose *after* this whole video was shot, and the shotgun's role in the suicide carried out once he'd expired.'

'What kind of sick fuck…'

They continued watching frame by frame as Nikolai's visible torso jerked from the shotgun blast. Beckford had seen it so many times, he reckoned he could draw any frame from memory. When the video ended, Hogan turned to him.

'I'm going to need more time to analyse this, John. Maybe get one of my composite monkeys involved. Kumar, maybe. That dude knows his shit.'

'Keep it contained,' said Beckford. 'This is sensitive material.'

'John, if the video is fake it's a professional job or by some fuckin' genius who's in the wrong game. In which case, when you find him give him my card will ya?'

He laughed, deep and loud, clapping a hand on Beckford's shoulder, who only managed to muster a smile.

* * *

The Fork & Field was much busier than the day before. Beckford slurped carrot and coriander soup, but couldn't get a table near the window. Instead, he was situated further towards back, near his friend the rubber plant. He could still see Dunning House and watched as students came and went, going about their lives completely unperturbed, having already forgotten about the blue lights, uniforms, local news crew and Chinese whispers surrounding the state of Nikolai Guskov's body when it was found.

Halloween of all nights, and what a mess it was too. Alcohol flowing like piss at half-time. Every floor of the building crawling with lubricated 20-somethings rapt in their own fabulous costumes and drug of choice. Who would have had the faintest idea that anything truly ghoulish was going on inside room 412?

Nobody had seen Nikolai all day; business as usual his neighbours said. That was according to the reports. Beckford rarely trusted other officer's statements. The thought had crossed his mind to go door-to-door himself. Rookies never asked the right questions and they never looked hard enough.

There's no time to look hard enough, John, he thought.

He'd heard that before. To any ordinary citizen, a crime could be the most severe and traumatising thing they'd ever experienced, psychologically changing them for ever. To the police, a crime meant work and the endgame of that work was statistics. The numbers had to go down or they were in the shit. On the surface, Nikolai was a cut-and-dried suicide and an easy box to tick for senior management.

Just another weirdo kid who killed himself.

He'd heard that before, too.

'What's going on, John?' he said to himself, the words quiet enough to assure him it was an internal voice spoken aloud and not a full-blown conversation starter that would squeeze him into a comfy straightjacket quite nicely.

After paying up, Beckford stood out on the pavement and looked up and down Dunning Street yet again. He lingered on the traffic camera, this time looking at it in awe, almost respectful of someone's deft ability to alter reality. *Perceived reality*, he reminded himself. Nowadays, thanks to the reliance on digital information everything was perceived reality.

A bus rumbled to a halt in front of him at a bus stop and released a pneumatic hiss. The doors swung open and passengers cascaded onto the pavement. In among the crowd one face stood out, but at first Beckford didn't know why. The young man was clad head to toe in black with matching shoulder-length hair. Walking to the rear of the bus he stepped out into the road and skipped over towards Dunning House. That's when it clicked.

'Hey, pal?' shouted Beckford over the traffic and ran after him. 'Wait up a sec!'

Darting over the road himself, he flanked the lad as they made the curb together. It was only then that the young man noticed him, too entranced by the heavy rock blasting through concealed headphones under his blackest of black tresses. The lad yanked an earbud free.

'Are you Robert Brown?' said Beckford. The young man's face struck a chord between shock and confusion.

'Why?' he said and continued towards Dunning House. Beckford kept pace.

'My name's John Beckford. I'm a police officer.' From his jacket he pulled his warrant card, but Robert didn't look at it.

'You're not in any trouble,' assured Beckford, 'I just need to ask you a few questions about Nikolai Guskov.' He slid his ID back into his rear pocket and cut Robert off at the entrance to Dunning House. 'You were friends, right?'

'Does sitting next to someone in lectures and living on the same floor constitute a friendship?'

'Maybe not to you.'

'Look,' said Robert. 'I already told the other bloke everything I know, which isn't a lot.' He went to push past Beckford who shifted to obstruct him again.

'What other bloke?'

'One of your lot, last Friday. Cornered me on the stairs. Proper stank of B.O.'

'Friday?' said Beckford, now confused himself. 'Statements were taken the day after Nikolai—'

'It was Friday. I remember. He was on his own. It was early too, like seven or something. I was on my way to work.'

'What did he look like?' said Beckford.

Robert shrugged. 'Just… like a copper. Wore a suit.'

'He showed you ID?' Robert nodded. 'Get a name?' Robert shook his head no. Beckford stared through him, processing the information, his mind filling in gaps with a multitude of theories. When the entrance to Dunning House made a clunk, Beckford was pulled back from his thoughts and noticed that Robert had already disappeared inside.

A lone detective?

* * *

He tried Victor first, buzzing the concierge button over and over for what would have sounded like a madman trying to enter the building. No matter, he had a copy of the CCTV at home, and yet for the duration of the 43 excruciating minutes it took him to get there a growing obsessive notion told him that his copy of the Dunning House CCTV wouldn't stretch as far as Friday. The further he got from Dunning House, the bigger the obsession grew. Tempted to turn back at every junction, he kept his foot down and carried on. It eased once he'd got past the halfway point, but then his mind switched obsession – if the lone detective was involved, the video would have been doctored too.

When he finally got home, he took the stairs up to his

apartment, knowing he'd easily outsprint the lift even if it was waiting on the ground floor with open doors. Out of breath, he barged into his apartment, turned lights on and headed straight to his study.

Shaking the mouse, his black monitors flickered into life. The Dunning House CCTV was still frozen on one of them – Nikolai, about to walk out of frame.

Beckford closed the file down and browsed the contents of the pen drive. The files were time-stamped, and with much relief he found the lobby footage for Friday. He played the video and slid the timeline from 00:00, when the footage started, to 07:00.

For 10 minutes he watched, almost willing a man in a suit to appear. That's all he needed.

Who could it be? Someone who's job or a con artist?

At the 10-minute mark impatience got the better of Beckford and he started skipping through the video in 30-second chunks.

At 7:14, Beckford slapped the space bar to freeze the footage. It was Robert Brown, heading to work. Which meant the confrontation with the lone detective had already taken place. Beckford continued skipping. A few students here and there, but not a suit among them.

Closing the video, he next loaded the rear door CCTV. The camera was in the resident's car park, positioned on the wall directly above the back exit. At that time on a November morning it was still dark, but the camera used infrared to improve visibility and the car park floodlights provided more than enough illumination to see anyone coming or going.

Beckford skipped to at 07:00 and continued to watch, his heart rate increasing with each passing second.

Slap!

There. 07:12. The man in the suit was overweight and

lugged a black holdall over one shoulder. Frozen, walking away from the camera, Beckford couldn't see his face.

Slap.

The video resumed. After the man took a few steps he turned and looked directly at the camera.

Slap.

Beckford stared at the infrared flares that bounced from the man's eyes like a cat. Beckford didn't recognise the man in the video… but someone else did.

Unknown to Beckford, his computer was being monitored. Members of the Studio would dip in every now and then to keep an eye on things, but their systems did most of the work.

The covertly installed Agnoscis software specialised in computer vision. Its machine-learning algorithms used pattern recognition and content-based image retrieval to scour any visual data it was directed towards. In a fraction of a second, it had scanned the image on Beckford's computer and recognised the man as Dominic Peltz.

With the degrees of separation recalculated to one, Comminatio raised Beckford's threat rating to 861 out of 1000. Amber turned to red, and within 60 seconds the Studio set in motion the procedure they had to follow.

EIGHTEEN

The glow of his computer screen made Beckford's eyes light up like bulbs. It was late for most people. After scrutinising the video of the lone detective, Beckford realised no matter how many times he watched it, it wouldn't make any difference if he didn't know the man.

Who would know him? If the man was job, Beckford had enough contacts in the Met to email a screenshot out and wait for a response. But he couldn't wait. It would also raise suspicions. Racking his brain for a solution, Beckford remembered a technology Willow had shown him once called Reverse Image Search. All he had to do was upload a clear screenshot of the man's face to any one of the many available RIS sites on the internet and the system would first scan the content of the image, then scan any other images in its database looking for matching properties. Willow had used the technology to work out whether people's profile pictures on dating websites were genuine or stolen from other websites.

After a quick search, Beckford found a suitable RIS site and uploaded a cropped screenshot of the unidentified detective staring up at the camera. It wasn't the best quality, but it only took a few seconds for the website to return results causing Beckford's heart rate to jack up again.

Out of the stack of near-miss images returned, one of them stood out – a professional photograph of the same man in a different suit, sat in front of a stock studio backdrop. Beckford followed the image link, which took him directly to a news article on the Metropolitan Police website.

The man's name was Dominic Peltz, a detective inspector who specialised in computer crime. The article interviewed Peltz about the state of modern e-crime and its increasing threats. The article was six years old, but it got Beckford excited.

Farber's notes contained the case register for all attending officers at the scene of Nikolai's dorm room, as well as all the involved Metropolitan Police employees back at base, right down to administrators and clerks. Dominic Peltz was not among them. Some jigsaw pieces were falling into place, but there was still no evident connection between a corrupt detective, Nikolai Guskov and Joseph Winterburn.

The article stated that Peltz had been involved in e-crime for three years, which could put his present experience in the field close to 10. Undoubtedly a man with much skill, Beckford thought, wondering whether Peltz's extensive resume included hacking, video manipulation and falsifying evidence.

Beckford flipped to Google and searched for his name, but it was clear straightaway that Dominic Peltz was a private man. A personal choice, perhaps, but Beckford banked on his absence from the ever-increasing, ever-intruding social networks to be more likely a "professional" choice. A few more instances of his name appeared across the Metropolitan Police website, but there was nothing worthwhile. All the main social networking sites yielded no results.

Next, Beckford logged into his Metropolitan Police email and browsed the address book. In the list of current employees he found an account under the name Dominic Peltz. Beckford knew that when Met employees left the service, their account was purged, so the very existence of the account he'd found told him there was at least one person active in the Met by that name. Whether or not it was the same man as the one in the CCTV he couldn't be sure, but the odds were in his favour.

Where could he turn to next? With only scraps of data online, Beckford needed to track the man down in real life. For a long moment he just stared at the screen, half-thinking, half in a daze. It was like his body started to naturally shut down as tiredness took over.

On autopilot, he dragged the mouse cursor to the browser address bar, highlighted the text and hit delete. Nothing happened. He hit delete again a few times. The address remained. Confused, he shook the mouse but the cursor didn't move. Frozen.

Before he could react, the screen flickered, flashing a website up in front of his eyes – a blue and white page with a configuration menu that Beckford didn't have time to scrutinise. He quickly glanced to the address bar, noting the address http://www.tork2me.com. The mouse, now controlled by someone or something else, clicked a button on the page labelled "Connect." It was then that Beckford realised the website was a web-based chat client.

Connecting to a chatroom called #PunkSmiley, the page displayed the room's only occupants – Beckford himself, known by a default alias Anon247, and another user – Anon143.

Beckford's body was rigid and he was no longer tired. Over the past year he'd investigated a number of hacks, but had never been the victim of one. Had the whole situation lasted longer, he would have savoured getting his hack-cherry popped, but as messages appeared on screen, everything that came after was a blur.

`[01:14] <Anon143> You don't have much time.`

[01:14] <Anon143> They've been watching you. I locked them out of your computer, but they've sent people to get you.

The black text on a white background burned into his retinas as he was suddenly plunged into darkness, the words lingering for few seconds before fading synchronously with the sound of the internal fans spinning down inside his now powerless computer.

For the briefest moment Beckford thought he had died, as if someone had fired a bullet through the back of his head and turning him off. But his senses adapted and he started to notice his own breath whistling through his nostrils and the deep thud of his beating heart. Then his ears picked up the quiet rush of a distant plane overhead and – with the help of the polluting streetlights leaking in through his curtains – he started to see the shape of his now lifeless computer sat in front of him as his eyes adjusted to the darkness.

For a few seconds more he sat frozen to the spot with fear, even though he knew he had to move. He had to do *something*. Whoever Anon143 was, whether a bullshitter or Beckford's guardian angel, he'd put the fear of God into him good and proper.

Determined to stay relatively calm, Beckford carefully prised himself out of the chair and grabbed his phone from the side. With only socks on his feet, he drifted quietly across the room and flanked his study door. He flicked the light switch, but nothing happened.

Has power been cut to the whole building?

The door was ajar, showing a strip of blackness into the hallway. With his back to the wall he held his breath and listened, but all he could hear was his own blood pumping round his head.

Da-dum, da-dum, da-dum, da-dum.

When he unlocked his phone, the light from the screen destroyed any adaptation his eyes had made to the darkness. A few taps later and a torchlight emitted from the device, illuminating the room. Swiftly, Beckford opened his study door and directed the harsh but not very powerful LED light into the corridor, catching only faint, inanimate shapes at the far end of the living room.

He crossed the hall to his bedroom, leading with the torch as he went straight to his wardrobe where he dropped to his knees and shifted aside shoes and an old box of knick-knacks. Under all the crap he pulled out a white plastic bag, the rustling of which seemed deafening in the dark. Inside was a black travel bag, which he urgently unzipped and slid out a .40 calibre Walther P99 semi-automatic pistol and a spare magazine of bullets.

There was nothing official about the gun; he'd confiscated it from a drug dealer many moons ago and, unbelievably, had forgotten to hand in. Over time he'd gotten used to its presence in the flat, but after Sally's murder it became something else. A security blanket, keeping him safe in the knowledge that if, somehow, Peter McGregor was ever released… there would be solution.

He wedged the gun in his waistband, chucked the mag into a shoulder bag and put on his trainers. Going back into his study he swept the phone light across his desk. Into his bag went the pen drive, Farber's paperwork and a few other printouts including the transcript of private messages between Joseph Winterburn and Nikolai. With the bag on his back he clasped the phone to the side of the gun like a tactical light and led himself out into the hallway.

Keeping agile on his feet, he first entered the bathroom, checking it was clear. He then pushed on into the living room, sweeping the shadows with light, his senses on overload. Being a sufferer of panic attacks he was familiar with the fight or flight sensation, but there was something different this time – he wanted to fight. He'd spent so many times running that he was now fed up, riled up and ready for whatever came his way. With his thumb he released the gun's safety mechanism with a soft click.

As he panned the barrel across his once familiar but now hostile flat, he was certain that if anything moved he'd put a bullet right through it or unload the mag trying, but unless there was a contortionist hiding in his fridge, Beckford was sure he was the only one in his home.

He crossed to the front door, noting the dark gap underneath that told him the motion sensor lights in the corridor weren't on. Placing the phone light against the door's peephole, he shook his hand a few times and the lights came on outside, illuminating a golden strip under the door.

Maybe all the flats are on a separate circuit…

Maybe it's just my flat…

Beckford tapped his phone screen a few times, turning the light off and the camera on. This time he held the lens against the peephole and a fisheye view of the empty corridor outside his apartment appeared on screen.

It had been a while since he'd been in any combat situation that required such speed, focus and good fortune. In CID, death was usually talked about in the past-tense. Now it was a near-future possibility.

Pocketing his phone, he grabbed the front door handle and a wave of adrenaline came crashing over him as he rode it out of his apartment, his eyes fixed through the iron sights of his gun as he spun one way and then the other in the corridor.

It was deserted.

He pulled the front door shut and moved quickly for

the stairs. It was only when he got to the door of the stairwell that he looked back at his flat and considered the possibility he'd been the target of social engineering, coerced into believing he was in danger.

Did they just want me out of my flat?

Have I left anything of value in there?

Is there even anyone on their way?

But what about the power?

The building's electricity might be controlled by an online unit, which could have been compromised.

The questions came thick and fast. Not wanting to take any chances, he pushed through another door into the stairwell and the questions suddenly stopped.

The forearm came across his throat so quickly and tightly that his Adam's apple was crushed against his windpipe, causing him to gag and drop the gun. With his empty hands he scrambled at the foreign limb under his chin and a sharp pain bit into his neck. Beckford knew that it was now or never. He didn't want to be a past-tense. Not yet.

With everything he had, Beckford swung his left arm back, burying an elbow into his assailant's diaphragm. A deep grunt roared down his left ear and he felt the man's grip loosen. Beckford spun around and drove the man into the wall, the pain in his neck biting once more as a syringe detached from his skin and clattered down the stairs.

The man's eyes were a piercing blue, staring through the gaping holes of a black balaclava. He was strong too; stronger than Beckford. Ferociously grappling one another, the man gritted his teeth and slowly got the upper hand, forcing Beckford away from the wall. Letting go with his right hand, Beckford slammed a fist into the man's nose. The connection was weak, stunning him only briefly before he pushed back with more power.

A few steps back and Beckford's right foot met with air and he dropped, falling down the first flight of stairs and pulling the man with him. Their bodies, like sacks of meat, fell without grace – rolling over one another, limbs flailing, bones thumping concrete. Beckford's backpack acted as a cushion for one tumble, before slipping off in the fray as both men battled with physics, each hoping to land with the best physical advantage.

Beckford found himself face-down and the man's legs swung into the back of his head like two baseballs bats, bouncing his forehead off the concrete. Numbed by adrenaline, no pain came but his vision went fuzzy. In a dazed scramble he managed get to his feet first, spinning around and planting a knee just behind the man's right ear – the impact sounding deep, almost wooden, and the momentum causing Beckford to topple over the man and crumple awkwardly to the floor.

In front of him lay the syringe, the plunger still primed. Just as he reached out, the man flipped over and clasped Beckford's jacket with both hands. In a flash, Beckford whipped round and buried the needle through the man's coat, just under the armpit, the force so strong that the plunger depressed on impact.

A fist whipped out and caught Beckford clean on the chin, jarring his brain enough to see stars. He hadn't felt a punch like that for many years and forgot how painful it was. As his focus returned, he saw the man standing over him holding a gun.

'Get up,' said the man's weak voice between gasps. He repeated the request by motioning Beckford to his feet with the barrel of the gun. Beckford took his time, overplaying his pain and exhaustion by first dragging himself upright against the wall, then raising himself to his feet. The man grabbed the handrail to steady himself.

'Stupid cunt,' he said, then dragged a two-way radio from inside his jacket and clicked the talk button. The channel crackled.

'This is Two… I'm…' the man blinked rapidly and his head started to sway. Beckford locked eyes on the gun's muzzle.

'…I'm… oh shhhh—' The man slumped against the railing and fell backwards to the floor, the gun skittering down the next flight of stairs. The radio crackled again and a voice came through.

'Copy Delta Two?'

Beckford was still in shock, his heart pumping like a steam engine. He watched the man writhe softly on the floor before slipping into unconsciousness.

'Delta Two, do you copy?'

Beckford grabbed his gun and bag from the stairs and shot down the next flight, two steps at a time. Curiosity stopped him in his tracks. He'd punish himself if he didn't go back and check.

Sprinting back up the stairs, he got down by the unconscious man. Was he sleeping or was he dead? Wondering what concoction was in the syringe, Beckford slid his hand carefully into the man's trouser pockets, wary of any further needles. He found nothing but a pack of chewing gum, a set of keys and some loose change. He looked at the man's head, and just as he slipped two fingers under the balaclava a loud bang echoed up from the depths of the stairwell as a door slammed shut. Beckford got up and arched over the railing.

Running footsteps, more than one pair, their shadows bouncing off surfaces, getting closer. Beckford fled back up the stairs and pushed through the doors onto his floor again. Down the corridor he ran, charging through fire doors, checking for danger over his shoulder as he went, the gun in his hand.

In the few seconds he had, in the throes of panic and with limited blood supply to his brain, Beckford conjured up a weak plan that consisted of two words: Fire escape.

Each corridor had one. And they were alarmed.

Through the final set of doors, the floor's fire escape ahead lay ahead. Without slowing, Beckford threw himself at the door's push-bar and slammed through into another stairwell. A loud siren wailed. Beckford flew down the stairs faster than he had moved in his life.

The shrill alarm would alert them to his whereabouts, but that didn't worry him too much because everyone else in the building would be clambering out of their beds now, soon to be filling the corridors and stairwells themselves. For the first time, the thought of an onslaught of pissed-off residents was a comforting one.

When he reached the ground floor, Beckford checked the safety on the gun and pushed through an outer door into the dim car park, panning the barrel across a row of cars. His body buzzed with erratic energy, but there was no stopping to smell the roses. He spilled out into the night air, ducking in among the shadows of the cars, eyes darting into every dark corner.

Voices echoed off the surrounding brick walls.

Down on his haunches, Beckford peered through the back window of an Audi, spotting unknown figures by the entrance to his building, looking up at the block. It was only after a moment of observation that he recognised one or two of them as residents, and that they were standing in the designated assembly point, most likely discussing which dickhead had set off the fire alarm.

Beckford stayed where he was for a moment, closing his eyes and trying to control his breathing. Thankfully, the physical stress gave him no manoeuvre for thoughts, and the voices, indecipherable murmurings, had an almost meditative quality to them. He listened unconsciously as he let his body recover.

When he became aware of the cold caressing his bare hands he decided to move. He kept low behind the cars, and it was only when he was free of the apartment grounds that he ran.

NINETEEN

Dominic Peltz sat at the dressing table of his hotel room, head in one hand, phone in the other. On his monitors were a range of live data windows, text scrolling, videos playing. He was still in his underwear, the phone having dragged him out of bed in the early hours. It had taken four calls before he heard it and five before he answered.

The past few days had been hellish, with Peltz working around the clock to contain Nikolai's "legacy" and to monitor the ever-encroaching movements of one John Beckford.

It was only after Peltz had answered the fifth call that he found out Beckford had identified him and that a team had been dispatched to his apartment.

But it hadn't gone to plan.

'Who made up the team?' said Peltz. 'Which incompetent fuck—'

'We don't know what happened yet,' said the vocoded voice, 'but the Studio will want answers for deeper discrepancies.'

'The Ukrainian's file was done and dusted,' said Peltz, agitated. 'Still is. It's not been reopened. How was I to know some bloody jobsworth was going to dig around like some obsessive beachcomber?'

'Risks weren't mitigated. You got lax.'

'I'm up to my bloody neck in it, that's why!' Peltz wanted to roar down the phone, but despite the soundproofing, he kept his voice hushed. Force of habit. 'You're putting too many resources into the Studio and not enough at my end. I'm the backbone. I can't run this thing on my own *and* go out on clean-ups.'

'Don't give me that,' said the voice, 'you put yourself on that job. It was your choice.'

'It's not me who's gotten lax, that's why. It needed to be thorough.'

Peltz hadn't slept properly since Nikolai's death. He'd known the lad. Not very well, but well enough. That wasn't why he was having sleepless nights. There were other things. Things that forced him into the dead of night, to Dunning House for his first clean-up job in years. The Studio would see it as an odd move – Peltz was a backend manager and dirty work was often left to newcomers and the odd one or two who actually enjoyed the thrill of sneaking around and killing people.

To avoid any suspicion of why he wanted the clean-up job, Peltz used his social engineering skills to convince the team he wanted to get back into the thick of it.

'I'm like a battery hen in this bloody hotel,' he'd said. 'I'm sick of it.'

But it couldn't be further from the truth. Peltz loved hiding away, where he had warmth, food and a safe distance from danger.

'Use the woman,' said Peltz. 'Get him out in the open.'

'So you'll have yet another stain to bleach?' said the voice. 'No. You said it yourself, we don't have the manpower to contain it. No more ripples. Not at the moment at least. Beckford will show up on the grid sooner or later.'

Peltz sighed and said, 'When do they want me?'

'You mean you're not dressed yet?'

Before he could respond the call ended with a click. Peltz stood up and paced the room, squeezing his phone like a stress ball. He spun and went to throw it at the wall, but stopped himself at the last second, freezing like some tribute statue. With another sigh, his body deflated. He let the phone drop onto the bed, then opened a cupboard under the dressing table and plugged in an iron.

* * *

Being well versed in panic attacks, Beckford had experienced the threat of death many times before, each just as terrifying as the last. With very little range of intensity, the terror experienced during an attack was nearly always a 10. It was the nature of the beast – convinced that the utmost worst was about to happen, the sufferer quite literally thought that they were about to die horribly.

The causes of an attack always seemed to confound anyone lucky enough to have never experienced one. External factors could exacerbate them, but their inception was internal. Mental. Completely irrational, yet entirely believable.

This time, the panic was rational, the prospect of death real and external. People had come to get him.

Unlike a panic attack, where the "flight" part of a fight-or-flight response was impossible – which was one of the reasons why they were so harrowing – Beckford could run from his assailants. And getting distance in the physical world was a hell of a lot easier than getting distance in the mental world.

It had taken him 20 minutes of navigating side roads and alleyways to reach Sudbury Golf Club, where he skulked onto the course to take refuge in among the dark trees to the left and just short of the 10th hole. It was bitterly cold. Crouched against one of the trees, Beckford warmed his hands and tried to set his mind straight. With his body still buzzing with adrenaline, he couldn't seem to grab hold of a single thought and it pissed him off. He *needed* his thoughts. Without them he was lost.

Pulling up the hood of his jacket, he closed his eyes and rested his head on his knees, shutting out the world around him. Breathing slow and deliberate, he visualised the cold air drawing in through his nostrils and pouring down into his lungs. Then he steadily exhaled out of his mouth. He did this a few times until finally he latched onto a thought.

Alison.

If they wanted Beckford, naturally they'd go to the next person he cared about the most. But did he care enough about Farber? And if so, did anyone know? Did *they* know?

They know everything, dickhead. You've probably been under surveillance – both online and in the real world – for weeks, if not months.

Beckford pulled his phone from his pocket and unlocked it. At the top of the screen he noticed the GPS icon – normally, he'd have it switched off to save battery. Beckford scrolled through the settings, found the GPS option and tapped to turn it off. Nothing happened. He tried again, but realised the button was disabled.

They hadn't just been in his computer.

Beckford sprang to his feet and ran out onto the 10th fairway. With all his might, he threw his phone far and high into the night sky and bolted, not even waiting to hear it land.

Across the golf course he ran, keeping close to the trees and doing his best to ignore every suspicious shadow or rustling bush. In his pocket, he held the gun tight, his index wedged behind the trigger to prevent accidental discharge. He had to keep his wits about him. If he wasn't careful, he'd put a bullet into just about anyone or anything if they appeared out of the darkness.

Once he was off the golf course, Beckford headed south-east into Alperton where he trekked up and down desolate roads in an attempt to lose anyone who might have been tailing him. Every now and then he turned back on himself or dropped into gardens to lie in wait. He thought about his phone, lying on wet grass on the 10th hole with radio waves seeping out of it like pheromones. It was a carrot he could have used to lead them into a trap or at least get a better look at them.

With public payphones on the decline, Beckford's journey felt longer and more frustrating with every corner he turned. Eventually, he stumbled upon a working phone box outside a closed-down library – another thing that was on the decline.

Inside the phone box, Beckford pulled free the plastic casing from the ceiling, exposing a length of wires that he yanked randomly until the blinding fluorescent shut off, plunging the booth into darkness and leaving sunspots in Beckford's vision. No longer reflected in the booth's Perspex windows, Beckford was able to see out into the darkened streets. A phone box wouldn't exactly be the best place to get jumped. A Perspex coffin.

With the greasy receiver clamped between his shoulder and head, he flicked through a handful of coins in his palm. He was still shaking and out of breath, his heavy gasps echoing in the isolated space around him. In his peripheral, a dark shape darted across the street, but when Beckford looked it had gone. Maybe a cat or a fox, he presumed.

He dropped a pound into the machine and dialled Farber's mobile. It was the only number he knew by heart and thankfully she hadn't changed it since they were together.

It rang. With every blast of the tone, the knot in Beckford's stomach tightened. After what felt like an eternity, the phone was answered.

'Hello?' said Farber, her voice raspy.

'Ali, it's me.'

She mumbled something, half-asleep, then said: 'What time is it?'

'Are you okay? Are you safe?'

'What…? yes, I'm asleep. I *was* asleep. It's two in the bloody morning!'

'Listen,' said Beckford, 'they were watching me. Every move, everything I was looking at on my computer. My phone. They know I'm onto them. They might have tapped your phone, I don't know. Don't answer the door to anyone.'

'Are you drunk?'

'This is 100% *real*, Ali. They sent people to my apartment. Masked men with guns. I was nearly a fucking *goner!*'

Farber stuttered a few times, not able to get any words out until finally saying, 'What…? Where are you? Let me call Ray.'

'Michaels? No. No way.

'What about Corden?'

'Don't call anyone. Don't message anyone. Don't email. Don't text. No communication whatsoever. Especially work people. Promise me.'

There was a brief silence while Farber contemplated his words.

'John, tell me exactly what hap—'

'*Promise me.*'

She sighed on the line and said, 'All right. I promise.'

Beckford closed his eyes and leaned his head against the grimy Perspex. 'I'm not saying anything else,' he said. 'It'll put you more at risk.'

'*More* at risk?'

'Go and get your biggest and sharpest kitchen knife and keep it on you.'

'John…'

'My phone is compromised and so is my apartment. I'll contact you in the morning. If anything happens to me…' He swallowed, wondering what his next line would be. If they were to be his last to Farber, should he confess how he still felt?

'If anything happens,' he repeated, '…you'll get everything I know.'

Before Beckford could say anything else, the line went dead.

His money had run out.

TWENTY

The lights of Canary Wharf twinkled in the distance as a light drizzle fell across a four-storey flat-topped building situated in the heart of the deserted docklands. Back in the nineties, the building was used as a training centre for the unemployed, but government cuts had forced it to close and for over a decade the building sat vacant along with most of the surrounding industrial estate.

It was now a living and breathing workplace, although nobody would know from looking at it. The building was covered in scaffolding and surrounded by a high blue-boarded perimeter fence. It looked like a building site and had done for years. The construction company had gone into administration. At least that was the story.

There were two entrances to the Studio – one for cars and one for personnel, both of which were controlled by a variety of digital recognition systems. For any black site, security was paramount.

Unable to drive himself, Peltz took a cab that dropped him two minutes away from the location. Sheltering from the drizzle under his laptop bag, he traversed potholes and uneven pavements, the sparse street lighting making his journey even more treacherous.

Peltz rarely wore suits anymore, and the only one he owned felt a lot more snug than the last time he'd worn it. The shirt too, the top button of which he was unable to fasten without choking himself. Instead, he left it undone and covered it with the wide knot of his tie. There were no slapdash appearances at the Studio. It was a place of business. They all wore suits.

Peltz skipped up to the personnel entrance, which first consisted of a metal turnstile and digital keypad. Entering a six-digit code, he pushed through the turnstile into a claustrophobic sally port where a frosted Perspex door faced him. At least it was dry in there. To the right of the door a small camera faced him.

'Please look into the camera and state your name,' said a pre-recorded woman's voice.

'Peltz, Dominic.'

For a split second, Peltz worried that the system wouldn't recognise him. If he remembered correctly, the facial recognition not only took into account features such as eyes, nose, mouth, cheekbones and their relative position to each other, but the shape of the face, which his room-service diet of late had certainly altered since the last time he was stood where he was.

Beep.

The door facing him hissed open and Peltz walked back out into the cold, wet night, and across the car park towards the seemingly abandoned building. Butterflies started to fill his stomach as he took note of the cars. A few big names were already there. *Great.*

Knowing how the Studio worked, Peltz was fully expecting to become the fall guy for the recent fuck-up. They had to pin it on someone, and besides their systems would have already identified Peltz as the root of the problem. Comminatio didn't just monitor external threats. The nature of their work was almost an oxymoron, which meant internal threats were often a very high possibility.

There was a time when Peltz felt safe in his role. He'd implemented many of the systems and infrastructure the Studio worked with. He was useful. But with younger, brighter members rising up through the ranks, he started to wonder if his days were numbered. Technology was certainly moving at a rate he couldn't keep up with. Maybe it was his age. Or maybe he just didn't care anymore.

He used to care, back when the Studio was a close-knit team of people with valid reasons to be there. That was nearly eight years ago. Things had certainly expanded since then, and with plans to build another site up north on the outskirts of Manchester there was no signs of it slowing down.

Secretly, Peltz wanted to pull the plug on the whole operation, but he kept that to himself, knowing any negative connotations targeting their mission would mark him as an outcast. And that was a death sentence. After all, the Studio's survival policy was to "protect the nest."

There was a time when he could have easily shut the whole thing down at the click of a button. It was no longer that simple, although it wasn't impossible – Peltz was just a coward and he knew it.

* * *

Morning came quickly for Beckford. After his phone call to Farber, exhaustion soon seeped in and overwhelmed him. All he wanted to do was sleep, and to go somewhere that wasn't there… and to be someone entirely different. Fortunately, for anybody wanting to lose themselves London was the ideal place to do it, and soon enough Beckford felt safe in the knowledge that he was no longer being followed.

Further south, Beckford had ended up in Ealing, where on a road of white stuccoed townhouses he came to a bank of neighbouring hotels, each one with grandiose names.

Walking up the steps leading to a hotel called The King's Royal, Beckford froze on the spot. There'd be CCTV in there, but would it be modern enough to be accessed by *them*? Also, hotels required a credit card, regardless of whether or not he was paying in cash.

They'll find you.

Shaking in the cold drizzle, Beckford contemplated every conceivable outcome that his fatigued mind could think of. In the end, fear got the upper hand and he descended the steps and continued on his way.

When he was a beat bobby right at the start of his police career, Beckford dealt with the homeless on an almost daily basis. It was only right then, with warmth and shelter merely yards away on either side of the street, that Beckford finally felt some kind of affinity towards them. Where could he go? If he slept outside, would he freeze to death? It certainly felt like it.

On a parallel road, out of the spotlights of hotels, Beckford started checking the doors of cars he passed – softly, not wanting to trigger his second alarm of the night and piss another load of people off. He focussed on older models, knowing he didn't have a chance against the keyless systems of newer cars.

After trying every old banger in two streets, the door of a 90s Renault popped open. With one last glance up and down the deserted road, Beckford crawled onto the back seats and quietly closed the door behind.

The seats were vinyl, cold and coated with a stale smell of cigarettes. Tucking in his clothes, zipping up zippers, pulling cords and fastening Velcro, Beckford covered up as many exposed areas of his skin as possible before finally putting his hood up and folding his arms across his chest.

Expecting to use the moment of peace for processing everything queued up in his mental buffer, all he could think about was how cold he was. He lay on his side, fantasising about hot-wiring the ignition and turning the little plastic dial that would pump the car with lovely warm air.

The fantasy started to shift and evolve as sleep crept up on him.

And then he was out.

He dreamt, too – but not of Peter McGregor or Nikolai Guskov. Not of Alison or any masked men chasing him down corridors. He dreamt he was back in school, in a building that would be unfamiliar in his waking life, but in the dream world it was *definitely* his school. His mind had tricked him. The smell of the corridors, the sensation of being there. It was as if he'd travelled back in time.

There was something he had to do, somewhere he had to be. An exam, that was it, although he didn't know where, and no matter how many classrooms he passed and how many doors he peered through he couldn't find it.

As time ticked away, anxiety started to build, and the sight of other pupils happily scrawling on their test papers only made it worse.

Then Beckford found himself in a darker, quieter area of the school, and then he was in the caretaker's room, a box of an office no bigger than a garden shed. On the table in front of him lay a single sheet of paper accompanied by a sharpened pencil, illuminated by a single desk lamp.

Not even finding it remotely unusual that his exam was in some off-limit part of the school, Beckford took a seat. The paper in front of him was full of questions, but there was nowhere to write his answers. Searching high and low he couldn't find any other paper among the array of dirty tools and knick-knacks that littered the office.

Panic set in and his breathing quickened. Dad would be mad if he didn't pass. Beckford started to cry.

When his eyes opened in the real world, his left cheek was wet where tears had slid onto the seats. If the clock in the car was correct, he'd got three hours sleep and a crick in the neck. It was some form of rest at least, but with the interior of the car like a cold chamber in a morgue, he was surprised he'd woken up at all. Perhaps it was the butt of the pistol digging into his hip that roused him.

For five minutes Beckford lay there, contracting every muscle in his body in a desperate attempt to keep warm. The drizzle had turned to snow in the night and covered the windows completely, but an incessant drip of water hitting metal somewhere outside the vehicle told Beckford the temperature was at least above zero.

Pushing aside the remnants of his fading dream, he attempted to replay the previous night in his head. At first only flashcard moments popped into his head. A fight. The syringe. A phone call. Farber.

His thoughts started to realign, as if aided by the metronome tapping of the drip-drip-drip outside. Details came to him, filling in the gaps like grouting. That's when he stumbled upon a golden nugget that gave him a much needed sense of security.

He was not alone.

Someone had helped him, watching over Beckford like a digital guardian angel. Without their warning, Beckford would have been toast, no two ways about it. Somehow, the sense of protection filled him with the illusion of warmth. He pondered the identity of his helper, thankful to have another living being on his side of the fence.

Living being?

How did he know his helper was a "living being"? All he saw was his cursor move across the screen, some web pages and a couple of lines of text. Any basic artificial intelligence coded by a school kid could produce that effect.

Am I being played? he asked himself again.

The warmth gradually left his body and an empty

sickness returned. In the blink of an eye he'd convinced himself that there was no hope, but before he could sink any lower, a car engine started up not too far from the one he was lying in. Not wanting to take any chances on the Renault's owner being a lover of lie-ins, Beckford waited for the other car to drive away before quietly leaving the vehicle.

The thawing snow wouldn't stick around all day. Beckford wondered if the same could be said for him.

TWENTY-ONE

It was an odd thing, being a wanted man. Generic thoughts and worries that normally occupied Beckford's head were now placed on the back burner in favour of more fundamental self-preservation instincts. He was reminded of Maslow's psychological theory on the Hierarchy of Needs – a pyramid diagram explaining five levels of human requirements, from the physiological needs on the bottom layer – food, security, sleep, warmth – to the more complex ones at the top, such as creative endeavours and the possibility of the self-actualisation of talent and potential. Only when a level was satisfied did the person seek and explore the next one above.

For now, Beckford couldn't see beyond the bottom two layers – safety. He needed food, warmth and rest, but he also had to be alert and ready to use his gun at the drop of a hat. Survival instincts were at the forefront of everything he did, and once the streets of Ealing came alive, his senses were heightened.

Strangers in the street were no longer easily ignored; any one of them could be an assailant. Would they jump him in broad daylight in front of people? He doubted even the best computer and video wizards could erase *that* from existence.

Holing up in the nearest cafe, Beckford bought a latte and a toasted chicken and bacon panini, which was extremely salty but very tasty. It was a lavish purchase considering he only had about £80 and some loose change in his wallet and using his bank cards was off limits. But he didn't care – the warmth of the cafe and the sight of normal people, living normal lives on their way to normal jobs, was worth the price alone.

It was only when he was halfway through his coffee that Beckford caught sight of yet another CCTV camera on the wall facing him. Of *course* there was CCTV in the cafe. There was CCTV everywhere! And where there was CCTV, there was the possibility of a pair of eyes or maybe even software that did the hard work for them if the system was online. Would a cafe have such a security system in place? Beckford couldn't take the risk.

Downing the rest of his hot coffee, he wrapped the panini in a paper serviette and headed for the door, keeping his head down the whole time. Back out on the busy streets, he started spotting CCTV cameras everywhere. The watchful eyes of his enemies.

To prepare for his move to cybercrime Beckford had read a lot, researching computing fundamentals of anything he could get his hands on. It astonished him how clever they had become, and one area that blew his mind was digital recognition – the ability to analyse and decipher any form of digital information such as video, audio and text.

Already widely used for automatic license plate recognition and biometrics (such as facial, thumb and iris recognition), there was one area that programmers often struggled to get right, primarily due to the vast range of dialects and accents that the software had to cater for. These days voice recognition was no longer a struggle. It was better than ever. The technology was so good that a listening process could analyse the live waveform of a phone call and identify words and phrases with 99% accuracy. The process could not only be told to listen out for particular statements, but for individual voices that would be matched against a source recording.

If Beckford was going to use modern forms of communication, he needed to be vigilant. Cramming himself into a phone box, he cycled through a repertoire of accents like an actor preparing for a role. First he tried a Geordie accent, which was a disaster, then Scottish, which veered into Irish, then Pakistani, an accent he found quite easy for some reason, until he finally went back to Irish. It was the most natural and less cringeworthy of the lot.

Graham Noakes was just about to leave for work when the call came through. The man was bemused to say the least upon hearing such a bizarre voice tell him it was John Beckford, then rattle off a list of things only those two would know about to prove his identity. Noakes caught on quickly, but Beckford kept the call brief and as cryptic as he could.

After the call ended, Beckford walked to the shops on Broadway and waited in the doorway of Primark until it opened. Avoiding eye contact with staff, he went straight to the men's department and disregarded style over comfort for functional and budgetary reasons.

It wasn't until he got into a changing room that he saw the damage to his face.

On his left cheek glowed a darkening shiner. On his right, an angry cut sealed with dried blood that had dripped down his face and joined another dried smear coming from his nostrils. He looked a state, which explained the funny looks he'd gotten from the cafe barista that had kick-started his paranoia.

He then started to take notice of aches and pains throughout his body, in places he didn't know existed. Had adrenaline been numbing him this entire time?

Using his old T-shirt and some spit, he cleaned up his face as best he could. He left the stained top along with his old clothes lying in a heap on the changing room floor, and apologised to the desk clerk for wearing the new clothes as she leaned over the counter to scan the barcodes of each item.

His new wardrobe was plain with dull colours. Two additions were highly important – a black baseball cap and a navy hoodie that he wore under his jacket with the hood up, over the cap. He looked like a chav, but ironically felt much safer, able to walk the streets and take the tube with the majority of his face hidden from prying eyes, human or digital.

He'd even tried on sunglasses, which would have given him an extra level of anonymity had it not been November. The only thing they did was remind him of the fact he hadn't been away for years, the last time being with Farber in the Costa del Sol. "Sunny," "loving" and "carefree" were some of the words that accompanied the memory. Words that no longer seemed to be a part of his everyday vocabulary.

From a secondhand shop, Beckford purchased a couple of mobile phones. They were severely outdated Android handsets, but that didn't matter. Beckford didn't want them to play games or take professional photographs, he just needed them to run a couple of bespoke applications he'd learned about at the HTCU. The first app encrypted data traffic to and from the phone, and the second app was a vocoder, transforming the voice of the call into what sounded like a robot from the 1960s.

From there, he went to the nearest Vodafone store and picked up a couple of free SIM cards with preloaded credit, then stood in the nearest Post Office where he wrote out the following note:

Use only this phone to contact me. It's encrypted and

alters your voice. Don't send any information that can be traced (names, addresses, etc). Keep everything cryptic. Confirm that you are all right by telling me the number of cats we saw that night in Nerja.

After dropping the note and phone into a padded envelope, he hailed a taxi and asked the driver if he'd courier the parcel to a police station in West Hampstead. It was a 30-minute drive and the cost the driver gave was extortionate, but Beckford needed to contact Farber. Make sure she was all right. And he couldn't take any chances.

With the phone on it's way, Beckford's next port of call was a self-storage facility he found through directory enquiries. It was a 20-minute walk away. Beckford paid in cash and used false registration information. What money he had left could only get a locker for seven days, but in it he dumped some of the contents of his bag – the pen drive containing the suicide video and CCTV footage, including the VHS tape from Fork & Field. Farber's case notes went in too, and his own paperwork that contained the evidence for the hard drive serial number. It was all the collateral he had. The only items that showed any inkling that something truly sinister was going on. As he closed and secured the locker door, he felt a surge of melancholy, wondering whether his eyes would lay upon those things again. A sobering thought… or a terrifying premonition.

Entering the foyer of the Ealing Central Library, Beckford headed to the front desk and purchased a new pen drive from a slight woman with white hair. The remainder of his loose change came in at under a pound, which he dumped in a charity box before heading to one of the computer suites upstairs.

He found a vacant machine at the end of a bank of

terminals where luckily the screen faced a wall. He was paranoid enough about people seeing his face; he certainly didn't want anyone seeing his screen.

As he sat down on the chair, a thought came to mind. Antibacterial hand gel. That's what he needed. He never liked touching the keyboards of other people's computers, let alone public ones that got fingered a hundred times a day by a plethora of filthy bastards. For a minute he stared at the computer, battling his OCD. Then, finding a clean tissue he'd taken from the cafe, he wiped down the keyboard and mouse, promising himself he'd scrub his hands thoroughly in the library toilets once he was done.

Logging into the computer using his temporary guest account with a one-hour limit, Beckford first went online and downloaded a freely available piece of software called Katana, which contained a collection of security tools for almost any situation, although most notably it was used for so-called "ethical hacking." *Yeah, right...* Beckford thought.

He wasn't going to break the law, he just needed to secure his computer. Public machines weren't only breeding grounds for bacteria, but computer viruses and other invasive digital nasties.

Copying Katana to the pen drive, Beckford restarted the machine and altered the computer's boot-sequence to load the operating system from it instead of the hard drive. When the computer finally reloaded, a menu appeared offering Katana's tool suite for selection – a smörgåsbord of versatile features that could let even the most amateur of hackers skirt round security and break into off-limit areas.

Tapping the arrow keys, Beckford selected a tool called "Puppy Linux" and hit enter. Katana then loaded a stripped-down, totally customised version of the popular open-source software operating system Linux, including a bombproof VPN, giving Beckford a sterile and secure environment to work in. To put even further distance between him and "them," he connected to a remote server that he had access to thanks to Davies. The server was located in Florida and physically sat behind a multitude of security solutions that would be a headache for even the most skilled hacker.

Only when his American desktop flashed up in front of him did he feel some sort of anonymity and protection. With the digital world at his fingertips, he had to be careful. Personal accounts such as email or social networks were strictly off limits. Depending on how deep they could get, the handshake process that occurred when logging into an online account could notify them of his access and lead them right to him.

Like an animal skirting too close to croc-infested waters, Beckford had to keep his distance. But there was still plenty he could do.

The moment in his apartment just before the power cut was a blur, but some pieces of information had stuck to him like pollen to a bee. Loading a particular website, Beckford ran a WHOIS check on the domain name www.tork2me.com. The site would tell him when the website was registered and, hopefully, by who. It was a long shot, and as the details flashed up on screen he had predicted correctly – the registrant had remained anonymous.

A library staff member passed behind him and Beckford expertly switched to the BBC Sports website, feigning an interest in the latest cricket score. When the coast was clear, Beckford switched back to his server and without hesitation typed www.tork2me.com into the browser and hit enter.

On screen loaded the familiar blue configuration that

had beamed at him the night before. Beckford glanced nervously around the rows of computers in the suite, double-checking that everyone was locked into their own online world.

Five minutes at the most, he told himself. If it was a trap, five minutes was how long it would take them to trace his location and get someone over there.

Beckford hovered the mouse cursor over the "Connect" button and, after a slight stall, coughed as he clicked it, as if to distract himself from his action like he was making an expensive and unwise online purchase.

Text spilled down the page as the site connected to the chat server. It said there were 844 chat rooms available, and 12,301 users. Beckford scrolled down the list and found #PunkSmiley, the room he'd been in when he was alerted of his assailants.

There was nobody in it.

Beckford double-clicked the room and saw, as Anon202, that he was the only occupant. Closing his eyes, he thought long and hard. It was possible the helper was still online, just not in the channel, but what was his username? Anon176? Anon114? It was impossible to remember. Beckford could search for all the Anons on the server and message each one individually, but he'd only be opening himself up to a world of trolls and abuse and derisive memes that would waste his time. Time he didn't have to waste.

Clicking around the page, Beckford discovered an option to change the channel's topic – a piece of text that sat across the top of the chat room for every member to see upon entering. Beckford changed it to:

`I have many questions… please tell me what you know.`

It was a long shot, but the only thing he could do. Leaving the chat room open in Florida awaiting a response, Beckford disconnected the library computer from his server. Looking around the suite again, his chair felt like a ticking time bomb. He'd already pushed his luck.

Quickly, he shut down the library computer and returned the boot sequence to its original settings. When he was sure nobody was looking, he rubbed the cafe tissue over the keyboard and mouse again, this time to remove his prints, then headed for the toilets.

TWENTY-TWO

Graham Noakes gripped the handrail and took the stairs to the third floor of the Ealing Central Library. Working his way down aisles of books, he eventually came to one dedicated to *Computers and the Internet*. It was a place he'd visited many times before, for the progressive speed of technology always assured a constant turnover of textbooks. The topics had certainly changed a lot since his early days, with the majority of modern tomes geared towards e-commerce and the development of frontend applications and websites. Noakes was more of a systems man, interested in the fundamentals of computing, but for his line of work he had to keep up with the times.

'Brushing up?' he said, sidling up to the only other person in the aisle.

'Kind of,' said Beckford, keeping his hooded head down in the pages of a dense textbook.

'What's the book?' said Noakes. Beckford held it up so he could see the cover: *Applied Network Security: Collection, Detection and Analysis.*

'There's a *third* edition?' said Noakes.

Beckford reopened the book at the page he'd bookmarked and said, 'Notice how all the computers are occupied downstairs, but there's not a soul other than me and you in this aisle?'

'Kids still read books.'

'Only ones who are willing to put the work in. Effort is hard to come by these days.'

'I won't argue with you on that,' said Noakes, giving him a once over. 'So is this your new look, yeah?'

Beckford mumbled something of a response. Noakes slid a rucksack from his shoulder and planted it by his feet.

'I've been telling you for a while to take some time off, but spending it on yet another computer project isn't exactly what I meant. This is Kelly's old one, by the way, but a pretty good spec. The battery won't take a full charge. Well, it might, but it won't last what you think it will. What's wrong with yours?'

When there was no response, Noakes reached out a hand and tilted Beckford's face towards him, catching only a glimpse of his profile before Beckford turned away.

'You sleep last night?' said Noakes.

From the pages of the book in Beckford's hands, he slipped out a folded piece of paper and handed it over. Noakes opened it, revealing a printout of a man in a suit, taken from the Dunning House CCTV. Across the bottom was the name "DOMINIC PELTZ" scribbled in black felt pen.

Beckford finally glimpsed at Noakes, needing to see the reaction on his face as he looked at the photo.

'Don't say the name out loud,' said Beckford, 'but do you know him? Have you seen him? Heard the name? Anything.'

As Noakes looked closer at the photo, Beckford reached out and gripped his shoulder, angling the man slightly more towards him. Noakes, confused at first, looked around and noticed a CCTV camera behind them, further down towards the opposite aisle. Noakes turned back, and it was obvious by the look on his face that he thought Beckford had lost his marbles.

Beckford needed to be taken seriously. He raised his hands and pulled his hoodie back.

'Christ almighty,' said Noakes, seeing the injuries on his face for the first time.

'Do you know him?' said Beckford again.

Noakes took a moment, then looked back down at the photograph and shook his head. 'Were you on the piss last night? What the fuck happened to you?' he asked.

Beckford ignored him and snatched the photo and folded it back into his jeans pocket. 'He works,' he said, 'or worked, for the Met. I need you to find him quickly.'

'After you tell me why you look like pummeled spam.'

Beckford stared into space, weighing up consequences in his head. A young woman entered the aisle and passed them, scanning the shelves. She gave them an unnecessary 'sorry' as she perused the books between the two of them, then quickly moved on. Noakes noticed her pull out a book on website marketing, then waited for her to get out of earshot.

'You're not going to let me in on anything, John? For Christ's sake, you make me meet you here like we're a couple of MI6 spies. You look terrible. Why do you need to know who this Dom—'

'Don't!' Beckford spat, cutting him off. 'Don't mention names. This is *real*, okay? People came for me last night. Masked men carrying guns. Look…'

He unzipped the top half of his hoodie and dragged it to one side, revealing a bruise the size of a tennis ball on his neck. 'That's where one of them grabbed me and stuck me with a hypodermic.' He zipped back up quickly. Noakes couldn't believe what he was seeing or hearing.

'I was looking for *him*,' said Beckford, patting the photo in his pocket, '…searching online, and they knew it. They were watching me. Watching everything I did. Online and in real life.'

He moved in closer, speaking in almost a whisper. 'The computer that Ali brought in…'

'The suicide?' Noakes asked.

'He was at Dunning House, this bloke. That's where the CCTV was taken from. I analysed the kid's computer and it was clean, but the next day I noticed something and realised the hard drive had been switched out. Maybe something was on there that our software didn't pick up.'

'No one has access to the Graveyard but our team.'

'I know. I checked access logs and the CCTV. Nothing. But it definitely happened.'

'How?'

'Digital wizardry. The kind we're not prepared for.'

Even to Beckford he sounded crazy, and he could see Noakes was having a hard time getting to grips with it. What weakened his stance was the fact that Noakes was one of a handful of people who knew the extent of Beckford's personal issues, which surfaced in a health report during his recruitment to the High Tech Crime Unit. That would teach him to confide in a psychological profiler. Despite that, not once in the year he'd been working under Noakes had he proven himself to be anything but an exemplary member of staff and extremely trustworthy.

'Graham… I'm not losing it. This is happening.

'Well if it's happening we should go public.'

'No fucking way,' said Beckford. 'This *has* to be an inside job. We go public and it'll scatter the roaches.'

'So you're just going to use yourself as bait?'

'If that's what it takes, yeah.'

Noakes glared, mouth open, his head ever so slightly shaking left to right. He checked the coast was clear again and said, 'How are your sessions coming along?'

Beckford turned away in anger, rubbed a hand over his face and snapped back. 'I'm going to fucking walk in a minute if you don't want to help!'

'Now hold on—'

'*Listen to me!* This isn't a cry for help or a death wish or a nervous breakdown or any bloody bollocks like that. I genuinely believe something massive is behind this and if we let it go now, well, we're not doing our job. Not the fucking job on paper, forget all that. A *real* job, one that takes genuine courage and sacrifice to see it through. I know you know what I'm talking about.'

Noakes took the statement on the chin. He turned to a row of spines on the bookshelf in front of him and mulled Beckford's words over for a moment. Eventually, he held a hand out towards Beckford's pocket, beckoning the photo with his fingers. Beckford obliged.

Holding the printout in front of him, Noakes took his phone out and loaded the camera app. Beckford snatched the printout back.

'What are you doing? I don't think you understand. They've got eyes and ear *everywhere*. Think about that on a technical level.'

'How far did you get tracking him down?' said Noakes, nodding at the photo. 'Did you go deep?'

'I didn't have chance. He's in the archives on the Met website and there's an account on the network with that name, but no accompanying photograph.'

'You know how many officers there are in the Met?' said Noakes.

'Around 31,000, give or take,' said Beckford without hesitation.

'You know how many active accounts there are on the network? This bloke might not be who you think he is. That name could be just a pseudonym. There's a lot of dark corners in the Met that not a lot of people know about.'

'There'll be records,' said Beckford. 'It doesn't matter how covert the unit is, there's always records. I need you to find them.'

Noakes looked at him intently. 'You've put me in a tricky position here, John. I help you out and something happens—'

'No one will know of your involvement. It's me they're after. Just be vigilant.'

'It's my responsibility to report this, you know. Please reconsider your options. I'll get you a protection detail, send this upstairs and open an investigation. I can pool resources, maybe get SCO19 tooled up and on the job if I can.'

'Not until I know who this bloke is and which pies his fingers are in.'

'Corruption in the service is at an all time low.'

'Yet it still exists,' said Beckford, 'and it always will – the exception that proves the rule.'

More silence followed as Noakes tried to figure things out in his head.

'Where are you staying?' he said.

Beckford shrugged. 'I don't want to use my cards so my options are limited.'

'Walk with me.'

From a nearby cash machine outside, Noakes gave him £500 – the maximum he could take out without having to go into a bank.

'I think you should get out of London,' he said, having to raise his voice to battle the noise of the street while maintaining a level of discretion. 'I'll do the legwork, you just keep yourself safe.'

'They'll find me wherever I go. At least there's people here I can trust. Speaking of which…'

'How much does she know?' said Noakes.

'Enough.'

'You two aren't…'

Beckford shook his head no.

'I'll sort out protection,' said Noakes, 'I know a couple of chaps. Decent chaps. Off the book, of course.'

'Thank you.'

When they said goodbye, Beckford left Noakes with some parting advice. 'If you go looking for him, make sure there's a three-foot thick lead wall between you and the internet. No, make it four-foot. They're *that* good.'

Noakes nodded. 'Keep in touch,' he said, adding, 'please.' But it went unheard as Beckford merged into the sea of people.

* * *

The officers took the lift to the sixth floor. Two detectives and two constables, one of which was wearing a protective helmet and carrying an Enforcer, also informally known as "the big red key" by those on the ground – a heavy red battering ram for when a friendly knock on the door just wasn't enough.

Out the lift they marched down the corridor, checking flat numbers along the way. Stopping outside flat 606 the leading DI – a chubby man with waxy skin – took one hand out of his trench coat pocket and rattled the door with authority.

Around 10 seconds of silence followed. With the heel of his fist, Chubby banged hard on the door. Again, nothing. He lowered onto one knee, lifted the brass letterbox and put his mouth up close.

'POLICE! OPEN UP! NOW!'

He turned his ear to the letterbox. The officers waited. A door down the far end of the corridor opened and a man in his underwear peered out, then ducked back in again at the sight of the Old Bill ready to break a door down. Chubby looked back through the letterbox and saw only a wall and a small section of the living area. There was no sound or movement. He let the letterbox snap shut, got to his feet and stepped out of the way.

The Enforcer officer stepped up and in one smooth motion swung the butt-end of the ram just to the left of the lock, smashing the door open with an explosion of splinters. Chubby rushed in first.

'Police! Come quietly, Mr Beckford!'

The rest followed quickly behind him.

TWENTY-THREE

Beckford couldn't think of anywhere safe to go. From the moment he'd left Noakes at the library, his anxiety started to bite with a vengeance. Walking the streets with his hoodie up, head down and laptop bag slung over his back, he felt he could blend in like a tourist or a student, but the bustling crowds and constant police sightings kept his nerves electrified to a torturous intensity.

At least the cap and hoodie helped blinker out the world around him, but it didn't stop the droves of bodies hurtling towards him, blocking his way. Every now and then he would look up to avoid collisions, but the sea of faces and the fear that someone would recognise him sent his eyes back down to the pavement.

At one point his heartbeat got too fast, his mouth too dry and his hands too sweaty, forcing him to take refuge in a small antiques shop where he pretended to browse shelves of ornaments and household decor, while taking long, slow breaths and quietly repeating the mantra: 'False Evidence Appearing Real… False Evidence Appearing Real.'

The acronym of the sentence was the word "FEAR," a mantra he'd been recommended as a calming tool by his therapist. He'd used it to great effect in the past, but it wasn't so effective in the claustrophobic shop. All he could think about was how there'd be no easy way out if he was ambushed. With panic rising, he turned on his heels and rushed back out onto the street.

Walking through the throng of strangers, a piercing hiss caught his attention – a bus, arriving for a queue of commuters at a nearby stop. *That's it*, he thought. He could get mobile. Recharge while on the move.

From a nearby newsagents, Beckford bought a one day Travelcard for zones one to four, giving him unlimited travel on trains, tubes and buses in and around Greater London. That way he didn't have to expose himself to any contactless system. It was a paper ticket, maybe somewhat archaic but entirely untraceable.

On Uxbridge Road he queued for the R70 bus in the freezing cold. Some 10 minutes later it arrived, and as he boarded the double-decker he felt a wall of humid air envelope him. It was lovely and warm and just what he needed.

Upstairs he headed for where it was quieter, with about a third of the seats full. Beckford kept his eyes down, but beyond the peripheral of his hoodie he caught a glimpse of a young goth couple canoodling and an older gentleman with hand gripped on the steel seat bar in front of him. The bus swayed as it pulled away from the stop and Beckford balanced his way towards the back where he took a seat.

CCTV was everywhere on the bus, but he knew that if he kept facing forwards, the camera at the front of the bus would be too far away to recognise him, and the one behind would only get the back of his head.

Learning against the very cold and foggy window, thoughts started to ricochet off the walls of his skull, tripping over one another. Closing his eyes just made him dizzy, like he was lost in a dense forest, ambling through the undergrowth and desperately seeking a sliver of clear daylight.

Quietly, he sighed and muttered to himself: 'What the fuck?' It's was all he could say. He didn't have the focus or concentration to think of anything else. Maybe sleep would help. Not getting the usual six hours had left his brain buzzing with a raw reserve of energy and he knew that it was finite. He inhaled deeply, then closed his eyes again and nestled his head back into the corner of the seat, listening closely to his breath as the air pulled in past his lips and teeth and surged down his throat and back again.

Farber had forced him into his first meditation experience. He'd fallen asleep then and there was no reason why he couldn't now.

After a minute of his desperate pseudo-meditative breathing, his frenetic thoughts began to flow less and ebb more, like a tide drifting out to sea. Aided by the blowing hot air by his feet and the rumbling of the bus, Beckford eventually slipped away.

* * *

Farber was just about to rip into the parcel when she was beckoned across the room by Chief Inspector Ray Michaels.

'Close the door,' he said, as she entered his office. He poured himself filtered coffee from the constantly brewing pot that gave his office a permanent Arabica aroma. He shuffled himself behind his desk and dumped a box of cigarettes into the top drawer. Michaels wasn't the healthiest of men, but no one would say that to his blood vessel-popped face.

Farber took a seat opposite, her heart already pounding. Was this about Beckford? She hadn't heard anything from him all morning. Was he dead? Was she implicated for not having raised the alarm?

'Alison, bear with me. I apologise for prying into your personal life, but I have an obligation here. Rumours have been circulating that you've been spending a bit of time with John Beckford.'

Farber knew very well to keep quiet under pressure. Let them do the talking. Consciously, she relaxed her facial muscles, not wanting to reveal anything, then realised she needed to pretend to be confused.

Michaels continued, 'Now, that's nobody's business but yours and his, but if it is true your assistance is required.'

'My assistance?'

'When was the last time you saw him?'

Farber hadn't prepared for this. Her stomach churned with nerves. She hesitated, but it was never a good idea to lie to a superior officer, and the lie was losing believability with each silently-passing second.

'Yesterday,' she said. 'With Staedler. What's this about?'

'I'll come to that,' he said, 'but have you spoken to him today?'

Michaels' face was statuesque, his eyes penetrating. Being such a physically imposing figure didn't help in such situations, but before Farber could say anything he cut to the chase.

'In the early hours of this morning, CEOP investigators traced online activity to a server hosting images and videos of child pornography. It was John Beckford's home computer. It falls under category A classification, and I don't need to tell you how bad that is. His apartment was raided and a warrant has been put out for his arrest.'

Farber's face finally took the shape of confusion, but this time it was real. Her first thought: *John is being set up*. It was the only explanation. The only one she wanted to hear, anyway, because the other far darker explanation made her stomach twist in knots. She was crazy for even thinking it.

No way. She would have known.

John wasn't like that.

Michaels stared impassively, awaiting a response. Tears started to well under Farber's eyelids.

* * *

A raucous commotion jarred Beckford awake. It took him a moment for his thoughts to realign, remembering where he was, why he was there and what he'd been doing. The shops outside the window he recognised as Richmond, meaning he'd gotten at least 20 minutes rest, and bite-sized naps would be vital.

But there was shouting going on somewhere towards the front of the bus. A slanging match. Beckford leaned into the aisle and saw a young male with a shaved head, stood up, confronting an older man who was still seated.

'You fuckin' what? You fuckin' what mate…?'

Skinhead's girlfriend was pulling him back, but the older man, who was probably mid-forties, just sat there, staring and saying nothing. Everyone else on the deck watched the drama unfold, trying not to get involved. This was all Beckford needed.

'Leave him alone!' shouted a woman sat in front of Beckford. Any other day, Beckford would have intervened. His warrant card was in his back pocket, the situation easily diffused. But that would put him in the spotlight as well as CCTV footage, which would put him at risk.

Mentally, he apologised to the man on the wrong end of the altercation, who then stood up and edged out of his seat into the aisle. Skinhead swung at him and the man took it on the cheek. The girlfriend screamed, but Skinhead was like a rabid animal, closing the man down as he backed towards Beckford.

'All right, stop!' the man shouted, as Skinhead swung again and missed. By this time, the man had shuffled back enough to be next to Beckford. The problem had reached him, and he couldn't just sit idly by. That was not who he was.

When Skinhead closed in again, Beckford sprang out of his seat like a coiled snake, shifting between the opponents and blocking the incoming punch.

'Police!' shouted Beckford to Skinhead, holding up his warrant card. 'You're nicked, mate.'

Upon seeing the ID in Beckford's hand, Skinhead's face instantly turned from anger to fear, his girlfriend still screaming at him, berating him for his behaviour. Reading the lad his rights, Beckford grabbed his wrist and twisted it behind him while using his considerable bulk to obscure his own face from camera, forcing Skinhead to face the front of the bus before marching him down the aisle behind his animated girlfriend.

A small round of applause broke out.

As they got closer to the stairwell, the first police officer appeared, her high-vis jacket rising like a blinding sun up the narrow stairway. Beckford stopped, his heart ratcheting from 0 to 60 like a Lamborghini. A second male officer followed up as the lady constable made her way towards them.

'Can you let go of him, sir?' said the constable. Beckford showed his ID again.

'I've already read him his rights,' he said.

'Oh,' said the surprised constable. 'That's fortunate.'

Beckford handed Skinhead over and the officer cuffed him, asking him if he understood why he was being arrested. Skinhead wasn't so mouthy anymore, and his girlfriend was almost comatose, the explosive tension of the situation having sapped her of energy. As the two were led away down the stairs, Beckford got back to his seat, wide awake now. He was worried. The CCTV would have snapped him for sure. The officers would probably be back up to take a statement. He couldn't go anywhere.

Claustrophobia kicked in.

With haste he shuffled across the back seats and let his forehead take the icy chill of the window on the street side. The male constable had taken Skinhead and his girlfriend to their car, but the lady constable had been joined by two other officers at the entrance to the bus. The engine continued to rumble at an idle pace while the officers talked. Something was wrong.

An unfamiliar ringtone rang out of Beckford's pocket, taking him off guard. It was his temp phone and only one person should have had his number.

'Hello?' he said.

'There were 19 cats,' said a vocoded Farber, her robotic voice hushed. '*Where are you*?' Something was definitely wrong.

'Why?' he said.

Farber sounded flustered as she reeled off everything as quickly and quietly as she could. The raid on his apartment. The child pornography. The warrant for his arrest.

'Are you being framed?' she said finally, the hope in her voice as clear as day.

The bus still hadn't moved. Beckford glared back out of the window and watched one of the officers talk into his radio while the lady constable and the other officer reboarded the bus.

News travelled fast in the Met, and an arrest warrant for a serving police officer went at light speed. Farber's voice buzzed in his ear.

'Come in to us,' she said. 'Michaels can protect you.'

Beckford hung up.

Feet bounded up the stairs. In the space of half a second he acknowledged every logical exit from where he was sitting, and that was when he arched his neck and saw a bright red emergency hammer clipped above the back window. A high-vis jacket rose again at the stairs. Beckford was a caged animal. Part of him wanted to stay, get arrested, reason with the law. He hadn't done anything wrong.

That didn't matter. Peltz and his team would be making sure he was as guilty as sin and any hard facts in Beckford's possession would either be erased or bent in their favour. The deck was stacked well and truly against him.

'Mr Beckford?' said the approaching WPC.

Beckford's decision was instantaneous. Leaping out of his seat, he gripped the emergency hammer from its clip and swung the pin into the bottom right-hand corner of the back window. The glass shattered with unbelievable efficiency, turning cloudy for a brief moment as miniscule fractures exploded across the pane, splitting into shards, then the bulk of it dropped to the road below.

Beckford heard the male officer yell from behind, but he was already up on the seats, bashing fragments of glass away with his rucksack. He slid himself through the now breezy opening and dropped from the top floor of the bus.

As his feet hit the concrete, his body crumpled, the slight off-angle sending him tumbling to one side. He tucked his head in and rolled – the bag slapping the floor, the laptop cracking inside – before he whipped back up with force, his arms clattering into the bumper of a parked hackney cab.

A few onlookers screamed. Beckford clambered to his feet, pain throbbing all over his body. There was no time to pinpoint exactly where he was injured, but straightaway he saw his right hand was dripping with blood. A voice bellowed: 'POLICE, STOP RIGHT THERE!'

Beckford didn't heed the order and stumbled through the traffic, car horns screaming and tires skidding around him. On the other side of the road he swivelled his head and saw yellow jackets in hot pursuit. Beckford would have been a field mouse to a group of feral cats if his lingering fatigue and lethargy hadn't been replaced by pure adrenaline once again.

Through the waves of shoppers he dashed, every now and then unavoidably banging into people, young and old, their faces plastered with shock as they went down like rugby players.

A tattooed man, attempting to be heroic, leapt out of the crowd, but Beckford's dashing momentum tore the man's grip from his jacket without missing a beat. Behind him, more shouts and screams followed. Every now and then he'd spin his head in the chaos and see a blur of yellow jackets. They weren't going to let him get away that easily.

A sharp left saw him heading down a short road ending in black gates that led to residential flats. Beckford skidded to a stop, took the bag off his shoulder and pushed it through the bars. With a small jump he clasped the top rail and, with extreme difficulty, pulled himself over. Security spikes on top of the gates prickled his body like a rash, and the drop on the other side made him think he'd mangled his knee. With the bag back on his shoulder he carried on sprinting as fast as he could, desperately sucking air in to douse the fire in his lungs.

Halfway towards the flats he turned and saw an officer help his partner over the gate. With all the equipment they carried, Beckford knew how difficult it was for beat bobbies to climb. He almost felt sorry for them.

Rounding the apartment block, Beckford shot through an almost empty car park and followed the driveway up to another road. Without looking, he darted out and a car took his legs out from under him, sending him rolling over the bonnet and up against the windshield, where he peeled off and landed in a heap on the tarmac. The driver – a

Greek man with glasses – frantically jumped out.

'Jesus, oh Jesus. You came out of nowhere my mate!'

Despite the objecting stings and aches that riddled his legs, Beckford somehow got to his feet. A prominent pain pulsated in the back of his head. Was it the windshield or the road? He couldn't remember. It bloody hurt, though.

'I'm fine,' said Beckford.

'I'll call an ambul—'

Beckford hobbled into a light jog. Every step on his right foot sent a sharp stabbing pain shooting through his kneecap. They'd catch him at this rate, but the wail of approaching sirens pushed him harder and harder, and he started to build up speed, the collection of wounds magically numbed again by another fresh surge of adrenaline.

At the far end of the road was a refuse truck, inching towards him, bin men swarming around it like worker bees. Beckford took to the pavement, then a few seconds later one of the distant police sirens suddenly popped into clarity. He could see the flash of blue sweep the houses and hear the engine racing towards him. He couldn't get enough air. Each breath felt like an inhalation of Tabasco sauce.

On his side of the street, two bin men had stopped what they were doing and watched him approach wide-eyed. A niggling feeling made Beckford think one – or maybe both of them – would try to be heroic like his tattooed friend on the high street.

Making a snap decision Beckford split left down an alleyway between some houses, dodging a pink bike with stabilisers and a worn out football next to it. The siren was deafening, the vehicle now stationary. They'd parked up. Beckford reached for the top of a peeling wooden gate, his hands landing in what he hoped was wet moss, then wedged the toe of his left trainer on the rusting handle.

Each movement pummelled his joints with agony, but he fought through it, pulling himself up and over the gate and landing in a small paved back garden with a thud. He sprinted towards the back fence, not noticing two young boys who'd stopped kicking a football. They watched in awe as Beckford vaulted it and dropped out of sight. A second later, the side gate clattered again and a police officer's head emerged over the top. The taller of the young boys pointed towards the back fence.

The officer dropped out of sight and his radio crackled: 'He's gone through onto the other street!' a voice yelled. The boys looked at each other and smiled.

'Muuuuuum!'

* * *

Four units, a helicopter and one hour later, it was clear – John Beckford had evaded police capture. Additional manpower had been pooled to canvas the Richmond borough. Witness statements were collected. The route of the chase was retraced and searched for evidence. Stop and searches were carried out on anyone matching the description (white male, approximately six-foot tall, wearing dark blue jeans, a black waterproof jacket and a blue hoodie). That was until word came through the radio that his jacket and hoodie had been found discarded behind a garden hedge.

After three hours, daylight started to fade and the officers were instructed to give up the search. It wasn't over though. The net had been cast wide, with John Beckford's profile sent to all London boroughs and an All-Ports Warning issued to major airports, train, bus stations and even ferry ports, just in case he made it that far.

For Beckford, the big smoke was getting smaller by the minute.

TWENTY-FOUR

The meeting lasted over two hours, and as expected Peltz was made to feel like an incompetent idiot. The main item on the agenda was Detective Sergeant John Beckford, a highly volatile individual who was now on the run. Beckford's case had threads – Detectives Alison Farber and Leonard Staedler, and most recently Chief Inspector Graham Noakes, a man whose skill and experience rated him instantly as an amber threat to the Studio. Each of them were being tracked, but the meeting started at the inception, where Peltz had to explain his negligence regarding Nikolai Guskov, a member that he himself was supposed to be watching like a hawk.

It felt like a disciplinary. Peltz lost his cool a couple of times, defending himself as best he could with his back pressed against the wall. At no point had he considered Nikolai to be depressed or suicidal. They monitored his online activity on the various computing devices he'd been issued, but this wasn't Big Brother – the Ukrainian had a degree of freedom to do as he wished. It wasn't out of the realms of possibility that he'd secretly acquired his own, unmonitored devices. In fact, Peltz had expected it, and no amount of room checks could prevent it. What was he to do, move in with the lad?

Next on the agenda was Joseph Winterburn and his involvement. Apart from the messages to Nikolai via the Survivors website, the only reason he was on the Studio's radar was because he was on Beckford's. And yet, like Beckford, they found nothing substantive about the man and the Studio could certainly dig a lot deeper than

Beckford could. Hominem, their profiling system, cast its net far and wide across the public and private domains, but the picture it constructed was nothing more than a depressed psychology graduate who'd been dumped by his girlfriend. There was no trace of any relevant tech experience. Why had Beckford been so adamant that he'd murdered Nikolai? Why had he been so adamant that Nikolai was murdered at all?

Some of the very best at the Studio analysed Nikolai's suicide video frame by frame, practically pixel by pixel, and even to them the idea that it was fake seemed far-fetched. Their bespoke Agnoscis algorithms found no anomalies in the images, but they held out for a second opinion – GyroFX's office communications were secretly filtered and monitored through a channel on Notitia, the software they used to analyse online traffic based on pattern recognition and keyword activity. If Gyro's VFX wizards were to find something odd about the video, the Studio would know in a heartbeat.

One anomaly did worry them. The report from the bungled attempt at Beckford's apartment stated that operatives had been "locked out" of Beckford's computer in the minutes leading up to the planned removal. Their team then cut the power to the building, just in case, but it was suspected that a third-party was behind the lock-out.

Was it Winterburn? Was he working for Beckford? It was possible the Studio were being played at their own game, but tenuous suspicions were banned in their organisation; suspicions had the tendency to grow and sometimes will themselves into existence. It was concrete data that, ironically, ensured the Studio's survival.

After the grilling, Peltz headed to the toilets and relieved himself at a corner urinal. It was quiet in there. No more stern, frantic voices, just the faint humming of an extractor fan above his head. If he'd suspected it before, it was more certain now than ever – he'd had enough of this circus. But there was only one way out of the Studio, as demonstrated by the Ukrainian and his somewhat extreme exit strategy. If Peltz wasn't such a coward…

The peace was interrupted by the door swinging open, followed by the clopping of shoes. Peltz turned and dutifully greeted the young man with a nod.

'They manhandle you again?' said the man, taking up the next urinal but one, leaving a barrier of social acceptability between the two of them.

'Certainly felt like it,' said Peltz, 'and I know why it is. They're losing their grip on the situation. They're panicking. It's only natural for them to start pointing fingers, but if they spent that energy on containing this fucking thing instead of waterboarding one of their own, they wouldn't be in this mess.'

'They've got a grip.'

'Bollocks,' said Peltz. 'Beckford's ahead of us. Winterburn? The videos? I wouldn't be surprised if *he's* taking us for a ride, not the other way around.'

'You know we got his stash, don't you?' said the man. The look on Peltz face confirmed he didn't. 'Yeah. Some storage facility in Ealing. Once we could identify him on the bus CCTV, Agnoscis stitched a timeline of everywhere he'd been since his outfit change.'

'What was in the stash?' said Peltz, finishing up.

'They didn't tell you?' said the man.

Peltz waited expectantly for an elaboration. The man remained silent, entranced by his own urination.

'No,' said Peltz, unable to hide his contempt and frustration. Why was he being treated like an outsider? The fresh blood spoke to him like he was a first-year computer science student. Were they preparing him for pastures new or something even more disagreeable?

The silence dragged out long enough for Peltz to consider flattening the man. He was about half his age, and clearly enjoyed the power of knowledge like all the other young, intelligent, self-righteous cunts who walked into that building.

'A VHS tape,' he said, 'taken from the CCTV of a cafe across the street. It shows another figure following the Ukrainian into Dunning Halls. We think it's Winterburn.'

Peltz walked over to the sink. 'You're saying Winterburn edited those other CCTV recordings?' he said. 'Seamless enough to get past our team? Get past Agnoscis?

The man zipped up and joined Peltz at the adjacent sink. 'We don't even know who Winterburn really is,' he said, 'and we won't until we find him. But those vids have been edited by someone. There's two possibilities – one, it's an inside job, in which case this place is fucked; or two, there's someone else. A freelancer maybe.'

The revelation came to Peltz so fast he thought the light bulb above his head had popped, sending sparks showering down around him.

'What about three?' he said, his wet hands poised to go into the dryer.

'*Three*?' said the man, mocking him. It was the same belittling attitude Peltz had become accustomed to, but at that moment he didn't care. He felt omnipotent. He'd figured something out that those smarmy pricks hadn't. Yes, they might have first class honours degrees from prestigious universities framed on mummy and daddy's dining room walls, and be so clued up on modern technology that if you blinked you'd be out of date. But they'd all been assembled in a factory, wired for purpose yet lacking the all-important life experience that Peltz had over them.

'Actually…' he said, backtracking, 'no, you're right. Just the two.'

As the dryer blasted his hands, everything started to fall into place. There *was* a third possibility and it stunned Peltz so much that he actually smiled in disbelief. The Studio – the outfit who specialised in modern deception – had themselves been duped.

* * *

Some doner kebabs contain over 2000 calories, 500 shy of the recommended daily limit for a grown man. Unlike a normal day, where Beckford would have been crushed with extreme guilt for eating such a hideously unhealthy thing – not to mention overwhelming concerns for the general hygiene of the place – the guilt never came. He was so hungry he could have eaten a scabby cat. Even the kebab shop's yellow, grease-stained walls – which gave everything, including the food, a rancid hue – had no effect on his ravenous appetite.

Hunger was one basic need that he was satisfying, but sleep had to wait. Every now and then, almost mid-bite, his eyes would uncontrollably close and he'd experience a few seconds of bliss. But like falling in a dream, he'd jolt awake again and continue tackling his food before the Turkish man behind the counter caught wind of how utterly wrecked he looked. The day had tested Beckford as much as he'd ever been tested before, the only comparable experience being the day he'd found out about Sally. That, however, was a purely mental battle, not physical. This had been both, his body and mind feeling like they'd been put through a tumble dryer. Flashbacks of the last couple of hours bombarded him as he ate.

Reviewing the events of the day he realised that evading

the Old Bill had taken everything he had. After ditching his jacket and hoodie behind a hedge, he'd sprinted down a few more streets before jumping into another garden where he came upon a bicycle, balanced upside down on its seat and handlebars, which – with the back door to the house wide open – looked like it was being worked on. A two-second analysis of the wheels and gears deemed it fit for the road and Beckford led the bike through the side gate and took off on it, making a mental note of the address and telling himself he'd compensate the owner, somehow, at some point in the future. If he was still alive and able to do so.

Cycling on main roads could gain a lot of unwanted attention, so Beckford stuck to the B-roads and headed east. A part of him just wanted to flee, head north and get as far away as possible. But that wouldn't have got him the answers he was looking for.

After 40 minutes of furious pedaling, his piston-pumped blood the only thing keeping him warm, a paranoia started to creep in. The bike certainly would have been reported stolen, but there could have been some sort of GPS tracking device on it – plenty were available online. Unable to shift his worries, Beckford left the bike outside a pub in West Norwood and limped to a nearby phone box where he got his breath back and took stock of his body, identifying where he was hurting and if anything was serious. His right knee was swollen like a tennis ball, but after a brief inspection he was pretty sure it wasn't broken. Everything else was either a gash or a bruise; nothing a warm herbal bath wouldn't sooth.

When darkness fell, he left the phone box and limped along the streets. Unable to put all his weight on his right leg, his pace was halved, making any chance of evading another pursuit slim to none. He needed another change of clothes to remain anonymous, but above all to keep warm as the evening settled in and the temperature plummeted.

On Norwood Road, he'd pretended to browse the window of a charity shop while trying to determine how modern their CCTV system inside was. It was difficult to see. In the end, Beckford had bitten the bullet and entered the shop under the luxurious doorway heaters. Thankfully, there was no store security. Beckford's distrust in the police had unconsciously spread to anyone wearing an authoritative uniform. To him, they now all seemed like fakes – the badge or ID card a prop, their uniform a costume. Was it still Halloween?

With a pair of dark jeans, black sweater and a North Face jacket off the racks, each in surprisingly good nick, Beckford had left the charity shop in search of food, which led him to the nearest fast-food shop.

Holding the remaining kebab together like a fat microphone, Beckford chewed the car-crash of meat, giving his jaw a tough workout. From behind the counter came a single cheer accompanied by a tinny roar of jubilation from a television.

'Did you see that mate?' said the Turkish man, the question and wide grin on his face snapping Beckford out of his reverie. Chelsea had just scored, apparently. Beckford did his best to smirk and acknowledge it, but mustering enough energy to do so felt like an effort.

His knee wasn't the only thing damaged in his fall from the double-decker. The laptop took a hit, a spider-web crack spreading up from the bottom right-hand corner of the screen. When the machine turned on, the hard drive made some ominous clicking sounds as it spun up but it still somehow worked. Beckford hoped to high heaven it wouldn't die on him; he didn't want to a chance it in another public library.

Polishing off the last of his kebab, he lazily wiped his mouth with a serviette and cleaned his fingers. Getting up gently, he limped to the counter and unplugged his phone from the wall, thanking the Turkish man again for letting him use the socket.

'No problem, my friend,' said the cook, tipping a bag of frozen fries into a vat of bubbling oil.

Beckford added feigned interest in the football score. Two–one, apparently. Beckford didn't even know if Chelsea were home or away. He wished he could be concerned with such trivial things like sport. What a luxury.

Holding down the power button on his phone, the screen sprang to life, loading its operating system and connecting to various networks. He hoped 20 minutes of charge would give him enough juice until morning. Farber would be worried sick about him. Wouldn't she?

In computer crime, kiddie porn was the digital equivalent of leprosy and even the most tenuous association with it, whether true or not, could tar and feather a person for life. Beckford was reminded of the story of the paediatrician whose home was vandalised by an angry and illiterate mob of kids in Gwent in 2002. In Beckford's experience, when dealing with suspected paedophiles the term "innocent until proven guilty" became so gossamer thin it was almost transparent. The more heinous the crime, the quicker people were to judge.

Those bastards, he thought. *Those stupid fucking bastards.*

When his phone finally connected to the network, it vibrated four times in quick succession as a queue of notifications came through. There were two missed calls from Farber's mobile, another missed call from a private number and a message from Farber that read: "Are u ok? X"

The unknown number intrigued Beckford. No one had his burner number but Farber and Noakes. It could have been Noakes, he reasoned, but he didn't understand why he'd make it a private call. Unless it was someone else?

Somehow, before he let himself get swept up an obsessive notion that something more ominous was behind it, Beckford convinced himself it was a generic cold-call and nothing else. He did very well, considering his state of mind. Maybe there just wasn't enough space in his head for any more mental and emotional bullshit.

Beckford sat back down in front of the ruins of his kebab and dialled Farber. Only one ring sounded before she picked up and her vocoded voice came through.

'Hello?'

'No names, remember,' he said, his voice raspy to his ears. He cleared his throat, took a swig of Sprite, then quickly added, 'Or places. Keep it cryptic.'

'What's happening? Bloody hell… where are you? Are you all right?'

'I'm safe. I'm okay, honestly.

A snort of disbelief came through the phone. 'Okay? You're *okay?* You're a bloody…'

The silence stretched a bit too long, long enough for Beckford to push the kebab tray to one side as a sickness uncoiled in his gut.

'…a bloody fugitive,' she concluded.

'Was that what you were going to say?' said Beckford.

'Yes,' she said. 'What else would I say?'

Beckford sighed and let his head hang to face the table. 'This is what they want,' he said. 'This is what they want. To ruin me. To shut me down, cut me off and destroy my credibility.'

'I believe you,' said Farber. It sounded authentic, despite the digital distortion, although Beckford had started to lose the ability to understand what authenticity actually was any more.

'Tell me what's been going on,' he said. 'On your side.'

Farber was silent for a few seconds, then started to unfold what she knew bit by bit.

Just after midday she'd been visited by a couple of CEOP officers who interviewed her for over an hour. She'd told them about her and Beckford's history – their relationship, their split, and their recent reconciliation involving the suicide of Ukrainian student Nikolai Guskov.

'Why did you do that?' said Beckford, attempting to control his anger.

'Because it's the *truth*! I'm sorry J—' she caught herself before saying his name, then continued '...I'm sorry, but the truth might be the only thing that'll save you.'

'If they realise they can use you against me, they will.'

'Why would they use me?'

Beckford kept quiet. How could Farber not think that there might still be remnants of something between them? Their relationship ended through events out of their control. Unfortunately, there'd been no bad stuff – no infidelity, drunken indiscretion or loathsome character flaw to hang a grudge on, which must have disappointed his pursuers.

'Anyway,' said Farber, 'it was a confidential interview.'

'*Con-fi-den-tial?*' said Beckford, accentuating every syllable as if it was the most preposterous thing he'd ever heard. 'They recorded the interview, right? Audio? Video? Now it's data, which means it's freely available to these people. Like stealing light from the sun.'

'I didn't tell them we'd been in contact since your warrant was put out. If they were going to use me against you it would have already happened by now.'

Beckford took a few soft breaths before he realised she

was probably right. These people operated well ahead of the game. Beckford kept falling into the trap where he thought he'd outsmarted them, but really that couldn't be further from the truth. They didn't need Farber as bait, they had every beat bobby in London looking for him now.

'The computers from my apartment, where are they now?'

'I'm still trying to find that out.'

Beckford sighed, 'I guess it doesn't matter, they're going to make sure there's enough incriminating evidence on them to put me away for good.'

'You haven't done anything wrong. Your name will be cleared, it'll just take some time.'

'I wouldn't live to see it cleared,' said Beckford. 'They want me inside so they can bump me off. That's the only way they'll cover this up.'

Beckford was so exhausted that the reality of the situation still hadn't hit home properly. It was as if he was talking about someone else in peril.

As another slice of silence passed down the phone, three young men entered the kebab shop looking slightly inebriated, one of them laughing hysterically at something. The laughing ceased when they reached the counter and the pressure of ordering came upon them.

'Where will you stay?' said Farber.

Beckford scrunched his eyes and squeezed the bridge of his nose. 'Don't worry about that. What can you tell me about the young man, the one who's missing?'

'Not much more than what you already know. Two friends knew about his depression but never got wind of any suicidal tendencies. No one in the dorms saw him on Halloween with… the other one. He's just disappeared without a trace.'

Beckford felt defeated. Each unturned stone he

approached seemed to yield nothing but dirt, and with his lack of funds, resources and freedom – not to mention his deteriorating physiological and psychological state – stone-turning was becoming difficult.

'Okay,' said Beckford, 'Look, I need to sleep. I'll talk to you tomorrow.'

'Be safe.'

'You too.'

Beckford hung up and put the phone in his pocket. Taking the laptop from his bag, he opened it out onto the greasy table and turned to the Turkish man who was in the middle of splashing vinegar over whatever the three louts had ordered.

'Excuse me?' said Beckford. 'Do you have wifi?'

'Next door,' said the man, nodding in the direction.

'You know the password?'

'Is not one.'

Beckford scanned for nearby networks and connected to the one with the strongest signal, managing to navigate the screen despite the large cracks across it. No sooner had the laptop gone online, he started downloading the necessary tools to ensure the hand-me-down that Noakes had donated was as secure as he could make it. Being connected to an open network was a risk in itself, even though he was running a Virtual Private Network that supposedly located him in Oslo.

After a few minutes, a green tick signified the system was clean of malware, viruses and spyware, and his inbound and outbound connections were monitored. Beckford then navigated to the only place he knew where someone might have an answer.

When his Florida-based server appeared on the screen, it was in exactly the same state as he'd left earlier that day – the website www.tork2me.com still open, awaiting a response.

And a small flashing icon told him there was one.

TWENTY-FIVE

Beckford leaned in closer to the screen, the blaring football match and general ambience of the kebab shop fading away around him.

[11:01] *Anon27 has joined #PunkSmiley
[11:01] you hav to stop...
[11:01] theres no way to beat them, they no ur every move.

The user hadn't said anymore but had remained in the channel. Beckford's fingers rattled the keys.

[22:34]<Anon199> hello?!!!!

Going by the timestamps of the chat, nearly 12 hours had passed since his mysterious helper had responded. Beckford typed '/whois Anon27' into the chat box, hit enter and information spilled into the main window:

Anon27 is Anon27@0545a479.tork2me.com * Anon27
Anon27 on #PunkSmiley
Anon27 using *.TTM [www.tork2me.com/]
Anon27 has been idle 14mins 42secs
Anon27 End of WHOIS list

The idle time gave a more accurate reading, showing the last time Anon27 had been active. The other information told Beckford that the website www.tork2me.com wasn't just a place to host a chat application, but appeared to be an all encompassing server and one that Anon27 was hiding behind. Beckford's fingers rattled the keys again.

```
/msg Anon27 WTF? HEY!!!!
```

The command would send a direct message to Anon27, popping open a new window on their screen and hopefully making a notification sound at the same time, alerting whoever it was to the fact that Beckford was there, waiting impatiently and desperate for answers.

And wait he did. He filled the drawn-out minutes that followed by chewing the skin around his nails and picking the leftover kebab meat out of the tray, which he rinsed down with the rest of his Sprite. Every now and then he'd type "/ping Anon27" that sent a transmission between the two clients to see if a reply bounced back. It did, which meant Anon27 was still online.

When the hoarse voice repeated the question for a second time, Beckford realised it was directed at him and he tilted his head up to the young lads at the counter.

'Bit late to be doing work, innit pal?' said one of them. He was young, maybe early twenties. Much too young to be having such a gravelly, worn-out voice. *Must be a smoker*, Beckford thought. The lad had shoulder-length hair and when he grinned he revealed a missing incisor. He was swaying too, and as he turned to his other two drunken friends they burst into fits of hysterics. About what Beckford had no idea. When he looked back down at his cracked screen his heart leapt into his mouth.

```
[22:36] <Anon27> hello
```

Beckford rapidly bashed the keys.

[22:36] <Anon199> who are you?

He sat and waited, oblivious to the fact the long-haired lad at the counter was still looking in his direction.

[22:37] <Anon27> I knew Nikolai

Seeing the name in text like that did all sorts of strange things to Beckford. His emotions flared with delight, but his stomach twisted in fear. Would their text crawlers pick that up?

He quickly minimised his Florida desktop and checked the incoming and outgoing traffic activity on the laptop. It was minimal, with no spikes. Maybe the Tork2Me server was encrypted. He maximised the Florida desktop again.

'Mate, what are you doin'?' said the long-haired lad taking a seat opposite him. 'Writing the next Fifty Shades of Shite? This ain't a fuckin' Starbucks.

He laughed again, turning to his mates to absorb their glee. Beckford sat back. The lad – or Huey as Beckford mentally dubbed him – was joined by his fatter friend Duey, who added: 'I don't think I've ever seen someone using a computer in a fuckin' kebab gaff before.'

'You see people use phones, don't you?' said Beckford calmly, opting for the intelligent yet probably least effective way out of the precarious situation. '…*they're* computers. In fact, I bet the phone you've got in your pocket has more power than this piece of shit.' He hit the laptop with a careless slap and smiled at them.

Duey dug into his jeans and pulled out his phone. 'You're right, mate. This is the latest top-end shit. Got all the whiz-bang bollocks there is. Cost me a few fuckin' quid, like.'

Huey fell into fits of laughter again, repeating his friend's words mid-heave. '*...whiz-bang bollocks...!*' Beckford smiled again, then chuckled lightly. If he couldn't beat them, he'd have to join them, and so he laughed some more, keeping his eyes on the two louts while blindly typing on the laptop:

`<Anon199> wait ther pleaes`

The third friend, Louie, shouted something over from the counter, confirming Duey's order and asked what sauce he wanted. This gave Beckford an opportunity to type a coherent sentence.

`<Anon199> how did you know him? don't make me ask questions please, just tell me.`

'What are you typin'...?' said Huey, taking the seat opposite him. Beckford thought of a quick lie, but it wasn't fast enough to deceive the intense, slightly aggressive and alcohol-glazed stare of the lad.

'An email,' said Beckford, glancing quickly at the screen. No reply. Louie, a shorter and more ordinary looking bloke, approached the table with polystyrene trays balanced on top of a pizza box.

'We're not eating here, are we?' he said. Duey jumped up at the food.

'Aw, gimme that shit man.'

Beckford pretended to pay attention to the ravenous trio, but in reality he was hoping long-haired Huey's focus would switch track, diffusing his own brewing anger by connecting again with the alluring idea of food.

'Show me,' said Huey, his glossy eyes penetrating

Beckford as he continued to ignore the other two, tucking into their junk food like starving dogs. Shit was about to hit the fan and Beckford knew it. The whirlpool of anger behind Huey's glazed eyes was turning faster and faster, and stopping it was near impossible. Not at this stage. Stealthily, Beckford pressed CTRL-ALT-DELETE on the laptop and locked the screen. There was no way he was going to let a group of pissheads derail him.

'Oi!' shouted Huey. Beckford looked at him. 'I said fuckin' show me what you're doin'…'

'Phil, fuck it,' said Duey, folding a slice of pizza into his mouth. Beckford guessed it wasn't just alcohol that Huey had been consuming. Cocaine was hard to reason with. Beckford could have shown him his warrant card, but he'd lost it after his spill from the double-decker. Yet there was still a chance to resolve the situation. He closed the lid of the laptop until it clicked.

'Look,' said Beckford, 'I'm a police officer. If you don't take your food and leave peacefully, I will arrest you for being drunk and disorderly. Your call.'

Duey and Louie froze, almost comically mid-bite. Beckford didn't break eye contact with Huey, whose jaw was now pulsating with tension. It was a confidence game. Beckford hadn't walked the beat for years, but it all came flooding back. It was still a scary thing, having to deal with people who weren't of a rational state of mind. They were fearless and disregarded any consideration for consequences.

In situations like that, police had to rely on each other to be an extension of their senses – eyes, ears and physical power. Beckford was alone, staring back at a pair of vicious eyes that could have belonged to a feral beast, poised to fight to the death. He was also outnumbered three to one. He looked at the Turkish man behind the counter, who was eying them nervously.

In a flash, the long-haired lad was out of his seat with the laptop in his hands. 'You're a cozzer, yeah?!' he shouted. 'Well fuckin'… arrest… *THIS*!'

Beckford was up, but it was too late. The laptop sailed through the large, single-pane window of the kebab shop. Jagged shards exploded out onto the street with ferocity, the rest of the pane dropping from the frame and crashing into the shop.

Beckford stared, frozen to the spot. Then, as if psychically linked, the trio of louts synchronously bolted, ditching their food in the process.

'Fucking assholes!' shouted the Turkish man who quickly picked up the phone and dialled. There was nothing Beckford could do but run himself, as best he could on his damaged leg. He skittered on the glass by the door, then once outside he looked down the road where the louts had already gained quite some distance. Beckford gathered his battered laptop from the glass-dusted pavement and limped off in the opposite direction.

* * *

In the shadows of a church cemetery in between rows of gravestones, Beckford collapsed to the grass and caught his breath. With only a smattering of light sleep banked in the last two days, he was amazed his body was still chugging along. It was his heart that he worried about – beating hard and fast, even at times of rest. The fear was never-ending. His adrenal glands must have looked like two dried old prunes.

If he wasn't so bloody stubborn, obsessive and intrigued, he might have just given up there and then, letting himself fall asleep in the icy grass among the dead, hoping to join them as worm food. But like a survival instinct, he wasn't going to go down without a fight. And there was no way he'd be leaving the planet with his name tarnished by the worst brush imaginable.

Pulling himself into an upright position, Beckford prised the laptop open beside him. It was too dark to see, but stroking his fingers across the keyboard revealed a few of the keys were missing. He pushed the on button and the hard drive clicked like a metronome. Nothing appeared on screen. With his ear held to the keyboard, his suspicions were confirmed. It was fucked.

The laptop may have gone the way of his buried companions, but if Anon27 had answered his plea it would still be there, recorded on his remote server in Florida. How could he connect and find out? It was surely too late for any internet cafes to be open, unless he headed towards the city. *Too risky.*

Then he remembered his phone. Why not just connect with that? The phone was old, almost redundant by today's standards, but it still had a functioning internet browser.

As he took his phone out of his pocket, it started to vibrate. The illuminated screen was blinding in the dark, and when Beckford's irises adjusted, he could see an incoming call from a contact called "2" – a number Beckford had assigned to the person to save himself entering their real name. Farber was "1." He hit answer and held the phone to his ear.

'Hello?' he said, his voice hoarse. He cleared his throat and tried again: '*Hello?*'

'It's me,' said Noakes, his voice digitally disguised as instructed by Beckford. 'I need to meet with you soon. It's about… that person you're looking for.'

'What is it? What have you found?'

'Not over the phone. Meet me outside Mansfield's old

house in one hour.'

The phone went dead. Instantly, the fear pumping through Beckford's heart was displaced by excitement. Involving Noakes was never part of his strategy, but he knew when it came to the digital domain the man's knowledge, experience and caution was second to none. He started to wish he'd gone to him sooner.

At the rear of the church, Beckford softly lowered the laptop into a bin and left the grounds. When he got to the high-street, a man and woman linked arm in arm pointed him in the direction of the nearest taxi rank.

* * *

When the phone left Noakes' ear, it was placed on the breakfast table beside him. He was in his underwear, shaking, his face beaten, bruised and bloody. Another larger wound above his left kneecap spilled blood down his leg that pooled by his bare feet.

He knew there was a gun. He'd seen it when they first got him, but he'd managed to avoid looking at it since. Both men were before him, their balaclavas masking everything but their eyes. With a glance to one another, a silent decision between them was made. While the man with the gun remained stationary, the other approached Noakes, passing him and disappearing behind the chair he was tied to.

In the following brief second or so, Noakes experienced an extreme fear that he'd only ever felt once before, when his phone once rang at four in the morning and he knew it would be the hospital telling him his wife was dead.

Noakes wasn't in any way religious, but he mentally begged a higher power to take his fear away so he could go join his wife. And it was then – amid the terror, guilt and regret coursing through him – that a long-lost image of Lydia came to him. She was looking at him, one eyebrow arched. Her hair was done up nice. *Where was this?*

He wanted to tell the men to stop, to give him a chance to at least identify the memory, but it was too late. From behind, leather-bound hands enveloped his face, smothering his senses as if he was being forced face-down into thick clay. One hand pinched his nostrils shut, the other clamped over his mouth. Noakes thrashed with panic, his legs and arms battling against the restraints. Desperately trying to hold on to the new moment with his wife, he hoped it would be enough to see him through to the other side. But the terror was relentless.

The man killing him was strong and used his chest to force Noakes' face harder into his palms, tightening his head like a vice, shutting off his mouth and nose from the precious air.

Through the man's leather fingers, Noakes could see blurred flashes of his kitchen and the man standing there with the gun. With his lungs sucking and blowing with no success in finding air, his fear peaked at a level known only to those who have not lived to describe it.

Then it all just ebbed away.

TWENTY-SIX

For once, Beckford counted himself lucky. It was the early hours of a Wednesday morning, which meant his cab ride from West Norwood to Croydon was quicker than at any other time of the day. The driver was foreign, perhaps Romanian and probably unlicensed, and he barely said a word for the whole trip. Peace at last.

On his journey, Beckford attempted to access www.tork2me.com on his aging phone. Unfortunately, the site was even more archaic than his phone and completely unresponsive. He sat there and mulled for a few minutes where, despite a desperate need to stay alert, the warm car and soft vibrations of the road sent his head lolling to the window and he drifted off.

He woke up just as the cab pulled up outside Selhurst Park, home to Crystal Palace football club. Beckford paid the man and no sooner was he out in the cold night air, he felt wide awake again, venturing deeper into the suburbs to navigate the dark and dangerous streets.

Beckford hunkered down in his North Face, which had no hood, the sharp cold wind incessantly lashing at him. He missed his hoodie. Not only would it have kept his head warm, it would have let him blend in better with any gang members or degenerates he was likely to meet roaming the street at this time of night.

Cleverly Avenue was a row of council houses dwarfed by tower blocks that stretched into the night sky. With his wits cranked up to 11, Beckford kept his fingers crossed that the sub-zero temperature would keep the teenage hoodlums indoors. It was a known fact that street crime increased during the summer, the heat sending people crazy. Tonight, the cold was his ally.

As he walked past the row of houses, Beckford spotted the porch roof of Mansfield's house poking out ahead; squinting in the darkness he could just make out a small, unidentifiable object sat atop. *It's still there*, Beckford thought. A gnome, somehow lodged there by local kids as a kind of warning after Mansfield's arrest. Although in truth the crude graffiti across his boarded-up windows was a more obvious giveaway.

Rupert Mansfield was a 61-year-old paedophile who had created a safe online haven for others with a similar interest. An obsessive hoarder of tens of thousands of images and videos, Mansfield shared his extensive collection with others who were willing to upload their own depraved content in return. At some point he had switched from being a "looker" to a "toucher," and outside of his comfort zone away from his hard drives and secure servers he soon drew attention to himself. At a funfair on a sunny afternoon, words were had, punches thrown and the police were eventually called, which set off a chain of events that saw Beckford – who was part of CID at the time – and Staelder take part in a raid on his house. Mansfield's computer was investigated live on-scene to preserve any running processes that could incriminate him further or expose any accomplices who might be online.

The memory was crystal clear – it was Beckford's first exposure to the evils of paedophilia. Numerous grisly murder scenes had given him a cast-iron stomach, but being present in Mansfield's house, knowing what was on those computers and drives... it had disturbed him more than anything. It was through the raid that Beckford first met Chief Inspector Graham Noakes, a contact who would facilitate his departmental transfer over a year later.

With every parked car he passed, Beckford crouched and peered through the frosty windows, expecting to see Noakes' waiting silhouette in the front seat. If the man had any sense he'd have the heaters on full blast, but Beckford couldn't hear any car engines above the gusts of wind.

Was he too late? Too early? Had something gone wrong?

A distant metallic click pulled Beckford's attention down the road. Someone was walking towards him, attempting to ignite a cigarette with a dud lighter. Beckford stayed on course as the unknown figure got nearer. Noakes didn't smoke, so it couldn't have been him. Maybe it was a bad-tempered teen with meth in his blood and a kitchen knife tucked up his sleeve.

With every step they took, the person's outline, shape and clothing improved in detail, until an overhead streetlight exposed a silhouette of a man too short and stocky to be Noakes. Beckford took his hands out of his jacket pockets and passed Mansfield's house without stopping. The man's thick boots thudded the pavement like a rubber mallet, and when they were 10 feet apart, he spoke unexpectedly with a deep and gravelly cockney accent.

''Scuse me mate, you gotta light?'

The seemingly ordinary question took Beckford's eye off the ball for the briefest of moments, and as the man came under the nearest streetlight, Beckford could see he was wearing a balaclava.

By which time it was too late.

From behind, a hand clamped his left arm, and as he turned, what felt like an intensely sharp bite pierced his neck just below his right ear. Every muscle in his body burst into flames as 3.6 microcoulombs of electrical charge surged through him. His knees gave way and he dropped, his right cheek smacking a Baltic block of mossy concrete. Fortunately, he was already unconscious and unable to feel any pain.

The man pocketed the stun gun and crouched, first shining a torch in Beckford's inanimate face – zombie-like under the harsh sodium light – then he shimmied up the sleeve of Beckford's left arm, exposing his bare skin. The second man, the smoker, pulled a capped syringe from his coat and got to his knees, prodding the flesh in the crook of Beckford's arm. Pulling the cap off with his teeth, he buried the hypodermic slowly to three-quarters of an inch and the clear liquid disappeared into Beckford's bloodstream.

Stun Gun popped open the door of a nearby car and the two of them carried Beckford onto the back seat. Smoker got in with him and Stun Gun quietly bumped the door shut with his hip before getting in the front. The engine rattled to life, and through the lifeless orange haze of the street the car made its escape.

Beckford's head flopped forwards, chin to chest, propped up slightly by the plastic funnel that poked out of his mouth. Latex fingers came through the window and grabbed a clump of his hair, lifting him up. Beckford was still unconscious, sat upright in the driver's seat of a car. A different car. And they were no longer parked on Cleverly Avenue, but grasslands where the soft whoosh of traffic from the nearby M25 floated in over the cold air.

Holding Beckford's head in place, Smoker poured whisky into the funnel. There was no reflexive gag, coughing or spluttering, the Famous Grouse just flowed as if he was emptying it down the sink.

When half a litre had gone, Smoker threw the open bottle into the footwell and pulled the funnel from

Beckford's mouth, a trailing two-foot long gastric tube attached to the end that slid from his throat like a snake. Smoker packed the contraption away outside the car, then leaned back against the window, fastened Beckford's seatbelt and turned the feeble overhead light off.

If Beckford had somehow woken up – his body perhaps immune to the cocktail of drugs and booze he'd been administered – he could have gone straight for the glove compartment where pepper spray sat nestled among a collection of old CDs. He'd have known it was there, because it was his own car he was sat in.

'Double-check the handbrake,' said Stun Gun from under the bonnet.

Smoker had already applied it but yanked it hard again to be sure. It was solid.

'Go,' he said, priming his grip on the brake. From under the bonnet came crackles and sparks and the engine roared to life, the high whiny screech of first gear hitting maximum revs. Stun Gun dropped the bonnet quickly and bounced it shut before getting out of the way.

Mentally timing his movement, Smoker dropped the handbrake. The revs instantly lowered as the engine caught the weight of the car. The back tires skidded, kicking up wet grass and earth. Smoker pulled himself free, but only just, buffeted by the door frame as the car sped off towards a black void in between moonlit trees some 100 yards away.

The car snaked but reached its target dead on, charging up an embankment and hitting air as it flew over and plummeted 25 feet towards a pitch-black lake. As the front of the car crashed through the surface, a deluge of water exploded up into the air, the impact launching Beckford forward in his seat. The belt locked against his chest, but the inertia pulled his head, legs and arms forwards like the limbs of a ragdoll, his muscles and bones stretched taut.

The semi-submerged car poised vertically for a second, until the back end teetered and slapped down onto the surface, thrusting Beckford back in his seat. For a moment, everything seemed to settle around him. Then the water came – ice cold and inky black, spilling in through the open window and pooling at Beckford's feet. The whisky bottle came to life and bobbed around his ankles.

The front of the car dipped at a quickening rate as water flooded the engine compartment and gushed out from under the steering wheel and glove box. In a matter of seconds, the lake had engulfed Beckford's legs and was racing up his torso.

From high on the embankment, the masked men observed. To them, the car was barely visible, but the bubbling sounds and flickering ripples told them the job wasn't done. Not yet. So they waited. With the dosage they'd given him, as long as the car went under and nothing came back up, it would be over. A few seconds later the car roof shimmered out of sight and the lake began its slow transformation back into a featureless mirror of the night sky. With their task complete, the men turned and left.

In the blackness under the water, Beckford floated inches off his seat, the remaining air in his lungs providing enough buoyancy to push against the belt that still anchored him down. Thanks to a diving reflex found in all mammals, Beckford was yet to take a breath.

The reflex had three main objectives – to slow the heart rate by up to 50%, restrict blood flow to the bodily extremities so it could reroute blood and oxygen to vital organs, and finally something called "blood shift," which was the movement of blood to the thoracic cavity to avoid the collapse of the lungs under heavy pressure in deep water.

Had Beckford been conscious, panic would have seized

him and his stored air would have depleted in seconds. Instead, he was suspended in ignorant bliss, the drug coursing through his bloodstream ironically assisting with his survival. But he wasn't superhuman. His time was limited. And after 20 seconds or so his supply of oxygen came to an end.

Instinctively, his airways opened. Water chased in through his nose and mouth but another reflex called laryngospasm sealed shut his trachea, stopping water entering his lungs. Any air left in him was coughed out as a result, pumping bubbles against the roof of the submerged car.

On auto-pilot, he siphoned in more mouthfuls of water, this time the liquid only finding its way to his stomach. That was when he started to shake and jerk, his diaphragm spasming as his lungs desperately sought oxygen. With each attempted breath, more water filled his stomach until his larynx began to relax and small amounts found its way into his lungs, each influx stopped by a fresh spasm snapping shut his trachea. As the spasms weakened, yet more liquid entered his lungs.

It could take approximately six minutes for the brain to die due to a lack of oxygen, but cardiac arrest would have most likely taken Beckford sooner as he floated there alone, drowning in blackness.

Only he wasn't alone.

Through the murkiness outside the car, a hazy finger of light probed the green-tinged water. The light struck Beckford's right cheek then flickered violently, as if the person holding it was moving at a frantic speed. When the source of light reached the open car window, a figure swam in. The waterproof torch searched for and found the belt buckle, and latex-gloved fingers pushed the release and the belt popped free. The anonymous swimmer heaved

Beckford's weighty body – now even heavier with his flooded lungs and stomach – through the window.

The lake was only 15 feet or so deep, but it felt twice that as the Swimmer had to swim for two. Eventually breaking through the surface of the lake, the Swimmer took in lungful's of air – the baritone exhalations of breath, which materialised as great plumes of mist caught in the moonlight, revealing in the darkness that Beckford's rescuer was male.

Treading water with a 12-stone weight was hard, and he didn't have enough strength to lift Beckford's head above the surface for any longer than a second without going under himself. So, with one hand gripped on Beckford's jacket, he managed to swim a short distance until the rocky lakebed touched his feet.

With each step out of the water, Beckford's body – his clothes soaking wet – got heavier and heavier. Finally dragging him free of the lake, the man lay Beckford face-up on the bank and dropped to his knees, getting his breath back. He'd be needing it.

Shining the torch in Beckford's face, the beam unsteady as he shivered in the cold night air, a lifeless visage illuminated before him; his lips dark and his face so bloodless it looked like he was wearing gothic makeup. The Swimmer peeled an eyelid open and was greeted with a dead stare. With an ear to his chest he could hear an unusual sound, which may or may not have been a heartbeat.

Lashing out, the man slapped Beckford on the side of the face. When there was no response he slapped him again, harder, the clap echoing off the encircling embankment. It was no use, he had to do it.

Laying the torch across a mound of grass, he directed the light at Beckford's face, casting a hard shadow on the other side of Beckford's profile. Going by what he'd read and what he had seen on TV, Swimmer parted Beckford's lips, pinched his nose shut, and with some apprehension exhaled into his lungs.

Beckford's lips were so cold that Swimmer was concerned he'd just kissed a corpse. He pulled away and watched Beckford's chest fall as his gift of breath seeped back out of the unconscious man. An eerie sight that delivered no encore.

Unzipping Beckford's jacket, he exposed a sodden T-shirt that clung to his skin. Swimmer prodded his latex fingers around the centre of his chest, unsure of what he was supposed to be looking for. There was no time for uncertainty. He placed both hands, palms down, roughly on the centre of the chest and pumped, just like he'd seen on TV. He did it five times, Beckford jolting with each compression. After the fifth he went back to Beckford's mouth and give him two more lungful's of air. Once again, Beckford's chest rose and the air escaped with a lifeless exhalation, like a bag deflating.

Swimmer went back, pumped again. Five times. Back to the head, three breaths this time. Beckford's sallow mouth lay agape like an unpainted mannequin. Swimmer quickened his efforts, feeling like every second that ticked down was counting the fading thuds in Beckford's chest.

Blow air.

Wait.

Chest – pump-pump-pump-pump-pump.

The transferred breath once again escaped through Beckford's slack mouth. He tried one last frantic time, breathing deeper, pumping harder.

Beckford lay inanimate but for the water still dripping from his clothes.

Swimmer stared, then rocked onto his back side,

clasping his hands around his knees as the occasional icy droplet abandoned his own drenched hair and trailed its way down his face. The wind whipped against his wet body, each sharp buffet of air wrapping him in a frosty chill. Above the wind he could hear his own breathing. Deep and regular. Teasingly so.

Dropping his head between his legs, he tried to convince himself that none of this was his fault. What would he do now? Drag Beckford back underwater and leave him in his car? His mouth was now covered with his own DNA. They'd certainly swab that. *Actually, that might work—*

A low, guttural sound interrupted Swimmer's thoughts and he snapped his head up. Beckford was moving, his back arching slightly. Another low groan came from within, followed by a trickle of water that dribbled from his mouth.

Swimmer bounced back onto his knees and tipped Beckford onto his side. A third buried croak emerged and a gush of water spilled from his mouth, disappearing into the grass. Swimmer patted and rubbed Beckford's back, something he'd remembered from childhood.

Beckford heaved a few more times, purging mouthfuls of water until he finally took an abrupt and desperate inhalation of air. He coughed violently, spluttering for a good 20 seconds as every last drop of lake water was unconsciously expelled from his lungs.

Swimmer could only watch, his own nerves finally settling as Beckford's respiratory system eventually stabilised and fell into a natural rhythm.

TWENTY-SEVEN

Dominic Peltz had managed an hour and a half before someone kicked the bed, jolting him back into the real world.

'Kit's here,' said a voice before leaving him. Peltz roused in semi-darkness where the worries he'd managed to escape from in the realm of unconsciousness came stampeding back like a two-ton enraged rhino. As he sat up on the fold-out bed, a familiar pain throbbed in the left side of his neck where it joined his shoulder. It was the shitty bed. The Studio invested heavily in the latest technology, with a rolling replacement plan that upgraded their equipment and core infrastructure every six months, pushing their yearly budget into the tens of millions, yet they wouldn't spend a few extra quid to buy some proper beds.

That's why he convinced them to put him up in a hotel. The six months he'd spent on a fold-out was fast-tracking him into becoming a decrepit invalid, not to mention the bouts of depression he got from being holed up there for days, even weeks at a time without seeing anyone. It was no quality of life, but once he moved into the hotel the concept of "quality of life" started to fade altogether.

He swung his legs out of the bed and stuffed his socked feet into his waiting brogues. Hanging on the wall was his suit jacket and tie, but he'd slept in everything else. His shirt looked like crinkled paper, and as he ironed it out with his hands the best he could his brain started to kick into gear – the risks, security measures, processes and procedures of the Studio were making his mind melt. Could his fuck-up have been a cry for help?

He yearned for the early days. They were golden. Less fingers, less pies. He managed the entire Studio single-handedly back then. People bought him drinks. Now he was lucky to get offered a coffee from the vending machine.

Peltz tucked in his shirt, slipped his tie off the hook and put it on – a double Windsor knot, as always. An odd skill for a man who despised wearing ties. Staring at himself in the small mirror on the wall, his thoughts drifted to John Beckford, a man who'd been on Peltz's radar for some time before the shit hit the fan.

On a personal level, Peltz had grown to respect Beckford. For someone to dig so deep into something so seemingly trivial, to formulate an idea out of a few scraps of data – that was a talent to be marvelled at. Peltz had even felt excited at how close Beckford got to exposing them – to setting him free. Now it was back to square one.

He yawned, scratched his head and reorganised his boxers under his suit. Slipping his jacket on, he fixed the collar and left the room, conscientiously closing the door quietly behind as to not wake the other two.

Down the carpeted corridor, he eventually came to a door labelled "Lab 1," where he pushed his thumb against a biometric reader. The door beeped and unlocked. They were already hard at work. On the central workstation was a single desktop computer and two laptops. The technicians looked like surgeons – hair nets, latex gloves, spotless overalls. For all intents and purposes they *were* surgeons, only they operated in the field of technology and not biology.

Taking a few steps into the lab, Peltz observed the computers that were being gutted with precision, the components removed with the tender touch of someone holding a newborn kitten.

'Passwords?' said Peltz. One of the technicians held up a strip of paper with some scribbled writing on it and then got back to work.

'Confirmed?' said Peltz. The same technician looked up, nodded and looked down again. Peltz's watch said 2:27 am. He leaned back and perched on a desk, crossing his arms as far as they could reach round his gut.

The computers belonged to Graham Noakes, and would unearth his final moments of digital activity before he was removed. With the wealth of 0s and 1s stored on the disks, Noakes' online life was about to be turned upside down. Social networks. Email. Instant messages. Web postings. Online documents. Cloud storage. All of it rifled through like an enormous filing cabinet. A comprehensive digital sweep of someone's life.

When required, the Studio had to break a few eggs. It was a policy backed by their motto, which was proudly emblazoned on a sign in the corridor by the drinks machine.

"It is the greatest good to the greatest number of people which is the measure of right and wrong."

To Peltz, Jeremy Bentham's words had – much like a lot of things in his life – lost all meaning. The Studio could design and build perceptions of what was true and what was false. Their fiction became everyone else's fact.

As Peltz watched the hard drive of Graham Noakes' desktop computer being cloned, the door to the lab beeped and thumped open. Barging in was an Asian woman in a business suit.

'He's still alive,' she said, breathless.

The technicians stopped and Peltz straightened up.

'Noakes?' he said.

'Beckford. He's in the Royal right now. Hasn't woken up yet, but he's stable. The Met are all over it.'

A volcanic pit opened up inside Peltz's stomach, searing his ulcer.

'How the fuck did he—'

'There's a meeting in 10 minutes.'

'What room?'

The Asian woman turned and on leaving, said: 'Check your bloody email.'

The door sealed shut behind her. Peltz pulled his phone out and refreshed his inbox. No new messages. When he looked up, the technicians stopped staring at him and went back to work.

Their containment plan had started with Beckford, but it was a priority for fires to be extinguished as they sparked and smoldered. Now it was desperately getting out of control. With the Met involved, the scale of the operation had increased dramatically. They'd been in a similar situation before. Studio personnel would be pulled from other operations. A "mirror team" would piggyback the Met's investigation, drip-feeding intel to the rest of them as they worked fast, building the necessary narratives to always stay one step ahead.

Peltz stared into space, thinking. It was no surprise that he'd been excluded from the meeting. It would be his future they were discussing. Depending on how much digging Noakes did, Peltz's name could very well be with the police already. Which meant he was a link, and the only links the Studio liked was the ones they could control.

With an index finger, Peltz loosened his tie. He'd sensed he was heading for pastures new, he just didn't expect it to be so soon.

TWENTY-EIGHT

By shutting down his body into an almost coma-like stasis, the near-fatal dose of GHB and ethanol in his system had kept Beckford alive. A couple of hours after the drugs were administered they started to wear off, and Beckford – although still heavily sedated – became conscious for the first time since his kiss from the Taser.

It was a bobbing motion, he felt. It could have easily been mistaken for nausea, and upon opening his sore eyes his first sight through the darkness was two small, white shapes, disappearing and reappearing one by one. Left then right.

It took him almost a minute to get any true sense of awareness before he realised the white shapes were somebody's trainers, and that he was being carried over the shoulder of that person. But his bout of reality was short-lived and he soon slipped back under again.

When he awoke a second time he felt the base of his skull lay softly on concrete. As his eyelids flickered open, a stinging pain pierced each eyeball and he struggled again with focussing on anything. When he rolled his head back he could see the outline of a person standing over him, backlit by a streetlight. The figure was looking away and wore a hoodie similar to the one Beckford had ditched.

In his delirium, Beckford started to believe the unknown figure was himself. Was he dreaming? Having an out-of-body experience? The figure's head then turned to him, but the hoodie swallowed his face in darkness. The figure crouched until his face was no more than 12 inches away from Beckford's. A dark void in a hood.

Death.

'You'll be all right,' the figure said, his voice peculiar.

Then he was gone.

Next, Beckford's retinas ached from a blinding fluorescent light. He was aware that time had lapsed, but was it seconds, minutes or hours? He clacked his tongue around his arid mouth, pathetically attempting to lubricate it. Out of the bright glare stepped a female apparition who leaned into him, and as his weak eyes slowly adjusted, Beckford smiled; a weak and feeble smile, but a smile all the same.

Farber beamed back at him, dabbing wet mascara from her eyes. He tried to speak, but only managed a hoarse whisper before he coughed, his throat igniting with a burning rawness. Farber took a glass of water from the bedside table and carried it to his lips, letting barely a sip enter his mouth before pulling it away.

He swallowed and coughed again, this time more violently. Farber rubbed his arm until his fit subsided and he was able to take in smoother, deeper breaths. He nodded to the glass in her hand and she obliged, letting him take another sip. This time he stopped himself from coughing, managing to control the urge, and consumed a good two to three mouthfuls before letting his head sink back into the pillow, the effort of keeping it raised having taken its toll.

With his eyes closed he caught his breath. Farber placed the glass to the side and cupped his IV-punctured hand, gently rubbing it with precise care. A moment passed before Beckford's eyes snapped back open, this time in a panic as anxiety flooded his body, electrifying his nerves with a freshly tapped energy.

'John,' said Farber, holding his hand tighter. 'John you're in hospital, it's okay.'

Beckford locked his bloodshot eyes with hers.

'You're safe,' she said. The sight of Farber's honest face was a comforting one, but it was only able to distract him momentarily from the searing pain that pulsed inside his skull. It felt like his brain was being mashed into a lemon juicer.

'Twatting hell,' he croaked, closing his eyes once more and gently resting fingertips on his forehead, as if the light touch might magically remedy the pain. 'Feels like I've been on the piss for days.'

'Have you?' asked Amelia Corden. Her heels clicked as she stepped forward, her crisp, business-like image rising up over Farber's shoulder. Seeing Corden gave Beckford even more relief. The way he was feeling, he wanted nothing more than to hand her the baton and call it a day.

Have you? he repeated in his mind.

Beckford struggled to think. The last 24 hours was nothing but a gaping chasm in his half-baked mind, with the occasional sensual memory coming to him – a strong smell of whisky, a pinch at the back of his neck, the sight of his hoodie under an orange streetlight and a faceless figure crouching over him.

Utterances fell from Beckford's lips as he wrangled with his thoughts.

'Start at the beginning,' said Corden, '…and by that I mean from the exact point you decided to start an investigation all on your own.'

Beckford glared at Farber but she avoided his ire.

'Commander,' said Farber, 'look at the state of him.'

'Not half as bad as I'm going to look if the reporters downstairs find out I'm here,' said Corden. 'If you want my help John, it has to be now so start talking.'

It was only then out the corner of his hazy peripheral that Beckford noticed a uniformed constable, clipboard and pen at the ready. With a wince, Beckford propped himself up and peered beyond Corden, through the window in the door to where another uniformed officer stood with his back to them.

'Is he to keep people from getting in,' said Beckford, 'or to keep me from getting out?'

Corden sat on the bed near his feet and straightened her skirt.

'First and foremost, John, I know you. I don't believe any of this bollocks they're throwing around, and if I could sweep everything under the rug I would. But this is an official meeting and the allegations against you are serious. Which means I have to be serious. The more information you give me, the more I can help you. It's as simple as that.'

Beckford felt his body go limp, a gazelle being run down by a lioness. Farber was wrong, he wasn't safe. They'd already tried to bump him off twice. Third time's a charm, and he was a soft target lying in that hospital bed. If they didn't get to him in there, he'd get shanked in a dank holding cell somewhere else.

He closed his eyes and took a deep breath. The machinery around him hummed. It was only when he heard Corden say, 'John,' that he peeled his eyes apart and realised he'd almost nodded off again.

Then he told her everything that he knew so far. The faked suicide video. The switched hard drive. The manipulated CCTV footage. Joseph Winterburn. The online messages. Dominic Peltz. The attempt on his life at his apartment.

Reeling everything off in one go without so much as a pause for breath was surprisingly therapeutic. It also gave him a fresh perspective on it all, and before Corden could rattle off any questions, Beckford whittled everything down to a more succinct explanation of what the hell he thought was going on.

'There's a criminal network,' he said, 'possibly led by Peltz, and it has the ability to hack into almost any system. They can manipulate data. They can remove data. And they can create it. I believe the network is partially formed by corrupt officers of the Metropolitan Police.'

He paused to cough, the pain inside his head pulsating with each hack. He lay a hand on his chest and shook his head when Farber offered more water.

'What they do or who they work with,' he said, 'I don't know, but Nikolai Guskov is the key to it all. Whoever was involved in his investigation – the suicide, from detectives to SOCOs, to the button mob guarding the doors – they need to be put under the bloody microscope. And I mean yes, get the IPCC involved.'

Corden lifted a hand to interrupt, but Beckford ignored it.

'Nikolai's hard drive was stolen from our lockup at Water Street and replaced with a dupe. Nothing on the CCTV or entrance logs to the room, department or entire building recorded anybody coming by during the only time they could have done it. There is a severe breach of security within the Met. Within *everything!*'

He dropped his head back onto the pillow, out of breath again. 'The Ukrainian had talent,' he added, 'Genius-level talent. I think Peltz groomed him, used him… maybe the kid found out something he shouldn't have or served his purpose, then Peltz had him taken out, covering the whole thing up as being a suicide.'

'Who's Joseph Winterburn,' said Corden, 'and where does he fit into all this?'

'A 29-year-old from Richmond,' said Farber, jumping at an opportunity to speak. 'He's been missing for over a week but we don't have any concrete evidence for supporting his involvement in—'

'We?' said Corden.

'Well,' said Farber, 'I'm one of the investigating officers on the misper, ma'am.'

'Winterburn works for them,' said Beckford. 'His record may only have one blemish for shoplifting, and his own mother thinks he's a psychology graduate who's into music, but like I said they're masters of deception. Just watch the video. It's him following Nikolai into the building. The whole message board stuff was just a set up. Nikolai didn't want to go. He was forced to.

'And Peltz?' said Corden.

'He's off grid,' said Beckford. 'Only things I could find were a few archived articles on the Met website and a PNC account. Maybe you're privy to more guarded information?'

'You're sure he's still in the Met?' said Corden.

'PNC accounts get purged the day you leave,' he said, then managing a weak smirk he added, 'Security, you know.'

'Why did you run?' said Corden. 'From the bus I mean.'

'You're actually asking me that?' he said, his words punching the air with annoyance. 'Don't you *see* what was going on? Why have a small group of people catching a mouse when they can enlist the entire Metropolitan Police Force to do it for them? That's why they fitted me up, because they'll have people on the inside ready to take me out for a pack of fucking smokes!'

'But you're worth nothing to them now,' said Farber. 'Everything's on the table.'

'She's right,' said Corden. 'I'll personally see to it that a thorough investigation gets under way as soon as humanly possible. We'll go public.'

'That's very sweet of you,' said Beckford, 'but the

damage is already done. These people are extremely good at what they do. In fact, in my time at Water Street I've not seen better. In the field of digital forensics we are told that Locard's exchange principle applies just like it does with physical evidence – "the perpetrator of a crime will bring something to the crime scene and leave with something from it." Everything leaves a trace. But after analysing Nikolai's computer and his "suicide video", I'm not sure there's any truth in that anymore. That's how bloody good these people are. They alter data at its most fundamental level, erasing information like it never even existed or planting it as if it always has. You can have the best lab technicians at the Yard scan my hard drive with an electron microscope, but there's no doubt in my mind that the vile shit they put there will appear like it's been on it for months. Maybe even years. Basically, I'm properly fucked.'

'If what John's saying is true,' said Farber, angling to Corden, 'it exposes considerable flaws in the numerous acts that our justice system is built on. Essentially, the system no longer works.'

'Only if what he's saying is true,' she said, turning to Beckford.

He was astonished. Corden was more to him than a Commander, she was a friend. Someone he'd grown close to, shared intimate details with and trusted unconditionally. How could she not trust him back?

'John,' she said, crossing her arms and finding a stray piece of lint on her skirt that she flicked away with a hand. 'Unfortunately your line of work makes this situation more difficult, you understand? The kinds of images and videos you have access to on a daily basis… any logical person would think you're using your job as a smoke screen.'

'John's not a paedophile!' said Farber with a flash of anger before restraining herself out of respect for Corden's rank.

'Doesn't matter,' said Corden. 'You can't prove anything by what goes on inside someone's head, only by what actions they make.'

'…or appear to make,' added Beckford. He took a hand to his face and rubbed his bloodshot eyes with his thumb and forefinger. After a few breaths, he seemed to take a hold of the situation from a more logical perspective.

'Look,' he said, opening his eyes and turning to the constable at the rear of the room. 'What's your name?'

'Peters,' he said.

'Are you staying?'

'I can leave if you—'

'No, I mean after this. Are you on duty?'

'Oh, I'm only here for this,' he said, raising the clipboard of notes.

'Okay,' Beckford pointed to the door and said to Corden: 'And him? Who's he?'

'I don't know his name,' said Corden.

'You don't know his…? Jesus fucking Christ, I'm *done* for.'

'John, he's been here all night,' said Farber. 'So have the doctors and nurses. You're safe here, despite what you think.'

'If I have *any* chance of seeing tomorrow, you need to find Peltz *today*. And you need to use people you can trust. Contact Graham Noakes.'

An awkward silence followed. Farber turned to Corden, as if waiting for an order.

'Do you remember anything else from last night?' said Corden. Beckford furrowed his brow, searching the recesses of his mind.

'A phone call,' he said, his eyes fixed on nothing in particular. 'He called me – Noakes called me.'

'And you involved him in this?' said Corden.

'I told him things, yes.' He glanced at the constable, who'd done a fine job up to now maintaining an impartial demeanour and scribbling down almost everything he heard. But now he was reading the fine print on a laminated sign stuck to the wall.

'John,' said Corden, 'Graham Noakes was found dead at his house this morning. He was murdered.'

The words didn't sink in straightaway. Beckford's thoughts were still muddled and for a brief moment he questioned whether he was either still asleep or that the after effects of the drug cocktail had made him audibly hallucinate. Both possibilities felt real for a handful of seconds until an undeniable sense of reality insisted otherwise, and it was the wet and reddening eyes of Farber that confirmed what he feared.

A battle of horror and guilt flooded his insides and he lowered his head back onto the pillow. With controlled anger, he released a lungful of air through his gritted teeth and let a fist fly, pounding it down into the hospital bed with a thud, making Farber jump. He opened his mouth to speak, his lips quivering, his cold eyes never leaving the ceiling.

'How?' he said, his voice low and controlled.

'Definitely?' said Corden. 'Too early to say. Probably? It looks like suffocation. An autopsy is scheduled.'

Beckford didn't react. Farber secretly hoped Corden would stop there; the additional circumstances surrounding Noakes' death had already made her sick to the stomach. But before she could think of any decent segue, Corden cut back in.

'We're pretty sure he was tortured before he died.'

Her monotone delivery took none of the heartache away. If anything, it only exacerbated it. Beckford continued his lifeless stare at the ceiling, trying hard not to lose it. Farber stroked his hand and forearm, but when he started to sob he pulled his arm free and covered his face to stifle the sound.

No one said anything for nearly a minute as Beckford let it all out, his pent-up emotions finally let loose into the wild, his sobbing uncontrollable. He needed it.

When there was very little left in his tank, Corden stood up.

'John,' she said, 'I'm sorry about this, but if the shoe was on the other foot I'd expect you to do the same.'

What was she talking about? Beckford wiped his cheeks on the bed blanket and looked up, catching her signal to the constable before turning back to him.

'John Beckford,' she said, 'I'm placing you under arrest for possession of indecent files and the suspected murder of Graham Noakes. You do not have to say anything, but it may harm your defence if you do not mention when questioned something which you later rely on in court. Anything you do say may be given in evidence.'

The constable was over, snapping handcuffs around his left wrist and the hospital bed's handrail. After a few seconds, Beckford realised he was smiling. He had to laugh. Whatever was happening to him was just too insane to comprehend. Everything was just completely fucking *nuts*.

While he battled the mind-boggling situation he found himself in, Corden gave him some reassuring spiel about doing everything in her power to find out who was responsible. Beckford was only half-listening and didn't respond. Farber then tried to speak to him, but again he just stared up at the ceiling and let his mind drift into a kind of meditative state.

He wasn't quite sure of when they left, but at some

point he'd slipped back to his dreams, where a mosaic of reality and imagination took to the cerebral stage. Blue pixels, millions of them, were spread out in front of him like a vast ocean; the magnetic weight of them pulling his body down as he fought to stay afloat.

On the horizon he could see a figure watching him, and no matter how hard he swam towards it, the ocean hit back – choppier, louder, the crashing waves around him relentless, growing with each swell until he was consumed by a rip tide of pixels dragging him under.

It was down in the depths of the digital water where Beckford saw the figure adrift – a hooded man, illuminated by a misty green hue shining down from the surface.

Beckford pushed his hands through the water and swam towards him, the black void where the figure's face would be getting closer, but revealing nothing but more blackness. It was when Beckford was just a few feet away that the figure's gloved hands came up and gripped its hood, and in one smooth motion pulled it back.

TWENTY-NINE

Farber still couldn't believe what had happened – a senior member of the Metropolitan Police murdered in their home in such a brutal fashion.

On her drive over there she kept the radio off so as to remain oblivious to whether media outlets had got hold of the story or not. It was the kind of attention that law enforcement agencies liked to avoid, and yet when Noakes' neat semi-detached on Melwood Avenue came into view the numerous news vans were already stacking up at the police cordon.

Squeezing her own car between vehicles, Farber wound down the window and showed her ID to a couple of entry control officers who were warming their hands with their breath. After letting her through, she drove down the winding cul-de-sac until it straightened out towards the end. Graham Noakes' house was one of the last on the street, bookmarked by a squad of police vehicles.

The closest Farber could park was a tight space between a skip and a black four-by-four. Neighbours were out and about, a morbid curiosity enticing them, fearful that something so terrible had happened on their doorstep while they slept.

Farber didn't particularly want to be there – she'd had that much shit shovelled on her in the past 48 hours, it was touch and go whether or not she was about to snap. The reason she was there was Beckford. He was understandably feeling a responsibility for Noakes' death, and Farber felt she had the opportunity to step in and help prove that wasn't the case. If she could lessen his torment somewhat, it would be enough.

On entering the house she was hit by a musty smell that reminded her of her mum's place. The layout was very similar too, with a narrow hallway made even more narrow by an old mahogany cupboard and side table; the stairs on the left, two rooms on the right and what Farber presumed was the kitchen straight ahead.

As she let a couple of SOCOs in jumpsuits pass, a deep and recognisable cough came from the kitchen, followed by Michaels, who took one look at Farber before continuing to violently hack into his hand.

'This fucking cough,' he said, his breath laboured. He wiped his hand with a tissue and placed it on a nearby CSI trolley.

'I've just got off the phone with Commander Corden,' he said, the accusatory tone enough to set Farber's nerves on edge. 'In here,' he added, nodding for Farber to follow him into the unoccupied front room. She did, and Michaels closed the door behind them.

'Were you going to tell me about any of this, detective?'

'Of course,' said Farber.

'Of course? When "of course"? I don't have to tell you that the CPS might consider your actions criminal.'

'My actions? Chief, Beckford kept me in the dark for most of it.'

'But not all of it?'

Farber felt her mouth go dry. 'He was an investigator on a case of mine.'

'The Russian?'

'Ukrainian, yes. It was closed, but John being John found something and couldn't let it go. Whatever it was put his life in jeopardy. They've fitted him up, chief. When all of this unravels, Beckford will be commended – not convicted.'

'Oh,' said Michaels, straightening up. 'So you believe him?'

Farber suddenly felt like an invisible wall had sprung up between them. It astonished her how the lies about Beckford had taken root and thrived, like a deadly virus growing and adapting and consuming. And it seemed like there was no way to contain it.

'The commander believes him,' she said, using her ace in the pack. Michaels' eyes – marble-like with tiny burst blood vessels that matched his pitted cheeks – shot over to the door as it opened. A young officer, realising she was interrupting a private conversation, held up an apologetic hand and closed the door again.

Michaels turned back to Farber and said, 'I know there's history between you two, and it *was* nobody's business… but that's changed, you understand? This is turning out to be the investigation of the year and you've just managed to get a front-row seat, Farber. Were you aware of his problems? Depression? The paranoia and anxiety?'

Farber had once spotted a pack of Xanax in his bathroom cabinet but thought nothing of it.

Michaels added, 'Did you know he was seeing a therapist?'

'Why would I?' said Farber. 'Our history ended with Sally. He's been through a lot, chief. You were there. I imagine things like therapy come with the territory.'

'Let me put it to you straight,' said Michaels. 'Try to disconnect yourself from him for a moment. Which of these sounds more plausible… this coming from a suspect with mental health issues. A hacking group, responsible for the murder of a young student, has faultlessly fabricated digital information to frame Beckford as a member of a child pornography ring *or* there is no hacking group and he's simply telling tall tales.'

Michaels had a way with words, and although Farber was usually immune to his influence, put bluntly like that anyone would pick the latter. But Farber was determined not to be swayed. What he was saying was all out of context. Michaels didn't know Beckford like she did.

'You've seen it 100 times, detective,' Michaels continued, 'the guilty always want a second chance and they'll invent any old cobblers to get one.'

'I know him, Chief. I *knew* him… we were in love. I think I'd know if he was a…'

'Would you?' said Michaels, his voice raised. 'One of the many things I've learnt in this shitty job, detective, is nobody knows anything about anyone. The secrets we keep, the things we choose to forget. I've got my fair share, I'm sure you do too. Not to sound like some corny movie, but life is full of surprises and not all of them are nice.'

The cogs behind Farber's eyes were trying to grind to a halt and change direction. *Don't let go*, she told herself. It was difficult. All the signs pointed to what she feared. As a dizziness came over her, she lowered herself onto a creamy white couch, upholstered with a small pattern of flowers sewn into the fabric. With her gaze lost in the pattern, she ran a finger over the arching shape of a single rose. Then tears came and snaked down her face.

Michaels took a seat next to her and said, 'If the truth is there, we'll find it. It's facts we run on, remember? Those facts that will either incarcerate John or set him free.'

Reaching into his jacket, he plucked out a handkerchief and handed it over. 'I need you to come to the station,' he said, 'but take your time.'

By the time Farber had mopped her face and blown her nose, Michaels had got up and left the room. She sat in a trance for what could have been 10 or 15 minutes, sifting through her thoughts, after which she'd managed to pull herself free from Michaels' spin. There was no way John wasn't the person she knew him to be. He'd had a good upbringing – a loving father and mother. He was good around children, and during their time together they'd had serious discussions about having their own.

There were never any issues in the bedroom either. He wasn't kinky, and never failed to perform unless a session down the pub had turned into eight pints, and even then it wasn't for want of trying. He wasn't precious about his laptop, desktop or phone; Farber regularly had access to all of them. He had nothing to hide.

The more she went over the facts in her head, the more she realised how much of an uphill battle Beckford faced and how terrifying the world had become. Was that all it took? A collection of indecent images dumped on a computer and the person was frog-marched to the gallows? Allegations like that were hard to shake, a "no smoke without fire" attitude common everywhere, even the police force. Farber blew her nose again, checked her face in an ornate oak-framed mirror on the wall and headed to the kitchen.

The body of Graham Noakes had been removed hours earlier. In its place, and dotted about the kitchen, were a variety of numbered yellow forensic markers, the sight of which caused Farber to cross her arms and tread carefully.

A lone pathologist was on her knees, headfirst in the cupboard under the sink. *Presumably examining the contents of the drain*, Farber thought. A deep thud came through the wooden worktop and the pathologist pulled back from the cupboard, rubbing the crown of her head with her latex fingers.

'Ow, ow, ow, fuck, fuck…'

'Ouch, are you okay?' asked Farber.

The pathologist pulled her facemask down. 'Right on

the corner,' she said, wincing. Farber recognised her as Dr Newman, first name Lucy or Lily.

'I'm nearly done here,' said Newman, '...just don't walk around over there.' She waved her hand in the direction of the kitchen table where a wooden chair had been pulled away and sat askew. Newman got back under the sink and Farber crouched down on one knee to peer under the table.

A splash of blood adorned the corner of the chair and dribbled down the front leg to the tiles, where it had dried to a brown crust.

'Ali,' said Staedler, entering the room. Farber turned and stood up.

'Did you go?' said Staedler.

Farber nodded. 'He's in a bad way,' she said.

'Physically or...?'

'He looked like he'd been run over by a bus. But yeah, not good in the head either.'

'Has he seen today's papers?' Farber's eyes widened, which told Staedler she hadn't.

'Oh God,' she said.

'Fucking tabloids. They know what they're doing... how fickle people are. True or not, a defamatory headline is all it takes to ruin someone's life.'

Farber had known of cases where people had hung themselves, inhaled car fumes or taken a dive off a bridge because they'd been wrongly accused. The more terrible the crime, the less likely an innocent person was likely to recover from the false accusation. And they both knew that accusations of paedophilia was up there with the worst of them.

Staedler reached out an arm and pulled her into a hug, which she took gratefully for a second or two before pushing off him.

'Don't,' she said, 'I'm sick of crying.'

'I can't imagine how John's feeling right now,' said Staedler. 'Were him and Noakes close?'

'I think so, yeah.'

'Fuck's sake.'

'You get anything?' said Farber, pointing at a notepad clenched under his arm.

'Uniforms are still door-stepping,' he said, handing the notepad over, 'but this is all from in here. You know he was tortured, right?' Farber's stomach twisted again.

'They tossed his house,' said Staedler, 'but were at least courteous enough to leave it tidy. It was his computers they wanted. There's a couple of laptop bags and peripherals in the back room, but no actual hardware. Upstairs, the base unit of his desktop has been taken, but everything else left behind; monitor, cables, mouse et cetera. Hold on, I'm just nipping upstairs to see if they've finished with the loo.'

Staedler disappeared and Farber flipped back a few pages in the notebook to where he'd scribbled the date, the victim's name and a brief description of the crime. Farber was an expert at translating his almost hieroglyphic-like handwriting, which was always accompanied by doodles and other incoherent squiggles.

-No sign of forced entry.

-Laptop bags by living room couch, both empty.

Farber scanned the page with her index finger.

-Time of death sometime before 12:00am.

-Punctured knee. Possible shattered kneecap. Bloody screwdriver found in kitchen bin. Extensive signs of torture.

She flipped the page and continued scanning down until

she came to a list of telephone numbers, each one time-stamped and descending from most recent call. Staedler re-entered the kitchen, slightly exasperated.

'Knew I'd be pushing my luck,' he said. 'Any courteous neighbours around who'd let me use their bog?'

'That's John,' said Farber, pointing to the first telephone number in the list. 'He was using a burner. Told me Noakes had called him, wanting to meet.' She traced her finger across to the time of the call: 11:22 pm.

'That was the last call made from Noakes' mobile,' said Staelder. 'Which we can't find, but we got his Vodafone receipt, which was enough to get his number. Think it was a burner too. Purchased yesterday.' Farber's finger slid to the second number in the list:

- 212-6919-2200… 11:21pm

'What's that?' she said. 'Is that even a real area code?'

'Dunno,' said Staedler. 'Goulding's getting them to send over the full list later on today. Was that a McDonald's back out on the main road?'

'Yes.'

'You gonna be okay? I'll only be 10 minutes.' Farber nodded and Staedler dived out the room again. Getting her mobile out of her bag, Farber held up the notepad and dialled.

THIRTY

After waking from his dream, Beckford spent a while alone with his thoughts, stitching together what stray memories he could gather, hoping to form some kind of tenuous logic as to what happened to him the night before.

The gnome… yes, I remember Mansfield's house.

A lighter sparking. Who's lighter? Did it burn me… round the back of the neck?

Everything went dark. Was I knocked unconscious?

There was the faintest smell of whisky too.

Whisky? I don't remember that.

Cold, wet grass though… pressing up against my face and hands.

Wetness. There was water. I was coughing up water.

And there he was…

…crouching over me.

In his dream, the figure had pulled back its hood and Beckford saw nothing – no head, no face, just an absence of light. During the groggy few minutes upon waking, his subconscious had filled the black void with the face of Graham Noakes, but now, wide awake, he knew that couldn't have been true.

The door to his hospital room clicked open and a young nurse entered. She checked his vitals, recording the information on a clipboard at the end of his bed, but at no point did she look at him or say anything. Maybe she was just too busy, like all nurses, but that reasoning wasn't enough to quell Beckford's paranoia. She would know why there was a police officer stationed outside his room. And she would see that he was cuffed to the bed. The whole hospital must have known.

She thinks I'm a fucking nonce.

His stomach turned, already sick with nerves and god knows what else that had been pumped into him in the past 24 hours. After a deep breath, he rolled himself slowly onto his side, aches and pains firing across his body all at once. It was awkward, with his left arm still cuffed to the handrail, but he needed to change position.

He stared out of the window at the grey sky and put his past on the back burner to begin deliberating his future. Things were destined to go from bad to worse, that was certain. If he was to ever get out of the hospital room it would be at a doctor's discretion, and from there he'd be transferred to a local prison. That's where his real troubles would start.

Branded with the term "paedophile" guaranteed a much worse time inside than any serial killer or rapist. A paedophile police officer was practically a death sentence. It wouldn't even matter that Beckford was only being held for trial – innocent or guilty were quite often forgotten terms when someone was accused of such hideous behaviour.

It was then that Beckford started to feel a strange and unwarranted sympathy for Rupert Mansfield, the convicted nonce that Beckford helped imprison. A frail old man. *A dirty old fucker.*

What a nightmarish time he must be having.

Serves him right.

Is he still alive?

Better off dead in a place like that.

Beckford had to get out of there. He winced and rolled back to face the room. The nurse had gone. Through the door's window he could see the corridor wall and nothing else, although he knew the guarding officer was just a few feet to the right, sat down, most likely on his phone or reading whatever garbage magazine he could get his hands on in the ward.

Beckford had seen him look in a few times, keeping an eye on the prize, but there was no predicting of when he would do it. It's not like Beckford had an escape plan anyway; he was shackled to the metal bedframe, and without a key or a picklock he couldn't do anything about it.

That was when he noticed it – the cuff was no longer linked to the steel handrail that Constable Peters had first snapped it to. It was linked to a lower section, just below the mattress. When Beckford leaned over the bed, he could see that the new bar was open-ended. Without any effort, he simply slid the cuff all the way to the end and pulled it free.

What the hell?

Beckford glanced at the door.

Nothing.

He quickly slid the cuff back onto the bar and lay back to wait, observing the door like a twitcher.

How had his handcuffs been repositioned? Unless his anonymous helper was the officer outside his door, there was no way anyone could get in the room undetected.

Unless…

…*Alison*? It was possible. A standard issue key opened all the standard-issue handcuffs used by the police.

The officer's face appeared in the window, then dropped out of sight again.

It was now or never.

A spike of adrenaline numbed his pain, giving him enough strength to push himself up into a sitting position. He slid the handcuff free, swung his legs over the edge of the bed and eased his feet down, letting his bare soles hit the cold tiles. Slowly, he stood up, his jelly legs vibrating as a rush of blood pumped through his body and congregated in his head where a dull pain surged through his skull.

His mind was still foggy.

Using the IV stand to steady himself still, he closed his eyes until the pain ebbed, then peeled off the tape on the back of his hand and pulled out the cannula, which clattered against the stand.

He glanced at the door.

Not a peep.

What was he to do next? He was wearing a gown and had no shoes – opening the door and running for it wouldn't be his best option.

What would?

The windows in his room were locked, but if he managed to get one open, could he abseil to freedom? It looked pretty high up. Four, maybe five storeys.

He scanned the room, eyeing fixtures, equipment, furniture – anything that could assist in his escape.

The IV drip. Is it a sedative? Are there any syringes lying about?

Beckford shook his head. Who did he think he was? James Bond?

Maybe there was only one way out.

The same way Nikolai went.

Outside of the room, Constable Mark Riley sat reading a dog-eared gossip magazine. Every visitor that had passed he'd scrutinised, well aware that there were no depths the paparazzi wouldn't sink to. A ruse to visit a dying mother would be an easy way to get a photo of the hospitalised e-crime detective John Beckford, arrested on child pornography charges and the suspected sadistic murder of a police chief. For a front page national newspaper, a decent snap would be worth more than a few bob.

Riley glanced at his watch – 45 minutes before his shift was over, then he'd head to the supermarket on his way home. As his shopping list idly scrolled through his head, he stood up and stretched, his Achilles aching from an injury he sustained a few weeks back playing five-a-side football.

Casually, he glanced into the hospital room, expecting to see what he'd seen all day.

But he didn't.

Riley snatched at the door handle and charged into the room. The bed curtain had been drawn, but through it – backlit by the fading daylight outside – he could see a tall, dark silhouette upright on the bed.

Riley stripped back the curtain to reveal Beckford, facing away from him. He was kneeling on the bed, suspended by a taut IV tube wrapped around his throat and tied to the metal grid that the ceiling tiles were meant to be attached to. The two removed fibreglass square panels lay on the floor.

'Oh shit,' said Riley. 'No. Shit, no-no-no, please…'

Riley clambered onto the bed and hooked an arm around Beckford's waist, lifting him as he tried to untie the tube from around his neck.

'No, no,' said Riley, '…HELP!'

Finally loosening the knot, the tube whipped free and Beckford slumped forwards. Riley grabbed him with both arms, then felt Beckford's body go tense. In a flash, Beckford's head whipped back, his crown smashing into Riley's nose.

There was pain of course, but it took Riley a good few seconds before he realised he was on the ground, the world around him spinning and a crimson river coursing down his chin. Beckford dragged the dazed constable into a blind spot by the door and unclipped his radio.

'Don't be getting any ideas,' said Beckford, unbuckling the man's belt.

It had been a while since Beckford had worn a police uniform. As a plain clothes detective, a suit let him blend in with the crowd. Now that he was wearing Riley's black trousers, white shirt and tactical duty vest, he'd be getting the public attention of a celebrity.

Handcuffing the bloodied and dazed Riley to a water pipe Beckford promised him he'd send in a doctor shortly, then waited for the coast to clear before leaving his room.

Despite his own cuts and bruises, Beckford hoped that the authority his uniform exuded would be enough to influence any confrontational hospital staff. But no confrontation came. No one even recognised him. Nurses and doctors just scuttled past him like worker ants, lost in their own busy responsibilities.

A few corridors away, Beckford informed a male nurse of a man bleeding profusely from his nose in room 514. Being a man of his word, Beckford didn't want Constable Riley to bleed to death. There was no room left in his conscience for that.

With the male nurse on his way, Beckford was on a timer. Once he'd made the stairs he shifted gear and dropped three at a time, pains shooting through his knee with each landing.

At the bottom of the flight, Beckford dumped his tactical vest and any other item that would mark him as a police officer. With just the shirt and trousers, he could be mistaken for a lax security guard or office worker.

Along the ground floor corridor he walked, casually but quickly, guiding himself through waves of visitors that clogged up the reception. Only when he bundled through the Royal London's main entrance onto Stepney Way did he start to jog, slowly at first, still struggling with the stabbing pain in his knee.

Then, like a slap on the arse of a racehorse, a wail of ambulance sirens made him jump and he sprinted, thankful that the cloak of night was creeping in.

With no money, no phone and only a short-sleeved shirt keeping him from the cold, Beckford had no idea where to turn. He was heading deep into the city, where his name was mud. It was only a matter of time before the city police were informed of his escape. So he kept on running and headed north towards Hackney.

After a while, his lungs were on fire and his knee felt like it was going to crack like ceramic. Slowing to a stop, he took refuge between two rubbish containers at the back of a pub where he stretched his leg and got his breath back, still unable to comprehend what was going on.

Was he still dreaming? He slapped himself hard across the face and it hurt like hell. Shame. A part of him wished he was back in the warm hospital bed. At least there he could slip back into dreamland, away from all this.

Dreams were his only escape. Even if somehow, magically, everything was reversed, the truth exposed and Beckford's name cleared… there was still one thing that couldn't be fixed. Graham Noakes' was dead and it was Beckford's fault.

Involving Noakes was a selfish act on his part, but entirely born out of desperation. There was a risk they'd be listening or watching, or that Noakes would drop his guard just long enough for them to trace him. Beckford had trusted that he'd look after himself. If he had known what was in store for the man, what lengths they'd go to, he would have kept his trap shut and carried on just trying to figure it all out by himself, as per usual.

Consumed in his thoughts, Beckford let an angry fist fly, crushing his knuckles into one of the steel bins. The clang echoed around the staff car park and a pain welled up in his hand and fell into step among all the other pains that consumed his body.

He hung there for a moment and closed his eyes, the distant sounds of main roads slowly fading as exhaustion pulled him closer towards sleep. Thoughts whizzed by unconsciously, with Beckford just a casual observer. Noakes' face made an appearance – his strong jawline, his silvery hair, his fearless eyes. Beckford felt a tingling at the back of his nose as a surge of emotion rushed up from his stomach. His eyes began to swell under their lids until it burned, then he sobbed again. The lonely, surrendering cry of a broken man.

Graham Noakes was as selfless a person as Beckford had met. A trait that constantly highlighted his own selfishness. The reality was that Beckford saw Noakes as a kind of father figure. During his darkest times, Noakes was one of a handful of people he could really talk to. It wasn't just about offloading worries and negative thoughts, it was about learning from them. Noakes was like a wise elder, passing down knowledge and experience from his generation to the next. That source of information was like a safety net for Beckford, and now it was gone he felt lost and alone.

Pushing his face into his shirt sleeve, Beckford wiped away the tears and savoured the almost euphoric feeling that occurred just after a big cry. His thoughts then turned to the tide he'd been battling against ever since he took apart Nikolai Guskov's computer. And as he crouched there in the dark between the bins, a preposterous thought entered his head.

Farber.

Yes, she'd delivered the computer to him, but why would she be involved?

Why would she want him dead?

It was preposterous, but could anyone blame him for thinking it? It was his job to see things from multiple different angles. Sometimes it seemed like the whole world was against him.

The only person he knew for certain that he could trust was now dead; Noakes' murder an unfortunate demonstration of his loyalty. And yet, as Beckford berated himself in the dark a glimmer of hope shot across his path, lifting his spirits.

Noakes must have found something they didn't want anyone to find.

THIRTY-ONE

On a quiet road in Crouch End, a 10-minute walk from Finsbury Park, a National Electrics van pulled up to the curb and parked. Two engineers got out, both wearing the same getup of heavy-duty boots, black overalls and high-vis jackets – the ultimate urban camouflage. No one even glanced at them as they went about their work.

One approached a British Telecom junction box on the pavement, tight up against a garden wall. Down on his knees, he unlocked the cabinet and started disconnecting cables while the other one watched.

A young woman passed wearing a thick coat and a skirt above her knees, a black and brown dachshund skipping at her heels. The watching engineer gave her a smile and ogled her arse as she went by.

From the cabinet, the other engineer pulled free an electrical device no bigger than a hotel bible. The cabinet was then locked again and the men got back into the van and drove off.

* * *

'Just the one node?' asked the Asian woman. Peltz nodded across the desk, then she added, 'What could he have gained access to?'

'Without usernames and passwords, not much.'

'Not much? Much of what? Be specific.'

Peltz sighed. 'Just the general configuration interface, which offers up no worthwhile information.'

'What about the usernames and passwords? Could he

have brute-forced his way in?'

'Only if he had a way to crack 128-bit encryption. Which, may I remind you, is pretty fucking difficult.'

The Asian woman's lips tightened.

'I'm sorry,' said Peltz, 'I'm knackered. Short fuse and all that. The node's on its way over. When the lab gets hold of it, they can tell you more.'

'How did he trace it in the first place?'

Peltz was really fucking tired of all these silly questions. 'How?' he said. 'How did the Chief Inspector of a Metropolitan Police e-crime unit, who's been in computer security for 30-odd years, trace the node?'

This time, the Asian woman tilted her head to the side, only slightly but enough for Peltz to know her patience was waning. 'You don't seem to be very phased by this breach, Dom.'

'I've had three hours sleep in the last 48. In that fucking closet with the stale farts of two other grown men. I am done in.'

'How could he trace the node?' she repeated.

Peltz sighed, lifted more coffee to his lips then realised he'd drank it all. He clinked the mug back onto the table, pressed his thumb and forefinger into the corner of his eyes and said, 'Notitia tracks keywords. Words we tell it to track. Noakes had my name and had gone looking for information on me, which is when he was flagged up on the system. We went digging in his computer and maybe that's how he did it – followed our inbound connection. But like I said, I don't think he got any further than the node.'

'Unless he's good at hacking 128-bit encryption?'

'Well… yeah.'

'But that's "*pretty fucking difficult,*" right?'

'There you are,' said Peltz, 'you learn something new

everyday.'

She looked at him with a face like thunder. Peltz waited, expecting there to be a slanging match, but she somehow managed to swallow whatever bile she was going to spit his way and told him he was free to leave.

Out in the corridor, Peltz felt far from free. Every conversation he'd had at the Studio had been laced with an accusatory tone – the ripples from Nikolai's suicide widening, the cost of their cover-up ballooning, and with all threads coming away at the seams their threat system Comminatio was throwing a wobbly.

With his name out in the public domain, Peltz felt tarred and feathered. People at the Studio were looking at him differently. Like he was a leper. They had the power to help him – to weave a story that put Peltz in a positive light. The only problem was it was always easier to spin bad lies than it was to spin good ones.

Back in the sleeping quarters, Peltz packed his things.

Ironically, he was somewhat omnipotent if he stayed in the building. They wouldn't do him there. "Don't shit where you eat" and all that.

But Peltz couldn't stay there for ever.

Without saying goodbye, he left the offices and rode the lift down with one hand in his bag, the feeling of the gun's grip comforting in his palm.

As he walked out across the dark car park, he held his head high, hoping to retain a glimmer of dignity if he were to just go out like a light bulb.

When Peltz was out of the grounds, he was in no man's land and dignity went out of the window. Jogging through the dark industrial estate, he swivelled nervously to the sounds and shadows around him.

The cab was late. Peltz stood under an overpass for what felt like an eternity, finger on the trigger at all times.

When the cab finally arrived, Peltz was wary. As he opened the door, he pretended to drop some loose coins in the gutter, giving him an excuse to get on his knees and check under the car's chassis. Apart from a slight oil leak, it was clear. They'd used that one before, certainly.

When he got into the back of the cab, he was surprised to see the same driver who'd dropped him off the day before. Coincidence, no doubt.

Peltz spent the journey back to his hotel chatting amicably with the man, the barrel of his gun buried into the back of the driver's seat where his driver's spine was located. It was how it was going to be until he found an escape. Or someone else did it for him.

* * *

Farber swiped her pass at the back entrance of HQ and pushed through into the car park. A cold wind lashed her hair to one side, but it was welcomed, blowing away the stuffy, humid office air that had clung to her like dust.

Taking a deep breath, she filled her lungs. It had been a hell of a double-shift – Beckford in the morning, Noakes in the afternoon, then the moment she got back to the station a couple of Richmond borough detectives were on hand to take her statement. What made matters worse was word of Beckford's escape came in halfway through the interview. That's when the detectives got really pushy. It was quite an emotional skirmish, and then some.

After the interview, she crept back to her desk under the prying eyes of her colleagues. Staedler sidled over and slid her a can of gin and tonic. It was warm, but Farber cracked the ring-pull and downed half of it straightaway. It settled her nerves, and with a taste for it she earmarked a bottle of rosé at home as her next victim.

The final hours of her shift dragged by, Michaels insisting she stick to admin work and stay station-bound for the meantime.

When she got into her car, she slammed the door shut and waited for the tears to fall. None came; too tired to cry. Revving the engine, she noticed a small strip of paper trapped under her one of her windscreen wipers. Winding the window down, she leaned out and snatched it.

You look like a drink

"You look like a drink" was an in-joke between her and Beckford. On their first date they'd gone to a North London wine bar called Ladel's. It was while Farber was being served that a sozzled man 20 years older than her leaned into her ear and said the now infamous line.

Farber stared at the words, contemplating a number of scenarios. Having just been through the ringer with Michaels, the Richmond duo and the soon-to-be IPCC bods, Farber wasn't sure meeting a known fugitive was a good idea. Then again it was her fault he escaped, which meant she could do with a drink.

Having been highlighted by the investigation team as one of Beckford's priority contacts – and rightly so – Farber doubled back on herself a few times. Then, leaving her phone and any other electrical device in the car, she grabbed the tube at Archway and went on a mini-adventure, jumping from line to line until she was fairly sure she wasn't being followed. By detectives or whoever.

It was karaoke night at Ladel's, which Farber thought was unusual for a trendy Camden wine bar. It was only when she got inside that she realised the place had taken a nosedive in class, now filled with a much younger crowd, predominantly city workers and what appeared to be a couple of hen-dos.

At one end of the main bar were two large women on a tiny stage, wailing Celine Dion in tandem. One of them had a great voice, but only one of them.

Farber made her way to the bar, straining to identify anyone through the coloured lights and drunken debauchery.

There was no sign of him.

Ordering herself a gin and tonic, she perched herself on a stool and scanned the room. It was not a place to remain sober.

She sat there for five minutes, eyeing everyone in sight and silently praying to god the lighting rig would drop and take out the Celine Dion wannabes, putting everyone out of their misery.

After a few minutes more, she took her drink and stalked the place, finding a quieter area at the back of the bar where the toilets were, a few arcade machines and seating booths backed onto a large mirrored wall.

Farber stood by a sparkling fruit machine, glad of the fact she wasn't epileptic as the flashing lights battered her retinas. All the booths were taken, occupied by groups or couples, apart from the last booth where a rough-looking man with glasses and a shaved head stared at her.

Farber turned back to the machine, and, as if the flashing jackpot light was above her head, the penny dropped.

Walking over to the man with the shaved head, Farber planted her drink on the table and slid onto the leather bench opposite.

'That's not a good look,' shouted Farber over the noise.

'There are worse aspects about my life,' said Beckford.

His head, shaved to the skin, was pock-marked with patches of hair and the occasional gash. It was far from a professional job. He wore what looked like a builder's coat with a thick woolen jumper underneath.

'Gone to the dogs, this place,' said Farber, then pointed at his drink. 'What's that? Rum and coke?'

'I don't know,' he said, 'it's not mine. I have no money. Everything I have is stolen.'

'Let me get you a—'

'I'm not here for a drink, Ali. I don't know why I'm here actually. Maybe just to see if you would turn up… or if someone else would.'

'John, I *believe* you. You wouldn't be sat here if I didn't.'

Beckford subconsciously rubbed his wrist where the handcuffs had bitten, then said, 'If I was in your shoes, I would have condemned me already. The evidence is all there, Ali. It's right there.'

'That's bollocks. Since when have you accepted any evidence on face value?'

'What if…' He let out a sigh, contemplating what he was about to say. 'What if… it's all true?'

He looked at her, expecting a dramatic change in her sympathetic look, but Farber's face remained the same. He continued.

'My head is so… I mean… I don't think I'm well. I haven't been for a while now, Ali, and… isn't it possible… that maybe I *did* do all those things?'

'You're not crazy, John.'

And you're qualified to make that diagnosis, are you?'

He shot a fidgety glance to a moving figure in his peripheral – just a swaying patron on a mission to the loo.

'Remember when we found out it was McGregor?' Beckford asked. 'You remember that? The manhunt… I spent those 16 nights wide awake, wondering where he was. I even thought that if I really tried I could somehow sense his location, like I was fucking psychic or something.

Now I'm the prey.'

'You're not like him, John. Don't say crap like that.' Farber leaned over the table, trying to keep quiet over the god-awful Axl Rose impersonator failing to hit the high notes. 'Look, people have tried to kill you twice and very nearly succeeded. That's more than most people can handle. Throw in all the stuff with Sally… you're probably suffering from some sort of PTSD. None of what you're feeling or thinking is because of who you are, it's just a reaction that anyone else would experience.'

Beckford looked down into the drink abandoned on his table, then lifted it to his lips, pausing before downing the whole lot. He grimaced slightly, perturbed by his action of going against the grain of his old OCD self. The one bonus from his exhaustion and desperation had been a reduction in his neuroticism, but it hadn't been worth the hassle. Not by a long way.

'Rum and coke,' said Beckford, smacking his lips together. 'Well done.'

'What are you going to do?' said Farber.

'Drink myself to death seems appealing right now.'

'I can give you money. Not for booze, for a hotel. You need rest.'

Beckford put his elbows on the table and started chewing the nail of his left thumb. 'You know,' he said, 'I think this is how they operate. I was a threat at one point. They wanted me gone quickly and quietly, but as soon as I went beyond their grasp, they put all this shit in place to frame me… and now I'm no longer their problem. I'm starting to wish they'd just snuffed me out on the stairs outside my apartment.'

'John, Corden believes you too. When you've got someone that high up in your corner, you're safe. Come on, think of all the many names we know who've had their arses saved by those on high. *And* they were guilty.'

'Maybe that's my problem,' said Beckford. 'Not corrupt enough.'

Farber took a sip of her drink then slid it over to him. Beckford took a mouthful and pushed the glass back.

'Anything on Noakes?' he said.

'They took all his computers.'

'Of course they did.'

'But there was one thing.' Farber pulled her phone from her bag, loaded up her pictures and swiped through a few until finding the one she wanted. She zoomed in and handed the phone over to Beckford.

'This is the number he dialled moments before calling you.'

Beckford examined the digits, scrawled in Staedler's messy handwriting.

212-6919-2200

Expecting his brain to kick into gear like it normally did when fed cryptic information, the revelation or insight or whatever it was never came. Instead he just stared, the pistons not firing. The numbers were numbers and the combination of his mental and physical fatigue made him feel like a superhero stripped of his powers.

'What's the area code?' he said.

'Doesn't exist.'

An idea popped into Beckford's head that made him uncomfortable.

'Maybe,' he said, '…maybe he was terrified and in pain and couldn't dial properly. Or they did it for him and he just rattled off a random number.'

'Maybe,' said Farber, nodding. 'Do you have a phone?'

'Only just. I "found" one on the bar.'

Beckford had stayed put while Farber went to the nearest cash machine. When she came back she stuffed £500 into his hands, which he quickly squirrelled into his jacket pocket. They agreed to meet again the next day. Same time, same place.

Farber left Ladel's alone as Beckford sat in the back, nursing the remains of her gin and tonic. For once, his thoughts were absent, blocked out perhaps by the ear-piercing version of Gloria Gaynor that filled the bar.

He turned the glass in his fingers, but it was only a minute or so before his eyelids felt heavy. Then he was out like a light.

While he slept his stockpiled thoughts started to unravel. Unrecognisable, intangible shapes and ideas clattered into one another like accelerated particles, every so often producing rare moments of clarity – Graham Noakes' bloodied corpse, accompanied by the unmistakable aroma of rotting human flesh. A hospital bed with a sweat-soaked pillow. Corden, her attire dark, almost fit for a funeral. Then it was Nikolai's dorm room and a bookcase that towered into the sky beyond which Beckford's eyesight could not reach.

Peter McGregor was then staring at him, his eyeballs turning to marble.

Then it was Farber's touch – her tender, soft skin. She was crying, but then she was bright eyed and beaming a smile, her face having switched in a microsecond like someone flipping a TV channel.

In the real world, Beckford had leaned back into the corner of the booth, his mouth slack; a sight not unusual for such a rowdy, alcohol-drenched boozer at this time of night.

Back inside his mind, he found himself up in the clouds at night as cracks of lightning whipped across the Earth.

Falling alongside the streaks of light, he edged closer and closer until a charged bolt absorbed him and struck the ground, its fingers surging through power and communication grids like digital tentacles.

Beckford could feel everything and everyone. He could hear people talk – millions of conversations happening simultaneously, overlapping each other in a cacophony of violent resonance that contracted into one focussed stream, a single note and then splitting apart again like microscopic fibres.

He could see them too – every person, every shape, every size, every colour – fluttering in front of his eyes at such speed it blurred into static.

The dream would have made no sense to an observer, but Beckford knew and understood what he could see, hear and feel. It was a representation of *information*. The lives of everyone on the planet, depicted by raw data that was – and had ever been – recorded.

'Come on, mate.'

Like being pulled through a wormhole, Beckford was tipped and dragged back to the noisy chaos of Ladel's.

An imposing doorman in black loomed over him, nudging his arm.

'You pissed, yeah?'

Beckford shook his head no, and unsteadily shimmied himself out of the booth and headed for the exit, bumping into people as he threaded himself through the crowd. He was still half-asleep, his brain elastic and open, continuing to process his thoughts subconsciously.

When the memory of Staedler's handwriting popped into his head, he froze to the spot, just before the doors. A middle-aged man was screaming ZZ Top, but Beckford wasn't paying attention. All he could think of was the telephone number, crystal clear in his head.

Only, it wasn't a telephone number.

THIRTY-TWO

Tossing and turning in a light slumber, Farber rolled over and opened her eyes. Sleep just wasn't happening, and the more it wasn't happening, the more frustrated she got. But how could she with everything that was going on?

Turning her head to the bedside table, she reached out and grabbed her phone. The screen blinded her for a second before her eyes settled on the time: 4:55 am. Only two hours had passed since the last time she'd checked.

Lying there with her phone still gripped tight, her thoughts naturally drifted to Beckford, hoping he was somewhere warm and safe. What did his future hold? Or hers, for that matter?

When her phone started buzzing in her hand, she jumped. Staedler's name flashed up and her heart leapt into her mouth.

'Len?' she said, answering.

'They've found him,' said Staedler.

'Who?'

'Who? John! He's at the Bell Tower Hotel in Westminster. They're sending a small army there right now. I'll be outside your door in five minutes.'

The phone went dead. Farber lay motionless, unable – or unwilling – to comprehend the words that had come through her phone. Beckford's future had finally caught up with him.

By the time Farber had got out of bed, tied her hair back, put on fresh underwear and her work suit, Staedler was waiting outside.

'What the fuck is going on?' said Farber, clicking in her

seat belt. Staedler floored the car and flicked the wipers on to battle the sleet.

'Unbelievable,' he said. 'A few hours ago, John sent an email to the National Cyber Crime Unit, spouting all sorts of stuff like he didn't do any of the shit they're trying to pin on him, blah blah blah. I've got a copy on my phone. Anyway, they traced the email's IP. Michaels is leading the raid, reckons he could be suicidal and needs a friendly face.'

'*Michaels*?' said Farber. 'Familiar, yes, but friendly…? Where's Corden?'

Staedler shrugged.

Farber stared out of the window and picked her nails. She had his number. She could message him to warn him, but it was probably too late.

* * *

Mohamed pulled the last stack of newspapers up onto the ice cream cabinet and slipped the Stanley knife under the plastic binding. There was a commotion outside of his shop and Nigel, his delivery man, came storming back inside in a huff.

'Can't you just let me get going?' he said over his shoulder to a police officer who followed him in. 'I've got to make six more stops in the next 20 minutes mate.'

'I understand this is an inconvenience, sir,' said the officer, 'but we will inform you when the operation is over and it is safe to leave. In the meantime, please keep the door closed and stay away from the windows. Thank you for your cooperation.'

The officer left, closing the shop door behind. Nigel stood there, steaming, as Mohamed crossed the store and peered through the window. He'd never seen so many people outside at five in the morning.

The Bell Tower Hotel was a 19th-century building boasting six stories and 110 rooms. Converted from a Victorian mansion house, the majestic orange and beige-bricked building sat proudly towards one end of Harrington Road on the south side of Hyde Park.

Despite its high-class exterior, the Bell Tower was only a three star, popular among tourists for its reasonable price and easy access to many of London's main attractions such as the Natural History Museum, Buckingham Palace and Harrods. Access wasn't so easy today. Both ends of Harrington Road had been blockaded by Armed Response Vehicles and swarming police officers. Units had also been deployed to the rear of the building, ensuring every exit was covered.

Around 50 yards or so from the hotel's main entrance were two marked vans parked on double-yellows, hidden from view of any hotel window by an outcrop of overhanging trees from the grounds of a neighboring building.

The van doors slid open and a team of Authorised Firearms Officers spilled out onto the pavement, clad head to foot in black and blue. Michaels was among them, suitably attired in Kevlar, although he was the only one unarmed.

The AFOs lined up against the wall where they ran last-minute checks on their equipment, each member carrying a Glock 17 pistol, with a few of them also bearing Heckler & Koch MP5 submachine guns.

'All right, listen up,' said Michaels, keeping his voice low. 'Beckford may be armed, but I don't want a single drop of blood on them carpets, understand? He's alive when we bring him down those steps.'

The team synchronously nodded and muttered affirmations. Michaels turned on his heels and off they went – a string of armed officers moving in single-file towards the hotel entrance, watched on by their uniformed colleagues and a small crowd of civilians.

Snaking up the stone steps of the Bell Tower, the officers poured into the hotel.

The reception was clean, but had a decor that belonged in the seventies – red patterned carpet, cream walls and oversized potted plants. An enormous glass chandelier levitated above a grand staircase of dark oak banisters and iron scroll balusters trailing up and out of sight.

The receptionist – a large woman with a name tag that said "Lynne" – sat behind the front desk reading a Lee Child novel. When her eyes lifted from the page she did a double-take as the lobby flooded with armed police in less time than it took to lose her place in the book.

Michaels approached the desk with haste and slapped a couple of sheets of paper in front of her.

'Good Morning, miss,' he said, pulling his ID lanyard from under his vest, 'I'm Chief Inspector Ray Michaels and for this Metropolitan Police operation we require your full cooperation.'

Lynne was speechless. She managed a nod, albeit a subtle one, and Michaels continued.

'We understand a man by the name of John or Jonathan Beckford is staying here, although he's most probably is using an alias. This is a photograph of him.'

He tapped the printout in front of Lynne, who leaned forward to take a look. Not recognising the face, she shook her head and turned to her computer, click-clacking away. After 30 seconds she looked back at Michaels, shook her head again and said, 'There's no one booked in under those names.'

Michaels nodded and slid the photo to one side, tapping the sheet underneath. 'In that case this here is a warrant that permits us to do a full room-to-room search of this hotel. Miss, we require a complete list of all occupied rooms and as many sets of master keys as you can give me. Thank you.'

The hotel rooms were whittled down by best-matched suspects; couples and families were ruled out, as he'd almost certainly be staying alone. The AFOs went up in pairs. One per floor, starting at the top and working down.

The corridors oozed even less class than the lobby with faux candlestick lamps on the walls and old generic paintings with brushed gold frames. Michaels accompanied a seasoned AFO called Carla O'Brien. At five foot two, O'Brien was dwarfed when she stood alongside Michaels, but what she lacked in height she made up for in strength. "Built like a brick shithouse," some might say, and when she wasn't storming buildings she was hurling weights down the police gym and practicing Brazilian jiu-jitsu.

On the fourth floor O'Brien led the way, her MP5 clamped against the crook of her arm, barrel pointing down. There were three rooms on the fourth floor that housed possible suspects. Passing a number of doors, they reached the first on their list: 406. Sliding his palm over the peephole, Michaels rattled his knuckles on the door.

'Room service,' he said softly.

There was no answer. Michaels slid the keycard into the handle, producing a green light and a beep. He primed the handle, nodded to O'Brien, and pushed open the door for her as she propelled in, weapon raised.

'Armed police! Armed police!'

A young Spanish man, no older than 21, shot up in bed, launching his arms into the air. Michaels checked the bathroom and pulled back the shower curtain. O'Brien looked under the bed and in the wardrobe.

'Sorry to disturb you,' said O'Brien and they left, closing

the door behind them.

Further down the corridor they stopped outside room 413. O'Brien went to knock this time but Michaels stopped her. He shook his head and slotted the key card into the door.

Beep.

O'Brien entered first.

'Armed police! Armed police!'

He was sat at the dressing table in his underwear, fingers still on the laptop keyboard. The shock took his breath away, but when his eyes landed on Michaels, his face changed.

'What the fuck are you doing here?' he said.

And that was the last thing he said. His body jolted and his eyes bulged as two muted pops punched 9mm holes into his chest. O'Brien swivelled to Michaels who was already crossing the room before Peltz's body had slid off the chair.

Pitching the barrel of her MP5 pitched towards the carpet, O'Brien took slow, uncertain steps into the room, confounded by what just happened. As Michaels placed a smoking, silenced Glock on the dressing table, she noticed he was wearing latex gloves.

'Jesus,' she said. 'Ray…?'

Michaels took three small pen drives from a pouch on his vest and slotted them into each of Peltz's laptops.

'I need you to trust me, Carla,' he said, eyes glued to the screens. O'Brien just stood there, the respect she'd harboured for Michaels over the years drying up in an instant. Looking back over her shoulder, she saw that the door to the room was now closed. Michaels had planned this.

Flashing up on the laptop screens were crude images of mushroom clouds, an application called "Nuclear

Meltdown" loading up on each. With haste, Michaels clicked the buttons labelled "System Wipe." Warning messages popped up on each screen, which he quickly clicked "Yes" to, one by one, as progress bars appeared, visualising the data as it was being removed.

'Ray. You know I'd go through hell for you…'

Michaels wasn't listening. The system wipe completed in a matter of seconds and automatically rebooted the laptops. Dragging the pen drives out one by one, Michaels inserted another set into each.

On the screens, a pre-packaged script executed, running through a number of commands. Michaels left them processing and began rummaging through one of Peltz's suitcases that lay alongside his corpse.

'Ray…' said Carla. 'Fucking hell, say something! Who was he?'

Michaels moved to another suitcase, digging around and pulling dirty clothes free.

'What are you involved with here?' said Carla.

Michaels finally looked up at her. It was the first time O'Brien had seen any kind of fear on the face of the Wolf.

'Why did you have to partner me, Carla?'

His hand pulled free of the suitcase and two deafening blasts followed. O'Brien shuddered and clasped both hands around her throat. She dropped to her knees, blood spitting through her fingers from a hole in her windpipe. As she gargled, she fell forwards, hitting her head on the side table and landing awkwardly.

Michaels let the gun clatter to the side of Peltz's corpse, then got on his radio.

'OFFICER DOWN! OFFICER DOWN!' he shouted. 'ROOM FOUR-ONE-THREE. REPEAT, FOUR-ONE-THREE.'

The radio crackled with acknowledgements.

The next few seconds were crucial.

Grabbing the Glock from the dressing table, Michaels unscrewed the silencer and pocketed it. With the same gun, he got down on one knee and clasped one of O'Brien's limp, blood soaked hands around the grip, careful to avoid contaminating himself. He then unclipped O'Brien's issued Glock and wedged it under his vest, out of sight.

By that time, the scripts had finished processing and had shut down the laptops. Michaels unplugged the pen drives and peeled off his gloves, pocketing the lot. With O'Brien's corpse blocking his way, he rolled across the bed, opened the room door and got into place in the hallway.

The scene was set.

Ticking a checklist in his head, Michaels processed the forensic information and sequence of events that would be scrutinised in the coming months. On the surface, it was a fairly simple fit-up, but he knew even the smallest infraction could see the IPCC take him to court.

The only piece of data that would expose him as a murderer was the serial number on the Glock lying in O'Brien's bloodied fingers. But by the time he'd even had the thought, the switch had been made. It was O'Brien's weapon now.

Taking a deep breath, Michaels prepared himself as the sound of running footsteps vibrated through the ceiling and unseen corridors. If there had been even a hint of shock in his system, he could have used it to theatrical effect. After all, it had been well over a year since he last took someone's life.

But there was no shock; that only affected the minds of the inexperienced.

Michaels had done his job, and despite the combined friendship of Carla O'Brien and Dominic Peltz totalling 20-plus years, any emotion was dismissed with an enforced discipline. It was the way things were and the way it had to be.

THIRTY-THREE

Beckford had watched the entire scene at the Bell Tower unfold from the roof of another building 500 yards away. From the moment he clicked "send" on his email, it had taken 27 minutes before the first of the fleet came rolling into town, then a further 15 minutes before the deserted road was a flash mob of police activity.

An impressive turn out, he thought, and it was all thanks to Noakes and his mysterious telephone number.

Only, it wasn't a telephone number. It was an IP address.

212.69.192.200

In Noakes' final moments, with his soon-to-be killers waiting for him to make the call, he'd punched the IP into his phone, pretending to dial Beckford before palming it off as an honest mistake and dialing the real number.

When the realisation came to Beckford, it was like the pins dropping in the tumbler of a lock. He needed to get to a computer fast – and in the early hours of the morning, he knew only one place he could access one.

* * *

He'd decided to take a cab, using 50 of Farber's hard earned pounds to get him to where he needed to be. Once by the side of Willow's house, he peered into the back garden; above him loomed a small black box, which – when his eyes finally adjusted to the darkness – he identified as a motion sensor floodlight.

Her parents were certainly tucked up in bed, but Willow on the other hand was probably battling soldiers from the future on an alien planet. Three in the morning was early for her.

Hugging the house, Beckford crept under the floodlight until he arrived at the first of two sunken windows that led to the basement – Willow's bedroom/bunker.

Getting down on his haunches, he peered into the dark, frosted window. Either Willow was in bed or she had blackout curtains fitted. Either way, he needed her help, but with his knuckles primed to knock the glass, the floodlight clicked on and filled the garden with a stark beam.

'Who the fuck are you?' said Willow, stood no more than 10 feet from Beckford. In the harsh light he could see she was carrying a cricket bat.

'Sshh,' said Beckford, gingerly getting to his feet and side-stepping onto the grass and into the light. Recognising him straightaway, Willow's face screwed up in disgust.

'The fuck happened to you?'

'Keep it down,' said Beckford.

'Calm your tits,' she said, 'they're in Wales for the week.'

Beckford let his shoulders relax a bit, then said, 'I take it you don't watch the news, then?'

'Why the fuck would I poison my mind with that nasty shit?'

Without having to give an explanation for his presence at such hour, Willow invited him inside, leading him through the kitchen and into the hallway, through a locked door and down a steep set of rickety stairs that took Beckford back a year to the day he met Willow.

'You're gonna have to gimme your phone,' she said, stopping at another locked door at the bottom of the stairwell. Beckford patted himself down and held up his empty hands.

'Phoneless,' he said.

Willow's eyes narrowed, then she turned to the door, cupped the keypad and punched in the code.

The basement, while cramped, was no ordinary basement. There were no shelves carrying tins of paint, no mountain bike stacked against the wall and no washer dryer shuddering away on a cycle.

The last time Beckford was down there was to confiscate Willow's computer from a small table at the foot of her bed. The rest of the space had been a teenager's paradise – faux-leather couch, massive TV, surround sound speakers, games consoles, mini fridge and a tower of pizza boxes stacked high like a Greek column.

Things had certainly changed since then.

On either side of the room were two large desks, each with back-to-back computer workstations and banks of monitors that made Beckford wonder if Willow no longer worked alone, and that perhaps she'd started a business managing hedge funds.

Where was the mess? Her gaming zone?

In a recess at the back of the room was a seven-foot server cabinet that whirred, flashed and pumped out heat, which was counteracted by two portable air conditioning units, both of which had their exhaust pipes running up and out through the wall. On another wall was a strip of TVs showing a variety of network monitoring interfaces, live cryptocurrency values and CCTV from locations in and outside of her house.

'Where's your bed?' said Beckford.

'My brother's old room. I sleep up there now.' She turned to him and folded her arms. 'Is *that* what you came for?'

Beckford realised what he'd said, but before he could try to worm his way out of it, Willow snickered and took a seat at one of the desks.

'I do watch the news,' she said, logging into the computer.

'Then why did you invite me in?'

'Because I've met kiddie fiddlers before, and you ain't a kiddie fiddler.'

Knowing how brazen Willow was, Beckford wouldn't be surprised if she spent some of her online time being a vigilante, honey-trapping perverted men and ruining their lives. It would certainly help appease some of her racked-up guilt from her other illegal activities, assuming she had any.

'I take it you need my help?' said Willow.

'That depends.'

He gave her the number. A taster of what was to come. Pulling up a chair, Beckford sat and watched Willow open a command prompt and type: '`ping 212.69.192.200`.'

She hit enter and the screen filled with text:

```
Pinging 212.69.192.200 [212.69.192.200] with 32 bytes of data:
Reply from 212.69.192.200 : bytes=32 time=30ms TTL=58
Reply from 212.69.192.200 : bytes=32 time=32ms TTL=58
Reply from 212.69.192.200 : bytes=32 time=32ms TTL=58
Reply from 212.69.192.200 : bytes=32 time=28ms TTL=58
```

It was alive. A computer, a router, a phone – whatever it was, Noakes' discovery was now making a digital handshake with Willow's network, sending a buzz of energy vibrating through Beckford's battered body.

'What is it?' said Willow.

'That's what I need your help with.'

Beckford had every intention of protecting Willow from the same bastards who'd murdered Noakes. He kept it brief and cryptic, but Willow wouldn't stop asking questions, causing Beckford to get flustered, his brain too slow and mushy to keep up with her incessant requests for details.

'What do you mean they can change things?' said Willow, getting impatient.

'They can access any data,' said Beckford, '...anywhere, and change it to anything they want.'

With a disbelieving smirk on her face, Willow said, 'DarkBrain? Do fuck off.'

'Dark-what?' said Beckford. 'Dark*Brain*?... What the hell's that?'

'A myth,' said Willow, turning back to her computer. 'Few years ago, word got round about a new botnet by that name. Apparently it could get behind any firewall and give total, unrestricted access to the user. The only problem was people couldn't prove it existed. Personally, I think it was a fucking rumour started by some prick script-kiddie, but it stuck for a while and caused a boom in botnets, with every noob trying to write their own.

'Including you?'

'I wrote MagNet *wayyyy* before DarkBrain came on the scene.'

'You don't think it's possible then? For software to exist that can get into anything, anywhere, undetected?'

Willow looked at him again, the same smirk on her face.

'Are you fucking serious? GCHQ? NSA? *Helloooo…* those cunts are watching us *all the time.* I wouldn't be surprised if they're the ones framing your ass.'

Great, thought Beckford. *First bent cops, now the government.*

'You wanna know where this IP goes or what?' Willow asked.

Before she was first arrested, Willow spent most of her time on a crappy computer, annoying people on the internet for the "lulz" – a phrase that just meant "amusement," typically at someone else's expense.

A lot had changed in a year. There was a sophistication about her lair now, and while Willow had never discussed her own exploits as they drove around the block trading prescriptions of Lexapro and Xanax, Beckford got the impression she had relegated "lulz" for more serious jobs. The type of serious jobs that paid serious money. The kind of money needed to purchase the serious kit surrounding them now.

Willow had more digital fingers in digital pies than Beckford had anticipated, and after agreeing to her help he sat in awe watching her do her thing – fingers dancing across the keyboard like an automated machine; windows popping up on screens, flooded with information; software and prompts, from which she blitzed strings of commands at an almost inhuman speed.

Beckford struggled to keep up, losing his place at times. Every now and then he had to interrupt her with queries like, 'Is that for—' and Willow would interrupt him back, answering his question by completing his sentence for him.

There were aspects of the hack Beckford couldn't make head nor tail of; it was technically superior to anything he'd learned or applied at the HTCU. He wasn't a big believer in natural talent, but witnessing a 16-year-old girl make child's play of top-level security systems tested his knowledge.

There was no doubt about it, Willow would be a highly valued employee at Water Street. *Christ*, he thought, *she could be working for the NCCU, army or the government.* But where was the fun in that?

On screen, Willow started to construct an SQL query, which told Beckford she'd found a way into the database, past the firewalls, gateways and other incredibly secure barriers that were supposed to prevent people like her doing what she was doing.

'Is that BT's customer database?' said Beckford, leaning in and trying his best to contain his almost childlike excitement.

'One of them,' she said.

Davies had always been Beckford's ISP man. What would he think if he knew Beckford was an accomplice to the security breach of the largest telecom companies in the country?

That was when Beckford's excitement morphed into panic.

What if they were watching?

What if they traced it back to them?

He'd warned Willow to be extra vigilant in covering her tracks, but she just laughed at him and said, 'purr-leaaase.'

The SQL query she'd written was long and convoluted, and given a few minutes Beckford could have probably worked out precisely what the hell it was doing. For now though, he had the gist of it – to match Noakes' IP and date of the day he died to a vast consumer database.

Willow hit enter and a progress icon appeared, circling on repeat as the query searched the hundreds of tables, thousands of rows and millions of cells of data.

Finally, one match came back:

```
Mr James Melling
The Bell Tower Hotel
11 Harrington Road
London
SW7 3EQ
```

Beckford was confused. He'd expected to see a name he recognised, but James Melling drew a blank. A quick web search revealed he was the ex-manager of the Bell Tower Hotel, his name just hadn't been updated on the ISP account.

Beckford leaned back in his chair and sighed towards the soundproofed ceiling.

'A hotel?' he said, '…a *public* connection? Why did it have to be a public connection?'

In the world of computer forensics, public internet connections were like town bikes, letting any anonymous user jump on without so much as swapping names. If only the IP address had led them to one device and one person; everything would have been a hundred times simpler.

Opening her second can of Coke that hour, Willow asked him what he wanted to do. Beckford mulled it over. How had Noakes discovered the IP in the first place? And what significance lay behind it?

Beckford had desperately wanted it to be Dominic Peltz. Maybe it *was* him… a guest at the hotel. Beckford had read about hackers who'd set up camp in hotels. It was ideal for them, blending into the fast-turnover crowd with the ability to up and leave if things got too hot. It gave them the physical anonymity that they were so used to in the digital domain.

While Beckford sat in silence, chewing the skin off his index finger, Willow turned back to her computer and got to work, fingers click-clacking across the keyboard. After

10 minutes Beckford had drawn blood, and Willow wheeled back in her chair, unveiling a list of names on her monitor – all current guests at the Bell Tower.

Beckford didn't recognise a single one of them. Why would he have? Peltz, or whoever, would be using a pseudonym. Every name on the list could have been a pseudonym. And why would he even take it at face value? Willow could have just typed it up herself for all he knew.

Standing from his chair, Beckford stretched and started pacing the room, hoping to get the blood flowing. Willow started typing again.

'What are you trying now?' said Beckford.

'Vetting the guest information,' she said. 'If we can find even one abnormality or erroneous—'

'You're not getting it,' said Beckford. 'They can *invent* people. People with real histories, real jobs and real families. You could spend your life chasing breadcrumbs down a path, but they'll always be one step ahead of you.'

'Well, one of those names on the list might be your guy.'

'You're right, but what can I do then? Go and knock on each door in the hotel and ask, "*Hello, are you a hacker?*"'

'Not you,' said Willow, '...but how about we get the police to do it?'

An hour later, after slipping through the entrance of an apartment block at 34–50 Harrington Road, Beckford found himself on the roof, observing the street below through an old pair of Nikon binoculars belonging to Willow's dad.

It was 4:22 am.

For the most effective disruption, Beckford had sent his email to a number of well-managed public addresses in the Metropolitan Police, including the National Cyber Crime Unit. It had to be seen by many in order to lower the chances of intervention and manipulation.

From the moment the first duty officers arrived on scene, Beckford was glued to the action like James Stewart in *Rear Window*. He was the host of the party, and it was exciting and terrifying in equal measures.

If Beckford's suspicions were correct, the Bell Tower was a hideout for corrupt Metropolitan police officers. But what if the raid found nothing but charming staff and a viable option for dirty weekends? If it wasn't for the fact that Beckford had been framed as a paedophile and almost killed twice, he would have felt guilty watching taxpayers' money pour out of the accumulating vehicles below.

But he had to put his trust in Noakes.

With no way of identifying the user behind the IP address, Willow and Beckford had inverted the problem. What if they made the police think it was *Beckford* behind the IP?

Using a popular hacking technique called spoofing, Willow was able to route Beckford's online traffic through Noakes' IP, making it appear to any digital expert that he was inside the Bell Tower.

Its ingenuity was two-fold. By sending his email, he'd surreptitiously coerced legitimate police to flush out the hotel for him. And if his enemies really had their fingers on the pulse, they'd want to be there to control it. With that in mind, and a personal morbid curiosity, Beckford was intrigued to see who'd turn up to his party.

But he never did.

THIRTY-FOUR

It was him. He was sure of it.

After the AFOs entered the hotel, Beckford waited with bated breath, searching the pavement below; observing groups of onlookers and the officers who floated between them. It was still dark, which – even with the help of Willow's dad's Nikons – made it difficult to identify any staff who'd turned up for the show. Every now and then, random faces would materialise under streetlights, but it was usually too fleeting for Beckford to get a good look.

As the magnified geography of Harrington Road panned inside his binoculars, an image flashed up like a single frame slotted secretly into an old film.

A skull, illuminated in the darkness.

Before he could even question it, it had disappeared beyond the scope of the binoculars and he couldn't find it again.

A skull? Was he seeing things? It had been over 24 hours since he'd been drugged. Enough time for it to have left his system, surely.

With his eyes buried in the Nikons, he frantically searched the canvas below, left to right, up and down, blindly hoping to stumble on the image again.

Then it dropped back into view and Beckford refocussed.

The skull had big, cartoon eyes and was turned slightly to one side, its tongue sticking out like a rock star. It was an image synonymous with youth and music, but there was an unnatural familiarity to it. Where had Beckford seen it before?

As he panned up, he saw the skull was printed on the back of a black jacket worn by an unknown figure. The person had their hood up and was facing away towards the hotel entrance, which was the focal point of everyone in the vicinity; everyone but Beckford.

Like a dream, the remnant memory of the skull could have easily been lost for ever. But upon seeing it again, a chasm opened from which Beckford unravelled a slew of memories from the night he was dragged from the lake.

He remembered the blood rushing to his head as he was carried over someone's shoulder. Lying in the wet grass and the incongruous sight of a phone box. A hooded figure peering down at him and saying something, then turning away, the sudden orange blast of a street light hitting his sensitive retinas like a supernova.

It was at then, after his vision had settled, that he saw the skull for the first time. A devilish apparition that he'd carried with him, skirting the outer limits of his thoughts as he drifted in and out of consciousness in his hospital bed. It was only now that he held the memory in a firm grip.

With the bins still glued to his eyes, Beckford got to his feet. The figure was stood on the corner of a side road, peering around a row of shops a good distance away from the escalating police activity. The figure's body language implied fear, dipping out of sight every now and then to avoid being seen by the cops.

'Joseph…' whispered Beckford.

Had he been his anonymous helper all along?

Beckford needed to know, and with the raid already in progress, the skull was as solid a lead as he could have wished for. Quickly, he made his way down the fire escape, the rusty structure ratting with his urgent footsteps, pulling on the fixtures and sending steel squeals bouncing off the adjacent building.

Once he was on Harrington Road, he could hear the operation in progress – the soft pattering of feet, radio chatter, vehicle doors sliding open and slamming shut, orders spoken, not shouted. Beckford wasn't watching any of it though, his eyes were looking at the empty space that the hooded figure occupied less than a minute ago.

Beckford carried on, drifting in and out of cars, avoiding streetlights as best he could, making sure not to veer too close to the police perimeter. If it wasn't for the fact he was wired with adrenaline and on a mission, he'd find the whole situation almost amusing – an army of police storming a hotel, looking for the man who was running up and down behind them, mooning and sticking two fingers up at the back of their heads.

No one would believe it.

The shop where the skull had lurked turned out to be an estate agents. Beckford stopped at the doorway and faced the ongoing operation with feigned interest, casually throwing glances up and down the road, searching, hoping. The excitement that had bubbled in his belly barely minutes before had now turned acidic. Anxiety was coming, and he reconsidered something that had been increasingly frequenting his thoughts of late: was he in fact going mad?

How else to explain the inexplicable?

Warming his hands with his breath, he found himself caught up in the operation outside of the Bell Tower Hotel. Now closer to the action and equipped with a pair of binoculars, Beckford was able to identify a few of the officers, some of them his immediate colleagues. All ex-colleagues now.

As he lowered the bins and looked down the side street behind him, two distant pops echoed from the hotel, causing him to snap his head back around. The civilians out on the street would have thought someone had just stood on a crisp packet or two, but every police officer on the scene knew a firearm had just been discharged. A nearby radio crackled.

'Shots fired! Shots fired!'

In an instant the atmosphere outside the hotel transformed. Ambulances were radioed in. Car engines revved up in order to clear the way. A second group of AFOs stormed the hotel entrance, some taking up position outside, weapons raised for a worst-case scenario with fingers on triggers. Beckford was transfixed, his mind whizzing through a raft of questions:

Who fired shots?

Was anybody hit?

Where in the hotel was the incident?

Was it Peltz or just some random shooting?

Along with his curiosity came a sense of self-justification. Baiting a sizeable chunk of London's police force had been a pretty bold – or stupid – thing to do. But now the gunshots had vindicated him.

As police activity increased, Beckford retreated into the shadows of the estate agent's recessed doorway. When he flicked his eyes away from the drama, he froze. On the other side of the road, where the side street continued, was the hooded figure, similarly drawn to the action like a moth to a flame.

He then turned in Beckford's direction – a black void in the hood of his jacket. A death-like apparition. Beckford remained statuesque, unsure if he could be seen or not. The hood stared for what felt like an eternity, until it turned back to the hotel as a pulse of blue lights whipped across the buildings and cars.

Unaware of his decision to move, Beckford found

himself sprinting flat-out, taking advantage of the distracting ambulance to rush the hooded figure like a leopard from the bushes. And like a gazelle, the figure saw him and instinctively turned and darted up a side street.

There was no pain in Beckford; he felt like he was running faster than ever, as if he had younger legs and younger blood. Up ahead the figure would disappear then reappear under each streetlight. A fast runner, but Beckford was faster, and for each sleeping shop they passed Beckford gained a few feet, closing in on him like a heat-seeking missile.

Turning on a sixpence, the figure dodged between parked cars and into the road. Beckford copied his move step for step, his lungs heaving, recycling the icy cold air. At the end of the road, headlights turned in exposing the figure's silhouette, his hood having fallen down.

He peeled off into the parked cars on the other side and Beckford did the same, reaching the pavement just in time to see the figure take a left at the junction. A few more seconds and he made the turn himself, slamming on the brakes and skittering to a stop.

On the pavement the figure lay in a heap, grunting and gripping his leg in agony. Just in front of Beckford was a sheet of ice reflecting the harsh streetlight above. He'd have crouched down and kissed it if it wouldn't have taken his lips off.

'Don't run,' said Beckford between breaths. The figure pulled his hood back over his head and eased up onto one leg, but he gasped through gritted teeth. Beckford put money on a fracture.

'You need a doctor?' he said.

The figure – who from the sound of his panting was young, possibly in his twenties – continued his attempt at walking, limping on one foot and barely letting the other touch the ground before quickly shifting his weight back to the left. It was futile, and yet he continued.

Bypassing the ice patch, Beckford walked up close behind him, his heart jackhammering in his chest and showing no sign of slowing down. It was excitement. He'd finally got him.

'Oi!' he shouted. 'I said do you need a doctor?'

Turn him around.

Look at his face.

It was as if Beckford was teasing himself; a cat with an injured mouse, toying with it, savouring the moment. The suspense was almost unbearable.

'No doctor,' said the figure.

Beckford was jarred. He'd never heard Joseph Winterburn talk, but it was only now that he questioned the accent. It was the same voice from the lake. Definitely. The one that had echoed through Beckford's mind as he lay in hospital. The voice that – at the time, muddied by the drugs and whisky and exhaustion – now sounded crystal clear, as if the biting temperature had frozen the air molecules in perfect harmony, allowing sound waves to travel without effort.

The lad had stopped. Beckford did too, unsure of what was about to happen.

'Turn around,' said Beckford.

'I helped you. Just let me go.'

'You did, and I want to know who to owe my gratitude. Turn around.'

A car came down the road, the headlights blinding until it hit a speedbump and they both saw the unmistakable blue and yellow decals on the chassis. Beckford dropped behind a parked car, and the lad did the same with the next one along. The police car passed and turned up the road they'd just come from.

As the car's engine faded away, Beckford watched the lad make himself comfortable on the pavement, leaning back against a car and testing a variety of movements on his damaged leg.

Enough of this shit.

Beckford got to his feet and walked over, grabbing the lad's hood and pulling it back.

Eyes looked up at him. *Those eyes.*

Like Beckford, the lad's head was shaven to the skin, but it was his nose, his mouth… his *fucking face.*

Beckford blinked, the shock so great he expected to wake up back in the hospital, ready to blame the drugs for addling his mind. It would have made more sense. Anything made more sense than *this.*

How could it be true?

The bitter breeze slapped Beckford's cheeks, reminding him he was awake, alert and in the real world, no matter how fucked up everything seemed. Then Beckford finally spoke.

'Nikolai?'

THIRTY-FIVE

He didn't talk much.

Beckford wondered whether Nikolai's English was any good at all, this being the only time he'd heard the lad speak outside of the carefully scripted video that had burned itself into his memory. The video that was now confirmed to be, as suspected, entirely fabricated.

Unless…

'You're a twin,' said Beckford, crouching over him, still in abject shock. Nikolai looked down and muttered something in Ukrainian. The last morsel of Beckford's patience vanished in an instant, replaced by a red mist.

He dropped a knee on the Nikolai's damaged leg and the lad let out an awful yelp that echoed off the surrounding shops and flats.

'AM NOT FUCKING TWIN!' he spat.

Beckford lifted his knee, allowing Nikolai to roll over and caress his leg with both hands, muttering things to himself. Beckford straightened up and glanced down the street. Windows were still dark and there was no new movement. He wanted to interrogate the lad right there and then, but he could still hear the Bell Tower operation in progress.

'Can you stand?' he said, holding out a hand. Nikolai looked up venomously, his face accentuated by the street light brushing his strong cheekbones and forehead, making his eyes look like sunken pits of oil. When he shuffled into an upright position, he grimaced and let a pained puff of air escape from between his teeth. Beckford grabbed him under the arm.

'I can do it!' said Nikolai.

'There's no time for pride,' said Beckford. 'The sun'll be up soon.'

Nikolai hesitated, then finally let Beckford take his weight and they slowly but surely rose to their feet. Beckford pulled Nikolai's arm up and over his neck and got a strong whiff of cigarettes and body odour.

'If you can't walk on it, it's probably broken.'

They took a few steps forward, Nikolai only managing to hop lightly on his right leg before jumping back to his left.

'No doctor,' he said.

'Well where do you want to go then, eh? We're smack-bang in the centre of London and you can't walk.'

Nikolai put his free hand in his pocket. Beckford saw the glint of steel, and in a fraction of a second he'd driven Nikolai up against a brick wall, twisting his right arm behind his back and adding extra torque to be sure. Nikolai let out another cry and sunk, his injured leg giving way.

Unclenching Nikolai's immobilised hand, Beckford heard a metallic jangle as a set of keys came loose. Nikolai hissed another slew of vehement Ukrainian, most likely a chain of obscenities, possibly involving Beckford's mother.

'My bike! My bike!' said Nikolai, pointing to a lamppost where a chained mountain bike leaned. Leaving Nikolai to hobble back on his feet, Beckford approached the bike, trying various keys in the lock until he found the right one.

'Can you sit on this?' he said, wheeling the bike over. Nikolai took hold of one handle and with great effort and agony, lifted his damaged leg over the crossbar and lowered himself on to the saddle, slumping forward over the handlebar and catching his breath. Putting his good foot on a pedal, he pressed down, but the bike sprang back as if attached to something.

'I'm not letting go of this seat,' said Beckford.

Nikolai craned his neck. 'You think I ride with this leg?'

'If you can fake your own death, you can fake a broken leg. Now, let's move.' Beckford pushed him on and Nikolai placed both feet on the pedals, making it look oddly like a father teaching his son how to ride.

'We go to my place,' said Nikolai.

'No, you're coming with me.'

'No, no, no… please. We go to my place. Please.'

Beckford stopped the bike. Even though he had the upper hand in the immediate situation, he still felt totally lost. Who was this greasy adolescent he was pushing on a bike? A digital magician? Was he even Ukrainian?

Take him to Willow's and tie him up.

'I don't want to go anywhere else,' said Nikolai. 'Please John.'

The use of his name made Beckford feel uneasy. It was obvious Nikolai knew a lot more about him than he knew about Nikolai, and with the lad's face buried in shadow it added an apt visual representation of his deceit and Beckford's inability to read him. That was where Nikolai had the upper hand. But it was the kid's voice that swayed him; full of the same fear and paranoia that Beckford had become accustomed to. Sure, it was possible that Nikolai was a just good actor. No, an *amazing* actor, but Beckford hadn't met many computer geniuses who were so connected to their emotions.

Is he even a computer genius?

Beckford started pushing the bike again, interrupting his thoughts before they inevitably snowballed into madness. As soon as they'd be alone and in private, Beckford was going to get answers.

They travelled for 20 minutes in silence, heading towards the Thames, the only sound between them a dislodged brake pad on the bike's back tyre brushing the wheel rim every two steps.

'It was you, wasn't it?' said Beckford, cutting through the dead-air. 'Anon27?'

There was no reply.

'How's the leg?'

Nikolai sat up on the bike and slapped his good leg. 'Fine,' he said, leaning back over the handlebar. Although Beckford couldn't see his face, he sensed a smirk.

'I'm trusting you here, Nikolai.'

He wasn't, he was just placating the situation while screams of paranoia echoed through his own conscience. '…I hope you're not planning on pulling any shit.'

Nikolai let out a tut. 'If I wanted you dead, I would have let you drown.'

A memory. The rush of water spilling from his lungs and mouth. A liberating sensation, as if someone had just popped a Champagne cork. He also remembered the skull on a black jacket again. The same skull he was now looking at, sat on the bike he had hold of.

'I'd be halfway round world if it wasn't for you,' said Nikolai. 'You like digging nose into place it does not belong. I feel responsible for you.'

Regardless of the reason why Beckford had almost become fish food in his own car, the Ukrainian had saved his life and most likely put his own in danger. It pained Beckford more to withhold any gratitude than it would to lower his guard and let the lad have it, but he had to maintain dominance.

A further 10 minutes and they'd crossed the Albert Bridge and headed south into Battersea.

'Down here,' said Nikolai, turning the bike left. They entered a cul-de-sac, long enough for a handful of town houses. Halfway down Nikolai put the brakes on and they stopped outside a row of garages. He limped off the bike and held out a hand.

'Keys.'

With his wits dialled up to 11, Beckford handed over the set of keys, all the while scrutinising Nikolai's every move with intense focus, bracing himself for any kind of unexpected and unwelcome surprise.

Nikolai hobbled to one of the garage doors, unlocked it and – with a slight jolt as pain shot through his leg – heaved it above his head, revealing a gaping hole of blackness.

Hobbling back, he grabbed the bike and pulled. Beckford still had hold of it. They locked eyes.

'You want to stay out in cold?' said Nikolai, gesturing to the street. He had a point, Beckford's right hand gripping the bike saddle was like ice. He relaxed his fingers and the bike released into Nikolai's control for the first time since he'd hopped on it. Beckford buried his ice-block hands in his pocket and his fingers started to throb like he'd been carrying heavy shopping for too long.

Wheeling his bike into the garage, Nikolai disappeared into the darkness. Beckford didn't move. He could hear sounds, but couldn't see anything. Shuffling. Clanging.

What's he up to? Should I run?

Nikolai had the advantage now. He also had access to guns. Beckford's skin started to tingle, then a single bulb flicked on, illuminating the garage. Nikolai was in the far corner, leaning his bike against the wall and turning on an electric fan heater.

Taking a few cautious steps inside, Beckford looked around.

In the opposite corner to Nikolai was a fold out camping bed with a blue pillow and dark green sleeping bag. Next to the bed was a chest of drawers, on top of which sat cooking utensils such as a camping stove, paper plates and a handful of real cutlery. An open drawer revealed tins of food.

'Close, close,' said Nikolai, pointing to the door. Beckford did so, his pessimism having somewhat lifted.

'Lock.'

Beckford turned the handle and the steel locking mechanism slid into place. He watched Nikolai slump down onto the camp bed and stretch out his injured leg.

'You want drink?' he said, tapping a kettle on the floor with his good foot. He grimaced again and massaged his bad knee, then sat up and rolled a small wooden keg between his legs that he used as a table. Beckford presumed most of the junk in there came from rubbish skips. In an eclectic, free-spirited sort of way it kind of worked, decoratively speaking. It wasn't much worse than the lad's shithole of a dorm. At least this place had character.

Nikolai unfurled a pouch of tobacco and papers onto the keg and started constructing a cigarette.

'Smoke?'

Beckford shook his head. To his immediate left, two laptops sat atop a table built out of a flat piece of wood – possibly the door of a cupboard – with one end resting on a small steel cabinet and the other on a mini-fridge with a few thick textbooks to pad it out and level it. Underneath the table whirred a computer tower. A server of some kind?

'Who pays for the electricity?' said Beckford.

'Electric company,' Nikolai replied, not looking up from his cigarette workstation. Spying a thick white power cable, Beckford followed it as it led up the brick wall and into the ceiling. Wherever it went, he guessed it wasn't legal, after which his sarcastic inner voice said, *You think?*

As he watched Nikolai roll his cancer stick, he tried to latch onto questions that flew through his head like a swarm of starlings, only managing to pluck mundane and tedious ones like 'who are you renting this place from?' and 'does anyone know you're living here?'

Why was Beckford procrastinating? Was it the suspense he was feeding off? Like a child who'd just seen an incredible magic trick, he knew that once the secret was revealed it would strip away any sense of wonder.

Get to the fucking point, John.

Maybe it wasn't just that. Nikolai was fragile, that was obvious just from his appearance and body language. Sessions with his own psychologist had taught Beckford a few things, and if he went straight for the jugular, Nikolai would recede, retreat into himself. With no foundation of trust between them, how could he expect the lad to reveal his deepest darkest secrets? Beckford was well versed in all that, having been on the receiving end of those types of penetrating questions himself.

'Look, Nikolai… or is Nikolai even your real name?'

Engrossed in his cigarette, he gave no response. Beckford took a step forward.

'You may think you know me, but you—'

'I don't think that,' said Nikolai. 'Why would I waste such time learning about a nobody?'

'Okay. Well, we're in the same boat here…'

Nikolai's eyebrows knitted with confusion and Beckford realised the idiom may have been lost on him. Retranslating, he said, 'We're both in the same… situation.'

Nikolai let out a muffled laugh, cigarette clenched between his lips. 'No we are not,' he said, sliding open a box of Swan matches and striking one on the concrete ground.

'Why are you running from them?' said Beckford.

The smirk lingered on Nikolai's face as he drew on the rollie, letting a lungful of smoke plume across the garage.

'So smart,' he said, dropping his head and planting his

elbows on his knees. Beckford had to suppress his anger. For the first time he finally felt an affinity for his colleagues, past and present, who complained on a weekly – sometimes daily – basis about their petulant teenage kids. Only this one wasn't staying out late, getting pissed or smoking weed – he was fucking with Beckford's life.

The smoke reached him and he felt it seep into his clothes and pores. The only windows were in the garage door and they were covered with blackout material secured with duct tape.

Sliding out an old oak dining chair from Nikolai's workstation – its leather seat faded, worn and cracked with time – Beckford took a seat.

With his life in the hands of criminals, rewritten on-the-fly, it had made Beckford question almost everything. And as he stared at the crown of Nikolai's head, a young man confirmed dead and yet, there he was, alive and kicking – it made Beckford believe that anything was possible.

The rules had changed. Pushing the supposedly dead Ukrainian on his bike through the cold streets outside, Beckford mentally picked the jigsaw pieces from the rubble and analysed them from a renewed perspective.

At first the possibilities seemed endless, but slowly and surely the pieces were tested, back and forth, over and over. It was trial and error searching for the logic. And it wasn't until Beckford finally sat down in the garage and a sudden surge of exhaustion swept across his aching body – making it feel like he'd doubled in weight – that the last piece of the puzzle fell into place.

'You're good with computers,' he said, stating the obvious. 'You're *very* good at programming. Fucking exceptional in fact.'

Nikolai's head remained hanging while he smoked, apparently not paying any attention to what Beckford had to say.

'You built DarkBrain,' said Beckford.

Nikolai blew smoke at the floor, then raised his head.

That got the prick's attention.

Not wanting his catch to wriggle off the end of the line, Beckford talked fast.

'…a botnet that can get beyond the walls of almost any digital fortress. But DarkBrain is a myth. How can it be real if no one can prove its existence? Like the Higgs boson or Bigfoot. But it *does* exist and you were tracked down by people even smarter than you.'

'Smarter than *me?'* said Nikolai, scoffing and taking a big drag of his cigarette. 'A thousand of them couldn't develop anything like DarkBrain.'

'Don't get me wrong,' said Beckford, 'you certainly outclass them at technical ability, that's why they came to you. But they beat you on psychology. They social engineered the shit out of you.'

'Fuck you.'

'Look at where you're living.'

'I'm here because of you.'

'You're here because of *them!* You let them control you, get inside your head, use fear to get you to give them free rein on the fucking thing. It's powerful. It's dangerous!'

'Only dangerous in wrong hands,' said Nikolai, repeatedly stubbing his rollie into a dirty saucer.

'You wanted to escape, right?' said Beckford, 'get off the grid? With DarkBrain at their fingertips they'd find you. They can do anything. What you said in your suicide video: "*there's only one way to disconnect*" – those words stuck with me, but it's not true, is it? There are *two* ways, and I've been thinking about the second one from the moment you looked up at me. I saw the photographs of your dead body. Your face *gone.* But that was part of the plan, wasn't it?

Because that corpse wasn't you, it belonged to someone called Joseph Winterburn.'

Nikolai inspected the end of the cigarette and then dropped it into a plastic carrier bag by his bed. Beckford's breathing had quickened. He was on a roll.

'You're a smart fucker you, Nikolai. You lured a young lad to your dorm… someone with a similar build, hair colour, weight, complexion, but most importantly someone who wanted to leave this planet as much as you wanted to be set free. You both dumped 24 paracetamol and waited. Only yours were placebos. Once Joseph collapsed and slipped into a coma, you strung him up and blew his face off with both barrels of a 12-bore, picking the perfect night for the sound to be drowned out by the Halloween madness outside your room.

'You'd spent months perfecting your CGI and VFX skills and set your computer up with an automated script to wipe everything apart from the video you'd stitched together – skillfully, I might add. What happens when forensics run checks on the corpse's dental? There's no record. Prints and DNA? There's a match: Nikolai Guskov. How that's possible? Simple. Joseph Winterburn had a criminal record, meaning both his prints and DNA are stored in the National DNA Database. A mere pinprick of data. Kilobytes. Using DarkBrain you hacked the NDNAD, created a false profile for yourself and switched the sample references so when forensics came to test the body, it was your name that popped up, not Joseph's.'

What a sense of satisfaction. It was like Beckford's body had been inflated with helium, the heaviness that had been so evident before dissipating into a cloud of euphoria. There was no other feeling quite like it, and the only thing he wasn't happy about was that he wished he'd recorded it. In the mental state he was in, he didn't trust himself to remember any of what he'd just said, yet he hoped it would be tattooed in the fabric of his mind for ever.

Still entranced by the concrete floor, Nikolai chewed the skin around his middle nicotine-stained finger, causing Beckford to subconsciously feel the skin around his own digit.

'There was nothing simple about any of it,' said Nikolai finally.

'One thing I still don't get,' said Beckford. 'If you wanted to fool these people, surely they'd know you faked your own death?'

Nikolai finally looked up at him. 'Do you have idea how much money your government put into security for the NDNAD? It gets lot of unwanted attention. Lot of people have problems with it. Ethical issues. Privacy. It is one of most secure systems in your country.'

'And yet DarkBrain got in.'

'No. It did not. It can not.'

Beckford's heart fluttered and he took a sharp breath, sitting upright as he did so, hoping he wouldn't collapse, faint or drop dead before he heard Nikolai's side of the story. With the excitement almost too much to bear, he started taking in long, deliberate breaths, hoping to quell the adrenaline that was pumping through his veins and jacking his heart rate through the roof.

I'm so fucking close here.

'They had me constantly developing,' said Nikolai. 'Streamlining better propagation system. That's how my botnet works. Replicates with just few lines of code beyond whatever security is in its way. Then, like egg, it grows, fed by more bytes of data, slowly, over time, until matures and makes connection home. It is organic process. Always changing. They introduced me to people in, how you say… house office?'

'Home Office,' said Beckford quickly, his heart leaping into his mouth.

'Yes. People who looked after DNA database.'

Beckford was well aware of how the NDNAD was governed, but he kept quiet and played ignorant, not wanting to stop Nikolai in his tracks.

'…they educated me on infrastructure, security, protocol.' He paused, as if he was conflicted about carrying on. Beckford held his breath, freezing every muscle in his body. It was as if Nikolai was hypnotised and even the faintest sound or movement could cause him to snap out of his trance and realise he was confessing liquid gold.

'I was employed as white hat,' said Nikolai, 'by Home Office.'

Beckford couldn't believe his ears. Nikolai… a mole? Sent in under the fence? Too many questions scrolled before his eyes.

'I carried out penetration tests and investigate security breaches. It was all a pretend.'

'Pretense,' Beckford corrected before he could stop himself.

'It only take two weeks before I breach security, unnoticed. I did what they wanted, but knew discovery would have big consequence, so I kept it from them. That was over year ago, and they kept pushing me to a find way in…'

Nikolai stopped again, then slapping a flat hand to his chest he exclaimed, 'I am not bad person!'

He lay back on his bed. Beckford's mouth was hanging, waiting like a begging dog, but Nikolai remained silent, staring at the ceiling. As Beckford digested the revelations, the past events – from the moment he received Nikolai's home computer up until now – were remolded. The muddy waters were clearing, and so too was the air coming into his lungs and the colours of everything he could see. The truth had risen. It was all going to be okay.

But he realised Nikolai had abstained from revealing an important nugget of information. Probably *the* most important nugget, and with hope that his guard was still softened like warm dough, Beckford straightened up and came right out with it.

'Nikolai. When you say "they"… who are you talking about?'

The silence was unbearable. Nikolai's rolled his head to face him. Beckford wanted to hear the name "Dominic Peltz" so much that he almost willed it into the lad's mouth. But when his lips parted, Beckford heard something entirely different.

'The police, of course.'

THIRTY-SIX

Beckford didn't say a word, hoping Nikolai would expound. More silence followed.

Come on lad. Come on.

'When I was arrested,' said Nikolai finally, 'they kicked door down… drag me out of bed. I had no time to dispose anything. Amateur back then. They had DarkBrain from that moment. It was encrypted of course, but they promise me freedom if I gave control.'

'These were legitimate police officers?'

'Yes. For first few months I was interviewed by cybercrime officers and computer specialists from different agencies. They had a lot of interest in my methods. I think they had hoped on reverse engineering my botnet, but they could not. I was released on bail and started work closely with a – how you say it – a "handler"?'

'Handler, yes.'

'…I had some freedom, but they wanted me close so enrolled me in London University. My work there was simply disguise.'

'Did he have a name, this handler?'

'Calls himself Dominic Pryor, but I don't think that is real name.'

Beckford was standing without realising. It was a known fact that informants used their first name when assuming a new identity, primarily so that they didn't forget to respond to it when spoken to.

'He *calls* himself…?' said Beckford. 'You still see him?'

Nikolai said nothing and rolled over on his bed. Beckford started searching himself, then stopped. He wasn't even wearing his own clothes so the printout of Peltz was long gone.

'Did he ever use,' said Beckford, 'or have you ever heard the name Dominic Peltz?'

There was no response. Beckford felt rage swell in him again. He was sick of the lengthy silences. Storming over, he kicked the kettle to one side before grabbing Nikolai's arm and yanking him so hard he almost dragged him off the bed.

'THIS IS IMPORTANT!' screamed Beckford.

'Fuck, man!' protested Nikolai.

'There's no point keeping anything from me, we're both in the same shit!'

'Same shit?' said Nikolai. 'I don't think so. One of us is safe.'

'Why are you protecting them?'

'I protecting *you*.'

Beckford let go of his arm. 'Well, great job you're doing. To the outside world I'm a wanted murderer and kiddy-fiddler. Thanks a fucking bunch, pal.'

Nikolai sat up, shifting his bad leg with care. 'I tell you everything I know, what can you do with it?'

'I'm a police officer. I uphold the law.'

Nikolai started to laugh one of those high-pitched, annoying laughs that Beckford associated with ignorant adolescents who hung around on street corners.

'You think you have more power than me?' said Nikolai, his laughter tailing off. 'You have uniform, warrant, a stick to hit people with… maybe a Taser? You have flashing blue lights. You write forms that people above you read and sign. And they have people above them. And so on. You are small fries. I don't answer to nobody. I go straight to source and do whatever I want.'

'I'm not doubting your skills,' said Beckford, 'but this is

police corruption on a major scale, and in order for me to blow it wide open I need information and I *must* follow procedure. The law will protect us, do you understand?'

'That law is *irrelevant*. They have too much control now. They listen and watch all the time. We are like bugs. We get in way, they squish.' Nikolai screwed a fist into his palm.

'How many of them there are?' said Beckford. Nikolai shrugged. Tenderly, he got up on his feet, gradually applying weight to his injured leg.

'Not fracture,' he said, hobbling over to his laptops with a less-pronounced limp. Taking the now vacant dining chair back to its original place, Nikolai sat down.

'DarkBrain is backdoor to almost any system worth accessing,' he said.

'Why don't you just pull the plug?' said Beckford, walking over. Nikolai logged onto both laptops and filtered through data almost faster than the eye could read. And Beckford thought Willow worked quickly.

'I no longer have access to command and control server,' said Nikolai. 'I used to only develop upgrade modules that took weeks, sometime months, before approved for deployment. I suspect they analysed my code with a… tooth comb?'

'Fine-toothed comb.'

'Yes, to be sure I wasn't adding backdoor access. They severed all my access after I "died." The botnet has mind of its own. It only grows, not shrink, but reality… it cannot do anything unless human asks it to.'

'Where do they control it from?'

'Anywhere they want. Building. Boat. Plane… outer space. There are hundreds of connection nodes. Thousands of proxy hops. They use computer, phone… whatever, and have instant access to DarkBrain client network.'

Beckford deflated. He'd never predicted the scale of their operation to be so big and illusive. Tracking down anyone involved in ruining his life seemed like an impossible task. He chewed the inside of his bottom lip and stared hopelessly at the back of Nikolai's head; laptop screens glowing beyond each ear.

'There is the Studio, however,' said Nikolai. Beckford stopped chewing. 'My handler let slip in conversation. You see, DarkBrain is only facilitator. Key to door. Once inside door, what happen then? These people are digital artists. They alter external perception of events using everything available – video, images, audio, transactional data, social networks, anything online. Anything to modify history that will alter future. And they need place to work from.'

* * *

She was out the car before Staedler even had time to engage the handbrake. Wading through a mass of black and blue uniforms, Farber held her ID from her neck like a mother searching for a missing son. The strobing blue lights of an ambulance acted as a beacon and with each determined step she took, fear gnawed away at her insides. That was until a gap opened up in the crowd and she saw the body bag.

A pained murmur escaped her lips that went unheard above the din. On the curb sat an AFO in tears, being consoled by a colleague.

'It's not him…' said a deep Scottish voice as the flashing blue lights were blocked by Michaels' enormous frame.

'He's not here, detective,' he said. 'Beckford's not here.'

Relief flooded Farber's system, steadying her breathing enough to let her respond quickly in an unphased manner.

'Who is it, Chief?'

Michaels didn't get a chance to answer as a short fat man in a faded grey suit tapped his arm and said, 'The car's waiting, Ray.'

Farber clocked the man's ID badge, the letters "IPCC" emblazoned at the top standing for "Independent Police Complaints Commission." Michaels nodded to him and, not saying anything else to Farber, followed him into the crowd. Swept up in the chaos at the Bell Tower, Farber didn't think anything more about it. Michaels was a busy man and dealt with the IPPC on a weekly basis. Business as usual.

The hotel room smelled of damp clothes. As she entered, Farber automatically honed in on the crimson patch burned into the cream carpet by the end of the bed. From a distance it looked like a bizarre map of the world turned on its side.

'O'Brien entered first,' said DI Goulding, a woman of advancing years who'd been in the racket longer than Michaels. Farber always thought her makeup was too heavy for a DI. And too immaculate. And at seven in the morning it was taking the piss.

'No sooner had O'Brien reached the wardrobe Peltz opened fire. They both let off two rounds each, both taking the other out. Chief said it happened like *that*,' she snapped her professionally manicured fingers.

Farber peered over the bed but realised the king-size was too wide to see where Peltz had fallen.

'He'd been living here since May,' said Goulding, 'according to the front desk.'

'Only two shots returned?' said Farber. 'Wasn't O'Brien armed with a sub?'

'She used her handgun as her primary. Close quarters.'

A vibration started pummeling Farber's right breast. She reached into her jacket and pulled out her phone. The number was Beckford's – the phone he'd "found" in the karaoke bar. Shockwaves of fear pulsed through her body.

'Excuse me,' she said, looking superficially calm and collected.

The hallway outside the room was still swarming with SOCOs and uniforms, but Farber hit answer anyway and held the phone by her side. She took the door to the stairs, walked down two floors, then out into the second floor corridor where she cornered herself by a small bay window.

'Hello?' she said into the phone.

'It's me,' said Beckford. 'Where are you?'

'Where you're supposed to be. They traced your email, but—'

'I heard shots.'

'Shots? Where are you?'

'I'm safe. Tell me what happened there.'

'It was Peltz. He was staying here in the hotel. Did you know that? He's dead. Opened fire on Michaels and an AFO. She's dead too.'

'Michaels?'

'That's what I said. Were you even here at all?'

There was silence on the line, not for an unreasonable length of time but enough for Farber to start panicking.

'Hello?' she said. The next stretch of silence filled her with dread, then two distinct beeps confirmed it. Their call had been disconnected.

Beckford stared in shock at the shattered pieces of plastic and circuitry spread across the garage floor. Nikolai had already started shutting down his laptops, clapping them shut and stuffing them into a large rucksack.

'Why did you do that?' said Beckford.

'She mention names!'

Beckford's stomach lurched. How did he not notice?

'Move!' said Nikolai, pointing, 'Under bed… canister, canister.' He started pulling disk drives from the computer under his makeshift desk, stacking them carefully in the rucksack.

Beckford got on his knees and reached under the bed, pulling out a plastic canister that sloshed half-full with liquid. Unscrewing the lid, his nostrils were instantly assaulted by the harsh fumes of petrol.

'Start that side,' said Nikolai, coiling cables. 'Everything. Hurry, hurry.'

Beckford got to his feet and did as asked, heaving the canister back then letting petrol fly all over the bed and walls; the potent, intoxicating stench seeping into every corner of the room like a toxic gas.

'This side!' shouted Nikolai, wheeling his bike out of the way. Beckford sloshed the fuel over and under the table, drenching the computer unit which now lay on its side with its guts exposed.

With his heavy rucksack strapped to his back, Nikolai dragged the garage door open and pushed his bike outside where the morning twilight had coated the road in a cool blue.

As the last few drops of petrol trickled from the nozzle, Beckford ditched the canister on the bed and turned to leave.

A match sparked in Nikolai's hands. Beckford froze on the spot. Nikolai was stood by his bike, holding the flame to a full box of matches. Beckford didn't need to look to know that his own feet were coated in fuel.

'What are you fucking waiting for?' said Nikolai. 'Come, come!'

Beckford's paranoia finally unlocked and his legs started

working again, propelling him forward and out into the bitterly cold morning air. Nikolai dropped the match, and as the box went up like a mini-bonfire it was thrown end over end into the garage.

It seemed like nothing happened for a second, then a fierce explosion of flames ignited and engulfed the interior in an instant, the heat almost welcomed by the two of them, but intense enough to push them back a few steps.

Shielding his face, Nikolai pulled the garage door closed, leaving a gap at the bottom for airflow. Hypnotised by the licking flames, Beckford watched the blackout cloth melt from the windows, the door lighting up like a spacecraft charging for lift-off.

'HAVE TO GO!' shouted Nikolai, ditching subtlety and cranking the gears on his bike. Beckford had to sprint to catch him up, and once out of the funny little road they turned right and continued at a pace.

Back in the public domain, and with the dark sky above their heads brightening with each passing second, their senses were electrified to any movement, sights or sounds.

'Need to split up,' said Nikolai, panting. Beckford felt bittersweet about the idea. There were still too many stones left unturned, and it was more than likely this would be the last time they'd see each other. But the lad was right, once the sun was up they'd stick out like sore thumbs.

'How can I contact—'

Beckford's last word was cut off by the coarse grind of an engine roaring to a stop, brakes locking tyres and screeching across the tarmac.

The white van had halted askew 20 feet from them, "POLICE" printed across the side doors in bold capitals.

THIRTY-SEVEN

'Go!' shouted Nikolai, pedalling into an upright position on his bike, the spokes starting to blur as his speed increased.

The van's side door split and screeched open. Beckford didn't hang around to see the occupants pile out, but as he bolted he heard boots thudding onto the road and shouted statements straight out of the handbook.

They were probably armed, and for the first 50 yards or so Beckford expected a bullet to just turn out the lights, dropping him dead in the street. Smoothing that one out would surely be schoolboy stuff for those at their Studio; plant a weapon on him, or go one step further and make him a wanted terrorist. A couple of clicks of a button and "*ding!*" one deep-fried fundamentalist convert called John Beckford waging his own personal jihad taken out. Computers made everything easier.

Somewhere behind him, beyond the collection of heavy boots thrumming the ground in unison, the van's engine coughed and growled into first gear, then into second almost straightaway.

Beckford knew Battersea well, but he needed an escape route, and as each new side road or alley way presented itself, he only had a fraction of a second to determine whether it'd be the right choice – a sprint to freedom or literally a dead end.

He'd ran a lot that week, but this time was different. Knowing what he knew now, the impetus to stay alive was even greater, his selfish responsibility having evolved into an altruistic one. This thing was bigger than him by a country mile, and as a serving officer of the law he no longer owed the truth just to himself – he owed it to the nation.

When he reached the end of the street, he spilled out across a main road on the other side of which was Battersea Park enclosed in its wrought iron fencing. He charged at the gate but it was locked. Without pause for hesitation, he clung to the spikes of the fence and pulled himself over, turning in the air and landing backwards, the inertia throwing his body to the ground, slamming him into the cold, moist grass.

With a wince, he looked back through the fence where blue lights strobed the iron bars like searchlights. Figures swarmed in the road. A pop fired and a whoosh of air flew by his right ear. Tranq darts typically used to take down wild animals. Beckford was on his feet again, fleeing across the park towards the rising sun that peeked out over the distant trees, crunching the frosted grass under his feet. With winter on its way, leaves had fallen and the nearly-bare trees gave him nowhere to hide.

Across the park he ran, his lungs on fire, the icy cold air doing nothing to douse the pain. He wanted to look back, see who was on his tail, but he was scared to do anything other than run as fast as his legs would carry him.

When he reached the bandstand in the centre of the park, he couldn't take it anymore and turned. There was no one behind him. Slowing to a jog, he spun around, giving himself a 360-degree view of the park.

Apart from a warden, spotted in the distance, Beckford was the park's only other occupant. There were certainly no Kevlar-clad officers storming his way. That made him even more uneasy. No blue lights. Where had they gone? Who fired the tranq dart at him?

He carried on towards the sun, then took a path

signposted for the Russell Page Terrace. In the morning sunlight the area looked beautiful, but he didn't stop to smell the roses and headed north, sprinting up more winding paths until he came to a large white pagoda, beyond which was the Thames.

Beckford looked up and down the promenade, spotting two dog walkers and a jogger. He took a moment to get his breath back, and although he wasn't anywhere near the Bell Tower, he thought he could still hear the faint whisper of sirens coming from that direction. Had the cold air carried the sound, like a rattling train in the dead of night?

Beckford looked east again towards the power station. Then back towards the Albert Bridge, which he'd crossed with Nikolai an hour before. He so wished he had more time with the Ukrainian. There were still too many unanswered questions, especially now that Peltz was dead.

To his right, the jogger was approaching, heading in the direction of the bridge. Beckford took his coat off and walked across to the railings, leaning over to the river below. With only a T-shirt up top, the cold breeze made the hairs on his arm stand up.

He waited.

When the jogger passed behind him, Beckford threw his coat over the side and started running in the man's wake, figuring that if he kept close to him, he'd look just like a running partner. To Beckford's advantage, the jogger wore large over-ear headphones, allowing Beckford to keep a close proximity without alerting him of his presence and freaking him out.

It took them a minute until they were at the end of the promenade, where Beckford scanned the busy traffic, eyes on the lookout for police vehicles. When they reached the road, the jogger took a left and headed south from where Beckford had come from. From where *they* had chased him.

Confidence was the key, and Beckford decided to continue tailing the jogger, closing the gap between them to just 10 feet or so.

Down the length of the park they ran, then all the way over Albert Bridge Road until they hit a pub called the Lighthouse where the jogger crossed over and took a left. Beckford followed suit.

Getting into a rhythm, Beckford's mind wandered, thinking back to Nikolai's garage. It should have been a mass of wet, smoking cinders by now, surrounded by firemen and police. He could hear the distant wail of sirens again, but this time it was real. An ambulance, somewhere beyond the buildings ahead of him.

Finally parting with his running partner, Beckford found himself turning into another road where the siren was louder and clearer. Why was he following it?

Ahead of him, a mob of people had amassed on a road bridge, peering through a chain-link fence to whatever was down below. It was imperative that Beckford kept moving, but something just didn't feel right.

Jogging closer to the commotion, he watched a woman pushing a pram let curiosity get the better of her. She leaned over to look through the chain-link and a bystander pointed something out to her – quickly, she turned away like someone had thrown sand in her eyes, her face distressed.

Beckford didn't want to look, but he had to. It wasn't just curiosity, it was the underlying feeling that it was all connected.

Crossing the road, he slowed to a walking pace. With his apprehension already maxed out, there was a numbness as he approached the bridge. Closer still, the distant wail became plural, and he scrutinised the gathering crowd, suspicious of all of them.

Finally, Beckford skipped onto the pavement out of breath and peered through the fence, down below. The bridge overhung a bank of four train tracks that ran a few hundred yards before bending out of sight. A train had stopped halfway into the bend, but that wasn't what everyone was looking at.

Lying up against one of the tracks was Nikolai's black jacket with the white comical skull sticking its tongue stuck out. It was on Nikolai's back, but there was no head or legs, just a dark patch of blood and some pink viscera.

A bit further up the track were his legs, separated from each other like discarded logs, one lying across railway sleepers and the other propped up on the track. Nikolai's rucksack sat upright in the bushes at the side, but his head was nowhere to be seen.

Beckford leaned to one side and wretched, regurgitating nothing but a trickle of burning bile that he promptly spat out. He hadn't attended a train accident for a long while, but it wasn't the gore that made him vomit.

'Here,' said a woman's voice, her warm palm resting on the middle of his sweaty back. Beckford turned to her, an older woman – maybe in her sixties – handing him a plastic bottle of water with the top screwed off.

'I'm fine,' he said, 'but thank you.' The woman nodded and carried on her way. Beckford turned back to the fence and saw police and paramedics strafing the tracks either side, heading for Nikolai's remains. A few hundred yards away another bridge crossed the tracks, but unlike the one Beckford was standing on, there was no chain-link fencing to stop people throwing things off it… such as themselves.

There is only one way to disconnect.

The congregation surrounding Beckford were giving each other a running commentary on what had happened, but Beckford only caught snippets. He was too busy trying to identify any of the attending officers below, wondering if they were legitimate or not.

There is only one way to disconnect.

As Nikolai's words rang in his head, his doubt expanded. Was that really Nikolai's body down there? What if the whole thing had been some form of elaborate hoax? His death had already been faked once before.

Maybe it was his vulnerability or desperation, but by the time they'd left Nikolai's hideout, Beckford trusted him implicitly. Everything he'd said about DarkBrain, his arrest, the Studio… it all made sense and slotted into Beckford's wider picture like laser-cut floor tiles. But was any of it true?

There was no warning.

Lost in thought, Beckford didn't hear the vehicles pull up behind him or the gasps from the surrounding onlookers. The first thing he knew was being driven forwards and getting a face full of the wire mesh.

'John Beckford, you're under arrest.'

His arms were pulled behind him with expert force as his Miranda rights were read to him. It was all so fast, Beckford couldn't do anything but submit. He couldn't fight any more. Plastic strips were pulled taut around his bare wrists, pinching the skin, and as he locked eyes on the bloody lumps that used to be Nikolai, the words continued to loop like a broken record:

There is only one way to disconnect.

There is only one way to disconnect.

There is only one way to disconnect.

He was spun around to six – maybe more – masked officers, standing there like an imposing crew of drunks about to lay into him. They looked like SCO19. From the few words he caught from the arresting officer, he was being charged with murder and possession of indecent material with intent to supply. It *sounded* legit.

Bundled into a van he was sandwiched between two officers, and just before the door slid shut he caught one final look at the cold morning light, the cloud-free sky and a row of astonished faces from onlookers.

Then the door shut, the engine roared to life and they were moving.

Beckford wanted to speak, but fatigue and shock wouldn't let him get any words out. The facing officers just sat there, staring at him through their tactical masks, their eyes giving away nothing to their identity.

There's still a chance it's a genuine arrest, Beckford thought. He fucking hoped so. If push came to shove, it was definitely the lesser of two evils. A legitimate trial could give him time. If he lived to see it.

Beckford's fate was sealed and he knew it.

With that realisation, he felt his body relax and his vocal chords loosen.

'I know who you all are,' he said.

There was a silence, then a pair of hands fumbled something, somewhere behind his back. Beckford wasn't even scared anymore. He just wanted it done quickly.

A deep voice behind him said, 'Then this'll need no explanation.'

Beckford could hear a faint rush, then a pair of headphones slipped over his ears, making him jump. All he could hear was a constant hiss of static; no engine, no rumble of traffic, no clanging of equipment in the van. Just a deafening hiss.

Then a black bag was dragged down over his head and he was completely shut out of the world.

THIRTY-EIGHT

Michaels had sat in on many post-incident interviews before, but had never been on the receiving end of one. It was an unusual ordeal, but being well-acquainted with both officers administering the rub down and his familiarity with the procedure, he was confident that he'd walk away with his pride and reputation untarnished.

The irony was he felt as filthy as horse dung. Forensics hadn't let him shower until they'd picked as many samples off him as they needed. It wasn't the blood spatter or gunshot residue clinging onto his sweaty skin that made him feel slick with muck, it was the pang of guilt that followed every operation like the Bell Tower.

He headed straight home after the interview, and as the warm, cleansing water trickled over his bald head and down his huge frame, a name came to him: *Jimmy O'Brien.* He thought back to meeting Carla's husband at some charity ball a few years back. They were expecting their second child now.

The emotions toppled like dominoes: anger, pain, guilt, self-loathing. He let himself take them all on the chin, knowing it was a necessity to feel them at their fullest for his system to purge them quickly, allowing him to return to the fully-functional professional that he was.

He'd personally visit Jimmy. James. And he'd look directly into the man's tear-soaked eyes and told him how sorry he was for his loss, doing it with truth, regardless of the fact that he'd personally fired the two bullets that killed his wife.

A cultivated mental discipline was the only way any of

them performed their job at the required standard. It was all for a greater good – a philosophy that was drilled into them during initiation, from which a belief germinated. The stronger the belief, the less guilt they felt when someone – through no fault of their own – had to be "removed."

Carla O'Brien was a soldier, unwittingly and unknowingly on the front line. She died for a true cause.

Michaels turned the taps and the shower fizzled off. It was only then that he could hear his phone ringing in the bedroom.

* * *

From the moment the hood was thrown over him, plunging him into darkness, Beckford anticipated panic in all shapes and sizes. Not the panic he was used to, which latched onto him at inopportune moments like an annoying friend. No, he expected something new; something beyond any terror he'd experienced before. And yet it didn't come.

What started out merely as discomfort and confusion became almost therapeutic, the sensory deprivation disconnecting him from the world he'd grown tired of. So he just sat, meditatively, with the rush of audible static acting as a mental composer, giving him a focal point and keeping his thoughts off the beaten track where unfavourable memories and premonitions lurked.

Every now and then an image or sound would enter his head, threatening to dig himself out of the safe haven he'd made for himself. Then, like he'd learned to do through meditation, he drew his attention back to the hiss and the sound once again took centre stage.

The static was so constant and unwavering that after

some time he began to hear things in it. Random echoes of reality. His eyes played tricks too, projecting shapes and colours from his mind onto the blank canvass of the opaque black hood.

Sometimes the van would turn and sway, dragging him back to reality and causing him to lean to one side, into the body of the officer sat adjacent to him. And he'd feel the tension of the sharp plasticuffs digging into his wrists, his swollen fingers entwined with one another.

The van would halt at times too, most likely at traffic lights, and each time it did Beckford fully expected the engine to cut out and for him to be frogmarched into a field where the rest of his senses would be shut off as well.

Time, however, was a mystery to him.

The first few minutes felt like minutes, because he was able quantify them by the temperature of his body, still defrosting from the bitter streets outside. But with molten blood pumping through his veins and the van's heaters blowing full blast, he thawed quickly and his perception of time started to warp, eventually disappearing altogether.

If he could determine how long they'd been driving he'd at least have some idea of how far from Battersea they were. At times, when he'd get dragged away from his relaxing trance, he'd imagine exactly what road they were on and which direction they were heading in. Then the van would unexpectedly turn, the gravitational shift not matching up to his imagined location, and he'd be dumped right back into a blind maze.

Switching back and forth between reality and his dreamlike-state, he started to think about Nikolai again – his body parts strewn along the train line like fly-tipped rubbish. The real thing or a special effect straight out of a horror film?

Pretty elaborate set up, he reasoned.

How would they know I'd come back that way and peer over that bridge?

The van went over speed bumps and Beckford's organs jostled, causing the aches and pains across his body to flare.

What about Noakes? Did anyone see his body?

Reviewing the events of the past week, Beckford began disassembling each one into manageable, bite-sized components, questioning whether any of it was real or that maybe he was quite simply going insane. It was the best explanation he had, and – exacerbated by having his sight and hearing disengaged – the notion began to stick. The whoosh of static. The blackness. Swimming thoughts of paranoia and doubt. He wouldn't be surprised if he was actually lying on a hospital bed, electrodes taped to his temples, brain cells frying on 100,000 volts.

That would be one way to keep me tight-lipped…

The van slowed to a stop and the shuddering vibrations of the engine cut out under his thighs, causing the terror that he'd expected to finally show up. He felt the van door slide open, the rumbling of which came through the floor under his feet and travelled up his body. With his insides flooded with fear, the van yawed and pitched, caused by what he presumed to be departing bodies.

A strong hand slid under his arm and he was pulled to his feet. His legs were a wobbly mess, and a wave of nausea suddenly hit him, caused by either a blood rush to the head or the dizzying sensation of being submerged in a black swamp of static feedback.

His first few steps in the van were as unsteady as a newborn deer's, and as he shuffled slowly in the direction the hand was pulling him, a chilly breeze hit his bare forearms and exposed neck.

The guiding officer dropped a few feet in front of him and Beckford followed, gingerly dangling a leg from the doorway as he lowered. He expected to hit soft ground – grass or soil – envisaging his execution to be carried out in woodland.

Just like Sally…

But when his toes touched down, followed by his heel, they landed on hard ground, possibly concrete. Bringing down his other foot his jelly legs almost crumpled beneath him but he was held steady by the strong grip under his arm. Then they were moving. Beckford could do nothing but follow the lead of his escort.

Only a few lungful's of freezing cold air made their way past Beckford's lips before a curtain of warmth swept over him and he was indoors again, his feet slapping a smooth surface. Laminate, perhaps. He could smell floor polish and bleach.

The immediate clues quickly settled Beckford's heart rate. It appeared he wasn't in some dodgy disused building or deserted woodland. It smelt like a living, breathing place with purpose and cleaning staff. The smell was not unlike a few police stations he'd been in, which would have raised his spirits somewhat had his black-bag journey not been so unconventional.

On the walk, he focussed his thoughts again. A right turn was taken, then a left. They entered a lift at one point, which Beckford deduced only by the shift in gravity. He only managed to count to seven before they were leaving again on a different floor, meaning they weren't too high up.

The next part of the journey started to confuse him, but nevertheless he attempted to draw a mental map of the route, from where he'd started in the van to where he was now, creating a blueprint of the building. But it got hazy pretty quickly.

They went up a small set of stairs at one point and

passed through a number of doors, maybe three or four, which Beckford deduced through short pauses in their travels. By the time they'd taken another couple of turns Beckford's mental map started to look like an H.R. Giger lithograph.

In fact, the blind journey had been so mentally consuming, Beckford had entirely forgotten about the rushing static that was still blasting in his ears. The sound only became deafening again when he was held stationary for a moment while a number of hands patted him down from head to toe. Very thorough and very professional. They dug into his pockets, down his legs, around his socks. His trainers were removed one by one and his belt was also taken.

Without warning his trousers were dragged down by to ankles and followed by his underwear. A foot kicked the inside of each leg, forcing Beckford to spread them, and a hand on his shoulder pushed him down into a squatting position. The static in his left ear eased up as the headphone was lifted.

'Cough,' said a man's voice.

The headphone slapped back on to his head and Beckford did as he was told, the grunt of his cough only audible from within like a deep thud through a wall. He was pulled upright again, along with his underwear and trousers, and pushed forward with force, almost stumbling as he took a few steps to steady himself. The hood was ripped from his head and harsh fluorescent light blasted his eyes, causing his pupils to shrink like a camera lens.

The cuffs were the next thing to go and finally the headphones, which were yanked from his ears, the static sound lingering behind like an audible sun spot.

Re-gifted with sight and sound after such an intense stint was overwhelming and disorientating. Beckford couldn't help but squint, his eyes pulsating with a sharp pain. But it was his hearing that took him off guard. The simple sensation of being able to hear the air around him reacting to his breath and movement – it gave him an unexpected sense of space and depth that was usually taken for granted.

Before his senses had chance to stabilise, a door slammed shut causing his head to spin like an owl. He instinctively grabbed for the handle, but there wasn't one. A heavy lock clunked somewhere inside the steel door. Beckford pressed his ear up against it, but couldn't hear a thing. No voices. No footsteps. It was only when he turned back to the room that it was clear he'd been imprisoned in a cell.

THIRTY-NINE

'You want a Coke?' said Michaels, holding the door open for her, '…the machine spat out two, so fill your boots.'

Farber entered his office like she'd done a thousand times before, but deep down she knew something was wrong and that it was going to be about John. Did Michaels know she'd been in contact with him?

'How's everything with you, Chief?' she said with a dollop of concern as she sat down. 'I heard you went to visit…' she tailed off, hoping Michaels would chime in with the rest.

'I did,' said Michaels, rounding his desk and taking a seat. 'It wasn't good, obviously. Never is, is it? He was in pieces when I got there. Kids were at school. So close to Christmas too.'

He sat back in his chair and let out a weighted sigh, aimed at the ceiling. Farber took the opportunity to look at something she'd spotted in her peripheral – a pair of headphones sat by Michaels' phone, the cable snaking off his desk and, presumably, into his computer underneath. At the end of his sigh Michaels looked at her.

'This is a tough job, Farber. I don't say that often enough, probably because none of us need to hear it to know it's true, but every once in awhile I think we need reassuring. To keep us in check. Make sure we're not going totally fuckin' doolally.'

'Chief, surely Staedler can cover you for a day or so? No one's going to nick your bloody chair if that's what you're worried about.'

A very brief smile flashed across his face, then he held

his hands apart like magician and said, 'What would I do? Catherine's at work. The dishwasher's on the blink, which I had a go at but I think I just fucked it up even more. If you know a good plumber…'

Farber had never seen a more sombre Michaels, but in a strange way she was glad. Maybe he just wanted to talk to someone, get things off his chest. But then his face solidified again and his stone-cold eyes set upon hers.

'Alison,' he said, 'I know you don't need reminding that perverting the course of justice is a serious offence, especially for an officer.'

Farber knitted her brow, trying every trick in the book to portray innocence. Michaels saw right through it.

'Don't bullshit a bullshitter,' he said, 'I know you've been in contact with him. Now, I don't want to lose a perfectly good – no, an *excellent* detective – from my branch.'

'Who?' said Farber, 'Contact with who…? John?'

'We have your phone logs. And I'm not talking about your personal or business phone. I'm talking about the burner that he supplied you with. For the past week you've been under investigation.'

Farber's eyebrows unlocked and her stomach tied in knots. Under investigation? She felt violated, as if someone had just grabbed her handbag and tipped her life out onto the table.

'I authorised it,' said Michaels. 'Your history with John… the rumours that have been flying around this office. We're talking about *very* serious allegations here.'

'Allegations that aren't true!' shouted Farber, taking him off-guard. Through the office windows, a couple of curious heads turned their way. Michaels got out of his chair, walked over to the glass and twisted the blinds shut.

'You care about him,' he said, 'I understand that—'

'No.'

'—but you can't deny there was an obvious, dramatic change in him after Sally's murder.' He walked back to his desk but remained standing.

'I've seen it happen before,' he said, 'not on quite the same scale, but an officer I knew up north. Constable he was. His wife was blackmailed. Photos of her in the knack. They wanted 50 large. The paranoia got to this fella so much that he couldn't perform in his job and was eventually dismissed. A member of my team picked him up a year later camelling pills.'

Farber looked at him, unsure of how to respond.

'All I'm saying is,' said Michaels, 'some people go off the boil when they become the victim.'

'John may have been withdrawn,' said Farber, 'even depressed, but could you blame him? As for going off the boil, he's made quite a name for himself down at Water Street, and has never been anything less than a model employee.'

Michaels chewed the inside of his lip while the air filled with an ominous silence. Farber had an inkling he wasn't giving her the whole story. Eventually Michaels took a seat.

'There was a phone found on Beckford after his swim in the lake,' he said. 'That's how we got the number for your burner. CEOP investigators traced John's calls to directory enquiries where he'd asked about storage facilities in Ealing. Officers were dispatched bearing photos of John to all listed storage facilities in the area. No one identified him. It wasn't until three days later that they received a phone call from one store, acknowledging that the person in the photo had come in recently, opened an account and deposited personal belongings.'

Michaels reached out and swivelled his computer monitor around. A paused video was on screen, showing

Beckford entering the facility's reception area carrying a rucksack. Farber sat upright to get a better look. It was him all right, but Beckford had warned her about believing what she saw on a screen.

'That was where they found Graham Noakes' laptop,' said Michaels.

Farber did a mental double-take. *John* had *Graham's* laptop? The split-second conclusion of any detective hearing such information would be that Beckford was at Noakes' house the night he was murdered, but that was bollocks and Farber knew it.

Michaels angled the screen back towards him and with hand on his mouse started navigating the screen.

'Graham was a stickler with data,' he said, '…a paranoid android. A lot of his material was highly encrypted, but CEOP managed to uncover something quite substantial.'

Still clicking away, he reached out with his free hand and slid the pair of headphones to Farber, finally acknowledging their presence.

'Noakes used to record all his phone calls.'

Farber took hold of the headphones with trepidation; but instead of giving herself a chance to consider the bubbling, disastrous thoughts that started running through her head, she slipped them over her ears as quickly as possible. The sooner she knew, the sooner she could deal with it.

After a couple of muffled clicks of Michaels' mouse, a ringing tone filled Farber's ears. Two bloated chirps rang out before the call was answered.

'Hello?' said Noakes. There was a slight pause before the other person spoke.

'Gray… look, I said I'm sorry.'

Beckford sounded despondent and slightly out of breath. There was another pause, punctuated by a breath exhaled through a nose, then Noakes spoke again:

'You can't— I'm not the one who requires an apology, John. I don't know who that is. Yourself, maybe.'

'I'll get help. I'm looking for help. I'm going to—'

'John…'

'I promise!'

The desperation in Beckford's voice triggered a very familiar feeling of helplessness in Farber. It was a voice she had tried to forget. The next line threw her for a loop.

'Have you always been… like this?' said Noakes.

Farber's insides erupted with nerves. She closed her eyes, focussing all her attention on the sound. It *couldn't* be John.

'I don't know,' said Beckford quietly. 'After Sally my head went south, didn't it? Everything went fucking south. Don't put me in with those other sickos, all right? I've never done— I'm not like them, okay? I've never done anything to anyone. It's just… it's just the pictures that I like.'

Farber's eyes snapped open. About to tear the headphones off, she saw Michaels' stony face willing her to continue listening.

'It's just the pictures,' said Beckford again, 'I've never done anything else, Gray. Never. I never would, either.'

The voice was definitely Beckford's. Farber's devastation came in the form of a single tear that snaked its way down her nose and leapt off onto her skirt.

'Gray, don't grass whatever you do. I told you I'll stop. Don't you believe me?'

'You're a friend, John. A good friend. But, like yourself, I have my ethics. And this is… I just can't put it into words. Heinous.'

Farber shook her head from side to side and dragged the headphones from her ears, dumping them with a clatter on the desk. Her hands were trembling. A ball in her throat swelled as more tears skied down her cheeks.

'That's not John,' she said, her lips quivering. Michaels didn't say a word, he just watched from across his desk as her face contorted with heartache. She dropped her forehead into a supporting hand, and as more tears fell amid gasps for breath, all she could think about was how she hadn't helped John enough back when he really needed it. Their relationship post-Sally had a futility that she just accepted, but she shouldn't have given up. She should have fought.

'You're not to blame for any of this,' said Michaels, as if reading her thoughts.

He was stood by her side, pushing a box of Kleenex in front of her. She took a couple of tissues but let the rest of the tears drain out of her before she started mopping them up.

'It looks like he fooled almost everyone,' said Michaels, 'apart from Noakes. And now we know.'

Farber couldn't respond, her breathing spluttering like an old car. She stood up and walked to a water cooler where she filled a plastic cup and downed it in one. By the time she'd filled her second cup, she'd gone from thinking sympathetically about Beckford to regarding him with hostility.

They'd made love – a thought that now made her head spin and her skin crawl. Anyone with a secret that dark would take it to the grave, no question. And that scared Farber more than anything. What if their relationship hadn't ended? Would she have ever found out?

'This doesn't make any sense,' she said, her voice cracking, desperate for some sort of loophole to emerge and blast everything they now knew into oblivion. She wanted reassuring that John was John – the caring, intelligent, well-rounded person she had only ever thought he was.

'That bastard,' she said, and for a further minute she stood by the cooler, drinking water and mopping her face. Michaels just let her get on with it.

After a long while spent fumbling with a tissue, Farber said, 'Does Corden know?'

'This is where it gets tricky,' said Michaels, 'I'm wondering if she knew all along.'

'Excuse me?' said Farber, incredulous.

'Corden was the one who set John up with his therapist last year,' said Michaels. 'A good friend of hers called Rachel Elway. Now, I've known many people who've lost someone close to them in terrible ways, people a lot closer to them than Sally was to John. And you know what they did? Grieved and moved on. Don't get me wrong, I'm sure the pain has left them with scars, but they didn't jump off the deep end like Beckford. Which makes me think something else was afoot, underneath that damaged surface of his.'

Farber's disbelief came out as a snort of laughter.

'It gets bigger,' said Michaels. 'All three of Dominic Peltz's laptops were filled with filth too. You can see where this is going, can't you? We believe Beckford and Peltz were part of a child pornography ring.'

Farber stared into space as the pieces fell into place around her. Michaels cracked open the second can of Coke on his desk, then from his desk drawer placed a small recording device. He pressed a button and it activated with a beep.

'What I need from you Alison is the truth. Everything John Beckford told you. It'll at least give me some chance of saving your job.'

FORTY

A turning lock shook Beckford awake.

Springing upright, his head swirled with fatigue and confusion as he glared about the room, reminding himself where he was and the shitty situation he was in. Before he could even muster any kind of deliberation over his imprisonment, such as who was about to enter the room or his impending fate, he simply felt amazed that somehow, in that grim and narrow room on the stained hard mattress, he'd fallen asleep.

And not just any sleep. A peaceful, dreamless one. The negative and terrifying thoughts, sounds and images that usually crowded his subconscious like hell's waiting room were non-existent. For once his mind had been clear, and Beckford wanted to savour the sensation one last time.

The door opened inwards on silent, well-oiled hinges. Shifting on his backside, Beckford swung his legs over the side of the mattress and instinctively primed himself for defence or attack. Three men entered, all wearing suits; two of them dark grey, the other navy. Nothing fancy, just run of the mill, well-worn business suits. They also wore black gloves and balaclavas, the latter making their heads look like black bowling balls with neckties.

Navy Suit and the shorter of the two Grey Suits approached him. Navy Suit carried what looked like a music stand with a screen attached, the other carried a small black case that looked like it might contain diamonds. The third man stood by the door, holding what looked like a toy gun – bright yellow, with a blue cap on the end. It was aimed directly at Beckford, and he recognised it as a police-issued X26 Taser. He'd used one himself in the past. They fired two wired barbed probes that hooked into the skin and delivered an almost lethal charge of electricity. The sight alone made Beckford's neck twinge where he'd felt a Taser's bite just a few days earlier.

Navy Suit positioned the music stand a few feet in front of Beckford, lowering the screen to eye-level. Shorty opened the case on the bed, revealing a couple of gizmos that were unrecognisable to Beckford. First to be taken out was a circular band, which the man placed on Beckford's head, the material cold like steel. The second device looked like a thimble and was placed on Beckford's index finger. There were no wires.

The man with the case then left the room, leaving the other two behind. Navy Suit finished setting up the screen, and as it turned on he moved upstage. From the screen, another suited and masked man stared back at Beckford.

An agent? A spook? Beckford had no idea. The man was heavy-set, the suit jacket stretched over his rotund torso, and he was sat at a desk in front of a beige-coloured wall. The anonymous eyes, the mask, the bare room and the washed-out video looked like an ISIS execution recording to Beckford; something he'd not even contemplated until that moment.

'Please don't try anything stupid,' said the man, his voice digitally disguised and made even tinnier by the screen's inadequate speakers. 'Even if you somehow managed to overpower your minders, you wouldn't escape the corridor. We use state-of-the-art biometric security here.'

Beckford couldn't deny that the open door and now only two guards certainly tempted him to consider an escape.

'Before I begin Mr Beckford, I want to congratulate you on the work you've done so far.'

Beckford's eyes narrowed. With the altered intonation in the digital voice it was difficult to determine whether the man was being sarcastic or not.

'We've been in operation a long time and you're the closest anyone has ever come to unmasking us – no pun intended. We're impressed, but then again having read many of your old case files it doesn't come as a huge surprise. You're as meticulous as they come. You know why that is? Curiosity. Now we know what happened to the curious cat, but I don't want you to worry, Mr Beckford. Not at all. Let's pretend we're making a documentary about your life. This is your moment, and the meticulous behaviour that you implement so deftly in your work I want demonstrated right there in that very room.'

The man momentarily leaned out of view and coughed – the sound quiet and muffled through the speakers. Coming back into view, he lightly cleared his throat.

'I'd just like to make it clear that our priority as an outfit or an organisation or whatever you want to call us, regardless of what we do, is to remain undetected. That's how we operate. How we continue to exist. And from what we understand – what we've learned from watching and listening to you, and what we've theorised by certain events, i.e. you spending time with our Ukrainian friend – you've come into the possession of information that may or may not put us at risk of discovery.

'Obviously, you're here now in our custody, but you may have left a trail – sent someone a message; dropped a piece of litter with a phone number on; made a note on your burner and discarded it, even old fashioned talking to someone about recent events. Data that could still exist in some form and might lead back to us. Now, before you contemplate authoring stories, please know that we've been doing this for a long time – we are a highly professional organisation. The camera you're looking at and the devices attached to you are connected to a system we call Veritas. It's a lie detector that actually works, so we only want the truth. And if you don't tell us the truth, the absolute truth, we will *make* you. Do you understand?'

Beckford nodded, then in case it wasn't clear added, 'Yes.'

He glanced up again at the two suits in his cell. Apart from the stun gun and the fear-inducing balaclavas, there was nothing too threatening about them. Actually, they looked quite feeble with their casual stances and almost hunched postures. Not at all like the imposing, sophisticated and utterly ruthless criminals he'd seen in movies.

'Also, do not presume what we do or do not know Mr Beckford. We've determined how meticulous you are, so your answers should be abundant in detail, as if informing a layperson for the very first time. Is that clear?'

'It is.'

'Good. Let's start with an easy one. Are you aware of anything in the outside world, physical or digital, that if found could lead back to us? This could be information you've gathered about us on your own or information you've shared with someone. Absolutely anything at all – even the tiniest thread can unravel the largest jumper.'

The man glanced to his right and reached off screen, as if navigating a different interface, adding, 'I understand you've been a busy boy in the last week or so, and you may need to think. So please take your time.'

Just as he awoke, Beckford's mind was blank again – a long, desert-like plain stretching out towards the horizon. Was it tiredness? Fear? Had the rejuvenating sleep wiped his memory? Had *they* wiped his memory?

Silence filled the room. Beckford didn't want to panic,

not again, not now… but he simply couldn't think straight.

He opened his lips and muttered, 'I…'

The man on the screen looked back at him, his white eyes buried deep in the mask, catching the light in a way that made them look illuminated.

'I…'

Those eyes.

For a brief moment, Beckford's anxiety was interrupted by a desire to identify the man on the screen. The eyes could be anyone's, the camera not good enough or close enough to make a positive identification, and yet Beckford still felt like he knew them.

'Yes Mr Beckford?'

'I… can't remember.'

He could almost smell the incredulity emitting from his captors. Before the silence had a chance to drag out, he cut back in, 'I'm being truthful,' he said. 'It's blank, my mind's blank. I've been running on empty… three hours of sleep a night, max.'

'Think *hard*, Mr Beckford.'

The statement was loaded with enough Semtex to blow up the Houses of Parliament. Like an animal cornered in a cage, Beckford could think of nothing other than his own safety. The more they pushed, the less likely he'd be of any help. Resigning to whatever they had lined up for him, his head was suddenly filled with a memory. Nikolai's jacket, scattered on the tracks. So much blood.

'What happened to Nikolai?' he said softly.

With a loud and commanding voice, the man on the screen said, 'Mr Beckford requires a little help.'

The man by the door took a few steps forward. Beckford saw the blue cap at the end of the stun gun pop off before everything went white. The pain was agonising, channeling its way through his rigid body, sparking each and every neuron in his nervous system like a trillion match heads setting alight.

When the pain drained from him a few seconds later, the room came back into focus. He was lying supine on the hard floor with the echo of a scream dying softly in his ears, his voice hoarse. Each breath he took was accompanied by a contraction of his vocal chords that sounded like weak cries for help.

He rolled his head to the sound of scuffing shoes, his cheek now pressed against the cold floor. A pair of dull leather brogues clopped right by his face, then the screen was placed in front of him, the eyes beyond the screen man's mask now more piercing and threatening.

'How about now?' said the man, his digitised words even more monotonous than before; no accommodating formality, just deadly gravitas.

'I…' muttered Beckford. 'I…'

He peeled his cheek from the floor and looked up at the ceiling.

'I… don't…'

He shut his eyes and thought harder than ever before. *Why is it so difficult?*

Nikolai… I remember him.

He killed himself.

No, he didn't… that's a lie.

A fallacy.

Manipulated video.

They're manipulating everything.

It's all a lie.

You're not even here. You're not even here?

The words stuck. Regardless of whether it was true or not, it made him smile. A comforting belief, like a kind of blind faith.

You're not even here.

His smile grew.

'I'm… not… even here,' he said quietly, the words barely escaping his lips.

'What was that, Mr Beckford?'

Louder, his smile bigger, he said, 'I'M NOT… EVEN HERE!'

The pain slammed into him like a bus and the room went white again, his senses tripped with the blazing current pouring through the darts in his chest, clenching every muscle in his body and taunting them to burst through his skin.

A few seconds felt like an hour, and the ravaging current never seemed to end. Just before he passed out, he saw an image of Sally smoking a cigarette and laughing at a joke he'd told.

Then everything went black.

FORTY-ONE

For the days following Beckford's capture, the Studio reassigned many of their now available operatives to one person – Alison Farber.

Farber first appeared on Comminatio's radar as an amber threat and hadn't risen or lowered outside of that rating for over a week. Now it was crunch time.

The story they'd constructed about Beckford was set in stone, having reached many millions of people via news and media outlets. Notitia gave the story a 92% impenetrability rating, tested even under the most severe scrutiny – a level beyond human ability. And yet, Farber's emotional ties with Beckford meant there was a high probability of doubt and – depending on her susceptibility to their story – a half-life to her inquisitiveness.

If her doubt caused her to dig deeper, how long would she dig for? This was Notitia's concern, and while it knew a hell of a lot, there were physical variables out in the real world that it couldn't account for. And although the system's analysis always factored in an apportion of unknowability, it was programmed to err on the side of caution.

With that, Farber was marked as the prime suspect for unravelling their story.

Heated discussions had taken place at the Studio regarding Farber's possible removal, but with Beckford already flagged, the complexity of whitewashing compounded significantly with each additional target. It was decided that such a severe course of action for Farber would be a last resort, and no further discussions were had on the matter.

After the Studio received the interview between Michaels and Farber, merely minutes after it had concluded at the station, the audio was run through Veritas. Farber's answers were deemed to be genuine, although without any visual aid the system could only rely on one element for analysis. Two was better, and unsurprisingly resulted in a 50% improvement in accuracy.

As instructed, Michaels had sent Farber home after the interview, telling her to take the week off as compassionate leave. It was clear by the email she'd sent to Staedler soon after that she suspected her role as a police officer was coming to an end, presuming her compassionate leave was preemptive gardening leave, and that the moment she'd click send on her email and left the office, Michaels would get her work and systems access revoked.

But that wasn't the case. The Studio were simply interested in seeing what she'd do. Naturally, Farber still had a million questions about Beckford, the primary one regarding the Ukrainian's role in everything. If there really was a child pornography ring, was Nikolai part of it or a victim? And if so, why did Beckford bring the lad's computer back to her attention, having gone to great lengths to investigate the suicide and propose the notion of the whole thing being fabricated?

It was a plot hole that the Studio fixed with a sprinkle of magic dust that wasn't too far from the truth – Beckford was losing his mind. A cocaine habit had been sewn into the story, which explained a recent increase in Beckford's paranoia; so much so that his browser history was filled with government conspiracies and advice on "hearing voices." On a deeper level, it could be explained that keeping Nikolai's case alive was a cry for help. Farber would make that assumption herself once his coke habit was disclosed internally within the Met.

That evening, Staedler dropped by on his way home from work. He'd listened to the stomach-turning phone conversation between Noakes and Beckford after someone he knew in the NCCU sent over the sound file to his personal email. With the concept of fabrication in the air, there was of course doubt.

'Those voices could have been impersonators,' said Staedler, the transmitting microphone installed behind a downlight in Farber's kitchen. '...or spliced together from a thousand other calls.'

Farber wasn't convinced, and they soon led into the uncomfortable topic surrounding Beckford's sexual preferences.

'Before you two got together,' said Staedler, 'me and him... we'd go out quite a bit. On the piss. Not that you want to hear this, but... well, he was pretty successful. With women, I mean. I was kind of like his wingman... married bloke, off-limits, "let me introduce you to my mate..." all that sort of shit. He was always up for it, just like any single bloke would be. What I'm saying is I don't think he was just sleeping around for a cover story. I mean, fuck's sake, you were with him for what, two years? You knew him better than anyone. Did it ever cross...'

Operatives at the Studio heard Farber break down crying. A minute later her phone rang, interrupting them. A private number. With her mobile constantly monitored, the Studio identified the caller as a James Thomas, a journalist from the *Daily Mail.* Farber didn't have nor require any such system to suspect it was yet another reporter, and she ended the call without answering.

They then moved into the living room and started to pick apart subtle things about Beckford that went previously unnoticed. It was there that the walls of their doubt were finally tested and the Studio's story started to embed itself.

As their recorded conversation filtered through Veritas, then through Comminatio, Farber's threat rating began to fall, spreading relief among the Studio's labs. It wasn't over, though. Not by a long shot.

Even if Farber's interest in Beckford disappeared altogether, the human mind was unpredictable. It didn't work like a computer. And due to her stake in the plan, it was already necessary for the Studio to put in place open-ended surveillance on Farber for as long as she lived. It was too dangerous otherwise.

Luckily, constant developments in their systems made it easier to automate the process, and Farber would just join a growing list of permanent targets, or "constants" as they were called. Any deviations in her patterns would be alerted back at HQ, and Comminatio's recommendation would be adhered to.

Farber spent the first half of the week feeling like a prisoner in her own home. Reporters knocked and called constantly, and through the blinds upstairs she identified an unmarked police car parked a few doors down.

Staedler was her only trusted source of information on Beckford's case, but with his shift finishing at eight each night, she had to spend most of her day consuming mainstream news that was at least 24 hours behind.

'There's still no sign of him,' said Staedler, tucking into a prawn cracker from the Chinese he'd brought with him. 'They think he might have travelled north, or…'

'…or what?'

'You know.'

'John wouldn't do that.'

'Suicide isn't a personality trait, Ali. It's always a surprise.'

On the Wednesday, Farber couldn't take anymore and decided to go and stay with her mum in Dover for a couple of days. They enjoyed long walks along the cliffs, ate pub lunches and went to the theatre. Lydia was 67 and attributed her positive demeanour to a lifelong abstinence from news. She was none the wiser about Beckford, which helped Farber slip back into normality for a day or two. The people who'd followed her there made sure to keep their distance.

On the Thursday, Staelder called to tell her Joseph Winterburn had been found.

'...or what was left of him,' he said. 'Scattered along the tracks in Battersea. Sunday, I think. Could only ID him by DNA, you see.'

It was only after discovering that Nikolai was alive that the Studio became aware of the mechanics behind his disappearing act. It caused quite a stir of excitement in the labs. A truly fabricated body swap was seen as a game-changer in their line of work, and with a dedicated team set up to investigate Nikolai's methods of penetrating the NDNAD, they had a renewed hope of replicating the process and pushing the boundaries of their operation into the new frontier.

'It's still not clear where Winterburn had been all this time,' said Staedler.

'Has Elaine Winterburn been informed?' replied Farber.

Veritas transferred their conversation to Comminiatio, which recalculated Farber's threat rating and increased it for the first time in days.

For each target monitored, Comminatio used a library of historical data about the subject, applying fundamentals of digital psychology to determine predicted outcomes.

It wasn't just what Farber said that had caused the increase but how she said it, and the inflection of concern in her voice had indicated sympathy.

Comminatio knew that Alison Farber had a mother called Lydia who lived alone and was just a year older than Elaine Winterburn, who also lived alone. The system also knew that Farber was very close to her own mother (87%), and that due to the familiarity heuristic she'd most likely treat Elaine Winterburn with a similar respect and admiration (72%). Therefore, the possibility that Farber would revisit Elaine Winterburn increased (84%), which in turn increased her possibility of analysing the Joseph Winterburn case (85%), meaning her distance of separation from the Studio reduced significantly (53%).

The scales had tipped, and the containment team at the Studio prepared themselves.

FORTY-TWO

A thick rheum had glued Beckford's eyelids together. With great effort, he peeled them open, feeling like a two-ton elephant was sat on his chest, weighing him down.

It was the pills.

When he'd slipped unconsciousness after 100,000 volts had juiced his body, they'd dumped sedatives down his throat and let him sleep for 14 hours straight. He wasn't any use to them otherwise, not with his mind scrambled like a box of secondhand Lego.

The next night Beckford asked for the pills, examining them with extreme suspicion before popping them into his mouth and washing them down with water.

If they wanted me dead, I'd already be dead.

The night after that, Beckford didn't even think twice about the pills. He popped them like sweets and hunkered down in his bed as if it was a work night – the deluded practice most likely a common defence mechanism for any desperate, imprisoned soul.

Where the pills did only 90% of the job, the kooky reveries did the rest.

Gotta be up early tomorrow, John.

Busy day!

For his first fully conscious day in his cell, Beckford was interviewed long and hard. What started out like an interrogation straight out of a Bond film soon turned into an exhausting and mundane daily routine.

The day would start early, or what he perceived as early. With no windows and no clocks, it was difficult to determine what time it actually was. The first sound he would hear was the door unlocking and breakfast sliding into his room. Unsweetened porridge and black coffee.

Beckford estimated he had 15 to 20 minutes to eat before the suited and masked men would enter the cell and set up for the day, moving with efficiency and speed.

A small table and three chairs were placed in the centre of the room, on which the video-link screen was set up, facing a lone chair for Beckford to sit in. Two of the men sat on the other side of the table, each of them tip-tapping into laptops of their own.

As always, Beckford was fitted with the lie-detector and ushered to his designated seat. One guard always remained to the side, stun gun pointed directly at Beckford. The "incentive."

The men never spoke.

Breaks were regular, and a shift-change halfway through the day would introduce new guards of differing shapes, sizes and smells. On the odd occasion Beckford would notice a woman in the mix, but they were always masked and never said a word. The only voice Beckford heard in his cell, apart from his own, was the rusty robotic one that leaked through the tinny speakers of the screen in front of him.

And it was always the same man interviewing him, who – since their first encounter – had become much more accommodating, allowing Beckford time to compose his thoughts before responding to the questions thrown at him.

It had been made perfectly clear by the way they Tased Beckford with the yellow gun on his first day just how important it was that he gave honest and detailed answers. And despite the leeway Beckford had been gifted, he never lied. Not once. Not even to test the almost tacky sci-fi props that sat on his head and finger.

Were they even real? He didn't want to find out. Their strategy to condition him had worked and the sight alone of the stun gun made Beckford squirm and grip the chair beneath him.

There'd be times during his sessions of interrogation where he'd struggle with his recollection of events, and the metallic voice would only have to recite the simple words, 'Do you need any help?' and Beckford's body would stiffen and shiver with fear.

'Gimme a sec!' he'd plead, closing his eyes and slowing his breathing, desperate to focus his attention on the task at hand.

Weak and at their mercy, his days in the cell felt like the longest of his life, made even longer by the expectation that they were also his last.

During the time spent recounting his journey from first powering up Nikolai's computer in the lab at Water Street to the seat he was sitting in – in among daily fluctuations of fear, desperation, anger and false euphoria – his head was filled with muddled, half-baked ideas about his captors.

It was obvious by their blunt, efficient yet professional demeanour that some of them, if not all, were either former or currently serving police officers. One thing that wasn't obvious was their intent.

Not once, not in all the days he was interviewed, did they ever let slip of anything – verbally, physically or psychologically – that could assist him with the picture he'd been painting in his head. The masked guards stuck rigidly to their routine and never so much as coughed.

All Beckford had to go on was the colour of their eyes, their marginally visible skin and hair and their gait; not enough to crack their anonymity, but that didn't stop Beckford substituting the nameless spooks with real people he'd met in the service – people he wouldn't bat an eyelid at were they to reveal themselves as turncoats.

The interviews themselves were extremely thorough. The questions specific and detailed to an obsessive level – a level that Beckford was all too familiar with.

Then they went beyond that.

Ephemeral moments that Beckford could barely remember were suddenly pushed under the spotlight and scrutinised to the nth degree. The inquiry became so fastidious that it led Beckford to muse about the possibility that his captors were robots, or that he was in fact part of a computer program like in the movie *Tron*. The sheer audacity of such thoughts only convinced him more that he was losing his mind, a notion that was exacerbated by the stretch he'd spent encased in his cell with his destructive thoughts feeding on themselves.

The pills are laced with something.

They're hoping I'll go insane and forget everything.

Every now and then, Beckford would be reassured that he wasn't alone with his mental battles. The spooks themselves were obviously extremely paranoid, specifically about data security but even more so about the protection of their identity.

A few years back, Beckford went through a phase of reading about Freemasons in the Metropolitan Police after a friend of a friend introduced him to someone at a party who drunkenly revealed himself to be one. The man gave Beckford a card, told him to give him a call and Beckford did what he normally did when a subject piqued his interest; he read up on it, quickly learning that the secret society of the Freemasons was a hotbed for police corruption, prevalent across a number of lodges where officers made easy links with organised crime.

Maybe that's who these people are…

The theory took hold quickly for Beckford: *A group of corrupt police officers with the ability to infiltrate any computer system, take any information and manipulate it in any way they wanted.*

They were pulling the biggest trick the British judicial system it had ever *not* seen. But *why* were they doing it?

Beckford tried to keep it simple. In all his years fighting the war on crime, he knew the number one motive was money. With that in mind, his conclusion came quickly.

They provide a service to the criminal underworld. For the right price, entire crimes can be created, edited or erased.

Before the digital age, the scrutiny of physical evidence was much more a manual process, the responsibility of the analyses 100% in the hands of human beings.

Now it was less. Much less.

Technological advancements garnered governmental trust by making the capture and delivery of forensic analyses faster, cheaper and with an extremely low margin of error. The downside to the increasing use of technology was that it invited tampering and hacking.

Questions were constantly raised about the integrity of digital information, yet as the technology got better, so did the hackers, and the so-called "security experts" often had to sprint to come in third.

If a team of hackers were truly able to re-engineer every facet of a crime completely undetected, the perfect crime was indeed a reality. Beckford's head spun when his theory snowballed to such a conclusion. It made more sense than he cared to admit.

A sickness bubbled inside him. It was as if someone had shone a light across his past, where his job to uphold the law – what he believed to be his purpose in life – had been all for nothing. It was a joke. The people before him could have been in operation for years. Who knew how deep their roots went?

The more Beckford considered his theory, the more questions he had.

To provide such a criminal service, the organisation's secrecy would be paramount, which explained their extreme interest in the subject. Security would have to be so tight that even the crooks they were doing business for wouldn't be allowed to look under the bonnet. Assignments would have to be conducted through close-knit syndicates by people who they could trust implicitly. Trust, perhaps, due to some sort of lifelong pledge.

Like the Freemasons.

The concept was a nose-hair away from being the plot of an old cyberpunk novel, and would have seemed far-fetched until the recent revelations of phone hacking, government spying and ever-increasing leaks and data theft of personal information from major corporations, banks and social networking sites. Hacking groups were growing in numbers and improving in talent. Anything seemed possible. Such as the fabrication of a suicide.

Ensconced in his head once more, Beckford revisited Nikolai's video, the images now available on demand in his memory for ever.

Nikolai's suicide looked real. It *was* real, officially – on paper he'd killed himself and the investigation was closed.

One young man with hacking skills and off-the-shelf video editing software. And no one batted an eyelid.

The masked people that Beckford faced were professionals; a team empowered with the ability to enforce altered perceptions on the rest of the world.

And nobody but Beckford knew about it.

FORTY-THREE

On the Friday, Farber said goodbye to her mum and took the train back home. Despite spending her days in Dover being watched like a hawk, Farber had managed to disconnect from everything, if only a bit, helped along by her mum's total obliviousness to the scandal that waited for her back in the big smoke.

But as the train rumbled on towards London, her stomach filled with nerves. A part of her wanted to turn back, go and live in Dover. Go live *anywhere.* London was tainted now, but never one to shy away from anything Farber had to face the music and dance.

'If you were to come in,' said Michaels on the phone, 'I can only have you on restricted duties. You wouldn't be able to get on any system, not while the investigation is ongoing. They're still looking through your accounts.'

'I see,' said Farber, putting out fresh cat food for Mitsy.

'You're not going to lose your job, Alison. I'll see to that.'

Apart from her initial emails concerning Nikolai Guskov's computer, Farber was comfortable that there'd been no other communication between her and Beckford through work, incriminating or otherwise. Her access there had only ever been legitimate.

'...and they want to interview you on Monday,' Michaels added.

'Right.'

'Standard stuff, Farber. Let them know the position you were in, your history together. Talk about his instability. How you were in danger.'

'I wouldn't say that was true.'

'Who said anything about the truth, detective?'

The line went quiet. Farber considered the implications of lying to protect herself. Would it be fair of her to benefit from Beckford's demise? Would it make any difference?

'Who's heading the investigation now?' she said.

'Burrows at Scotland Yard. Corden's overseeing.'

'Corden? But, but what about—'

'I'm keeping that ace up my sleeve for now – see how this whole thing pans out. It's a fine line I'm walking. Corden could strip pips off my shoulder in a heartbeat if she wanted to, but I'm interested in seeing what she does – see if she's got the integrity to volunteer such information.'

'Where did you get the lead on John's therapist in the first place?'

'I don't think so, Farber. You've got enough implications on your plate as it is. Let me handle Corden, you just rest and prepare for Monday, all right?'

'You know, Chief, I don't need my work computer. I can go old school. I've got a stack of paperwork to keep me going. You can even lock me in the post room if it'd make you happy.'

Michaels sighed on the line, then said, 'Want me to tell anyone you're coming in?'

'That's up to you.'

She procrastinated while getting ready, unable to shake off the apprehension. People at work would look at her differently; suspiciously, perhaps, but most definitely piteously.

As she glided from room to room, getting changed and gathering her things, her thoughts stumbled over Elaine Winterburn. Then, when Farber perched on the end of her bed and hooked an earring, she thought about her properly.

It happened every now and then, where a victim's relative, friend or lover would fill the idle, off-duty thoughts of a police officer. Farber had been lying on a beach in Zante once when the memory of an 84-year-old man who'd lost his wife in a car wreck came flooding back like the crashing waves in front of her.

Or the time she was queuing for popcorn at the cinema, and found herself thinking about the junkie who'd been stabbed six times and died in her arms. There was no easy explanation for why they cropped up like that. Poor souls adrift in a sea of memories.

Every officer had scars.

When Farber finally left her house she held a middle finger up to a photographer across the street, then got into her car and instantly regretted it. *Whatever.* A minor infraction in the grand scheme of things. There were more important things to think about right now, and she'd already decided to make an impromptu house call before heading to the office.

The doorbell chimed; an older, traditional sort of ding-dong. Farber stuffed her leather-gloved hand back into her jacket. It was just above zero and there was frost still on the ground where shadows had protected areas from the winter sun.

On the drive over, Farber had rifled through classic phrases of consolation, trying to find the best one to say when she saw that sweet face appear around the front door. But having used them all at one time or another in a professional capacity, none of them felt sincere enough any more. Instead, she took a gamble and hoped the right thing would organically pop into her head and out of her mouth. Sincerity couldn't be prepared.

When there was no answer, Farber gave the bell another

go – twice this time, and then rattled the door knocker that may have gone unused for a while. She waited longer this time, eventually pressing an ear to the door.

There was no sound.

Trying the side gate, she found it unlocked and entered the alley, stepping over an unravelled hose on the ground. The back door was wide open. Panic only had a second to manifest itself before Elaine Winterburn rounded the house from the back garden.

'Elaine—'

'Good heavens!' said Mrs Winterburn, stopping in her tracks and instinctively slapping a hand to her chest. She was wearing gardening gloves and carrying a small plastic bag with twigs and leaves poking out of it.

'I'm sorry,' said Farber, 'I'm so sorry. There was no answer round the front.'

'Detective…?'

'…Farber, yes, that's right.'

Mrs Winterburn closed her eyes, took a breath, then opened them again. She lifted the lid of a bin next to her and dropped the bag in.

'…I'm just clearing a few things out back here,' she said. 'They're putting down new flags on Tuesday next week. It's about time, the old ones are so uneven. Are you here about Joseph?'

Farber wasn't surprised by Mrs Winterburn's casual demeanour; it was classic denial and happened to the best of them.

'Well, firstly I'd like to say how—'

'How about a cuppa?' said Mrs Winterburn with a cheery smile.

Farber sat in the same armchair as her first visit, and once again perused the same eclectic ornaments that decorated the living room. Down by the fireplace was an old money box that had a clown holding a hoop. On one side of the clown was a dog and on the other a wooden barrel. Farber presumed the coin went in the dog's mouth and a trigger made it jump through the hoop, depositing the coin in the barrel. To satisfy her curiosity she picked it up. It was weighty, most likely cast iron.

'That's Joseph's,' said Mrs Winterburn, carrying in a tray with the same beautifully presented tea set. Farber put the money box back and made space on the coffee table, picking off a candle jar, photo album and a copy of the *Richmond and Twickenham Times*.

'I bought it for him on a day out at the Albert Dock. Up in Liverpool, you know? Think he was only about seven or eight at the time. Never saved a penny mind, he just liked it.'

Farber took one glance at the front page of the paper and quickly folded it back up in her lap.

'Full of rubbish those things,' said Mrs Winterburn. 'Norman, my neighbour… next door but one. Funny bloke. I mean funny in the head, not ha-ha funny. He brought it round thinking that explaining what happened to my boy might somehow bring me a kind of peace. I thanked him for his concern, then told him to shove off.'

Farber smiled and placed the candle down by her feet, leaving the paper and photo album on her lap. Mrs Winterburn took a seat opposite and poured the tea.

'You think I'm crazy, don't you?' she said, her eyes remaining fixed on the cups.

'Excuse me?'

'Because my son is dead and I'm not sat here covered in a blanket of tissues and drowning in tears. That's what's supposed to happen, isn't it?'

'Mrs Winterburn—'

'Oh please, call me Elaine. You've been to my house

twice already, surely that's enough to drop the formalities.'

'Elaine. There's no right or wrong way to deal with this, just *your* way. I'm not really supposed to be here, but, well, I've had some personal problems myself and the death of your son just happened to catch me off guard.'

'I've had lots of wonderful support,' said Elaine, 'Markus, one of yours… lovely, lovely man.'

DS Markus Wainwright had been Mrs Winterburn's Family Liaison Officer. Farber watched Elaine as she sat in a trance, staring into the cup of tea gripped in her liver-spotted hands. Then when her face cracked she said, 'Oh god,' and threw a hand to her mouth while managing to land her cup of tea onto the table with a clatter.

Farber got up quickly, the paper and photo album slipping off her lap as she rounded the table and perched herself on the chair, putting arm around Elaine who sobbed quietly, stifling cries with her hand.

'Let it out,' said Farber, welling up herself. 'That's it…'

She wished DS Wainwright was there. He was much better at handling these moments than her, and what made it harder was the strange, mirrored sensation she felt, cradling Elaine, having been held in a similar way by her own mother in times of grief.

'Oh lordy,' said Elaine through the gasps and tears. 'I'm so sorry, detective. This is no way to present oneself in front of a guest.'

'Don't you be silly,' said Farber, 'what about our informalities?'

Mrs Winterburn hurriedly freed herself from Farber's grip, got to her feet and dashed out of the room, fumbling a tissue out from one of her sleeve. Farber could hear her feet trudging slowly upstairs, interspersed with sobs and sniffles that faded into nothing.

Sliding herself into the chair, Farber took two deep

breaths in through the nose, sucking back her own tears. *Elaine needed this*, she told herself, reassuring her justification for being there; although it did nothing to scatter the feeling that she'd outstayed her welcome.

Deciding she'd leave once Elaine came back downstairs, Farber took two large swigs of her still scalding tea.

That was when she saw the photo.

Placing the tea back on the tray, she bent to the floor and pulled the open photo album back onto her lap. On each page, a collection of colour prints were presented behind clear plastic. The photos were perhaps 10 to 20 years old, and the poor quality implied that they'd been taken with a disposable camera.

One photo in particular intrigued Farber. It showed a younger Joseph Winterburn in his late teens or early twenties. He had long, greasy hair parted down the middle, and was laughing – his acne-scarred face turned side-on to the camera.

Being a close-up photograph, it wasn't clear where the picture was taken, but what caught Farber's attention was a white plaster, slightly smaller than a playing card, that was taped down the side of his neck, starting under his left ear and ending up down by his collar bone.

Elaine's movements drifted through the ceiling and she started down the stairs. Farber kept the album on her lap and took another sip of tea.

'What must you think of me?' said Elaine on entering the room.

'Please, Elaine… no more apologies. Not to anyone. This is your house and if you want to cry, you bloody well cry, okay?'

Farber felt she might have gone too far with her blunt approach, but Elaine laughed it off with a sniffle, prodding her nose with a tissue. She then noticed the album open on her lap.

'Oh, I see you've—'

'I hope you don't mind?'

'Of course not, that's what photos are for, aren't they? Handsome boy, wasn't he?'

Farber nodded. 'What happened here?' she said, landing an index finger on the photograph she'd been looking at.

'Yes, that was just after a little operation. A mole. It was benign, but you can never be too careful. September 10 that was. The day before the attacks. Odd how that event anchors so many memories.'

Farber stayed to finish her tea. They hugged before saying goodbye and Farber scribbled her mobile number on a notepad in the hallway, under which she wrote:

If you want to talk.
(Detective) Alison Farber
x

On her way out, Farber started to manifest a fantasy where her mother and Elaine became best friends. Both of them were lonely women. Perhaps it was unfair to call her mother that; she wasn't lonely per se, just… solitary and accustomed to that way of life. For Elaine, the solitude would be the start of a whole new world, made tougher by the fact that older people were generally more resistant to change and generally less likely to have a choice about it.

It was possible Farber would return in a couple of months to see how Elaine was getting on. But no sooner had she driven to the end of the road, her idle thoughts turned to Nikolai Guskov and whether he'd been cremated yet.

FORTY-FOUR

'Dark in here, isn't it?' said Peter McGregor – his rough Northern Irish accent coming out from every angle.

Beckford was perched on his bed staring into blackness, his hands pressed into the mattress. It wasn't often he sleepwalked, and when he did he didn't always remember doing so. Alison was usually the one to remind him. When she was there.

'Where are you?' Beckford asked.

If there was any light in the room, Beckford's eyes would be pink, his eyelids droopy. But there was nothing – a total absence of light.

Standing up, Beckford took a few steps forwards, his hands outstretched like a blind man searching.

'Where are you?' he repeated.

'I didn't mean to kill her, John,' said McGregor. 'It just happened, you know? The heat of the moment. I should have just paid up, like a good boy.'

The rage was already inside Beckford and bubbling. His heartbeat pounded his chest, deep and heavy.

'All is forgiven,' said Beckford, 'just let me know where you are.'

His fingers touched the wall on the other side of the room, and he started to follow it around, shuffling his feet, thinking he may be crouched on the floor.

'You forgive me?' said McGregor. 'I find that hard to believe.'

'It's true.'

Beckford's fingers passed over the heavy door, feeling the ridges around it. He carried on going, leading with his hands and feet.

'I didn't even like my sister,' added Beckford. 'She was a cunt to me. A cunt to everyone in fact.'

'Now that's not a nice thing to say.'

McGregor's voice sounded distant. Beckford turned to face the middle of the room and started to shuffle forwards.

'I'm not a nice person,' said Beckford.

'Oh yeah?'

Hands outstretched, he reached desperately back and forth in the darkness. 'I'm a killer,' he said.

'A killer? Is that right?'

Beckford sensed he was getting warmer. He could almost smell him.

'Yes,' said Beckford. 'Let me at you and I'll prove it.'

McGregor's voice changed, now louder, closer and full of arrogance. 'I'd like to see you try, matey,' he said.

Beckford stopped. His anger bubbled over and he let fly a fist, yelping in agony as his knuckles cracked into the hard plaster wall. He took a step back and lost his balance, falling to the floor.

He was wide awake now, cradling his useless hand, the agony having dragged him out of his trance. The door to the room unlocked and a blinding light poured in, followed by people. He felt a needle go into his arm and a drowsiness came over him.

When he woke a few hours later, the light in the room was on and his right hand was wrapped tight in a bandage. It throbbed, but he could move his fingers without too much pain. On the floor by the side of the bed were two blue pills sat next to a glass of water. Beckford presumed they were painkillers and took them without a second thought.

He wouldn't forget his sleepwalk that time.

As he lay back on the pillow, self-pity started to consume him. And bitterness. McGregor would have had light. He would have had his bed, his routines and people to talk to. Beckford was worse off than his sister's murderer, and that ate him up inside more than anything.

Closing his eyes he focussed on his breathing. But as he tried to meditate, wishful thoughts clouded his mind. Fantasies of escape. If only he had a gun. Or a grenade. Something to do the most irreversible damage to the most people. It was pure anger. It needed to be let out.

When he inspected his hand again, a different worrying thought came along: *How long had he been a prisoner?*

Was it four days…? Five…? 20? Each day had been the epitome of routine, causing them to blur together and offer no frame of reference. It was hard enough not having any windows in his cell. Time was estimated based on the punctuality of his captors; using their arrivals, breaks and departures as a kind of barometer.

Interview begins at 9:30.

First break at 11.

Lunch at 1:00 pm.

Afternoon break around 2:30.

Finish at 4:00?

It was a guess, although he was confident the schedule was in proportion, giving him at least some kind of metronome for the day.

What day, though? Friday?

If it was Friday, it meant he'd been cooped up for four days.

'…and you say that the Florida proxy was the only one you rented or operated from?' said the man's metallic voice.

Beckford rubbed his eyes with frustration and said,

'You've recorded everything I've ever said in here. I'm not repeating myself.'

The masked man looked into the camera, his panda eyes piercing the lens.

'You've been very patient with us, John, and we appreciate that, so in return I'm going to give you a little something as a reward. An insight into our world. I don't think you fully understand the lengths we must go to for our operations to succeed. Let me expound.

'You're being framed as the leader of a child pornography ring. It was a backstory our team came up with that fits nicely into the context of your living and working arrangements, but also gave us a credible reason to make you disappear.'

Beckford's skin prickled with heat. The man was so casual about it, as if he was telling him the results of an MOT or giving a quote to have new windows fitted.

'On the surface,' said the man, 'it's just a simple cover story. But what we've learned over time is that the number of facets a story relies upon to promote it from suspicion to 100% truth is insurmountable. Truth *cannot* be fabricated, but beliefs can, and we only need to go so far. If we come at the story from the side of the law at every available angle, we find the cracks and fill them in.'

Beyond his anger, Beckford was baffled. More than that, he was intrigued.

'How,' he muttered, '...how can you be sure you've covered every logical gap of any given scenario? That's not humanly possible.'

'Ever heard of a computer, Mr Beckford?'

The sarcasm didn't translate via the digitised voice, but Beckford got it loud and clear. And he was stunned. He started to piece together a picture in his head of some extremely advanced artificial intelligence that was able to take input, such as a crime scene, and calculate every conceivable physical and digital element, ordering them by the probability of importance and discovery.

'We're storytellers, Mr Beckford. It's just that people believe the stories we tell.'

Beckford let breath after breath escape his lips. The sensation of being lost and helpless overwhelmed him more than ever before. For these people to have been in operation for the length of time that they had must have meant they were very good at what they did. It also meant Beckford had no chance of overturning the despicable story they'd inserted in his past. A past conceived in a meeting room, brainstormed on a whiteboard, constructed by technicians, put in place by computers and taken as fact by the rest of the world.

Beckford took a deep breath through his nose and let his eyes glaze over.

Weakly, he asked, 'What day is it?'

'That's enough information from us for today, please can you confirm whether the Florida proxy was the only—'

'What *day* is it?' said Beckford, his anger blatant enough to bring the guard by the door slowly to his feet. It didn't matter to Beckford anymore; hope had just evaporated before his eyes. There was only so much prodding a lab rat could take.

The moment right before it happened was bizarre. Time felt suspended, the cell taking on the atmosphere of an exhibition in a modern art gallery. Somewhere in the room a chair nudged, the foot of the leg scraping the floor.

Pouncing like a snake, Beckford reached forwards and grabbed the screen. Then he was on his feet. The two captors opposite shot up like oil geysers and at the same time the guard by the door fired the Taser. One dart pierced Beckford's inner right thigh, but the other missed completely, the wire spilling out across the floor like silly string.

Swinging the screen with his bandaged hand, Beckford let it fly at the closest guard. Spinning like a discus, the device impacted the man's temple with an explosion of plastic and metal, causing him to let out a sound like a whale and keel back over his chair. The adjacent guard lifted a foot and stomped the edge of the table, driving it into Beckford's pelvis with such force that he doubled over, slapping down like a slab of meat on a butcher's block.

A solid grip took hold of his neck and a fist pelted the back of his skull. Everything vibrated and dimmed and he slid back off the table, half-landing back in his chair, causing him to flip onto the floor on his front.

Then hands were all over him.

A knee buried hard into his lower back and his arms were pulled taut behind. He didn't struggle. He couldn't. Everything was dark, his head swamped and spinning, like he was sat in the next room with the light off, listening in to the chaos.

With his left cheek pressed into the cold tiles, plasticuffs were zipped tight around wrists and ankles once again. Through the murkiness came mutterings. Voices. It was the first real words Beckford had heard since his incarceration.

'Is he out?' one of them asked. A hand slapped Beckford's right cheek lightly. Then harder. For Beckford, it felt like someone else's cheek. It was strangely comfortable where he was, somewhere in the back of his mind. Peaceful even.

'What about *him*?' a different voice said.

'Fuckin—'

'Sshhh.'

They didn't say anything after that, but Beckford could hear movement. The door opening. More feet. The shifting of things, table and chairs. Sweeping up. The cell door finally closed and locked, leaving nothing but absolute silence.

Beckford lay there, suspended in a semi-conscious state for what could have been hours. When his energy levels raised somewhat, he slowly phased back to reality, and when he opened his eyes the room spun into focus and continued to sway and bob for a further 30 seconds.

A dull ache throbbed from where his neck had been twisted on the floor. With his hands and feet still secured behind him, he slowly rolled himself onto his side, and as he turned his head back the other way he gasped, the pain intensifying and travelling up his neck to where he'd been punched at the base of his skull.

He closed his eyes and looked back the other way, stretching out his neck. If they came in again he'd ask for more painkillers, but somehow doubted they'd be so accommodating.

Looking around the floor, something caught his eye down on the tile by his midriff. A plastic shard, about four to five inches long, with one end coming to a point – a vicious and lethal looking point.

I must have been lying on it when they cleaned up.

Aware that the cameras watching him, Beckford made a meal of his struggle to roll over onto his back, all the while masquerading his attempt to push the shiv under his bed. Realising his hands and feet were no use to him, he managed to flick the plastic slice out of sight with his knee.

Luckily they didn't come back in for a while, which gave him enough time to work out the best way to use it.

FORTY-FIVE

'Watch your footing,' said Dr Lindt as they headed down a narrow stairwell. 'One misstep and you could end up on one of my tables.'

He laughed, a raspy smoker's chuckle. Farber laughed along, but guessed it was a recycled joke he made with all his visitors. Heeding his words, she gripped the handrail and angled her feet to one side as she descended the steps.

Having been in a number of morgues, the smell of disinfectant and sight of pink puddles on white tiles were nothing out of the ordinary for Farber. In fact, during the final year of her degree she became obsessed with the BBC drama *Silent Witness*, which made her want to become a pathologist when it first aired in the mid-nineties. But after talking to people in the field it became clear there was an enormous lack of employment opportunities, so Farber turned to policing instead.

Walking down a line of a massive stainless steel storage cabinets, Dr Lindt looked like a librarian searching for a book.

'Guskov… Guskov. Ah, here we are.'

He stopped, unlocked a cabinet door and with both hands slid out a cadaver covered in a white sheet. Farber stepped closer. Nonchalantly, and without any degree of sensitivity, Lindt pulled back the cover, exposing a drained corpse. He was almost grey in colour, the blood having pooled and set some time ago.

The sight still revolted Farber. It was the head that she couldn't look away from. Like some sort of flowering tropical plant, the flesh peeled outwards from the concave implosion that used to be a face, making Nikolai Guskov look more like an animatronic special effect from an eighties low-budget horror film.

'Pretty one, this,' said Lindt, a half-smile on his face. Farber leaned in closer, her sight delving into the dark remnants of what used to be Nikolai's mouth.

'Is this why you couldn't get a dental match?' said Farber.

'There's enough of the jaw and some teeth to make a partial match, but nothing came back. There were a lot of cavities, so I'm wondering whether the boy ever saw a toothbrush let alone a dentist.'

Farber's eyes began to scan. Nikolai's neck, gaunt and plastic looking. She remembered jabbing her pen in and feeling some give. It'd be like stone now. Scanning further, her eyes landed on a mark exactly an inch or so above his left collarbone. It was faint, but stood out on the smooth, clay-like skin.

'A scar,' said Lindt. 'Most likely from a mole removal or skin tag… cyst, something like that maybe.'

Farber managed to keep the dizzying thoughts in her head at arm's length. 'A surgical procedure?' she asked.

'I'd say so, unless he knew someone who was a dab hand with a scalpel. It's as clean as I could make it.'

'Could you tell how old?'

Lindt shook his head and said, 'Medical records perhaps?'

'Nothing listed,' she said. 'Not in this country anyway.' Farber stared at the scar. Lindt watched her, waiting for anything else.

'What is it you're looking for, detective?'

Farber stood up straight and took a slow, cautious breath in through her nose. There were no repugnant smells, only a sterile aroma that reminded her of a public toilet after a deep clean. She couldn't have cared less either way, not with the insane ideas running through her head. Further DNA tests would prove it, but she was already convinced that on the tray in front of her lay the body of Joseph Winterburn.

Beckford is right – the suicide video is a fake, she thought.

It was only after such realisation that another slew of questions came to her, mainly why – if Beckford was involved – would he make himself appear to be so obsessed and intent on discovering the "truth"? Part of his cover up, perhaps?

It was a known technique used by the greatest practitioners of deception whereby revealing a portion of the truth, Beckford would position himself on the safe side of the lie.

'Dr Lindt,' said Farber. 'What if I told you…' She glanced at him. His cold eyes stared back and she cut herself off. The way he was looking at her… it was like he could hear her thoughts and knew she'd just discovered something she wasn't meant to. Suddenly Farber became conscious of the fact that they were alone in the depths of a morgue, and the jovial if slightly eccentric man who led her there was now a suspicious and creepy predator. Was he in on it too?

'Actually, no,' she said, 'Thank you, Dr Lindt. That's all for now.'

She ascended the stairs twice as fast as she'd descended them.

When she got into her car outside she sat still, the sounds of passing traffic squeezing in through the doors and windows. After a few minutes, she realised she'd been watching someone in her right-side wing mirror. A man, also sat in his parked car but too far away to see what he was doing.

Waiting for someone?

Waiting for *her*?

Farber started the engine and eased out of her spot, keeping check in her rearview.

The car didn't follow.

FORTY-SIX

The cell door unbolted and opened. Of the two masked men who entered, Beckford recognised one of them from the slightly faded black suit he was wearing; a loose stitch dangling from the front of the jacket. The other bloke looked like fresh meat, sporting a grey suit but continuing the trend of black balaclava and gloves.

With his feet and hands still zip-tied, Beckford had managed to shift himself into a sitting position on the floor, his back resting against the bed. A part of him wondered how the guard who took a screen to the head was doing, but it was only weak curiosity – Beckford couldn't give a shit if the fella was in a coma or not. As a matter of fact, he kind of hoped he was.

Fucking prick.

'Have you calmed down yet?' said the new guy, an office chair gripped in one hand. Beckford couldn't place his accent at all. It was south London, yet far too generic.

'...if you piss about pal, we'll PAVA you too. I don't need to tell you how much that fucking hurts, do I?'

As part of his police training, Beckford had felt the full force of PAVA before – a much more potent incapacitant alternative to CS spray. His tear ducts started to tingle at the thought.

'I've calmed down,' he said. Black Suit remained stationary by the open door as Grey Suit set the office chair down and took a seat in the middle of the room.

This is new, thought Beckford.

Hooking a forefinger under his balaclava, Grey Suit peeled it off his head in one fluid motion. It was the first real face Beckford has seen in over a week, including his own. The sight sent his heart galloping; not because he knew the man who was staring back at him – he didn't – it was because up until then the strict measures they'd taken to protect their own identity implied that Beckford could still get out alive. That obviously wasn't the case anymore.

Grey Suit was a man of about 45 years of age, short brown hair and a dark complexion. His eyes, nose and mouth were consistently wide, with deep laughter lines cut into his cheeks.

'The name's Richards,' he said, '…you recognise me?'

Beckford had heard the question but couldn't answer straightaway. He was still running through the consequential labyrinth of what seeing the man's face meant to his fate. Eventually refocusing his attention, he heard the question again in his mind before finally shaking his head no.

'No?' said Richards. 'Well I recognise you. From before all this nonsense. I taught you, in fact. At Hendon. I'm talking probably 10, maybe 12 years ago now. You wore glasses then.'

There were quite a few people Beckford remembered from his training days at Hendon. He was still in contact with some, but after shaking his memory through a sieve, the man before him didn't ring any bells.

'Nice to know I made a mark,' said Richards. 'Anyway, I taught there for a short while. Now I work here.'

'Congratu-fucking-lations,' said Beckford.

Richards smirked. 'I'm trying to help you here, pal. You don't need to start spouting hate just because you think we're gonna snuff you out. We don't work like that. We're not criminals. Not in that sense.'

'Fucking turncoats,' said Beckford. 'That's what you are. Let me guess… pissed off about budget cuts? Lack of pay rise? Your big, fat pension not juicy enough for you anymore?'

'John—'

'Only the weak and distrustful get lured to the dark side where money flows like wine no matter who's pocket it's coming from.'

'We're not about money.'

'You've murdered people,' said Beckford. His bottom lip started to tremble. 'DCI Graham Noakes. Not only one of the best I've ever worked with, but a decent fucking human being. And… and a friend. A good—'

He stopped, holding himself back from breaking down.

'I knew Noakes,' said Richards, 'and I agree. With everything you just said. Murder is deplorable and the majority would say there is no excuse for it. But not me, and not this gentleman by the door or a number of others outside of this room. There are bigger things at play here. Some incidents are unavoidable, carried out through the quick decision making of a very experienced team of people. Our secrecy is paramount, which sometimes – unfortunately – involves the loss of life. And that brings me to why I'm here.

'Thanks to your cooperation, our cover-up has a 90% probability of success. We were pushing 92 yesterday, but something has happened. Detective Farber…'

Beckford's stomach pole-vaulted his organs. 'I told you,' he said, 'she doesn't know anything.'

'She's started to dig in places she shouldn't,' said Richards.

'Don't touch her.'

'That's what I'm here for.'

'Please,' said Beckford. 'Look, I'm cooperating. I'll do whatever—'

'Calm down,' said Richards. 'We're going to give you an

opportunity to straighten this out. You can save her, but you'll need to do exactly what we say.'

Beckford sat for a while, staring, thinking. Then, leaning to one side, he attempted to get over onto his knees.

'Easy,' said Richards.

'I just want to get up.'

With his hands bound behind his back and his feet locked together, he struggled to get anywhere close to standing, squirming on the ground like a pathetic worm. Richards nodded to Black Suit and the man approached Beckford, pulling a pair of wire clippers from his jacket pocket.

'You'll behave, won't you?' said Richards, adding '…think of Alison.'

Out of breath on the floor, Beckford nodded. Black Suit crouched behind him.

Snip!

His ankles broke free. Then Black Suit went to his wrists.

Snip!

Beckford gingerly eased up onto his hands and knees. Black Suit didn't know what hit him.

Richards jumped out of his chair, drawing the stun gun, but Beckford had already shot up and swivelled Black Suit into a human shield, locking the man's left arm behind his back. Beckford's other hand – a white-knuckled fist – was pressed hard into the man's neck, the shard of pointed plastic digging into the flesh. A pained cry came from Black Suit's balaclava as blood trickled down his white collar.

'No one fucking move!' said Beckford, spit flying from his lips. He looked at Richards and said, 'This is right in his carotid artery. If I keep it there, he'll live a lot longer than if I rip it out.'

'Take it easy!' said Richards. 'Take it easy, John. Where

are you going to go, hey? What's your play here?'

Black Suit gasped for breath like a fish out of water. A third masked suit rushed into the room sporting a gun – a real gun with real projectiles that didn't just make your hair stand up straight.

'Come on, John,' he said, '…let him go.'

'Is that what you want?' said Beckford. Richards turned to the new arrival.

'Call an ambulance.'

'NOBODY MOVES!' screamed Beckford. 'You drop everything and kick it over here, to me, okay? I swear. I fucking swear, one twist and I'll open him up like a tin of tuna.'

'John—'

Beckford tensed his fist, digging the shard of plastic in and prising another agonising scream from Black Suit whose blood was now trickling down Beckford's arm and dripping off his bare elbow. Richards held up both hands.

'Okay, okay, fucking hell… all right.'

Richards glanced at the third man and they both slowly crouched to the ground, placed their weapons down, and with a small push slid them over to Beckford's feet. Slowly, the men returned to standing positions. Beckford watched them intently, knowing all it would take was one hesitant or wrong move and they'd pounce.

Beckford leaned into Black Suit's ear, 'Pick up the gun, real slow.'

The man, wincing and breathing heavily, bent at the knees and squatted. Beckford followed, mimicking him all the way down like some sort of paired Tai Chi movement. Unable to look down, Black Suit reached out with his free right hand and blindly patted the floor.

'Barrel end,' said Beckford.

The man's fingers finally found the handle of the gun,

then worked their way up the steel body and got hold of the barrel.

'Up,' said Beckford, and they slowly rose to a standing position.

'Hold it up,' he said.

Black Suit lifted the gun slowly, presenting the handle above his shoulder, 12 inches from Beckford's bloodied fist. Richards and the third man still hadn't moved a muscle, but he knew they wanted to. He could also hear footsteps and movement in the corridor outside the room. It was now or never.

With a squeeze of his fist, Black Suit cried out again and in one quick motion Beckford let go of the shard and snatched the gun, simultaneously pushing Black Suit forwards and causing the man to stagger and flail to the floor.

Beckford had forgotten how heavy guns were, slippery in his blood-soaked hand. He pointed it directly at the two remaining men while Black Suit moaned on the floor, putting pressure on his wound, the plastic shard poking through his fingers like a dirty piece of glass. Then a woman's voice came from outside the room.

'John, there's nowhere for you to go.'

There's only one way to disconnect.

'Oh yes there is,' he said and pulled the trigger. The blast was deafening in the confined space. The third man went down screaming, clutching his leg, the bullet having gone in just above his knee.

'Don't!' yelled Richards, holding out a halting palm. Beckford felt numb with power. Numb enough to very easily pull the trigger again.

'What happened?!' screamed the woman, her voice wrought with fear '...John?!'

'No one's dead,' said Beckford. '...but if you look on

the CCTV you'll see I've got two of your turncoats repainting the tiles in red. Only, this is *actually happening*.'

Holding Richards in the sights of the gun, Beckford bent down again and picked the Taser up off the floor. Addressing whoever was outside the cell, he said, 'This is what we're going to do! I'm going to lead the last turncoat out of this room with my gun. No one is going to try anything, because they won't want his death on their hands. I know you know I'm serious, because you're the ones who put me so deep in this shit that I can't crawl out of. As clichéd as it sounds, I'm a man with absolutely nothing to lose and that makes me very fucking dangerous.'

'What about Alison?' said the woman.

'Fuck her!' Beckford snapped back. Inside, beyond all the adrenaline, anxiety and exhaustion, Beckford felt a heartstring snap. He sold it so well that he wondered if it was a lie or not. Lowering his voice he looked at Richards and said, 'Turn around and raise your hands.'

Richards did as he was told. Beckford side-stepped the groaning men and pools of blood on the floor and approached him from behind, holding the end of the gun three feet from the back of Richards's well-groomed head. A couple of sessions of the Israeli martial art Krav Maga had taught Beckford not to get any closer, the hostage could easily turn the tables in a split second.

'If you move…' said Beckford.

'Yes, I get it,' said Richards.

Beckford called out, 'Everybody outside! Whatever doors are out there, I want them open and clear for us to walk through. Anybody out there with a nervous disposition or an itchy nose, leave now, because it might be hard to believe but I'm as jumpy as a fucking rabbit… a fart will get me pulling this trigger, and if I do I'm not stopping until I'm out of bullets or dead. Is that clear?'

He could hear frantic scuffling of feet on the corridor's linoleum floor.

'Walk slowly,' he instructed Richards. Beckford followed behind, step for step, keeping an eye on the two writhing suits as they headed for the door. Richards passed the threshold of the cell.

'Stop,' said Beckford. 'I want you between them and me.'

Richards looked up and down the corridor, then angled himself to the right.

'No one the other way?' said Beckford. Richards shook his head. A second later, Beckford popped his head out checked, confirming there was no one on the left but a set of double doors. He pulled back into the cell, composed himself, then stepped out fully into the bland corridor, the barrel of the gun fixed to the back of Richards' head.

Ahead of them, 20 feet or so, was a troupe of people, all professionally dressed and looking like something straight of out of the TV show *The Apprentice*. When the woman spoke, he finally put a voice to a face.

'Put the gun down John,' she said.

The shock hit him like a freight train, stunning him into a frozen stupor. If the posse in front of him had pounced right there and then, Beckford would have been toast. Were his eyes deceiving him like everything else over the past week?

That's not her.

It's a twin.

A sister.

A fucking HOLOGRAM.

With his jaw hanging he rejoined reality once more, realising his gun had lowered ever so slightly so that it was aiming past Richard's shoulder. He corrected it quickly and remembered to breathe, hoping to focus and regain control of himself.

The sea of faces ahead of him were anonymous, different shapes and different colours. But it was the woman dead-centre who he couldn't take his eyes off.

Commander Amelia Corden appeared calm, her hands clasped together in front of her like a schoolteacher.

FORTY-SEVEN

Beckford wanted to speak but couldn't. It was as if the neurons in his brain had seized up or gone on strike. Nothing made sense anymore apart from one thing. One concrete revelation: Beckford had finally found his last straw.

He just wanted to scream at the top of his lungs. Try to get the attention of everybody in the world to look at him. The situation he was in. It was madness. No one would believe him unless they were right there with him, but they weren't. He was alone and his fate sealed.

As he pondered such thoughts, the gun started to feel heavier. He focussed on the back of Richard's head and imagined a bullet travelling through it. It wouldn't be like the movies, where the head explodes in a shower of blood, skull splinters and brains. No. Richards' hair would just shudder, perhaps leaving a subtle gap where the bullet had entered. And he would just drop, like Nikolai in his video. Then Beckford would open it up to the floor, contracting his index finger as fast as humanly possible.

'John,' said Corden, taking a few steps forwards, her heels clopping like coconut shells on the linoleum, '…please put the gun down. This isn't you.'

Beckford could feel himself nodding. 'You're right,' he said. 'I haven't been me for a long time. What the fuck is this? What *is this*?'

He tried to remain calm, but his tether snapped, taking himself off-guard his as he roared like a gladiator, 'TELL ME THAT AT LEAST!'

The bellow filled the corridor, ricocheting off the shiny

walls and floor until there was silence again.

'If you let Richards go,' said Corden, 'I'll give you everything. You can even keep the gun. You have my word.'

'Your *word?*' said Beckford, his face contorting with abject contempt.

'I never lied to you John,' said Corden. 'I just skirted the truth. There's no skirting here, I promise.'

The idea of spraying everyone with bullets tempted Beckford like the last chocolate in the box. The only thing preventing him was a stronger desire for the truth. For Beckford, going without that would be worse than death.

'Go,' he said to Richards, easing his grip on the gun. With Richards' hands still in the air, he walked forwards, down the corridor, past Corden and past the other watchful suits until he disappeared through an open door.

'Everyone else, too,' said Corden over her shoulder. There was no movement until Beckford gave permission with a curt nod and they all slowly filtered out, heels and shoes scuffing the floor until the door closed and there was no one else in the corridor but the two of them.

'Please,' said Corden, 'I don't feel comfortable with that thing pointing at me. I was an officer too, remember, and have been privy to one too many accidental shootings. I'll keep my distance.'

Her voice had a rhythmic, calming quality. Almost hypnotic. A voice that had helped Beckford through the dark days of Sally's murder, and although his trust in her had now shattered it was her voice that ran deep, as if the words he could hear and the woman in front of him were two sides to one person. Good and evil.

Pushing the cognitive dissonance to one side, Beckford considered his immediate options.

Were the others coming round the back?

Was Corden armed?

If I keep the gun by my side, I'll still have a chance to finish her off.

Keep your ears open.

After one final scrutiny of Corden's stern face, he lowered the gun.

'John, your idea of what we do here is all wrong. We're helpers.'

Beckford was beyond bemused. *Helpers?* How could the woman before him, whom he trusted through such hardship in his life, be so deceptive, deluded and so damn *psychotic?*

'James Hitchell,' said Corden, out of the blue. It was a name Beckford hadn't heard for years. One dug up out of a shit-tip of late night, coffee-fuelled memories.

'Arrested for murder,' she said, 'stabbed his ex-wife in the heart and neck at her home one night when he—'

'Helen Hitchell,' said Beckford, 'Well, Helen *Sanders*.'

'That's right,' said Corden. 'You excelled on that one. Pilford and Bronson too, if I recall. We had that bastard in his cell bawling his eyes out, giving us everything. But could we back it up? Could we bollocks. The crux of any case: No. Hard. Evidence. CPS were about ready to tie his laces for him and kick him out the door. Do you remember?'

Beckford nodded softly, unsure of where she was taking him.

'Now,' said Corden, 'you've got to remember that this was a time when there was a ton of pressure on our department and me in particular… *sleep*? What was that? My grey hairs are a result of that period in my life. Half the time I looked like a dog had chewed me up and shat me out, sweetcorn and all. The budget cutbacks led to less staff, which led to rising workload. Same crap, different year. Things were desperate and we had to pull it together… raise the stats. So I took the initiative. A friend of a friend – naming no names but someone who's job involved having access to a vial of Helen's blood, gave some to me and one night, I – that's right: a 47-year-old Chief Inspector at the time – broke into James Hitchell's apartment…'

'The sole of his work boot,' said Beckford, entranced by the memory and Corden's revelation.

'Bingo. Now, two things. Firstly, was I wrong to do that? And secondly, if so, why didn't *you* tell anyone?'

The numbness that had encased Beckford dipped just enough to let in a faint sensation of surprise. He opened his lips to protest.

'I knew that you knew, John. Yes.'

'You trusted me to keep my mouth shut?' he said. 'Why?'

'Because I knew deep down that you felt the same way about the investigation as I did. It was as clear as crystal glass that you just didn't have the balls, or perhaps the stupidity, to take such drastic measures and act on it. You're a justice man through and through. You're the bloke who got bullied in school, but it wasn't the dent in your pride that pissed you off, it was the fact the bullies got away with it. It chewed you up inside something rotten. I completely understand. The people beyond those doors understand as well. We've all experienced injustice at some point or another.'

'You're talking about noble cause corruption,' said Beckford, feeling the picture widen, the vast swathes of information in his head slotting together like the precise and delicate internal workings of an antique pocket watch.

'I'm talking about justice,' said Corden. 'In three years we've gone from one of the worst police forces in the UK to one of the best in the *world*. Thanks to justice.'

'Justice is about truth,' said Beckford, 'and there's no truth in what you've done.'

Raising her voice for the first time, Corden said, '*Truth*? We live in a society where *everything* is manipulated, from the food that we eat to the shows that we watch to the politicians we vote for. It's all tailored to right the balance. Policing was a whole lot easier 20 years ago, let me tell you. Now you even can't sneeze without having to adhere to policy and procedure; to give the criminal a "right." No criminal should have a right.'

'Innocent until proven…?'

'We're not putting away just anyone, John. The figures and statistics tell us where to turn to. Some 16-year-old kid arrested for murder… we look at the evidence, his history, previous records, lifestyle choices. If he hangs around with bad apples then it's more than likely he is one. It's the law of averages. Manipulating digital evidence will put that bad apple away and make an example of him. The message spreads like wildfire. Numbers of actual crimes have decreased since we started operating, can you believe that? Murder. Rape. Burglary. Assault. All down. The system is self-perpetuating.'

Beckford's face hardened. 'What about Graham?'

'An unfortunate loss, but we have to protect the nest.'

'An *unfortunate loss*?'

'John, you don't fully understand how integrated we are in the whole policing infrastructure. Everything you see here is funded by taxpayers' money, not laundered notes. We're a legitimate sector of British law enforcement, yet only a handful of people know we exist.'

I'm dreaming, thought Beckford. *This must be a dream.*

'We're now so integrated that if we were ever exposed the damage caused would be astronomical; much worse than however unethical and immoral you think our work is. An ironic thought experiment, I suppose. The public's confidence in us is the highest it's ever been. They must *never* know what we do. Think of it as a magic trick; once you know the secret…'

Beckford felt the gossamer fabric of his world shred in front of his eyes. He was backstage at the world's biggest illusion, and she was right – knowing the secret showed him that it wasn't magic at all. It was sorcery. And the digital landscape made it possible for such spells to be cast.

What made it worse for Beckford was there was a part of him that completely understood their plight. He'd seen so many guilty suspects walk free. Inadmissible evidence. Human error. Lack of manpower. Corruption. The justice system was an ethical minefield, and unfortunately for everyone ethics were not absolute.

It was a subject that Beckford felt strongly about, right and wrong having been drummed into him from an early age. A distant yet pivotal memory came back to him right there in the corridor – being caught shoplifting sweets at the age of nine. It was as clear as day. And before he knew it, a whirlwind of other childhood memories swept him off his feet. Dad in his toolshed. The hot summers. Running free with friends without a care in the world. Gooseberry pie, the fruit hand-picked from the garden. Cycling in the woods.

In that one accelerated moment of nostalgia, Beckford appreciated his life more than ever before. A byproduct, no doubt, due to the fact it was about to end.

Feeling the heavy steel in his hand, he straightened his slouch and said the simple words that had lingered in the back of his mind since the first time he had heard them.

'There's only one way to disconnect.'

He raised the gun and planted the barrel under his chin.

'YOU CAN SAVE HER!' screamed Corden.

FORTY-EIGHT

Farber got the call just after three in the afternoon.

The number was private, like a lot of calls she'd received that week. She ignored it until it rang for the third time in a minute.

When she heard his voice her legs turned to jelly, forcing her to sit on the stacked paper boxes by the printer. It was no place for her to talk to him. Not in the office. After casually saying, 'Hold on…' she got to her feet and left the room, locking herself in the disabled toilet down the corridor.

The first question that she asked he cut her off. He said there was no time to talk. They were to meet in one hour by the statue of Eros in Piccadilly Circus. It had to be public and busy, then the phone went dead.

* * *

Corden had done what she was good at – she'd spun words like a politician and managed to lure Beckford off the ledge, first placating him with words of hope, then driving home the message that Farber's fate was really in his hands. Beckford felt the weight of it all and could do nothing but submit. He was given a shower and fresh clothes, but half an hour later had no recollection of washing or dressing. He was in a daze. Everything since his confrontation with Corden a hazy blur, like his mind had started to slowly recess into power-saving mode.

In his back pocket they stuffed the letter – handwritten by Beckford, transcribed verbatim from a script they provided him with. He was handcuffed again, headphones put over his ears and the black bag thrown over his head. The sound of static was a welcome return and he hoped it would offer an opportunity to digest what he'd learned, but his thoughts were slow and laborious. It felt like it would take years to digest everything they'd thrown at him. But he didn't have years. He barely had hours.

If they're going to kill you, why go through the trouble of masking you?

He was treated more gently this time as they led him blindly through the building once again; a reversal of the maze he'd already walked. When the fresh outdoors hit him, he took in as many lungful's of air as he could. It was the best few breaths he'd ever taken.

Assisted into a van, he sat down and was flanked again by two warm bodies. The engine rumbled to life and then they were moving, on their way to Piccadilly Circus. After what felt like 20 minutes or so of jostling and black static, the hood was pulled from his head and the headphones taken off.

When the disorientation settled, he was looking at Corden who'd been sat opposite him the whole time.

'How are you feeling?' she said with what appeared to be genuine concern. She was good at that.

'I couldn't describe it to you even if I knew,' said Beckford.

A masked and armed officer to the left of him sniggered and kicked his boot up on the seat in front of him. Just another day on the job.

'We have people stationed there already,' said Corden. 'You apologise, hand her the letter, then you come back to us. That's it.'

'Putting a lot of trust in me, aren't you?'

'I do trust you, John, and I trust you'll do the right

thing.'

'There's only one right thing,' said Beckford, 'and if I tell her that, what would you do? Shoot us both of in the middle of Piccadilly Circus? Good luck trying to cover that one up.'

'You won't tell her,' she said.

Her confidence made Beckford wonder what kind of ace she had up her sleeve. Corden was too smart to just let him loose with the knowledge he'd just been given without some sort of insurance. And the insurance required to cover a secret capable of tearing the whole country apart had to be pretty sizable.

'We know a lot about you John,' she said, stone-faced. 'We know a lot about a lot of things. That's our wheelhouse, of course. Data. Information is king and so on. I never told you this but I had a sister growing up. Charlotte her name was. Two years older than me. She was very pretty, which made her very popular. When she had sleepovers I'd stay up late listening to them talk about boys and periods and god knows what else.

'She died in a car crash when she was 17. Her and a friend, Sadie. Both young, both beautiful, both heading for great things. Both dead. The boy driving the car was some idiot called Max Gilfoyle. He survived, predictably.'

She pulled a shirt cuff straight then swept a hand across her skirt. A subtle fidget, but one that Beckford saw as a distraction from the heartache under her hardened exterior. It was perhaps the first genuine thing she'd done so far.

'Now…' she said, looking back up at him, 'I know where Max Gilfoyle lives. I've always known, ever since that day. I know where he works. I know his wife's name. I know his children's names. Because I, like you, have become attached to the vengeful fantasy of knowing the person responsible for heartbreak in my life is not enjoying theirs. How *dare* they?'

Since Peter McGregor had been taken from his council flat in cuffs, Beckford's fantasies had grown in strength and severity, whiling away the hours, days, weeks and months thinking about how he could get revenge on the bastard. As the obsessive thoughts escalated, he started to believe – given half the chance – that he could very easily kill Peter McGregor in cold blood. In fact, he was certain of it. It soon fuelled his anxiety. And that perhaps, like McGregor, Beckford had psychopathic tendencies too. A murderer; just one who hadn't got out of the gate yet.

Beckford had only ever shared his macabre fantasy with two people in his life – his therapist and Corden, if a somewhat watered-down version. It begged the question of why she had never opened up to him about her own, similar troubles.

A sister?

'Consider this, John,' she said. 'You're in the supermarket... buying olives or ketchup or whatever. You drop them into your basket, turn and Peter McGregor is stood there. Shopping, just like you. Living a normal life. Just like you.'

Beckford's face froze, the van's engine and everything else around him dropping away, leaving him and Corden in a black space, facing one another.

There it was.

The insurance.

The ace up her sleeve.

'He's guilty,' said Beckford, his voice cracking.

'There wasn't enough evidence, Jo—'

'HE'S FUCKING GUILTY!' Beckford screamed, causing the masked heads in the van to swivel towards him. Corden let the dust settle.

'I know he's guilty,' she said, 'we all know it, but he was going to walk.'

'No...' said Beckford, shaking his head, not wanting to believe any of it.

'Yes,' said Corden. 'What you thought was an excellent piece of detective work for Michaels and his team was actually us, behind the scenes, sculpting the case to get the verdict we all wanted. The *just* verdict.

'No...'

'The CCTV,' said Corden, 'the till records, the fibres in his car... he's behind bars because of our handiwork John. And that's why I know you won't tell a soul.'

Beckford was shaking, his stomach churning. Peter McGregor's face flashed in front of his eyes, then beads of sweat squeezed out across his body.

'Get his head between his legs,' said Corden. A firm grip took the scruff of his neck forced him forwards and down.

'Breathe deep, John,' said Corden. 'Calm down.'

Beckford followed her instruction subconsciously, his thoughts elsewhere, travelling back in time. Back to when he worked in CID.

So many late nights in his study, fuelled by coffee and Red Bull, surrounded by an ever-mounting pile of paperwork across his desk and scattered about the floor. Inevitably, the late nights would turn into mornings and he'd go to work on zero sleep. Michaels would only have to take one look at him before sending him back home. He was in no fit state to perform even the lightest of duties, but above that the other officers felt under pressure from him and uncomfortable in his presence.

Back at home, Beckford couldn't switch off. He'd be drawn to his study, consumed by reams of information like some JFK conspiracy theorist, pleading with himself to figure it all out and find the key that would lock Peter

McGregor away for the rest of his life.

As the trial approached, Beckford's nights disappeared completely. He lost count of the number of times he'd shudder awake, finding himself still fully clothed slumped in his study chair, a cold coffee sat next to his keyboard. He didn't have the time to sleep, but it was sheer exhaustion that often forced his head down.

When the time came, it was Farber who called him. He remembered her words exactly.

'*We got the bastard.*'

The CCTV at a petrol station showed Peter McGregor's taxi pull in. He filled up, bought some cigarettes, paid and left. There was a woman in the passenger seat the whole time. Blonde. Sally's build. McGregor had been working that night, but said he'd finished before midnight. The CCTV proved otherwise. He'd even used his debit card to pay for the fuel and fags. A mistake.

Guilty.

But the whole thing was a lie. There was no CCTV, no debit card payment. It was all created on a computer and deployed to the relevant systems to be perceived as the truth.

'John,' he heard Corden say.

Slowly, he sat upright, his sickness and temperature settling.

'John, I've wanted to recruit you for the longest time. Do you think you'd ever convert to our principals?'

He didn't say anything. He couldn't. He just stared at her.

FORTY-NINE

Piccadilly Circus swarmed with people. Tourists stopping to take selfies and time-poor Londoners scuttling from A to B like worker ants. Farber was one of the latter, pushing through the crowds towards the Eros like a laser-guided missile. Her heart had been in her mouth ever since she left the tube, pumping harder with each step.

Keeping her end of the bargain, she hadn't told a soul of where she was going or who she was meeting. A hundred worries filtered through her head. What if someone recognised him from the news, the two of them caught in cahoots? Worse still, took a photo of them together? After all, she was surrounded by people snapping pictures like crazy, the images uploaded instantly to the web for the whole world to see.

Everything was instant these days.

Reaching the fountain, with the statue atop its tall, ornate plinth, Farber turned to face the crowds, her eyes flitting from person to person, making her head swim. Beckford was already stood to her right, his disguise so successful that Farber had already looked at him once, believing him to be just another tourist taking a selfie. It was only as she panned for a second time that she did a double-take, finally recognising him underneath the cap, glasses and fake but very realistic looking beard.

About to say his name, she stopped herself, and they held each other's gaze for a moment.

'Like my new look?' said Beckford, but there was no humour in his voice. It was hoarse and weary. It wasn't just the outside that was hurting. It pained him to be so close to her, the smell of her perfume and the sight of her hair, curled and beautiful, reminding him of all the good times he'd spent nestled in her arms.

She looked at him differently. It might have been fear, but Beckford saw only disgust. Averting her eyes, he stared out at the crowds.

'I'm so sorry, Ali. About everything.'

A wire under his coat broadcasted his apology to listening ears – Corden in the van and a team of plain-clothes operatives out in the square, invisible among the hustle and bustle.

Beckford held out the folded letter, and after a slight hesitation Farber took it.

'Don't look for me,' he said.

Then he turned and disappeared into the mass of bodies.

The eyes on the ground trailed him like bird spotters, watching him saunter through the bustling crowd.

One of the operatives got on his radio and said, 'He's going the wrong way.'

Corden's voice came through loud and clear, 'Move to intercept.'

Like velociraptors in tall grass, the operatives zoomed in on their prey through the sea of heads, Beckford's cap bobbing up and down like a flashing beacon.

'Eyes on the target.'

Beckford wasn't running, he just walked like everyone else. One of the operatives pushed through a group of French students, getting to within six feet, but Beckford's jacket looked different. Reaching out, the operative spun Beckford around.

An older man with leathery skin faced him, eyes wide and alarmed.

'Can I help you?' he said, speaking in an Austrian accent.

The other operatives emerged and assembled in front of the man, who now looked terrified.

'What is it?' said the man, but the operatives ignored him and frantically scoured the frantic ebb and flow of people, peering above the crowds like meerkats. Their target was now a needle in a stack of needles, the probability of recapture shrinking with each passing second.

Five minutes ticked by, and they were still empty handed. Even their systems found nothing. Beckford was gone.

FIFTY

Farber took the Piccadilly line to Green Park, then changed trains to the Jubilee line. The letter remained unopened in her jacket pocket, testing her patience to its limits. There were just too many people around, too many prying eyes. She needed privacy. She wanted silence.

After getting off the tube at West Hampstead, she dove to a nearby Costa and ordered a hot chocolate filled with marshmallows. Taking a seat at the back, Farber pulled the envelope out of her jacket. Her hands were shaking. Carefully, she tore the paper and unfolded the letter in her lap.

It had been written in black biro on white A5 note paper. She recognised Beckford's big, looping S instantly, but tried not to get ahead of herself and rewound back at the beginning.

Ali,

There is no excuse for what I've done or who I am. I understand that no amount of apologising will ever warrant your forgiveness, but for what it's worth I truly am sorry. Not just for what you've heard in the news or by the water cooler, but for everything. The happiest day of my life was when we were walking along the beach in Sharm, hand in hand watching the sunset. I remember that as if it was yesterday and if I could somehow bottle that experience and emotion, I could prove to everyone that life can be such a beautiful thing.

But it also ends.

The investigation goes beyond what you know Ali, and your recent discovery in the morgue is part of it. Please do not dig any further. You must tell no one what you've found or you will be killed. I can't protect you. They are watching all the time. Live a normal life and they will leave you alone.

Love someone. Be happy.

It's over now.

J

PS Burn this.

By the time she'd finished reading, tears had collected at the end of her nose. She dropped the letter to one side and used the serviette under her hot chocolate to wipe her face. With rush hour approaching, the place started to fill up.

Farber sat there for almost an hour, the cacophony of customers washing over her as she sat, sipping her drink. Thinking. Wondering. Reminiscing.

Worrying.

* * *

For the next few weeks, Farber succumbed to an overwhelming paranoia. The subtle sense of invincibility that came with being a police officer – which protected her while walking the city she knew so well – had disappeared. The streets weren't safe for her anymore, and whether Beckford was telling the truth or not she sensed watchful eyes wherever she went.

With it came the sleepless nights, abetted by every

strange noise in her house from the central heating creaking the floorboards to the wind rushing through the roof tiles; all taking the form of something else – ominous things that her imagination wouldn't leave be.

An aluminium baseball bat became a close companion and she'd stocked up on CS spray from work – one in her bag, one in her coat and one in the car. Anywhere in arm's reach at a moment's notice.

They were the hardest weeks of her life, because unlike her true self – a person who was always open and liked to talk things over – she had to remain silent about everything, driving the stress and directing the worry inwards, causing only more mental anguish.

As time went by, Beckford's photo in the papers started to decline, the articles pushed further back in the pages and journalists stopped pestering her altogether. To the outside world, DI John Beckford had become old hat – yesterday's news. Farber only wished she felt the same way about him.

Never one for sleeping pills, she got back into yoga and practiced mindfulness, hoping for a natural antidote to her nervous disposition. It worked to some extent. An added bonus to the classes was the social aspect – being with other people, making small talk, ingratiating herself back into the community.

After a class one night, a man called Lance asked her for coffee. She refused and regretted it. Next time she saw him she apologised and paid for his latte. He was nice. A bit younger than her, but at the very least an appropriate distraction.

Some nights she'd spend with her mum on the coast, and some nights Staedler would pop round to keep her company, take her to the cinema to watch something big, loud and completely mindless.

Even after Beckford's manhunt had started its

inevitable winding-up, Farber was still wrought with worry over what she'd read in the letter. She could see in Staedler's eyes that he suspected she was hiding something from him, but he respected her enough to know she'd tell him if and when the time was right. The only problem was there would never be a right time.

One night while alone, hunkered on her couch in front of the fire, Farber made a fast decision, scaring Mitsy half to death as she leapt off the couch. Taking an old *Encyclopedia Britannica* off the bookcase, she let the pages part to where John's letter had been concealed. She read it one last time from start to finish without stopping, then with no hesitation threw it on the fire.

As the page burned, she expected a pang of regret to start eating her up inside. It never came. Instead, liberation was what she felt, confirming not only that she'd done the right thing, but that she should have done it sooner.

From the loft she brought down a box she'd been keeping, a sort of time capsule containing everything she held dear from her and Beckford's past. Back then there were too many memories among it all to just get rid. Now it didn't matter. Whatever would burn went into the fire. Everything else was bagged and given to charity. It was the best episode of catharsis she'd felt for a long time, outdoing any yoga class or mindfulness session she'd attended.

By her wishes, Staedler stopped keeping her in the loop of what he'd heard on the grapevine regarding Beckford's investigation. After that, she started getting better at forgetting about him, letting life get in the way instead.

It was sometime in the New Year that – unknown to her – she went an entire day without thinking about him at all. And that was just the beginning.

FIFTY-ONE

The cigarette glowed like a miniature volcano, smoked down to the filter.

Sam Lawson stubbed it out in the wet grass and kept hold of the butt. He hated litter, and the unspoilt hills surrounding him were beautiful and peaceful, untouched by the human waste that clogged the cities and towns. Out there, the palette was filled with greens and blues – two colours he rarely saw in London.

A voice carried over the wind. It was Mick, a farmer and Sam's employer, waving goodbye for the day. Sam still struggled to understand Mick's thick accent at times, but he mostly got by on intonation alone. It had also taken Sam some time getting used to his new name. He'd considering keeping his first name to make things easier – after all, "John" was one of the most common names in the country. But in the end his paranoia got the best of him.

Sam gave Mick a lazy wave back and watched the man usher his dog into the back of a muddy Land Rover. The vehicle took off up the road to the farmhouse on the hill.

Making his way to the barn, Sam watched the golden sun brush the horizon. With spring nearly upon them, the evenings were getting lighter and the work was getting easier. Putting the cigarette butt in the outside bin, Sam slid off his wellies by the door and went inside.

The barn was still halfway through being converted, and while the harsh winter temperatures made the place almost uninhabitable, it was becoming home. The deal he'd struck with Mick was a good one – he could live there rent-free as long as he put the graft in, and that was something Sam always did no matter where he worked.

With the nearest grocery store an hour's drive away, dinner nearly always consisted of home-grown produce such as potatoes and other root vegetables. Every now and then a neighbouring farmer would drop by with a freshly wrapped shank of lamb or slab of steak.

It was the simple things that gave Sam balance and contentment now, but there were still some things he couldn't live without.

Out in the wilderness, the internet wasn't so easy to come by, and that had become a hindrance to many of the businesses in the area. That was before Sam arrived on the scene.

With technical skills foreign to most residents of the northern Orkneys, Sam set up a satellite system on Mick's farmhouse, the elevation providing the best position for point-to-point wireless access points, serving high speed internet to many of the buildings nearby.

It was a revelation that soon spread across the island, giving Sam a little more local renown than he would have liked. After some reluctance, he finally caved in and set up a small non-profit business to roll out remote broadband to all 416 residents on the island. Their digital infrastructure improved by a factor of thousands, generating a positive knock-on effect to their economy for generations to come.

For Sam, it only provided one thing. A lifeline.

Each night after dinner, he'd stoke the fire and top it up with logs from the woodshed. Coffee was brewed in a pan. He'd lock the doors, close the curtains and drag his strongbox out from under the bed.

On the table he'd set out his laptop and files in order of where he left off the night before. Once online, he'd authenticate with a secure file-hosting service, each time praying for there to be a new addition.

Sometimes there was; sometimes there wasn't.

Considering the source of the documents, his contact had many obstacles to overcome. It took time. Vigilance was paramount. Nevertheless, Sam couldn't continue his work without her help.

And it was there, in the warm glow of a table lamp and the crackling wood burner, that Sam spent his nights revisiting the case that had tortured him for years. A case that was already closed, seemingly solved – a man incarcerated for life.

And yet, it was only with legitimate proof that a taxi driver called Peter McGregor murdered a prostitute called Sally Beckford, that Sam Lawson would not only be able to end his nightmare, but unleash to the world a truth that they were certainly not ready for, but unquestionably needed to hear.

ABOUT THE AUTHOR

Stewart McDonald lives in Liverpool with his wife. He works in IT and in his spare time writes novels, films and plays.

For updates on Stewart's next novel, join the mailing list at www.stewartmcdonald.net